To Avery, Enjoy the ride!

[signature] 8/7/2012

Book I

GAMADIN™

Word of Honor

Tom Kirkbride

EMERALD
BOOK CO.

Published by Emerald Book Company
4425 South Mo Pac Expwy., Suite 600
Austin, TX 78735

For ordering information or special discounts for bulk purchases, please contact Greenleaf Book Group LLC at: 4425 South Mo Pac Expwy., Suite 600 Austin, TX 78735, (512) 891-6100.

Design and composition by Greenleaf Book Group LLC

Publisher's Cataloging-In-Publication Data
(Prepared by The Donohue Group, Inc.)

Kirkbride, Tom (Thomas K.)
   Gamadin. Book 1, Word of honor / Tom Kirkbride. -- 1st ed.

   p. ; cm.

   ISBN: 978-1-934572-06-1

1. Extraterrestrial beings--Fiction. 2. Space warfare--Fiction. 3. Surfers--California--Fiction. 4. Science fiction. 5. Fantasy fiction. I. Title.

PS3611.I75 G26 2009
813/.6   2008930961

Printed in the United States of America on acid-free paper

10 09 08   10 9 8 7 6 5 4 3 2 1

First Edition

For my parents, Jack and Phyllis
And my daughter, Lara

There's no such thing as chance;

And what to us seems merest accident

Springs from the deepest source of destiny . . .

JOHANN CHRISTOPH FRIEDRICH VON SCHILLER
(1759–1805)

True sacrifice is not what we give up,

But what we ultimately gain . . .

ASSOCIATE JUSTICE OF THE SUPREME COURT,
CLARENCE THOMAS (1948–)

SHE CAME TO EARTH

BEFORE THE FIRST CORNERSTONE AT GIZA WAS SET,

BEFORE A WOODEN HORSE DESTROYED AN EMPIRE,

BEFORE ATLANTIS FLOURISHED.

SHE TRAVELED THE VASTNESS OF SPACE

FROM AN OLD AND FORGOTTEN PLANET NEAR
THE GALACTIC CORE,

AND WAITED . . .

WAITED FOR THE SPREADING DEATH
TO COME TO HER.

WHO WERE THE GAMADIN?

MANY, MANY THOUSANDS of years ago, when the galactic trading centers of Hitt and Gibb were the cultural elite centers of the Omni quadrant, the Gamadin ruled the cosmos, not in an authoritarian way, but as a protective force against the spreading Death of evil empires and their acts of conquest and domination. A wise and very ancient group of planets from the galactic core formed an alliance to create the most powerful police force the galaxy had ever seen. This police force would be independent of any one state or planet. They were called "Gamadin."

Translated from the ancient scrolls of Amerloi, Gamadin means: *"From the center, for all that is good."* The sole mission of the Gamadin was to protect the freedom and happiness of peaceful planets everywhere, regardless of origin or wealth. It was said that a single Gamadin ship was so powerful, it could destroy an empire. Unfortunately, after many centuries of peace, the Gamadin had done their job *too* well. Few saw reason for such a powerful presence in their own backyard when the Death of war and the aggressive empire building were remnants of an ancient past. So what was left of the brave Gamadin simply withered away and was lost, never to be heard from again.

However, the ancient scrolls of Amerloi foretold their resurrection:

"For it is written that one day the coming Death will lift its evil head and awaken the fearsome Gamadin of the galactic core. And the wrath of the Gamadin will be felt again throughout the stars, and lo, while some people trembled in despair, still more rejoiced; for the wrath of the Gamadin will cleanse the stars for all; and return peace to the heavens. . . ."

Chapter One

SOOK

THE BOLT OF white-hot plasma streaked across the battlefield and decapitated a stone god. The resulting explosion did not awaken the city of worshipers, for they had turned to dust eons ago. The sickly sweet fumes of smoke billowed upward into the dimly lit, rose-colored sky before it spread wide over the ruins of the city like a shroud of death. On the distant horizon, bright orange flashes split the heavens as the war continued. Emerging from the underground catacombs of Hitt, a perverted, winged creature took flight a moment before a Triadian soldier carried a wounded comrade away from the falling dust. Right on their heels, another soldier led two Neejan archaeologists to safety behind the severed head of the god. One heartbeat later, the caverns of the dead collapsed forever from the explosive force of a terra-busting thader.

"Drak!" Sook cursed. The Triadian's gauntlet hands and arms were covered with Chubal's sticky green blood. "How did the Voids beat us to Amerloi?"

Voids, those mindless soldiers of the Triadians' enemy Fhaal. Without their leader they were powerless and disorganized, the end product of mass replication without concern for the power of the mind to think quickly.

Lying flat at the bottom of the trench in the cold Amerloian air, first officer Chubal's dark, amber scales sizzled under the rust-colored metal of the protective uniform Neeja's elite Triadian squadrons wore. The special forces armor had no markings of rank or station. Triadians fought as one. The garment's color changed with the landscape, having no true color of its own. Under the brightest sun a Triadian was nearly invisible. In low light, he was. In the harshest conditions, as on Amerloi, the garment meant survival. Its thin, thermal sections gave the soldier warmth and provided him with a recirculating system for filtering the supercooled, poisonous gases he must breathe. The armor's layers, like its color, were deceiving. Inside its pocketed divisions were hidden rounds of blaster-energy magazines, toaders, rapier daggers, tough duro-wire, enviro-masks, nutrient cubes, and high-absorption fluids. Anything and everything a trained killer needed to fight a heartless enemy.

Mestra, the other heavily scaled soldier, grunted his distaste as he shoved the civilian scientists against the cold stone. "Civs . . . It had to be one of them."

Mestra and Chubal were Bedouin tharlics. Their thick scales protected them against the supercold air. The two soldiers were three times the size of the frail-looking Sook, with thin skin and air-breathing lungs. The Triadian was ugly. How could anyone who didn't "molt" be attractive?

Chubal agreed with disgust. "Incompetent civs have betrayed us," he wheezed.

Sook remembered how Primary had scolded the civilian scientists who had broken contact-silence just before their ship had landed. *Drak! How did they know?*

The frail Triadian wiped the clinging dust from the enviro-mask lens before pulling apart the mouthpiece and spitting at the severed stone head. The wad froze in the air and then instantly vaporized before it struck the glowing end of the rock. Sook glanced at the two scientists with contempt. *Stupid incomps!*

"Prime should be here now protecting our escape, Sook," Mestra announced bitterly.

Chubal moved uneasily, his wounds gushing green blood down his uniform as he twisted against the pain. "They have bigger problems. We're on our own."

Sook placed a steady gauntlet on Chubal's shoulder. "Easy, sir."

"Leave me here, Sook," Chubal ordered. The Triadian stiffened in protest, but the first officer stood firm. "I said leave me; that's an order!" His throaty voice coughed up a beak full of green ooze, cutting short his reply. "Get the civs to the ship."

"But sir, we can all make it."

"Negative. We're all expendable. You know that."

"We should inform Primary that we're pinned down and our first officer's been hit," Mestra said as he came up beside his fellow Triadians.

"We stay dark," Chubal countered. "We've been compromised. Can't take a chance on the Voids finding our location. Follow the dry wash to the temple. It will open onto a plaza. Sook's ship is hidden there." Chubal grunted savagely. "It will outrun anything the Voids have."

Sook glanced up to see the bright orange radians of the battle continuing to light up the heavens. *Chubal is right; Primary is worse off than we are.*

"Sook . . .," Chubal wheezed.

"I'm here, sir."

"Keep that chinner of yours in check or we'll have civ parts spread clear across this draking planet."

"I will, sir!"

Chubal took an extra moment to catch his breath. "Move quickly now. Get the civs back to the ship. We don't know how many Voids have already landed." A shot of pain rifled up the back of his dorsal. "Help me up, Sook," Chubal ordered, spitting blood.

Sook removed both blasters from Chubal's belt, checking the magazines to make sure they were fully charged before placing them in the first officer's bleeding claws.

Chubal waved his persidon in the air. "Quit fussing over me like an old Scantorian mother," he groaned. Sook couldn't help it, however. Triadians were special; they took care of their own. They were not expendable; each life in their unit was precious. "Help me up so I can kill more of those grogan-eating Voids," he added.

As Mestra trained his six eyes on the ridgeline of advancing Voids, Sook lifted the first officer to a prone position along the top of the mound.

Chubal wiggled his thick body plates in the powdery dust, making himself ready.

Sook's helmet lenses cut through the dusty mist. The protective helmet gave the Triadian soldier the look of a giant insect. All that was visible now were the slaughtered bodies of fallen comrades that lay scattered among the ruins of the city. *Drak! They shouldn't have died. They were too good to die.* Sook shivered with disgust, wondering who betrayed them. *You'll not die in vain. I'll see to that. Not until my last breath will I give up on you, comrades.*

On the far ridge Fhaal reinforcements were repositioning themselves between the tall columns of stone that had once held a great portico. The towering archways were now pitilessly worn and broken. Time had finally won. All this knowledge . . . to dust. Soon the dim red star overhead would meet a similar fate.

Chubal snapped the faceplate closed on his helmet. They didn't have time to reminisce. "Get those civs out of here, Sook. You can't fail."

"Yes, sir," Sook replied, glancing at the two archaeologists still huddled together like spawning cadwaks. Sook had recognized the smaller of the two civs when they were inside the catacomb. It was Xancor, the lead scientist of the mission. He was clutching a small satchel over his chest and breathing painfully. The other civ was unfamiliar. He hadn't been on the list of scientists to evacuate.

"Let me hold this for you, Xancor," the civ said, reaching for the dark blue valise in Xancor's grasp.

Xancor trembled, protesting. "No, no. I must hold on."

"You're injured, Xancor, you may lose it."

"No. I will hold it," Xancor insisted.

Disgusted that he could not relieve Xancor of his burden, the civ looked to Sook for help.

Two thaders, one low, one high, struck the pile of rocks, showering hot shards of debris over them. Sook, with both blasters drawn, stepped out from behind the rocks and emptied both magazines at the oncoming wave of Voids. From the rear, Mestra and Chubal added more firepower as Sook dove back behind the pile, bringing on a fusillade of yellow plas-rounds.

"You're going to get me killed yet, Sook. I ordered you to get out of here. Now go!" Chubal ordered angrily.

"Yes, sir."

Sook turned back to check on Xancor and the civ. The civ's head had been blown away.

Sook pulled the civ's body away from Xancor. If Sook didn't get Xancor to the ship and a med unit, he would be dead and his knowledge lost.

Chubal pointed. "Go!" Then he turned around and began laying a barrage of plas-rounds to cover their escape down the dry wash. At one time the wash had probably been an old street that extended for miles, but after a million years of neglect, what remained of a once bright and beautiful avenue had, like everything else on the planet, died eons ago.

The Triadian hoisted Xancor to his feet and the two followed Mestra, who led the way. There was no stopping this time. Starting and stopping would only aggravate the wound and give the Voids a stationary target.

Before they had made it fifty strides out, the plas-rounds began whizzing past their heads. *The incomps couldn't hit the Neejan sun if they were kissing it,* thought Sook.

With a firm grip around Xancor's waist, Sook practically carried the scientist bodily in the air, his tiny feet brushing the dust every few strides. The Triadian turned back, plucking off the Voids who were coming down off the ridgeline as they sprinted for the temple.

Sook called to Mestra, "How many mags do you have?"

Mestra checked his belt. "Three. You?"

Sook held up the blaster, displaying the butt end of the weapon, and shouted, "This is it!" Then fired again. Two more Voids joined their ancestors.

A blaster magazine carried ten plas-rounds each. A Triadian carried ten mags. A hundred rounds were plenty for a mission like this. But no one had expected this kind of breach. Sook had used five mags just getting inside the catacombs and another three coming out. What was left between them was hardly enough to fend off the horde of Fhaal Voids closing in on their position.

"And the chinneroth?" Mestra kept asking.

"Forget the drakin' thing. It's probably thader dust by now."

The group of three popped over a knoll, ducking below more orange bolts. Mestra searched the horizon with all six eyes. In the next breath, both he and Sook dropped oncoming Voids five hundred strides out as easily as if they were at point-blank range.

With an exhaustive sigh Sook pointed behind them while checking Xancor's condition. His only chance was the ship's medical unit. "The wash continues on the other side of that fallen portico. We follow it past the temple."

Mestra understood as Sook lifted the semiconscious Xancor like a feather and took off again in long, quick strides. As near death as the old scientist was, he clung to his satchel so tightly that not even Death could rip it away.

Suddenly, a loud crack exploded behind them. Bright shards of light shot skyward. *Thaders.* And then Chubal's blasters went silent. Sook didn't have to look back to know Chubal was now living with his ancestors. *Good-bye, old friend.*

* * *

The heavy background explosions continued to rumble across the shadowy darkness as the small group ran along the lifeless wash, kicking up the dust as they ran.

Looking up at the dim heavens, a splinter of light far away caught Sook's attention for a brief moment. *There! There is Neeja. My home. She is guiding our way.* The Neejan star was clear and bright, blazing red and huge, six light-passings distant. *You would be in such awe of her,* Sook told the ancient ones of Amerloi. *Neeja is so delicious with life! She is beautiful like my Rhulaana and covers nearly the entire sky at its zenith! Yes, life there abounds,* Sook bragged to the fallen gods of the dead.

Sook sighed deeply. The thought of Rhulaana's passing ran deep, the blood in the Triadian's veins screaming hot with revenge. Rhulaana had been one of the first to perish in the Fhaal raids on the outer colonies. Sook would never forget.

Such a beautiful heart . . . gone from me . . . forever . . .

The back of Sook's eyes stung.

The dream ended.

"I will always miss you," Sook said softly to the faraway star.

They ran on. There was no more time to lament.

Soon they arrived at the temple along the wash. Just beyond the temple was the flat, windblown plaza of cracked floors and broken pillars that Chubal had described. The ship was still there, waiting patiently on the far side. It was a Tri-7. He had not expected that. Long and sleek, the transport had carried them through many campaigns against the Fhaal. Sook prayed to the ancestors it would save them one more time. The recent modifications to the Tri-7's drive had given it greater range, but there was a price: the craft had no plas-cannons. It was defenseless.

"The ship is in sight, Xancor," Sook informed the half-conscious scientist as they started walking toward the ship across the open plaza.

Xancor could hardly keep his head up. He uttered weakly, "Gamadin . . ."

Mestra asked, "What's he talking about?"

Sook shrugged. Neither of them had ever heard the word before.

Xancor's eyes pleaded for Sook to listen. "Alone, Triadian." Whether it was because Sook had stood by him and carried him all this way, or some other reason the Triadian wasn't privy to, Xancor's heartfelt expression of trust was one Sook wasn't about to deny the dying scientist.

Sook motioned for Mestra to go ahead while helping Xancor rest against a nearby broken column of the ancient temple. As Xancor labored against the supercold Amerloi air, he told Sook of his recent discovery of a race of beings called Gamadin. They were soldiers much like Triadians. They had traveled the stars long ago, protecting the cosmos from the madness of war. Xancor held up a shaking finger. "One ship alone could destroy an empire. The Fhaal have learned this. They fear the power of the Gamadin."

"The Fhaal fear the Gamadin?" Sook asked. "But how, sir? If these guardians are gone . . ."

Xancor's eyes looked down. "Yes," he admitted, "they are gone. But their technology still exists. I'm sure of it."

Sook was shocked. Looking around the crumbling city of Hitt, with its temples fallen in decay, its streets covered by lifeless dust, its gods long ago forgotten, how could the Gamadin have survived where gods couldn't?

Xancor continued. "Millawanda lies hidden. You must find her, Triadian. Find the Gamadin. Bring them here to save Neeja."

Sook decided that debating the dying scientist was pointless. More important than that, however, time was short. Chubal was no longer protecting their escape. The Voids were not far behind. Everyone's lives were in peril if they didn't get to the ship now. "We must go, Xancor," Sook urged. "I can help you there. We can talk later when we are safely——-"

Xancor stiffened. "No. No time. You must find the Gamadin, Triadian." He opened the satchel he had clung to and displayed the contents to Sook. There were only three items: a large vial of a blue fluid, a metal cylinder the color of very old gold, and a small square of folded cloth. Remarkably, the plasma blast had not incinerated the items inside. They were blemished with black scorch marks, but not destroyed.

As Death came for him, Xancor's large, glassy eyes glinted with delight, knowing that what he had uncovered was an archaeologist's dream. "Neeja," Xancor gasped, holding Sook in his final moments. "You must save Neeja . . ."

With shaky hands, Xancor removed the square cloth and unfolded it until it was an eighteen-clat square. The surface of the cloth was old, but the symbols and writing were as clear as a holographic projection. When Xancor touched a strange blue flower at the lower right-hand corner, the cloth came alive. Sook was awestruck. Its luminous qualities were superb.

"This map," Xancor pointed out as he labored to breathe, "will guide you."

Xancor touched the flower again. The field changed to a hologram of a planetary system.

"I have never been to this section of the quadrant," Sook said.

"Beyond the quadrant."

Sook kept staring with fascination. "Beyond?"

Xancor coughed up blood but answered, "Yes. Eight sectors."

Eight sectors!

No one had ever been outside the far reaches of the quadrant. Turning toward the ship, Sook wondered if it could be done at all. It had been retrofitted with long-range tanks. But even with extended range, the trip would be one way only. Even six sectors was pushing the extent of its range. Eight was way beyond the ship's capabilities.

"But, sir . . ."

Xancor wasn't listening. "This map is as old as Hitt," he said.

Sook stared in amazement. *How could that be? Hitt is dust. Nothing that old could remain usable for so long.*

Then, Mestra signaled that something was moving fast in the shadows. Sook saw it too and knew what it was.

Xancor pointed to a thin blue line that ran horizontally through the flat disk shape near the top of the open holo-map. In a painful movement, as though the gravity of a giant planet was pulling against him, Xancor tried reaching for the ancient symbol. "Help me, please."

With Sook's assistance, the old scientist touched the map and instantly the scene changed to a quadrant-size section of unexplored space. "Look for this power signature, here," he counseled, his voice trembling. "That is the source. The Gamadin . . . will be there. I'm sure of it," he wheezed.

Sook's head darted back and forth between Mestra and Xancor. "What source, Xancor? What am I looking for?"

"Soldiers, Triadian," Xancor gurgled, and then swallowed hard before finishing, "like yourself. Gamadin. They brought us peace once many eons ago. Find Millawanda. She will resurrect the Gamadin against the madness . . ."

Millawanda? Gamadin soldiers like Triadians? These words were all mysteries to Sook.

An almost apologetic grimace floated across Xancor's face as he saw Sook's look of confusion. "Forgive me, Triadian; you would be like a child against such power." His eyes drifted. "The Gamadin came from the galactic core. They traveled the stars before our ancestors walked. They are good. Find them, Triadian. You must do this. If you fail . . . well, you will not fail. You will save our dear Neeja from the Fhaal."

"I . . . alone?"

Xancor touched the map again, returning to the three-dimensional holo of twelve planets. "Find this system."

Xancor didn't have the strength to refold the cloth. He stuffed it back into the satchel with the vial of blue fluid and the metal cylinder, then gave his prizes to Sook like a dying king passing the scepter of power to his heir.

Xancor gasped. "Take it, Triadian . . ."

Sook mechanically accepted the keys to Neeja's survival. What else could be done? "Xancor, I . . . Mestra and I—"

"Find the peacemakers for Neeja, Triadian." With his last breath, Xancor whispered, "Find them . . . find the Gamadin . . . resurrect . . ."

Sook carefully laid Xancor's head in the ancient dust. While folding the square cloth to a single clat again and putting it safely back in the satchel, Mestra stepped over to ask, "What did he say?"

Sook answered, "I'll tell you along the way." Mestra helped Sook place Xancor's body into a shallow trench off to the side of the wash.

"Now all we need to find is the chinner," Mestra grunted with sour distaste.

Sook's bug-eyes turned like a slow-moving parabolic dish. Something winged flew across the horizon, keeping low in the dimness. "Stop, Mestra. He is not your concern."

Mestra sniffed the supercool air while four of his six eyes continued scanning. "He was with us at the catacomb, then disappeared," Mestra explained as his long strides shook the ground. "He's around, alright. I can smell his rancid breath."

When they got to within fifty strides of the ship, Sook's scanners went crazy. "Voids," the Triadian said, stopping instantly.

Four heavily armed Voids in dark uniforms stepped out of the shadows. Leading them into the open, as though he had nothing to fear, was a strikingly tall military figure. But this oversized being was no Void, Sook thought. Its presence instantly made the chilly air even colder. This Fhaal commander not only demanded obedience but also would kill anyone, entire planets, without hesitation if anyone blocked his way.

He wore no helmet or hat of any kind. The thin atmosphere and subzero cold of Amerloi had no effect on him. His hair, combed straight back against his skull, was silvery white. When his head rotated, surveying the shadows, his stone jaw protruded defiantly. His eyes were small and close together and glowed bright like a wild animal's at night. But no light was being shined into this creature's eyes to cast a reflection; its eyes glowed on their own. They did not blink or move. They stared. They pierced the soul with chilling thoughts of lifelessness, as though Death had somehow taken on the mortal guise of a Fhaal commander and was confronting Sook and Mestra face to face.

Sook drew first. But as fast as his Triadian trained reflexes were, the Fhaal leader was faster. In one swift, blinding draw, he pulled his weapon and shot Sook's blaster from the gauntlet's grip.

Sook's overheated fingers stung like plas-fire. Angrily forcing another step forward, a second searing round ripped through the right shoulder. Now on the ground, it was obvious Daashaan was taking his time and enjoying the sport of chiseling small slices of life from the Triadian. Mestra stood still, watching. He made no attempt at all to help his injured comrade.

"Such irrationality is unbecoming of a Triadian, is it not?" the Fhaal leader called out, stepping victoriously forward.

Sook protected the relics while keeping a painful jaw pointed at the approaching Voids. "Drak you!" Sook jeered, knowing the Triadians had hidden their ships well, cloaking them with an energy shroud. No one should have been able to locate them, even with probes, unless . . .

Sook turned toward Mestra just as Daashaan, lethargically replacing his pistol in its holster, said to him, "You've done well." His smile was wickedly cold, like Amerloian stone.

Sook was stunned. How? They had survived many campaigns together. Fought side by side. Saved each other's lives too numerous to count. Why?

"You're Triadian, Mestra," Sook began.

Mestra thrust his persidon into Sook's mask-covered face. The heartbreak in Sook's voice stirred no compassion in him. "I am no one. I go to the highest bidder. I was planted many passings ago. The Fhaal have penetrated to the very heart of the Neejan military corps. The end is written. Your dear Neeja is lost, old friend," he said, his voice heavy with self-satisfaction.

"The Gamadin location, Mestra," the leader demanded. "You have it?"

Mestra pointed to Sook. "The satchel. What you want is in there."

Mestra's eyes changed their priorities. His two far-left eyes remained on the leader while the rest busily darted from side to side, searching the perimeter for something unseen that frightened him.

"You betrayed us," Sook said, glaring up at Mestra. "I swear that your ancestors will see you shortly."

"You'll never get the chance, Sook. The chinneroth," Mestra demanded, "where is it?"

Sook lifted up as though trying to expel the pain, but instead, let out a short high-pitched whistle. "Find him yourself, drak."

Mestra's heavy claw struck Sook across the side of the head, sprawling the Triadian flat.

One of the Voids pulled his weapon to finish off Sook and take the satchel.

"Stop!" Mestra cried out. "The chinneroth is a trained pet. If we kill the Triadian, it will become enraged and kill us all, Daashaan," Mestra cautioned. The urgency in his voice froze the Voids where they stood as they all searched the surrounding area for trouble. "We must wait until it shows itself."

Daashaan scanned the horizon with his glowing eyes, penetrating the ink-black darkness from the Triadian ship to the ancient pillars and into the far distant shadows of the ancients. Nothing moved. "You worry over nothing, Mestra."

Mestra's beak tasted the air. "His presence is near, I tell you."

For long moments, Daashaan and his Voids kept searching the shadows with their sensors. Still, they found nothing.

Daashaan came back to Mestra. "Enough. The Triadian is unarmed, and three of my guards have their weapons pointed at its head. The satchel, Mestra, or you will die with the Triadian."

"The chinneroth is all that is unholy, Daashaan. Heed my words. He slaughters all without warning. I have seen such death before."

"Stop, coward," Daashaan interrupted, "I will not be intimidated by shadows. The Gamadin satchel, Mestra, get it!" the Fhaal leader demanded.

Mestra removed the satchel from Sook's possession without taking his eyes from the shadows. "All that you need to find the Gamadin is here," he said.

Daashaan reached for the case, but Mestra held back. "First, my payment, Daashaan. I must know that you have it before I give you the source of the Gamadin power."

Daashaan's brow wrinkled. The shallow smile faded instantly. "Yes," he said dryly, "I have it here."

Mestra's eyes focused on the heartless glare just before a Void filled his back with a charged bolt of white-hot plasma. The tharlic's eight-foot body fell into the fine dust, joining the stone gods of the distant past. *You're right, Mestra,* Sook mused, *I didn't get the chance to avenge your betrayal.*

A horrifying shriek suddenly shattered the air before Daashaan could retrieve the satchel. The Voids, their weapons ready, searched the horizon for anything that moved. Sook reached for Mestra's blaster. As Daashaan was about to kill Sook with a shot to the head, a screaming shadow exploded out of concealment and latched its gaping jaw onto Daashaan's forearm.

The attack was so swift and unexpected that the Voids froze in place. They had never seen anything so hideously evil nor heard such high-pitched shrieks. It was like a winged demon from a hellish nightmare sweeping down from the darkened skies. Even the gods of Amerloi trembled in fear.

Its giant, dragon-like body supported a loathsome head that was huge and disproportional with its wide, gaping mouth. Green, sticky drool dripped from the needle-sharp tips of its long teeth. The beast's wings, spanning ten strides, fluttered with rage as mid-joint talons tore deep into Daashaan's arm, crushing bone and severing tendons.

Daashaan whirled in a desperate effort to throw off the clinging beast. It would not let go. Its claws were locked, unbreakable.

Then, suddenly, a bone-crunching sound split the air as Daashaan's forearm detached from his body, his fingers still twitching feverishly for his weapon.

Daashaan's glowing eyes filled with terror as he fell to the ground, grabbing his bloodied stump. The chinneroth quickly swallowed the arm whole before it opened its wide, saw-toothed mouth and turned mercilessly on the nearest Void. In a desperate attempt to kill the beast, the Void thrust the muzzle of his weapon at point-blank range. But the chinner was merciless, ripping the Void's head from its neck before it could pull the trigger.

Another Void fired, but the shot went wild. The sounds of mutilation and terror threw his aim wide of the target.

Suddenly the screams stopped. The second Void's head lay cocked to one side, dangling from his shoulders where the chinneroth's claw had ripped clean through his neck and armored chest. The remaining Void, wide-eyed with fear, hastily aimed its weapon at the preoccupied dragon. But before the last Void could shoot, two yellow plas-rounds collapsed it where it stood.

For one confused moment, Daashaan eyed the Void's discarded weapon. "I wouldn't," Sook warned him, holding Mestra's blaster. The chinneroth stepped over the weapon and urinated along the length of its frame; the acidified waste ate through the barrel like it was melting wax.

Daashaan's pain-struck face twisted with rage. "You will never leave the quadrant," he said in raw, rasping gulps. "My ships will hunt you down."

The chinneroth started to charge, its crazed yellow eyes fierce with death.

"No, Mowgi!" Sook cried out.

The chinneroth stopped a fraction of a stride from Daashaan. Its hot, putrid breath washed over Daashaan's face, daring him to make the slightest offensive twitch.

Sook then kicked the Void's weapon away before retrieving the satchel from under Mestra's dead body.

"No matter where you go, the Fhaal will find you," Daashaan cried out, still holding his bloodied stump.

Sook grabbed the relics and limped painfully toward the waiting ship in silence. There was nothing to say.

Daashaan tried to rile his enemy. "Kill me now, Triadian," he shouted to Sook's back, "for I will not stop until you are dead."

Sook paused, facing Daashaan one last time. Holding a bar for support, Sook simply nodded.

Daashaan had but a brief moment to think about crawling over to grab the dead Void's weapon before the chinneroth severed the commander's head with one deadly swipe of its claw. Daashaan's body fell forward, his head bouncing in the Amerloian dust, never to rise again.

* * *

After strapping in, the Triadian blew a short, high-pitched whistle. The bestial creature obediently flew to the top of the ship's fuselage where it began to shrink, turning into something small and harmless. When its transformation was complete, it crawled through the hatchway like a sticky-footed fly as it found its special place behind the Triadian's control chair.

The sleek Tri-7 transport roared to life. Slowly it rose above the ancient city of Hitt and hovered momentarily while its two star drives extended to their full lengths. The ship then angled skyward, flashed into the stratosphere, and was gone.

Chapter Two

THE SURVIVOR

KEVIN DORRITY NEARLY lost control of his red Studebaker convertible when the crack of the sonic boom rumbled across the high deserts of northwestern New Mexico. All Kevin really cared about before the boom was the Yankees winning the doubleheader against the Red Socks and how far he could make it with Becky Price tonight. He, Becky, his best friend, Eddie Greenberg, and Eddie's girlfriend, Matty Madison, were on their way to Parker's Knoll for some serious spooning. The air was dry and cooling off from the midday summer heat. The scent of sage and mesquite mixing with a warm breeze always felt fresh and clean. It was shaping up to be one of those romantic red and bruise-colored New Mexico sunsets. If there was a more romantic spot, Kevin didn't have a clue where it was.

Kevin pulled off to the side of the road to make sure everyone was all right. Ahead was the entry to Pete Delmonte's cabin, an old silver mine that had been left over from the late 1800s. "That was close," he said, looking skyward.

"I don't see any clouds, Kev," Eddie reported after a quick check of the skies and hills around the old mine.

Kevin stared to the south. "Me either."

"Could be a jet. I hear they make quite a loud noise when they pass through the sound barrier," Becky added.

Eddie and Kevin traded looks that said, "how would she know that?" She turned away from Kevin in a huff. "I'm not stupid, Kevin Dorrity."

Whenever Becky added his last name, Kevin knew he was in trouble. He looked again at the perfect sunset. He didn't want to jeopardize his chances later that night. "I didn't say anything, Beck," he explained, holding his palms open.

"You said enough."

Kevin tried putting his arm around her to make amends, but Becky wasn't going for it. She moved to the other side of the front seat, her bottom ruby-red lip stuck out. Just getting to first base at Parker's Knoll was looking grim. Not only that, Kevin was due back at the fire station by midnight. As a member of Aztec's volunteer fire department, he had to spend one weekend a month at the station during his summer vacation from New Mexico State University. Time was short.

Although the sun was already down, there was enough light to see the nearby mine vents popping out all around the nearby hills.

"There must be a hundred pits out there," Kevin observed.

Eddie agreed. "They say old man Delmonte's been digging since the war."

Becky's eyes lit up. "Has he found any gold?"

"It's a silver mine, Beck," Kevin said. At the top of the ridge was an open tunnel where narrow tracks emerged that ran to a tailings pile. Rusty digging equipment, broken ore wagons, and bent rails were spread all around the entrance to the mine shaft. "And from the looks of it, he didn't find much."

Just then they all saw a bright, fast-moving object drop out of the heavens followed by another boom that was so powerful it cracked the windshield of the car. The object then banked hard, flying right over their heads at unbelievable speed. When it flew over Delmonte's abandoned mine, the object suddenly slowed to a crawl and hung in the air like a tree ornament.

Eddie's mouth dropped open. "What is it?"

Kevin's mouth was just as hollow. "I'm not sure."

The slender craft dropped behind the black outlines of the nearby hills and was gone. After a short delay, a high-energy pulse crackled just before bright balls of light shot skyward and exploded over the hills in a giant fireworks display.

"The old coot may need help," Kevin announced. He glanced up the highway and pointed to an old gate. He knew what he had to do. "Does that lead to his place?"

"I think so," Matty replied.

"Maybe we should call someone first," Eddie cautioned.

"That would mean going back into town. There's no time," Kevin replied as they watched the bright glow continue to radiate light over the black ridgeline of the hills. "If that thing crashed, they might need help right away, Eddie."

Becky asked anxiously, "What if there are bodies?"

"You can stay here with Matty . . ."

Matty wasn't going for it. "I'm not staying in the car, Kevin. If anyone's hurt, I want to help too."

Kevin saw the determination in Matty's face. There was no talking her out of it. He turned back to Becky and said, "We have to go, Beck. There might be bodies. I won't tell you differently. But if someone is alive up there, we might be able to help them. We have a car, too. We can get them to the hospital if we need to."

Becky was scared, but what choice did she have? Everyone was going with Kevin. She would rather see a dead body than be left in the car by herself.

Eddie's eyes lit up as he reached for the camera in the backseat. Displaying a wide grin, he seemed to be the only one who saw their future. "The newspapers will pay big money for pictures of the crash site, Kev."

Kevin didn't care about money or pictures. His only concern as he shifted the car into first gear and gunned it up the highway for Delmonte's gate was whether someone needed his help.

* * *

"Stop your crazy howling!" Pete Delmonte yelled at his sixteen-year-old yellow Labrador retriever. At six foot two and as thin as Digger's short-haired tail, the cantankerous old U.S. Navy vet had come to New Mexico just after the war, divorcing his third wife for the second time and trying his luck at silver mining. Problem was, those that knew him said whatever he found of value in the earth went immediately to a bottle of Jack Daniels instead of the bank and the support payments for his ex. The only other thing he did do with any regularity, drunk or sober, was make payments to his stockbroker for a college account for his only son, two-year-old Pete Delmonte Jr. Delmonte senior may have been a screw of a husband, but little Pete Junior was going to get a proper education if the father had to dig all the way to China to do it!

At the sound of the thunderous explosion that shook the entire hillside and his rickety bourbon-fumed one-room cabin, Delmonte had awakened, fists flying at unknown Japanese Zeros as though he were under attack. Delmonte had nearly tripped over Digger as he fell out of his cot. "Dog! Get your flea-bitten hind end out of my way," he shouted. Delmonte grabbed the sides of the wooden crate next to his cot to steady himself. The clapboard sides of the shack creaked and cried out under the sudden percussion. His last fifth of Jack Daniels teetered on the kitchen table and rolled off.

"Oh, no!" Delmonte moaned as he watched the half-full bottle of amber bliss shatter into a thousand pieces of broken glass on the floor. *Not my Jack!* If it wasn't for the broken glass, he would have licked the floorboards. It would be two whole weeks before he made his next trip to town. "That was my last bottle!"

A bright fiery light flooded the inside of the shack. Digger continued to bark as Delmonte stumbled to the window dressed in the rumpled clothes and shoes he lived and slept in.

Trying to focus, his eyes caught a glimpse of a long object diving across the sky and exploding over the nearby ridge behind the house. The thought that someone could be hurt didn't occur to Delmonte. At the moment he was more upset with the responsible party who broke his bottle of JD than about anyone's well-being. "Dang it!" he cried out. They were going to pay.

Delmonte kept up his verbal tirade while he retrieved his 12-gauge scattergun next to his cot and headed for the front door. "Dang right, you'll pay. And two bottles extra for the trouble, too!"

Weapon in hand, Delmonte kicked open the door, ripping out the screws from its last good hinge. Delmonte didn't care about the door; it was payback time. He clicked back the hammer on his shotgun as Digger bolted out ahead of him. He charged up the hill, screaming obscenities the whole way. Ready to shoot first and ask questions later.

* * *

Eddie leaped out of the car and opened the broken split-rail gate that stood at the entrance to the property. To the side of the gate was an old rusty mailbox upon which the words "Delmonte's Place" had been scribbled in dirty white paint. An additional sign of splintered wood hung crookedly below the mailbox. On it was the message "Never mind the hound . . . worry about the OWNER!!" with a hand-drawn pistol under the letters. The pistol was a terrible likeness, but the intent was quite clear to everyone.

Eddie climbed back in the car, and Kevin's wheels spun in the dirt as he drove through the gate. "He sure does take his privacy seriously," Matty said, "but he won't shoot us. My father knows Mr. Delmonte. He's a harmless old coot. Besides, he'll know who I am."

About a half-mile up the road they came to Delmonte's clapboard shack and Kevin honked the horn.

"Why'd you do that?" Eddie wanted to know.

Kevin looked back at Eddie through the rearview mirror. "I take that sign seriously. He's alone out here and he doesn't like company. We're unannounced and something just exploded over the ridge there. Now, do you want to sneak up on an old warhorse in the dark who we all know drinks whiskey like water?"

"Good point." Eddie reached over Kevin's shoulder and honked the horn again.

Becky's nose wrinkled with disgust. "What's that smell?"

"Bourbon," Kevin replied.

"Delmonte lives here?" Eddie asked, looking at all the trash and empty bottles of Jack Daniels lying around the porch.

Matty stepped out of the car first and called out for Delmonte. "It's me, Mr. Delmonte, Matty Madison. Are you home?"

Except for the headlights of the car, it was all black and motionless both inside and outside the shack. No one answered her call.

"I don't think the old coot's around," Kevin said.

Eddie stayed close to Matty as they walked up to the porch and peered inside, past the broken front door. "Empty," Eddie reported.

"Delmonte probably heard the explosion and took off up the road to investigate," Kevin offered, pointing ahead where the headlights carved a tunnel of light in the darkness.

Just then they heard a dog barking off in the distance.

"Sounds like Digger, Mr. Delmonte's dog," Matty said.

Kevin looked off beyond the shack. "We should get up there. He might need assistance."

Becky grabbed Kevin's arm. "I think we should stay here."

"Stay in the car, honey, but I have to go," Kevin told her.

Eddie reached into the car. "Alright, Kev. I've got the camera."

* * *

Delmonte carefully made his way around an open, vertical mine shaft before he reached the top of the ridge. He knew the open pit was more than a thousand feet deep. He ducked under the old pithead timbers, trying to catch his breath. His throat was parched. He'd give a silver bar for a drink. But what he saw next was enough to make him forget his thirst.

Delmonte came over the top of the ridge and stopped dead in his tracks. Staring wide-eyed in wonder, he took in the crash site that lay before him. The largest sections of the dull-platinum-colored craft were a quarter-mile away on the other side of the wide ravine. The smell of burning sage filled the smoky air as Delmonte viewed the ring of fire around the jagged sections of the object. He reckoned it was some kind of airship, but unlike any he had ever seen. The main section was nearly a football field in length, with one window at the front of the sleek, slender hull.

As Delmonte stood awestruck, a small creature jumped out of an open crack in the hull. It was followed closely by someone or something crawling out from under the burning main section of the craft.

The creature didn't wait for the other being. It just scampered away into the bushes and was gone.

Barking nonstop, Digger took off after the trespasser just in case the little survivor thought to mark the wrong bush.

"Dang, dog! Get your hind end back here," Delmonte yelled. But Digger was fixated, hearing nothing. He charged on, protecting his backyard from any squatters.

Delmonte grimaced with resolve. With his shotgun shaking in his hands, he cussed all the way down into the ravine. Added to the debt he had to collect, he now had to round up his fool-headed dog.

He stopped just before the perimeter rim of the fire, looking up at the pulsing, thin blue light that illuminated the object's side. He wondered where the door was, what was the front and what was the back, and how anything like that could fly.

Where's the dang engine?

Digger suddenly stopped barking, and Delmonte watched him sniff one of the smaller sections of wreckage before dousing it with a territorial marker. "Dang it, dog!" Delmonte riled, followed by a swift kick to the old yellow Lab's rump. "Don't go squirting on people's property like that."

A sudden movement from behind him startled Delmonte as Digger disappeared through the bushes on his way to stake another marker. Whirling around, Delmonte's finger accidentally discharged the shotgun, knocking him on his rear. The 12-gauge double-aught buckshot's sparks ricocheted off the main section of the craft. Momentarily stunned, Delmonte took a few seconds longer before he realized a being in an odd gray uniform was standing over him.

"Holy cow, where'd you come from, mister?" Delmonte said, trying to find his legs. "Well, is this your, your . . . Well, what is it? Some kind of spaceship or somethin'?"

Light from the surrounding fires allowed him only small glimpses of the strange being. He was tall and muscular, with wide shoulders and long, slender arms and legs. Because he wore a helmet, however, Delmonte could not see the survivor's face.

Delmonte looked around for other survivors. "Anyone else in there?" he asked, pointing. Seeing no one else, he added, "I think she's a goner, mister."

The being stood there, silent for a brief moment before it let go a short, high-pitched whistle. Obediently, the small creature Delmonte had seen exiting the ship earlier trotted up next to the survivor. It had to be the strangest-looking pet Delmonte had ever laid eyes on. In general, it had the size and shape of a medium-size dog. But that was as close to describing man's best friend as Delmonte would take it. The creature had large bat-like ears, a long snout, and short dark hair like the furry side of a felt patch. Its long thin tail curled up like a circus whip. Hidden behind a layer of skin near its mouth were rows of teeth that appeared sharp and pointed as they protruded ever so slightly from the heavily muscled jaw.

The big-eared creature didn't appear to be threatening. With simple gestures and high-pitched clacks, the being had the creature well under control. But Delmonte felt uneasy in its presence, and edged away. The pet was obviously very protective. "Nice pooch. Kinda an odd duck, ain't it?"

Still wordless, the tall being reached down and offered Delmonte a helping hand.

"What are you doing here anyway?" Delmonte asked, gripping the hand. The survivor lifted him to his feet as though he were a child's toy doll. It then touched the side of its head, which flipped up the covers over its eyes. In that moment Delmonte caught a partial glimpse of the being's young face and the strange green eyes that had an intelligence about them that went way beyond his whiskey-soaked brain. The eyes were quite extraordinary in their jewel-like brilliance. Beautiful even.

"You look like you could use a bottle of Jack yerself, mister," Delmonte said, trying not to stare too much. "Sorry about the . . ." He stopped, amazed that there were no marks at all where the buckshot had struck the hull of the ship at point-blank range. He rubbed his fingers over the area. The satiny gray metal was smooth and warm. The ship's hull wasn't even dented.

Delmonte glanced back at the stranger, who was in obvious pain from injuries he sustained from the crash. *You stupid SOB,* the drunkard chided himself, *can't ya see the man's hurtin'? Where's your manners?*

Delmonte held his shotgun to one side as he grabbed the man around the waist so he wouldn't fall over. "Ah, geez, mister. We'll worry about the Jack later. You don't look so good. Maybe you should spend the night at my place. It ain't much, but it's a roof." As the two passed the wreckage en route to the trail back to the shack, Delmonte exclaimed, "You're darned lucky to be alive, mister."

A thumping sound broke through the crackling sounds of the small fires around the ship. Two seconds later an Air Force whirlybird popped over the horizon, causing Delmonte's neck hairs to stand straight up. These boys weren't making a social call, he thought. From experience he knew other whirlybirds would be spitting out squads of heavily armed troops, and he and Digger and their new friends would be right in the middle of it all.

* * *

Eddie helped Matty over a large rut in the road as they continued up the hill behind Delmonte's shack. "I smell something burning," she said.

Behind them on the dirt path, Becky pointed high in the starry sky as several beacons of blinking red and white lights came swooping down out of the night.

"They're helicopters," Kevin explained.

Heavy thumping sounds were just hitting their ears. "And coming from several directions, Kev," Eddie added, grabbing Matty's hand. "This is getting exciting."

"They might not want us around," Becky cautioned. "Remember during the war? The government doesn't like people getting in their way."

"The war's over, Becky," Eddie replied. "This is a free country. We got a right to be here as much as they do."

A chopper, flying low, suddenly flashed bright floodlights across the low-lying hills, exposing the overhead timbers of an open mine shaft. "Watch it, Becky," Kevin called out, grabbing her around the waist.

Kevin pulled Becky back to safety while almost losing his own footing at the rim of the open shaft. Loose rocks tumbled into the black hole, clanking only after long moments of dead silence.

"Thanks," Becky said gratefully.

Kevin turned to Eddie and Matty. "Watch your step."

"Maybe the girls should go back to the car," Eddie suggested.

"We're staying with you," Matty stated flatly. There was no arguing.

"I'm with Matty," Becky added, reaching for Matty's hand.

The four continued to the top of the hill. Kevin bent down low behind a prickly sage bush, pulling Becky down with him. "Everybody keep your head down."

Eddie wasn't so cautious. He wanted a picture of the crash site for posterity. He stood up and started snapping shots with the Kodak camera, looking like a landing strobe in the process.

"I said keep your head down, Eddie. The whole world can see you with that camera . . ." Kevin's voice trailed off as he stood up and came alongside Eddie and Matty, who had joined him. There, spread out before them, was the object that had fallen from the stars. They could feel the heat from pockets of fire and hot twisted sections of metal. The odors were pungent, reeking of burning sage and toxic fumes from the crashed vessel.

"Wow!" Eddie said in a low, raspy voice. "It's a-a-a—"

"A spaceship?" Matty said, finishing the thought.

Kevin agreed. "Looks like it."

"I never thought it was possible," Eddie said, continuing to click photos. "It's so big!"

"I wonder where it came from?" asked Becky, who had joined them.

"Mars. Maybe Venus," Kevin guessed. "Not from here, that's for sure."

Matty pointed at the burning craft. "Something's moving down there."

"Let's check it out, Kev," Eddie said. "I've never seen a Martian. Maybe he'll let me take a picture of him."

"Easy, Eddie," Kevin cautioned. "They might not be friendly."

Eddie pulled Matty with him while he held the camera in his other hand. "That's movie stuff, Kev. If they wanted to hurt us, they wouldn't pick the middle of nowhere to invade, would they? And then crash trying to do it?"

But before the couple had taken a step, several loud pops high overhead broke the quiet, instantly flooding the ship with bright light.

"Flares!" Kevin cried out. "Look at all the soldiers. How'd they get here so fast?"

"Better hurry before they seal it off," Eddie said, undeterred.

Kevin tried to grab his friend. "No, Eddie, wait . . ."

A heavy thumping broke through the hiss of the burning flares. Then a dozen more whirling aircraft came in from all directions, landing near the spaceship and quickly depositing more heavily armed troops everywhere along the perimeter. Kevin looked back toward Delmonte's shack and could see a line of headlights bumping up the dirt road.

Becky shook. "Kevin . . ."

Kevin put his arm around her. "It's alright, babe," he said to comfort her, but he felt anxious too. This was no place for college students on summer vacation. "We'd better get out of here."

Matty pointed at two figures next to the largest section of the burning spacecraft. "Hey, I think that's Mr. Delmonte down there."

"Who's that with him?" Kevin asked.

"Maybe it's a Martian," Eddie joked.

Kevin squinted, focusing on the two figures. "He looks human."

Matty added, "Delmonte's helping him along. He's injured, Kevin."

Bam! Crack! Bam! Bam! Bam!

Bursts of machine-gun bullets whizzed above their heads. Eddie jolted backwards, blown away by a round of fire. His body tumbled over Matty, knocking her to the ground. Kevin couldn't help his friends because he was holding Becky. Her eyes were open, but they were vacant and lifeless. She had been shot through the head and neck. Matty screamed as she, too, tried to shake Eddie back to life. But he wouldn't move.

Another wave of bullets struck the desert brush around them. In that instant, Kevin tore Matty away from Eddie's lifeless form and grabbed the camera as his fireman's training kicked into overdrive. For a brief moment he thought about putting his hands in the air and giving up. But some innate feeling cried out that it wouldn't matter. If he did, he and Matty would both be shot dead.

They crouched in the brush long enough for Kevin to remove the camera film and then, together, they turned to run back down the hillside.

"Kevin, what are you doing?" Matty shouted. "We can't just leave them there."

"They're dead, Matty," Kevin cried out.

Overhead, a barrage of orange tracers sizzled inches from their heads and into the night. Their loved ones could not be helped and, if they stayed, they would end the same way. Kevin didn't have time to explain all that to Matty. He put the film in his pocket and pulled her along as they ran—their only hope for survival.

* * *

A broadside of bullets screamed passed Delmonte's head. He tried to fire back. Click. Nothing happened. "Dirt for brains," he scolded himself, remembering he had spent his last rounds when he misfired his scattergun earlier. He checked his pockets. No shells, either. He hadn't thought of bringing more ammo with him when he left his shack. Well, who would have thought he'd be in a war? "Dirt for brains!" he cried out again.

Another fusillade tore his shotgun from his grip, driving him to the dirt. Bullets thumped against the vessel's hull and simply fell to the ground, flattened like pennies rolled over by a train. The survivor stood over Delmonte, appearing to be unaffected by the whole matter, as more bullets thumped against his flight suit.

Delmonte was amazed. He didn't quite understand how the suit could withstand such an assault. The survivor wasn't entirely unaffected, however. His right hand was covered with the dark blood that was oozing out from under his uniform sleeve. Tucked tightly under his arm was a satchel that he carried like Delmonte would a bottle of Jack.

Delmonte reached up and pulled the survivor to the ground. He wasn't taking any chances. He was either the luckiest partner he knew, or the dumbest. "Those are live rounds, son." The survivor's face was half hidden behind his flight helmet, but his odd green eyes conveyed that he was in pain. The way he held his right arm close to his side and his labored breathing told Delmonte that the gent was going to pass out at any moment.

"Ah, dirt for brains!" Delmonte cursed as he struggled to pull the wounded being to the back side of the wreckage, where they could duck under a sheet of the spacecraft for protection.

As the deadly rounds continued to thump harmlessly against the tough metal, Delmonte wondered what to do next. He was fresh out of both shells and ideas on how to stay alive. They had nothing to protect themselves with except a battered section of the ship. For a split second he toyed with the idea of giving up. He thought harder. He might have dirt for brains, but he wasn't a total moron. *Those soldier boys are out to kill anything that moves.* Neither his life nor the alien survivor's was worth so much as an empty bottle of Jack.

The survivor seemed to appreciate Delmonte's help until the old war vet tried to relieve the survivor of his satchel. In the blink of an eye, Delmonte was staring down the barrel of a wickedly lethal weapon the likes of which he had never seen before. It was black and heavy and had a 12-inch barrel that had no hole in the end of it where a bullet would come out. Delmonte had no doubt, however, that if the survivor decided to pull the trigger, what was left of his brains would be spread out across Aztec County.

Delmonte raised his hands. "I was only trying to help ya." He thought his time was up, but just then the survivor unexpectedly slumped over and dropped the weapon.

Delmonte quickly seized the weapon. *Might as well use it to crack open a crate of Jack for all the good it will do,* he thought as he examined the weighty piece of unusual hardware.

Delmonte surveyed the area and spotted an air vent for the mine shaft a ways up the hillside. *If they could just make it to the shaft.* It was a good thirty yards through prickly bushes and tumbleweed. Dang it! It was too far without protection. They would be sitting ducks without some cover.

The bullets didn't stop as dark uniformed soldiers kept methodically tightening the circle around them. He pointed the barrel at his nose to check the weapon over. Maybe there was something he missed. Suddenly a hand came out of nowhere and grabbed the barrel of the weapon. The survivor's bulbous green eyes stared at Delmonte like he was some kind of ignorant dork. "Well, dang it, partner, I don't know how this thing works," Delmonte said in his own defense.

It was all that the survivor could do to push the weapon away from Delmonte's face and nod toward the oncoming soldiers.

Delmonte took a quick breath and pointed. Dang, he needed a drink. He didn't aim at anything in particular. He just pointed the weapon away from them and prayed the thing didn't explode in his hand. He squeezed the only thing that remotely looked like a trigger. The weapon kicked like an Army Colt .45. Instantly, an incredibly powerful bolt of yellow-green light shot out of the barrel and struck a large rock a hundred yards away. The rock exploded into a fiery ball of tiny missiles, taking out a squad of oncoming troops in the process. "Whoa! That's the ticket!"

The next shot blew the tail off a chopper that had landed on the ridge a quarter-mile away. Several more shots stopped the troops' advancement; they all scurried back into the hills for cover. Delmonte didn't know how many shots he had left, but he figured now was the time to make a run for the mine vent. As good as the weapon was, it had only bought them a few precious moments of time.

"Come on, partner. It's now or never," Delmonte urged as he pulled the being along toward the vent. If they stayed below the tops of the sage, maybe they could make it before the soldiers regrouped. They had gone only a few yards, though, when the survivor held him up.

"We can't stop now," Delmonte protested.

The survivor removed a small device from his belt. With hands shaking, he twisted a dial and then pressed a tiny green light on the end of the device. A strange whirr sounded next, followed by a precision click coming from the craft. Delmonte's mouth dropped open as he watched the main body of the ship fold in on itself and dissolve right before his eyes. A few seconds later all traces of the craft had turned to a powdery white dust. "Well, I'll be good to . . ."

A burst of flares exploded overhead, shocking Delmonte back to life and lighting their way toward the vent.

For some reason he didn't quite understand, Delmonte felt close to the survivor. Maybe it was because he knew they were both doomed. Why had he come here? What reason did he have for landing in Delmonte's backyard, in the middle of nowhere? Would Delmonte ever learn the answers before the soldier boys killed them? Did it matter? *Why should I care, anyway?* he thought.

Delmonte and the survivor crawled forward on their bellies. They were almost there. A huge dread of responsibility flushed the old miner's senses numb. Somehow all the bullets whizzing by his head didn't seem to bother him as much as letting the survivor fall into the hands of the government. Dag gummit, how he hated responsibility. He had spent his whole life being irresponsible. He thought he should have longer than five seconds to grow up.

They kept crawling as bullets began pecking away at the dirt around them. The soldiers had figured out their destination. "Move! Move! Move!" Delmonte kept repeating, wishing he could make himself the size of an ant. *Crawl, you SOB, crawl* . . . he grunted and spat under his breath. *Just ten feet more* . . . They slithered under the sagebrush like frightened sidewinders and reached out for the vent.

* * *

It was pitch black inside the mine shaft as Kevin continued to lower himself and Matty deeper into Delmonte's old abandoned mine. Out of complete desperation, Kevin had done the only thing he could think of after watching Becky and Eddie get shot dead by the soldiers' gunfire. The black pit was the one place that offered him and Matty any hope of survival. When he saw the cable hanging down into the shaft, he told Matty to hang on just above him as they swung out into the blackness and down in the hole. Whether the shaft dropped down ten feet or a thousand didn't matter. It was simply the only place they could escape.

Soon after, however, Matty's grip began to weaken. She couldn't hold on much longer. Kevin didn't know how much longer he could hold on for both of them either.

"I can't, Kevin," Matty cried.

"You've got to, Matty," Kevin urged. "You've got to help me. I don't have the strength to keep us both from falling. It's not much farther."

After the first few feet of their descent, light ceased to exist. Everywhere they looked it was pitch black. Matty began to sob. "They killed Becky, Kevin. Eddie . . . they killed him too."

"I know, Matty. I know . . ."

Something in the dark stopped Kevin's descent. "Hold on, Matty. I've hit something." He reached out and felt down below his Keds.

Matty slid down beside Kevin. Both of them could rest their feet on a board, and they began to bounce. "Maybe this leads to a side tunnel," Kevin suggested. Still holding fast to the cable, he reached out with his toe and found nothing but air. "Easy, Matty. We're standing on a cross plank. Stay where you are until I can figure out what direction it goes."

Kevin looked up. A few stars shed a dim light that cut through the darkness. He judged that he and Matty were at least a hundred feet down. The air was much cooler and wet in the shaft. He just needed a little more light. His first step would be crucial.

Suddenly, a soldier's head popped over the side at the top of the shaft. "Halt!" he shouted, pointing a bright flashlight down the shaft. "Stop right there." Others soon joined the soldier around the rim as they poked their rifles down the shaft.

With the light came the opportunity Kevin and Matty needed. The catwalk was now clearly illuminated, and Kevin could see that the foot-wide plank stretched across the shaft and connected two horizontal tunnels.

"Hurry, Matty!" Kevin urged.

Kevin took two quick steps sideways and entered the lip of the cross tunnel. He almost lost his balance when the loose rocks from around the edge started to crumble beneath him.

He turned back to Matty to pull her in. "Watch the edge, Matty. You can make it."

Matty nodded. She understood. She let go of the cable and reached for Kevin's hand as she scooted sideways along the few feet of plank as Kevin had done.

Shots exploded inside the shaft.

A split second was all that she needed to reach the edge. Kevin had her hand; their fingers locked. He wouldn't let go for any reason. In that next second, however, her momentum stopped. Her fingers tore away from Kevin's grip, and in the blink of an eye, Matty vanished from his sight into the blackness.

"MATTYYYYY!!" Kevin screamed. He stood there helpless, staring into the abyss, unable to do anything to save his friend's life. He tried to see down into the shaft whether she might have caught on a ledge. Sparks flew off the wall from the ricocheting bullets. He had to know if there was the slightest chance she was clinging to life and holding on to something in the dark. In the movies the good guy always found a way to survive. *Matty was good. She would find a way.* But after an extremely long moment, he heard the demoralizing sound from far below of her body crashing, echoing her final reality.

In that instant Kevin realized this wasn't the movies. Even if a bullet had not killed her, the fall certainly had. Tears flowed down his face. He backed away from the shaft. He was sickened and stunned, all alone, as the onslaught of rifle bullets continued.

Why did this happen? Why . . .

Deeper into the mine he went, stumbling and shivering as he followed a pair of narrow gauge tracks, away from the sound of ricocheting bullets, away from the soldiers' scattered light. The shaft was devoid of all light, and Kevin was stepping blind. He had no idea where he was or where he was going, or if it even mattered. The sound of soldiers clambering down the shaft meant they would find Kevin soon and end his confusion forever—unless the mine claimed him first. If there was another vertical pit in his path, he would never know it. *Maybe it was just as well.* Survival didn't seem appealing anymore now that he was all alone without his friends.

Cold and wet, Kevin continued along the ore cart tracks, figuring they had to lead somewhere. He kept his arms extended in front of him to protect his head in case a low-hanging beam or some other obstruction blocked his path.

A short while later, Kevin nearly tripped on something in the dark. He used the side of the tunnel to steady himself, wondering why he should bother to go on. An odd rustling noise drew his attention to movement close by. Something scraped against the side of his pants leg. At any other time Kevin might have jumped away, startled. But he was too exhausted and disheartened to care. At this point nothing could scare him.

He heard the sound again. He wished he could see. The thing brushed his leg, back and forth, like a cat hunting for affection. Bending down, Kevin saw a pair of yellow eyes staring up at him. They seemed to glow on their own without light. He could also hear the creature's breathing.

He reached out and touched a short, coarse-haired animal. It was small, not much bigger than Becky's beagle named Bailey. The animal let out a short yelp. *What animal could lurk in the mines?* Kevin asked himself.

Kevin backed away as the eyes fixated on him and the creature made a kind of giddy panting noise. The animal wouldn't take no for an answer. It wanted attention from the thing it had touched even if that something was cold and wet.

Figuring the critter was harmless enough, Kevin squatted down and put out his hand. A rough tongue began to lick the back of it. He then felt two incredibly large ears that stood up like a bat's. When he rubbed them, the thing began to purr quite loudly.

Although he didn't picture the old coot Delmonte having a pet like this, Kevin wondered if it was, indeed, Digger, the mutt that Matty had scolded Eddie about.

More at ease that the animal was not a hostile beast, Kevin forced himself to continue along the tracks. At least he was not alone—a small comfort. He felt the roll of film in his pants pocket. He would never lose it. It was the only thing that linked him with his three friends. If he did survive, the film would have a purpose, he promised them. And someday, maybe, it would also avenge their senseless deaths.

Yes, one day the government will pay . . .

Just then a light flashed in his eyes.

"Who's there?" a gruff voice called out.

The voice was not familiar, but who else's could it be? "Mr. Delmonte?" Kevin replied.

"Yeah. Who are you?" Delmonte asked.

"Kevin . . ."

"What are you doing down here?"

"Running away, sir."

There was a definite edge to the voice. As the flashlight came closer, Kevin couldn't see the face of the man who held it. "Do I know you, son?"

"I'm a friend of Matty Madison, Mr. Delmonte."

The light flashed down the tunnel. "A friend of Matty's? Is she with you?"

"No, sir. They killed her."

"The soldiers?"

"Yes, sir."

Delmonte let out a string of profanities as Kevin continued. "We saw the crash and we were coming to your place to see if you needed help when . . . when the soldiers started to shoot at us. They killed my girlfriend and my best friend too. They killed everyone, Mr. Delmonte."

Delmonte reached under Kevin's arm to prop him up. "Steady, son."

"I was coming down the tunnel when I . . ."

The clanking sounds of the military were echoing down the tunnel.

Delmonte hissed, "They're after us too, son. They won't stop until they've killed us all."

"What can we do, Mr. Delmonte?" Kevin asked, letting the old man lead him farther into the mine. They hadn't taken but a couple of steps when Delmonte's flashlight fell on the little critter, startling Kevin.

"What is that, Mr. Delmonte?"

Feeling it in the dark was one thing. Seeing the critter in the light was quite another. It was the scariest creature Kevin had ever seen. Its eyes were oversized and bulged from their sockets like they would fall out of its head if it sneezed. Its mouth was narrow, but one could see the lethal tips of its teeth hidden under a layer of loose skin. The ears, like the eyes, were way out of proportion to its head or any other parts of its body. All that he had touched in the dark was unimaginable in the light. But as evil as it looked, its large, yellow eyes were still gentle and friendly.

Delmonte spit off to the side. "The thing belongs to the gent who climbed out of the ship. The little varmint gets along okay. Makes your darkest nightmare seem less evil, doesn't it?"

They kept on walking. They didn't have time to socialize. "Gent?" Kevin finally asked.

"Yeah, he's kind of a weird duck like his pet."

"He survived the crash?"

"Yeah, but he's hurtin'. He's back here a ways. He might make it, he might not."

Delmonte sped up the pace and Kevin hustled to keep up. As for the critter, it bounced along like it hadn't a care in the world, always staying near like it just wanted to be close to someone. At times Delmonte had to warn the mutt with a few chosen words to stay out of the way.

As they hurried along, Kevin told Delmonte that at first he thought the critter was his dog. Delmonte grumbled something unintelligible before he said, seething with deep hatred, "They killed 'im. Shot poor Digger dead. The dang soldier boys! Well, I'll fix them."

They went on for a short distance, crossing over fallen timbers and another open pit. After stepping across the plank, Delmonte pulled it across to the other side. "Maybe that will get a few." They walked along more tracks and climbed over a couple of old ore carts until they came to a fork in the tunnel.

Delmonte pointed his flashlight on a hunched-over body propped against the wall of the right fork in the tunnel. The survivor's flight suit was dark and he was holding something under his left arm. It seemed like he was having a hard time breathing.

"That's him there," Delmonte said.

"He looks human," Kevin said in a low whisper.

Delmonte wiped sweat from his face. It was cold and damp in the mine shaft, but the old miner appeared to be suffering from some other malady. "I don't know what he is, or where he came from. But he seems normal enough. Don't talk much, though. Maybe he can't. But he could have killed me with this." Delmonte showed Kevin the survivor's weapon. It was certainly different from any handgun his father had in his gun rack.

"You took it from him?"

"Hardly, son. He gave it to me to protect us because he couldn't use it himself, being all hurt. Don't let the looks fool ya. It's got a kick. Makes my scattergun seem like a BB gun."

The survivor reached up like he was trying to remove his helmet.

"He's been clawing at it for the last hour," Delmonte said.

"Maybe he wants to take it off."

"Well, how would I know that? The gent hasn't said a lick to me."

Back in the shadows of the helmet two glowing eyes stared at Delmonte and Kevin. For a moment Kevin thought the flashlight was playing tricks on him, the way the survivor's eyes appeared to shine like green jewels. But when the light moved away, they still glowed on their own. Neither human had ever seen eyes like that before. They were young eyes too, although understandably tired and weak. Kevin guessed the wounded alien was close to six feet tall, like himself. And fit like a soldier.

Delmonte went on with his story. "I almost killed him by accident, and still he didn't kill me. He's not here to kill us, son. I'm sure of it. I don't know why he's here, but my guess is it's important. He won't let go of that satchel he's carrying for no one. Almost shot my fool head off when I touched it."

The survivor groaned. His breathing was becoming more labored, as though he wasn't getting enough air into his lungs. Kevin recognized the symptoms. He had seen that before when people were caught in a fire and were suffering from smoke inhalation. The survivor's hand touched the side of his helmet again. Something metallic clicked, then a section under his chin slid to the side. The faceplate then opened fully and they could see the survivor's face.

He was indeed quite young, almost boyish in appearance. It caught both Delmonte and Kevin off guard. After seeing the survivor's pet, they were expecting someone a lot more grotesque, with purple skin and multiple eyes. Except for his glowing green eyes, the alien could have been anyone on Earth.

Kevin found it difficult not to stare. Their eyes touched, feeling like one. He tried to resist. This was not at all what he had expected. The sweet alluring fragrance that came from the survivor only made it more difficult for him. Embarrassed by his lust, Kevin broke his steady gaze.

"Maybe he's Air Force?" Kevin suggested, taking a breath.

"But they were trying to kill him as much as me."

"Yeah, doesn't make sense."

Delmonte grunted sourly. "Nothing does, son."

The survivor kept trying to remove his headgear, but the helmet appeared to be stuck. Kevin bent down and tried to lend a hand before the survivor passed out. As Kevin tried to find the release catches under the jawline, Delmonte kept the area lit with his flashlight.

Something clicked. "There. I think I got it."

Just as Kevin started lifting the helmet away from the head, the heavy movement of approaching troops echoed down the tunnel.

Delmonte switched off his flashlight in a hurry. "Alright, they're past the pit."

In the pitch-blackness, Kevin removed the survivor's headgear and put it aside. He then reached under the collar and unzipped the top of the suit clear down the front. Almost immediately the survivor was breathing comfortably.

Delmonte grabbed Kevin's shirt in the dark. "Come on, son. We don't have time to play nursemaid."

The survivor seemed to feel the urgency too. He grabbed Kevin's arms and they rose up together. Surprisingly, the survivor felt warm and strong in Kevin's arms like he was regaining his strength. Just the same, they both clung to each other like they feared separating in the dark.

Kevin swallowed, fighting against the urge to hold the survivor too close. "Ready, Mr. Delmonte."

"He can walk?"

"I think so."

Delmonte flashed his light for a split second. It was a short burst, but good enough to show the way.

As they moved quickly down the tunnel, Delmonte kept talking. "Listen up, son. We don't have much time. Those soldiers are right on our tails." Delmonte flashed his light again every few feet so they could get a bead on what lay ahead. "Here. Take this." He put the flashlight in Kevin's hand. "Follow the tracks for a ways. Be mindful, son, there's a couple of pits along the way. As soon as you cross them, kick the cross planks into the hole. Don't get lost. Stay to the right at every juncture, all the way. The tracks will guide you. You'll come out just above the highway. The soldiers don't know about it. Get across the road and follow the wash around until you find an old shack. There's a car beside it. Take it."

"You're coming with us, Mr. Delmonte," Kevin said, concerned that he wasn't.

He wiped the cold sweat from his mouth. "Someone has to slow those SOBs. You two can make it without an old drunk like me. The keys are on top of the front tire. It's got plenty of gas. I keep it full for emergencies like this. Don't stop for anything. And son . . ." Delmonte grabbed the light in Kevin's hand and shined it directly on to his bloodshot eyes so there was no doubt to his meaning. "Don't go home. Don't ever go home. As far as you're concerned, you *are* dead."

Kevin cocked his head as if he wanted to question why. But Delmonte stopped him. "Don't argue with me, son, you have to understand that. You're dead. The life you had is over. If the government thinks you have told your parents or anyone what you know, they will kill them too. You must never again talk to anyone you knew before . . . ever. Understand? Talk to me, son. Tell me you understand."

"Yes, sir."

"I know Fate's dealt you a sorry hand. You just have to live with it. There's nothing you can do now. With the end of the war, the Commies have the bomb and now this . . . If people know aliens have invaded the planet . . . Well, dag gummit, the world's goin' to go crazy, son. Believe me. They're all spooked. They trust no one. So you can't contact anyone that you know. Ever . . ."

Kevin shook inside as tears welled up and fell in heavy droplets down his cheeks. Delmonte gave them both a gentle nudge down the shaft. "Now git. And when you see the opening, turn the light off. Don't use it. Someone could see you. Stay low and keep running."

"Yes, sir."

Kevin felt their chances of making it were practically nonexistent. But somehow, if they could make it to the car, then maybe . . .

Suddenly the soldiers' lights came flooding down the tunnel. Too late!

"They're on us," Delmonte grimaced. They didn't have a thing to defend themselves with except the survivor's weapon. Delmonte pointed it at the approaching squad of infantry. The light on the side of the barrel wasn't as bright as before. He doubted if he had more than one shot left. For what he had in mind, he needed one last shot. But here wasn't the place. He needed a little more time to put his final plan to work.

Just then the survivor whistled quietly to the critter. The animal's ears rotated and it trotted off down the tunnel like it was going to take on the whole squadron by itself.

"How useless is that?" Delmonte snorted. "One round from an M1 carbine and Digger will have a playmate."

The survivor's face was still obscure in the darkness, but the glow of his eyes was callous. He didn't seem to be concerned about his pet at all.

"Hold on, son." Delmonte ran to them and put a key from around his neck in Kevin's pocket. "You'll need money. The bank's name is on the key. It goes to a strongbox. Take it all. You'll need every penny for a new start."

"Mr. Delmonte, I can't take your money."

"I've got plenty more stashed away behind the shack. The code word is Jack. Don't forget it."

He pushed them off again and the two of them took off limping together, the light in Kevin's hand bouncing, pointing down at the tracks as they moved away in a hurry. "You're a good man, Mr. Delmonte," Kevin called back to the old vet.

"Take care, son."

From somewhere down the tunnel came an incredible roar that echoed along the walls. Loud shots of machine-gun fire and rifle bullets thundered. "What in the name of heaven . . ." Delmonte turned around, focusing up the tunnel. Something huge and winged was silhouetted against the flashing lights of the soldiers. A giant creature had blocked the entire tunnel not fifty yards from where he was standing.

By all that's unholy . . .

A ferocious roar was heard again, scattering the soldiers back down the tunnel. Soldiers cried out in horrifying agony as their bodies were ripped apart by the crazed beast. While the soldiers were occupied, Delmonte now had time to finish his plan. "Run, son!"

* * *

Kevin and the survivor followed Mr. Delmonte's orders, keeping the light on the tracks ahead, staying right, and not looking back. Nearly falling at times, they kept clinging to each other, never letting go while the sounds behind them went eerily silent. Kevin wondered whether Mr. Delmonte had found another way out or maybe hid himself in a secret place somewhere deep in the mine. He prayed a little for the old coot, hoping one day they would see each other again. A nagging knot filled Kevin's throat at the same moment a massive explosion shook the mountain. Kevin knew then that Mr. Delmonte had had his revenge.

After a couple more right turns the tunnel's mouth came into view. Kevin turned off the flashlight and moved cautiously to the opening and looked out. Military vehicles were motoring in long lines down the highway, but no one was stopping here. They were continuing on to Delmonte's gate. Overhead, more helicopters with bright searchlights were continuing to search the hillsides for anything that wasn't military.

They had no choice but to creep out into the night together.

It was dark outside but not pitch-black like the mine. There was plenty of starlight to see by. Kevin and the survivor quickly followed an old path down from the mine tailings dump to the highway. The tire tracks from his car were still fresh and undisturbed. So, too, were the tire tracks in the dirt where he and his friends had pulled over after hearing the first explosion. He felt like he was walking across their graves, but he didn't stop. He trembled with the grief and horror of it all, but he kept moving, his tears flowing freely down the sides of his face.

Between convoys, they ran across the highway and down into the dry wash. A mile farther on they came to the old shack where Delmonte's car was located. Before going in, Kevin felt a softness brush the side of his face. He turned around, somewhat confused as to where the motherly touch had come from. The survivor was looking at him with kindness and empathy, and he continued to caress Kevin's tear-stained cheeks with long, tender fingers. The alien's green eyes were even more beautiful than before. His hair was light in color and very short. Typical of a soldier, Kevin thought.

Then over the survivor's shoulder Kevin saw a winged beast of incredible size fly westward toward the rising moon in the same direction they would be traveling. Kevin wondered if he had lost his mind entirely. *Such things did not exist in the real world.*

A sweetness in the air drew his attention back to the survivor. In the pale moonlight he could see that the survivor's suit was open, exposing the chest. Kevin remembered unzipping the front of the flight suit back in the tunnel, allowing the survivor to breathe. It seemed Fate had not finished with Kevin's altered life, for the survivor was not a man at all, but a woman . . .

Chapter Three

BEACH CLOSED

ONE YEAR AGO

42ᴺᴰ STREET, NEWPORT BEACH, CALIFORNIA

Sixteen-year-old bodysurfers Harlowe Pylott and Matt River-stone would have thought twice about ditching classes that morning if they had taken their science teacher's lecture on the consequences of a domino effect more seriously. For Harlowe, the ultimate high was standing at the water's edge, waiting for the precise moment in which to dive into the rip that would carry him out to the twenty-foot waves pumping in from the north. Riverstone wasn't quite so sure. "We could die out there, pard," he warned Harlowe as his bright hazel eyes scanned the shoreline with worry.

The sun had barely peeked over the Santa Ana Mountains when the lifeguards closed every west-facing beach from Pt. Magu all the way south to the Mexican border. But on days like this, when the swells were marching in like an invading army as far out as the eye could see, Harlowe and Riverstone didn't read signs. They kicked them over and stomped on their faces.

"Man up," Harlowe grunted, appearing unconcerned as his clear blue eyes studied the great glass walls of unbounded power. The waves had no rivals. They were unstoppable.

Harlowe and Riverstone were both tall and lean, with boyish good looks, although Riverstone would be the first to admit he was the uncontested face man of the two. This was the first day Harlowe was *legally* able to drive to the beach without an adult in his hand-me-down gold VW bug that was older than he was. Harlowe wore a tattered pair of dark blue No Fear surf trunks; Riverstone brought out the heavy guns for Harlowe's *legal* solo flight, wearing a pair of brand-new, bright red and yellow paisley Billabongs.

Already attached to their feet were pairs of thirty-inch black Navy Seal rocket fins that looked like they fit Godzilla easier than their size twelve feet. Approaching six feet even, and still growing, Riverstone was an inch taller than his childhood friend. They had just started their junior year at Lakewood High and had no idea what they were going to be when they *grew up*.

Riverstone tried a different tack. "The babes won't be out for a couple of hours, pard. We should wait. You could find a date for tonight."

"I'm not waiting."

"You're crazy, you know that?"

Knowing he would have a better chance arguing with the sun, Riverstone twisted around, taking his eyes off the giants for a moment while he scanned the nearly empty beach. A heavy shore mist from the swells kept them from seeing too far in either direction. Except for a couple of dog walkers and curious wave watchers, Harlowe and Riverstone appeared to be the only ones along the shoreline and, thus, with no common sense.

"What happened to Wiz, by the way?" Riverstone asked. "Does he know where to take Baby when our bodies come in belly up? The drift is pretty strong, dude."

"He knows."

"Well, I don't want to walk three miles back from the Wedge in wet trunks," Riverstone whined.

Harlowe didn't care.

After Riverstone had aired his concerns, he spotted a goddess materializing out of the morning mist, running along the soft sand. She had the strength and the stride of an Olympic runner. Her long yellow hair rose and fell in great waves as her long, gazelle-like legs propelled her along in a slow, rhythmic gait. She continued south in her powder blue Nike sweats, her bright green eyes glancing more than once their way.

Riverstone moaned. *I'm in love.*

Running beside her with incredible ease was a small creature that defied logic as to whether it was a dog or some prank Mother Nature had designed in jest. The "undog" cantered along on its four padded feet, whipping its tail playfully as its bulging yellow eyes and parabolic ears scanned the horizon as though searching for apparent threats.

After a heavy breath Riverstone leaned over to Harlowe and asked, "Did you catch that doe, pard? She was so hot, Harlowe, I would go to the end of the galaxy for a babe like that."

Harlowe said nothing. The giants were his only concern.

Suddenly, a bright orange lifeguard vehicle roared up fast and skidded to a halt at the top of the berm just twenty feet away from the two bodysurfers. The sound of breaking wood split the air as the four-wheel Pathfinder, with big knotty tires, demolished the A-frame sign that was lying flat in the sand. Broken pieces of wood tore through the undercarriage, making a loud crunching sound.

Harlowe ignored the noise. Nothing could disturb the moment. His long, tight, nut brown curls with sun-touched ends waved freely in the onshore wind, in sharp contrast to his keen blue eyes that were so focused he seemed to be locked in some form of symbiotic communication with the giants.

"What was that, Kyle?" the driver of the emergency vehicle shouted as he jumped out and slammed his door. "Did you kick that sign over, kid?"

Riverstone smiled at the overzealous guards in their official-looking dark blue sweatshirts, white crosses, and red swim trunks as he gave them a friendly wave and pointed south. "Who's the babe, brah? She had legs up to her neck!"

"Forget her, kid," the guard who was the driver replied. "She's way out of your league."

The other guard, who had ridden shotgun, came around the front of the vehicle to check the damage. "Wow, Brady, the wooden posts broke through the floorboard. The captain will have us picking up trash for a month."

Brady glared at Harlowe and Riverstone like he was about to go ballistic. "The beach is closed, kid."

Riverstone glanced innocently down the beach. "Closed? Why? Is there a problem?"

Brady pointed at the smashed pieces of the A-frame sign under the front wheel. "Because that's what the sign said, kid."

Groaning over the fading goddess, Riverstone repeated, "Sign?"

"Yeah, the sign you knocked over," Shotgun snapped, pulling loose splinters out from under the heavy black treads.

"What did it say, brah?" Riverstone asked, appearing to be genuinely interested.

"It says, 'High Surf Warning: No Swimming or Surfing by Order of the Newport Beach Lifeguards,'" Brady said.

Shotgun put a curved thumb to his chest. "That's us, kid."

Behind the two insurgents a massive wall of white came charging toward the shore. It would be on them in a moment. The wall's thunderous energy was deafening, so Riverstone nodded at the guards like he was willing to cooperate. "Well, he did it," he said loudly, pointing an accusing finger at Harlowe. "I told him not to, brah, but he's so whacked-out over the tubes, his mind has snapped. He's not listening to me."

The guards began putting the broken sign pieces into the back of the SUV. "What are you going to do, Brady?" Shotgun asked.

Brady's eyes went flat. "Grab the handcuffs." He turned back to Riverstone and pointed a hot finger down at the sand. "Get your sorry selves up here," he yelled, projecting his voice loudly over the roar of the ocean. "NOW!"

"Are you talking to me or him?" Riverstone asked calmly, pointing to himself first.

"Both of you!" Brady snapped.

Riverstone was dumbfounded. "Me? I'm dyslexic. I can't read signs. I didn't know, really," he pleaded.

"March, or we'll come down there and drag you up here!"

Riverstone kept the excuses coming. "Alright, man. But he's challenged. He doesn't hear well."

Brady glanced heatedly at Shotgun. "They're morons. We're taking them in."

Brady grabbed the bullhorn mike from the front seat, stretching the coiled tether to its max. Click. The speaker horn on top of the cab crackled to life. "STEP BACK FROM THE WATER. YOU'RE GOING TO JAIL!" Brady's booming voice demanded.

Too late.

Harlowe dove straight out, meeting the incoming wall head on, while Riverstone made a twisting back flip, timing his entry into the surge like a playful dolphin.

The guards could do nothing to stop them. The mass of swirling energy roared up the steep incline of the beach and grabbed the two bodysurfers as with a godly hand, their bodies seized in a fast-moving rip as though captured in a river of no return.

Chapter Four

SAR

COMMANDER SAR STOOD on the quarterdeck waiting for his Class VII battle cruiser to dock with his commandant's flagship. The seven bright blue stars of the Andonian Cluster reflected brightly off his silvery skin. Ordered from the battlefront, he and two other star-class battle cruiser commanders had been summoned by the commandant to this rendezvous in deep space. Sar had no idea why. The call was unexpected and cloaked in the deepest secrecy. A promotion perhaps? A compensation for his master strategy that was leading them to certain victory over the Andonians?

Nevertheless, Sar was angry. The battle was unfinished. His swift elite forces were virtually destroying the Andonian stronghold at Thatra, and he wanted to be there when the battle was won. His eyes glowed with pride knowing that his accomplishment would expand the boundaries of the empire to yet another unknown frontier. There would be glory for his command, but mostly for him, whose successes were already legendary. After the Andonian remnants were swept clear, his plan was to regroup his command for the next campaign. His ambition was a full battle fleet of his own that would have total quadrant dominion, a feat no other commander had ever accomplished, not even the great Paradon, Sar mused arrogantly, his deep black and yellow eyes glowing hot with brazen conceit.

Sar reached over and grabbed a large hunk of dripping flesh from a plate on the table. The forearm of an Andonian prisoner was fresh and warm, he pondered, satisfied. The hand was still twitching. After a ravenous bite, he tossed the remains behind him to his pet grogans. A large gaping mouth snatched the morsel out of the air and swallowed it whole before the second grogan could take its share.

Sar laughed and his eyes beamed with self-satisfaction at the grogans' ferocity. He had raised them himself and fed them only fresh meat. They went where he went and killed upon command. They had the body of a giant dog, black and hairless; the bright hot eyes in their enormous heads glowed in the dark. Their giant mouths dripped inky black drool and were filled with rows of powerful razor-sharp teeth, upper and lower, that interlocked when closed and could snap a three-inch bone as easily as one could break a dried twig.

Sar reached for the platter again. He picked the head up by the hair and tossed it to his other grogan. "Eat, my beauties. Gorge on the enemies of the empire." The grogan speared the morsel out of the air and bit down. The skull burst like an exploded grape, its hot juices splattering hunks of brain onto Sar's polished black boots. Sar laughed as the first grogan quickly licked the residue from the boot.

His pets satisfied, Sar turned his attention to the port side observation window and watched his battle cruiser maneuver toward the docking bay of the flagship. The other two cruisers remained outside the bay in stationary headings paralleling the mammoth ship. Apparently he and he alone was being summoned by the commandant. One cannot deny destiny its due, he thought arrogantly. My superiors have seen my ability and cannot deny me what I so justly deserve. A fleet command will soon be mine.

The giant doors of the flagship docking bays slid open, anticipating the arrival as Sar's battle cruiser deftly drifted through the portal and settled delicately downward. After a moment, a heavy clank sounded, followed by a sudden rolling movement. The battle cruiser was secure.

In the dim glow of the docking bay, Sar saw the special guard waiting for his disembarkation. Under different circumstances—when the battle for the Andonian Cluster was complete, for example—he would have expected more. An entire command wing at least.

One of Sar's subordinates opened his door and snapped to attention. Sar petted his beauties before he stepped lively out to meet his escort. The escort took him through a side door. Sar stopped.

"What is the meaning of this? A side door for a commander of the elite corps?" he growled. "I will not enter."

The subordinate looked up at Sar. His eyes searched for an explanation. He was obviously unprepared for the confrontation.

"Sar," a sharp commanding voice called out before another word was spoken. It was the commandant. His eyes were not as bright as they once were, Sar noted, thinking quickly back over the passings. They seemed weaker. A being not to be trifled with, however, he quickly countered. Many had been fooled by the commandant's demeanor; he would not be one of them. Sar had served the commandant well through many campaigns. This was a ruse to catch his enemies and, yes, potential betrayers off guard. Sar would not challenge his commandant today, nor any other day.

Yet, there was something else about him. Something uncharacteristic Sar had never seen in the old commander. It was unmistakable. Fear. Sar shook his mind, trying to clear the one single thought he never believed was possible.

Sar bowed respectfully, then stood upright with a clenched fist across his breastplate in salute. "Commandant," he snapped, "I am here as ordered."

"The campaign is going well?"

"Yes, my commandant. Victory is near. But my requests for thermogrym have gone unanswered. My ships need fuel, Commandant."

The commandant nodded his approval. "Yes, it is a fleet-wide problem. But once again you've proven your worthiness, Sar. Yes, you are to be commended for using your thermogrym wisely."

The commandant then waved the escort away. The black-uniformed troopers reversed direction as though powered by a single mind and fast-stepped away, back through a sliding hatchway.

Sar and the commandant walked down the corridor alone, and in silence. Unless his superior initiated the conversation, no words would be spoken.

As they walked, Sar balanced his initial negative response with the gravity he felt. Whatever it was that had brought him here was more than he had imagined. Much to his disappointment, he was now sure of one thing: this was no summons to confer a promotion upon him.

The commandant stopped in front of a small hatchway that was more reminiscent of a crew entry than one used by the fleet's high command. He passed his hand over the light activator and the door slid back. The commandant entered. Sar followed.

Nothing about the room belied the importance of what Sar felt would come from such a meeting. It had one window that looked out at deep space. Not toward the Andonian Cluster, as one might believe, but toward the unknown frontier. That frontier was all that was left for him to conquer.

An uninteresting old piece of stone that pulsed slowly with a dull blue glow sat in the center of a large table. That stone was much like the three beings that sat around it. Two were in uniform, one on each side of a high civilian, their insignias and breast decorations duly proclaiming their advanced ranks. Even though the Fhaal Empire was vast, a thousand fleets spread out over an ever-expanding quadrant, Sar knew the commissars, Keraada and Methota, both from the Imperial High Command. The civilian was familiar, but Sar could not yet place the name with the face. The lone empty chair was obviously for him.

"Most honored council," the commandant began immediately upon entering the room. He bowed respectfully, as did Sar, only Sar's bow was deeper because he was the lowest-ranking member of the gathering. "I present my most trusted officer . . . Sar," the commandant announced, straightening himself, his right talon clutched over his breastplate.

Sar likewise stood erect but kept his eyes forward as the three rose to greet him. The civilian spoke first. "I am called Paradon." Sar lifted his gaze. He bowed again as he began to shake. It was such a rare honor to be in the presence of such a being. Paradon continued. "I have followed your career. Your commandant has chosen well. Perhaps you already know the two other members of my council from the Imperial High Command, Commissars Keraada and Methota?"

"Yes, great one, I do." Sar saluted by tapping a closed gauntlet hard across his chest. Protocol did not require further embellishments.

Paradon extended his talon. "You may sit, Sar."

Sar politely refused. To sit in the presence of the great Paradon would be considered a weakness.

Paradon understood the soldier's pride and quickly moved on. "Very well. We should begin by telling you why you were brought here so abruptly, away from the battlefront."

Commissar Methota waved his talon over the edge of the table. An instant later a star map projection appeared above the table. Sar recognized the area immediately. It was a three-dimensional rendering of the Fhaal conquests over the last two hundred passings. In the lower right were the seven bright blue stars of the Andonian Cluster where his forces were now heavily engaged in battle. In the upper right of the quadrant, two parsecs in, was the imperial mother planet, Fhaal. Except for the bulge that encompassed the Cluster, there was a near circular shape to the Fhaal conquests.

Beyond the Cluster, however, the star projection was vague. Unknown. Sar stared with resolute determination at the vastness.

It was his destiny to extend the reach of the empire, to fill in the projection gaps with Fhaal conquests . . . his conquests.

Paradon pointed with his one-inch claw to a location ten light-passings away from their present position. Neeja, a star system the Fhaal had conquered more than forty passings ago. "A Fhaal scout ship," he began, "was on a routine expeditionary survey when it detected an unknown power fluctuation on its contact screen. At the time, the empire's efforts were being redirected along the Proth-hyra line here." Paradon's talon traced an imaginary boundary leading outward, halfway between the Neeja system and the Cluster.

Sar inhaled a slow breath, savoring the victories of the empire's grandiose design of total domination. He had studied to the last detail every battle fought, back to when his great ancestor Daashaan was commander of the fleet, before his untimely death on Amerloi.

"It was such a short burst of energy," Paradon explained, "and so distant, that our intelligence officers determined it was no threat to the fleet. The power marks were only momentary and did not repeat. So it was simply recorded as such. The incident was forgotten and explained away as a fluctuation associated with an impulse star most likely out of the quadrant."

Commissar Methota passed his claw over the table again and a holographic contact screen replaced a portion of the star map. On the contact screen, an unusual blue wave of energy moved across the matrix.

Sar studied the power signature with curiosity. Every cadet knows that every source of energy leaves its own identifying mark. No two are alike. Each star is different, just as each battle cruiser is different, and each being in the room that produces energy is different from any other source of energy in the room. There is no way of disguising or modifying the mark. It is an unalterable law of physics.

"You have seen this signature before, commander?" Commissar Keraada asked, noticing that the glow in Sar's eyes had brightened.

"Yes," Sar replied. "Recently. Within the last tilo. My battle wing had already launched its first attack on the Andonians. The incident was brought to my attention. My science staff found the source too distant, however; possibly out of the quadrant. So I gave orders to disregard."

"Understandable, commander," Paradon replied. "A common mistake."

Mistake? Sar recoiled. Others made mistakes, but not Sar. The power fluctuation was insignificant. He had given it the attention it deserved and disregarded it. That was *no mistake.*

The great one pointed to a small yellow star at the very edge of the projection. "We believe we have found the source of the signature."

Sar wanted to laugh. It was such a pointless star system, hardly worth *his* effort. But he had not been brought here on a whimsical escapade, he quickly noted. Nor would the great one and the two commissars from the Imperial High Command have traveled thirty-three light-passings to participate in such a farce. Sar waited patiently for the great one to continue.

"Have you ever heard of the Gamadin, commander?" Paradon asked.

Sar nodded. "Every child has heard the fables of the Gamadin. They were mighty warriors whose ships were thought to have the power of the galactic core itself. They were the guardians of the stars, created by the old ones to bring harmony to the galaxy. It was said that during the Period of Harmony no wars were ever fought."

"That is correct, commander. You know your history well," Commissar Methota said. "No wars were fought. All hostilities ceased. Warring empires were forced to destroy their fleets or be totally exterminated by the Gamadin."

Sar snorted. "But they were only children's parables, Commissar. The Gamadin cannot possibly exist." He looked at the projection of the small yellow star, then back to the three. Their eyes remained unwaveringly steady. "Are you saying they do?" Sar asked, his smirk dissolving.

Paradon leaned forward. "What we are telling you, commander, is that we know they did exist. The evidence is clear." His claw moved to the pulsating blue stone. Sar had never noticed it before, but an insignia had been cut into the stone's surface. It was a flat elliptic image with a glowing blue line beating through its horizontal axis. "This stone was taken from the ancient world of Amerloi where one of your ancestors, Daashaan, was killed by a Triadian soldier."

Sar's face hardened. "Yes, great one. My ancestor had led the Fhaal on many glorious victories before his death. The coward shot him from behind and was never found."

"His loss was unfortunate. The reason he was sent to Amerloi was to intercept a secret Neejan mission. We learned that they had discovered a way of defeating our forces, that they had found a vault under the catacombs of the dead city. And in this vault their scientists found direct evidence of ancient Gamadin technology. Like you, we thought the legends of the Gamadin were simply that—legends—until this incident occurred.

"The Imperial High Command took no chances. Our need for thermogrym could not be jeopardized. So we sent Daashaan to intercept and learn of the vault's contents. What was discovered was most enlightening. During the Period of Harmony the Gamadin had established an emergency network of beacons throughout this quadrant so they could be called upon over great distances to help during times of disorder. They could not be everywhere at once. We are uncertain whether their scientists made a call or whether it was an automatic mechanism set up by the Gamadin in case the source planetary system was unable to utilize the security network. We think not. Our scientists found the remains of the beacon and learned it had been dead for many thousands of passings. Therefore, we were quite certain the Neejan mission failed.

"The soldier that killed Daashaan escaped. His ultimate where-abouts are unknown. But we believe, since the beacon was found to be inoperable, that he was sent to search out the Gamadin and bring them back to Neeja on his own. The fact that the Gamadin did not return proves that his efforts were futile. But maybe not. The soldier who killed your ancestor was special. He could have survived long enough to locate a Gamadin outpost. He may have found their ship. If this happened, he would not have been able to use its resources alone. He would have to wait until the ship's prime directive had been switched on. Even then it is doubtful since he himself was not Gamadin."

Paradon turned toward the window of the frontier. "We just do not know. There are too many questions." He turned back again. "That is why we need you, commander. We want you to locate the Triadian soldier from Neeja and discover whether he has found the Gamadin mothership."

"How can we be certain this is the correct signature?" Sar asked, looking at the stone.

Paradon passed his claw over the end of the table and the contact screen divided in two. "Compare the signatures. What do you see?"

"They are the same, great one. Identical in every respect."

"Yes, commander. One is from the source found here," he pointed to the yellow, insignificant star at the bottom of the projection, "and the other is from the stone. They are identical matches. A statistical impossibility, unless—"

"They are powered from the same source of energy," Sar said, fin-ishing the great one's statement.

The old eyes of the great one brightened. "Find that source, com-mander, and you'll find the mothership."

"The Gamadin died out many thousands of passings ago. How can they still exist, great one?" Sar reiterated.

"The security of the empire is at stake, commander. The risk is too great to disregard. If it is a probe sent out by a Gamadin ship, which we believe it is, then we must act now. We must have it for ourselves. With it, our need for thermogrym will be no more. But if you cannot capture the mothership, you must destroy it and all associated with the technology before it destroys us. Is that clear?"

Sar nodded. He understood, but in many ways he did not understand. He was a soldier first, however, and he would obey his leaders without question . . . for now.

"Very well," concluded Paradon. "You must lead a strike force and find this planet where Millawanda hides. From the vault we have learned a great deal about the Gamadin. If the legends are correct, the ship has lain dormant, waiting to be found again. If this is true, we have little time. The Gamadin will not expect us. Find the mothership and destroy Millawanda before she can regenerate."

He thrust his talon at the tiny yellow star. "Your ship, commander, and the two other Class VIIs are the most powerful ships in the fleet. Go! Find Millawanda while she is still weak and unprotected. Kill her! Kill the world where she hides. Kill everything!" Paradon's eyes glowed hot, staring at Sar. "Understand this, Sar," he continued. "I have read the transcripts from the Neeja science research team. Read them yourself. Memorize them, as though your life depended on it. For if this mission fails, and the Gamadin ship escapes, the Fhaal are doomed."

Chapter Five

THE YELLOW PATHWAY

IAN WIZZIXS PUSHED his thick glasses back on his nose because without them, he was legally blind. Feeling the chill, he tucked his hand back inside his multi-pocketed, olive green surplus jacket while his other hand guided Baby, a vintage '69 Volkswagen bug, slowly down a narrow street called E. Ocean Front, looking for a parking place. Even wearing a thick, gray Champion sweatshirt under his jacket and Levi's and weather-beaten Ugg boots, he was still cold. E. Ocean Front was more like an alley than a street. There was barely room for two cars to pass. But the homes along the twenty-foot-wide pavement were the zillion-dollar beachfront variety.

Ian and his buddies had never been this far south on the Newport peninsula before. The beach bungalows and party shacks along 42nd Street had pulled a Cinderella here. These homes were the kind that graced the front covers of *Architectural Digest*. This end of the peninsula wasn't just rich, it was Bill Gates rich. And as he putt-putted Baby along, downshifting it into a low cruising gear, he gawked up at the two- and three-story beachfront homes in awe, wondering if all the money in the world wasn't centered right here in the back alley where he was driving.

Ian's friends, who were out bodysurfing the waves, had planned in advance to meet him at this end of the peninsula because the southerly drift was so strong they would be at least this far down the coastline when it was time to come in. Dead or alive, the only thing that would stop them was the Newport Harbor Channel jetty that ran a quarter-mile out from the shoreline. Ian knew he was in the right place. His cell phone's GPS had confirmed it. But even so, there didn't appear to be any way past the fortress-like homes he was driving by to get to the beach.

Just when he thought it would be easier to turn around and find a parking place at the pier two miles back, a tall, gray-haired man with hazel eyes and an easy smile came out of nowhere. Ian stepped on the squeaky brakes to avoid hitting the middle-aged man dressed in khaki shorts, a white Tommy Bahama silk shirt, and beat-up dock shoes.

"Sorry, mister," Ian apologized. "I didn't see ya."

The guy was totally cool, Ian thought, and didn't seem upset at all. "Are you lost, son?"

Ian pushed back his heavy glasses before answering. "No, sir. Just looking for a place to park. My friends are out in the surf and I was hoping to meet them when they came in."

The man looked concerned when Ian mentioned that. "I thought the beach was closed."

"It is. But my friends can't read on days like this."

"They're crazy?"

"Yep."

"They could be in trouble."

"That's a given."

"Maybe we should call the lifeguards."

"Trust me. They're on it, sir."

"You don't seem concerned for their safety."

Ian reached up and tore off a stringy piece of ragged headliner dangling in his face. "I don't argue with the sun, sir."

The man seemed amused by the reply, as though he had a little rebel in himself. He pointed to a row of empty spaces along the alley and said, "Park it over there, son. It's okay."

Ian stretched his eyes along the biggest beachfront mansion he had ever seen. The compound was at least a football field in each direction. The main house was a modern concrete and glass structure surrounded by a tall, white stucco wall with cool-looking glass lamps on top of thick pilasters every fifty feet or so.

"It looks private," Ian replied.

The man returned a confident wink and grinned. "I know the owner. He won't mind."

Giving him a big relieved smile, Ian thanked the man and whipped Baby around to the first empty slot on the far side of the seven-car garage. As he drove past, he spied a vintage 1937 blue Bentley in one of the two bays that were open. In the other open bay was a deep red, 12-cylinder Fiorano that Ian had only read about in elite European car magazines. Before today, he would have bet a five-year subscription to *Car and Driver* that Ferrari had only drawings of the sleek, 230-mile-per-hour missile.

Sooo cool . . .

The man had told Ian the fastest way to the beach was through the gate along the wall about a hundred feet farther on down the alley. "Follow the yellow brick path," he said. The man explained that it had been his daughter's creation when she was a little girl. "It will take you where you want to go. If you meet a big-eared oddity along the way," the man went on, "tell him you come in peace. He's the keeper of the land around here."

"What's the keeper's name?"

"Mowgi."

"He's harmless?" Ian asked.

The man smiled slyly, then winked. "To friends."

Ian nodded thanks and said, "I'll bring gifts," as he held up two Three Musketeers candy bars he had retrieved from a hidden pocket.

* * *

Leaving Baby in the man's care, Ian moseyed down the alley toward the gate in the wall. The gate wasn't difficult to find. It was right where the man had said it would be and solid like a vault. He punched in the code the man had given him, and sliding bolts snapped back inside the gate door like fine pieces of machinery.

Ian had thought he might need his dad's tow truck to pull the heavy door open. But to his amazement, the foot-thick metal door opened easily with the touch of his finger. Beyond the doorway, just like the man had said, was a yellow brick pathway that was lined with dense tropical ferns, bamboo stalks, and broad-leafed trees that encased the pathway like a shady tunnel.

A brief but subtle clicking sound, followed by a clack, brought his attention back to the right. Strangely, he saw no movement or anything unusual in either direction. Everything was still and eerily quiet.

Ian stepped through the threshold of the gate and announced, "Hello, anyone here?"

No one answered, but Ian heard again the same faint clickity-clack sound that had greeted him earlier and had an undeterminable origin.

The path forked almost immediately beyond the gate, and in either direction it was pretty much the same. Problem was, which way to the beach? The man hadn't mentioned that Ian would have a choice. His chances of guessing which direction to take were reduced to fifty-fifty.

The gate behind him slowly closed on its own, surprising him a little in the way the heavy bolts slid back into place with such finality. Ian looked around for a combo pad like the one on the other side but found nothing but dense leaves and stringy vines. He tried the latch, but it didn't budge. Apparently, the entrance was the one-way kind.

You're in it now, pard. Stay cool.

Realizing his friends would be coming out of the water soon, Ian knew he needed to make a decision. He was about to make a wild guess and go right when a man's voice, speaking with a very proper British accent, asked him, "May I help you, sir?"

Ian thought that if he looked up the word *butler* in the dictionary, the lanky, elderly man striding toward him with a kind smile would fit the description to a tee. His dark tailored suit, conservative green and blue silk tie, polished black shoes, and white, white shirt had not one wrinkle anywhere.

The dude was walking cool.

Ian pulled his right hand from his pocket and pointed to himself. "Well, yes, maybe. I'm looking for the beach. The man outside on the street said I should go through that gate there. But he didn't say which part of the path to follow."

"Mr. Mars?" the tall scarecrow in the nice suit asked.

"Kinda tall dude with tan shorts and old deck shoes. Right out there by the garages."

"That would be Mr. Mars."

Ian's eyes turned serious. "Who owns all this?" he asked the butler, looking around with his arms outstretched.

"Mr. Mars does, sir."

"That's cool. Pretty loaded up, huh?"

"Very, sir," the scarecrow replied with cool self-assurance.

Ian nodded his understanding. "Well, ah, he said this was a short-cut to the beach."

"He did?"

"Well, yeah. It is, isn't it?"

"It depends on one's perspective, I guess." The gentleman then pointed behind Ian. "But if you follow the sign, it will show you the way, sir."

Ian rotated around, and not two steps from him, just off the yellow path, was the Tin Man standing among the towering shady ferns.

Well, not exactly *the* Tin Man.

But for a child's creation, it wasn't bad. The tubular man was about eyeball to eyeball with Ian's five-foot-six height. He wasn't a tarnished tin color either, but dirty gold, and its head was shaped like a Chinaman's hat instead of a tin funnel. In place of stovepipe extremities, this tin man had long thin tubes and stood soundly on round flat feet. Its legs, arms, and torso were connected by baseball-size metal balls. Ian didn't recall seeing the statue the first time he looked inside the gate, but then, everything was so eye-catching, the possibility that he had missed him the first time around was high.

Three signs held together by rusty tie wire dangled from one of the tin man's tubular arms. The small sign on the left hand read: "Emerald City that way." The small sign on the right hand simply read: "Beach." Finally, the biggest sign that hung around the statue's neck read: "Enemies of Neeja Beware; Chinner on Guard." All the writing was done in a child's hand.

Ian tipped his head, "Thanks, ah . . ."

The scarecrow bowed slightly at the waist. "Jewels, at your service, sir."

Ian smiled broadly. No one had ever treated him so grown-up before, or called him "sir," or never once mentioned his coke-bottle glasses. Ian extended his hand. "Thanks, Jewels. I'm Ian, but my friends call me Wiz. You're cool."

"May I call you Wiz too?"

"Everybody else does."

Jewels shook Ian's hand. Ian was impressed by his strong grip, which was firm and confidently dry. It seemed so strong to Ian that if Jewels wanted to, he could break a man's arm with a snap of his wrist. No one else had ever shaken his hand in that way except Harlowe's dad, Buster. An ex-Marine, Mr. P was the strongest man Ian had ever met.

Ian pointed to the right, just to confirm the direction. "This way, Jewels?"

Jewels nodded affirmatively. "Just follow the yellow brick path, Wiz."

* * *

After one more thank-you, Ian walked along confidently, feeling like Dorothy on the yellow brick road, wondering what other surprises lay ahead. After all, he had already met the scarecrow and the tin man. *Could the lion be far away?* he giggled to himself.

Not far down the path he came to another sign hanging awkwardly on a tree. The sign read: "Chinner Country; Enter at Your Own Risk." Above it, another sign pointed almost straight up. Ian pushed the leaves aside and read: "Neeja, 311. 32 light-passings." As on all the other signs, the writing was done in the same uninhibited style.

"Do-do-do-do. Do-do-do-do," Ian whistled, imitating the old *Twilight Zone* theme song.

As eerie as the yellow brick path felt, he was enjoying the peaceful quiet, the succulent sweet aromas of the strange blue flowers that lined the path, and the whimsical signs that kept him amused during his journey.

He tried several times to check his position with his GPS, but his cell phone was dead. The overhead growth might have been too dense to allow him to get a good satellite lock. Still, he thought the phone should have been picking up some kind of a signal. Ian was flying blind. *And this was a shortcut?* He flippantly thought either the Emerald City or the cowardly lion would be around the next bend. Just then, a frightening creature indeed jumped out of nowhere and stood defiantly in his path.

Oh my gosh! Toto, what happened?

Ian froze, not willing to test the snarling rows of long knives peeking out from the creature's curled upper lips.

"Did you eat the lion, brah?" he asked.

He didn't quite know what to do. *Mr. Mars had mentioned a keeper of the land, but not Toto on red kryptonite.*

Careful not to make any sudden moves toward the radar-eared beast with bulging yellow eyes, Ian held up the candy bar as an offering. "Greetings, keeper, I come in peace."

As though Ian's words had a magical meaning, the undog sat back on its hind legs, panting energetically. Its dark green tongue stuck out in a sort of wicked smile as it waited for the payoff. Ian didn't bother unwrapping the bar. He just tossed it in a tall, lazy arch toward the creature. But before the bribe began its descent, the keeper leaped effortlessly five feet in the air and snagged it out of the sky. The candy, paper wrapping and all, was gone in a heartbeat.

Ian gulped, wishing he had brought an entire box of bribes. Not knowing what kind of a beast it was, he wasn't sure whether he was its next toss-and-fetch buddy or its next meal. He had almost decided not to tempt Fate and to turn around when a woman's voice said, "He likes you."

Ian turned to the voice as the goddess came floating toward him like some spiritual being.

That's awkward . . . Glenda?

He wondered where the Good Witch of the North had come from. There appeared to be no place to hide along the path. Yet, there she was, a goddess, tall and beautiful, with long blond hair flowing like waves over her wide, tanned shoulders. She came toward him, moving gracefully as though stepping on a cloud of air. There seemed nothing about her that was not lean and energized. She wore a silky pink and blue sundress, split up the sides, which left nothing hidden under its sheerness. But what captivated him more than her beauty were her eyes. They were green and faceted and held him, not like an evil sorceress, but like a good witch welcoming him to her land.

Ian tried to talk but found his mouth stuck open and dry. "I-I thought I was lunch," he managed to stutter.

The Good Witch smiled. "Mowgi already feasted this morning."

"Lucky me."

"Are you lost?"

"Well, I . . ." he pointed back down the path. "The scarecrow . . . I mean Jewels, said the beach was this way."

Glenda nodded her understanding. "You're almost there."

Ian sighed, relieved. "I thought I'd see the Emerald City first," he joked.

Be careful what you wish for . . . his mom had always warned him.

Glenda pointed, and behold, there it was. A tall fountain of emerald green glass and stone, ten feet high, with sharp angles reaching for the heavens. It was surrounded by a pond of hundred-year-old koi. But instead of being orange or white, these koi were a deep emerald green and had large yellow eyes. It *was* the Emerald City.

"My daughter's idea, I'm afraid. Makes for an interesting stroll through Oz, don't you think?"

"All I need is a pair of ruby slippers."

Glenda laughed. "And you are?"

"Ian Wizzixs, ma'am. But my friends call me—"

"Wiz?" Glenda interrupted.

Ian was caught a little off guard. "That's right, Glen– I mean, ma'am. How did you know?"

"You look like a Wiz." Glenda bent down and picked up Mowgi before she offered her hand and introduced herself. "I'm Sook. Harry's wife. Nice to meet you, Mr. Wizzixs."

Ian's knees nearly buckled as he took her hand. "Is it animal, vegetable, or mineral?" he asked, forcing his lungs to work. Mrs. Mars smelled as wonderful as she looked, fresh and intoxicating, kinda like his mother's roses did in the morning sun. He sighed when she let go of his hand.

"Mowgi is a chinneroth," Sook replied, stroking the beast's head.

"A chinneroth? He looks rare."

"One of a kind, I'm afraid."

Ian nodded, then his face lit up. "Hey, was that him my friends and I saw trotting along Newport Beach with you this morning?"

"My daughter," Sook stated coolly.

Her daughter? Ian was stunned. He guessed anything was possible but the difference in ages between the babe he saw running on the beach this morning and the woman that stood before him couldn't possibly be more than a few years. Five tops! They were nearly alike in every respect. Like two angels from the same cloud.

"He wasn't breaking a sweat."

"He keeps her company."

Lucky him.

"Well, don't let me keep you," Sook said, her voice melodic yet strong and confident. A lot like Harlowe's mom's voice, Ian realized.

Ian broke out of his trance. She had that kind of beauty. Night could have fallen and he would not have known. "Oh yeah, right. My friends. They're out bodysurfin'. I'm their ride."

As they walked together along the yellow brick path, Ian told her about his friends Harlowe Pylott and Matt Riverstone and how they were surfing the big waves in front of her house.

"I thought the beach was closed," Sook said.

Sook's fragrance filled his senses. *Better than an engine block.* "Oh, it is. My friends can't read."

Sook smiled. "They sound like my daughter. She's out partying on a boat now. They're supposed to stay in the harbor, but Simon can't read signs either." She looked away in obvious discomfort. "Well, don't get me started."

"I wouldn't worry, ma'am. No one, except my stupid friends, would be out in that surf."

"Oh, Simon Bolt is plenty stupid."

"The movie star?"

"An arrogant drak is more like it," Sook stated with a definite sour edge to her voice. "I don't know what my daughter sees in him."

Ian had no idea what *drak* meant. But it was four letters, and from the tone of her voice, he had a pretty good idea. He was surprised that Sook would use such coarse language, though. Harlowe's mom was just like her in many ways. Strong and gorgeous, Tinker could swear like a Marine when her juices were stirred.

"A toad brain, huh?" Ian said.

"A toad brain?"

Ian pointed at his head. "Yeah, void of gray matter."

Sook stopped and stared at Ian oddly. "Yes, a Void. How did you know?"

He remembered reading about the famous actor who played the brave and handsome Captain Julian Starr in the just released sci-fi blockbuster, *Distant Galaxies*. The movie had already grossed over a hundred million dollars in the first weekend. "I know a couple."

Sook laughed as they came to the end of the yellow brick pathway where the tropical forest met the sandy beginnings of the beach. "You're a good boy, Wiz. I'm sure your parents are very proud of you."

"They have their doubts sometimes, ma'am."

Sook opened a small gate that marked the oceanfront boundary of the estate. On this side of the compound it seemed that merely a small wall was necessary to keep out the winged monkeys. She kissed Ian on the forehead, giving him the protection he needed to cross the sand. "Well, I hope your friends are safe when you see them," she said to him.

With a bright red face, it was Ian's turn to laugh. "Safe is not a word I would use with them, ma'am."

"Are they in trouble?"

Ian's chest expanded with a hopeless moan. "Constantly, ma'am. It's the monkey on their backs."

"I would like to meet them. Won't you have lunch with Harry and me on your way back?"

Ian put his hands back in his coat pockets. "Sure." On most days, after surfing, Harlowe and Riverstone trolled 42ⁿᵈ Street for quail. But once they saw who was fixing lunch, they would be panting like dogs, scrambling for the chair next to her. "They eat a lot, ma'am."

Mowgi jumped from Sook's arms to the nearby wall, where it stuck to its narrow top more like a fly than a cat. "I'll tell Jewels to make extra."

Ian flashed her a thumbs-up. Then, with a heavy sigh, he turned his head into the wind and mushed across the wide-open sandy beachfront. The shoreline was still a fair distance away. Although the high dunes blocked his view, he could hear the thunder of the giants pounding the shore. The ground trembled beneath him, growing stronger, just like the turmoil in his gut, as he pressed on toward the top of the berm.

Chapter Six

NO POWER

AFTER BURNING OFF earlier in the day, the clouds over the Newport coast rolled back with a vengeance. By the time Brady and his duty partner, Kyle, had fixed their punctured tire, the surf had turned gray and ugly. Visibility at this southern end of the Newport peninsula was less than a quarter-mile out. The giant faces were hidden behind the fog, but their monstrous walls of water kept marching into shore in relentless lines of destruction.

Brady and Kyle didn't care about the sun. They were after the two lawbreakers who had kicked over their "Beach Closed" sign and damaged their Pathfinder that morning. They were just waiting for them to beach themselves so they could trade their fins for a pair of handcuffs. The last section of the beach suitable for bodysurfing before the rocky channel opening was known as the Wedge. Only a select few in the world could tame the Wedge. The waves broke so hard in the shallow water that broken bones and smashed vertebrae were a common statistic. If the two didn't come out here, they would either be a statistic or plastered against the granite stone blocks of the channel.

Brady held up a black pair of binoculars and searched the horizon at the same moment a beautiful white yacht from the harbor came motoring into the channel from Newport Harbor. Onboard, the party was rocking out to the loud thumping beats that pounded across the beach.

"Can you see them?" Kyle asked, raising his voice above the blaring music. He was looking through his own pair of binocs to try and spot the two lawbreaking bodysurfers.

"Not yet, but they're out there," Brady replied.

"What? The music, Brady, I can't hear you."

Brady put down his glasses. His attention turned to the sixty-foot craft steadily moving along the channel that led out to the open bay. No one, it seemed, was paying attention to the giants exploding against the side of the channel's protective jetty. "Not yet!" he yelled again over the loud mix of music and surf.

Kyle noticed Brady's concerned facial expression and turned to the channel. "Where does that dude think he's going? Is he out of his mind?"

Brady stepped up on the running board of the Pathfinder to take a better look at the boat. "That's all we need." He pointed at the dash. "Get on the horn, Kyle, and have the harbor police radio that idiot to turn back."

"Aye, aye." Kyle dove across the seat and picked up the radio mike. A few moments later, he stuck his head out the door and said, "They're on it."

"They're not turning," a voice said from behind the officers.

Brady turned to the voice. It was a thick-spectacled kid with a silly smirk, looking out at the water like he was searching for someone. "How'd you get here?" Brady asked.

The kid pushed back his glasses then pointed behind him. "Through the Black Forest."

Brady grunted as he looked back in the direction the kid pointed. "Yeah, right. You met Mr. and Mrs. Mars?"

"They're cool people, dude." The kid pulled his jacket collar up around his neck. "The babe from the north wants to have lunch with me and my buddies."

Brady looked around. "What buddies?"

The kid nodded forward. "The ones in the water now."

"Forget lunch, bug-eyes, the only thing on the menu is jail for your pals," Kyle said, almost giddy.

"I'll let her know." The kid looked out at the raging sea. "Have you seen them?"

Brady was too worried about the yacht to continue a conversation with a wise-ass kid. But like an irritating fly, the kid wouldn't go away.

"Isn't that Simon Bolt's?" the kid asked of the beautiful yacht continuing to motor toward the open sea.

Brady grabbed his binocs and looked at the stern of the boat. He could barely make out the name through the fog, but the graphics of a *Distant Galaxies* starship meant only one person: Simon Bolt. Brady had seen his yacht tied up a number of times in front of Woody's Bar, partying 'til dawn. "Yeah, that's his," Brady finally replied.

"Mrs. M's daughter's on that boat, brah," the kid added.

Kyle came around the front of the Pathfinder. "Whose daughter, four-eyes?"

The kid removed a hand from his pocket and pointed behind him again. "Glenda's."

Kyle looked worried as he turned to his partner. "He's pointing at the Mars' place, Brady."

Brady's face went slack. "Leucadia Mars is on that boat, bug-eyes?"

The kid returned his hand to his pocket. "Yeah, Mrs. M said Simon Bolt was a toad and that her daughter was on his yacht. So, if that's his boat, chances are she's on it."

"Tall blond lady? Gorgeous?"

"A twelve."

"With a big-eared mutt?" Kyle added.

"The keeper."

"Of all the stupid . . ." Brady cried out. The boat was already bumping up against the deep troughs when the radio crackled to life with a call from headquarters.

Kyle slid back into the cab and answered the call. A few seconds later he came back to Brady and relayed the message. "They can't reach the boat, Brady. No one's answering their calls so they're sending a launch Code 3 now. They want us to head for the jetty and see if we can reach them with the bullhorn."

But the boat had already left the protection of the channel. There was nothing Brady could do to turn it around even if he turned the bullhorn up full blast. Brady had watched as an arrogant, and obviously drunk, young man with blond hair took over the controls from the onboard captain. After he had recklessly gunned the engine over the tops of a couple of ten-footers, he turned the boat sideways, paralleling the deep troughs, in an effort to turn the boat around and head back to the channel. Instead, his maneuvers killed the engines, just as if someone had suddenly ripped the power cord out of a wall socket.

Brady dove inside the cab and grabbed the mike. "Break, break! Emergency! Code 3! Code 3 to the Wedge! All vehicles! Code 3! I said Code 3 to the Wedge! All vehicles! We have got a boat . . ." Brady kept pressing the mike switch and suddenly realized he was getting nothing but dead air. "What happened to the radio, Kyle? It's dead."

Kyle tried turning the radio switches on and off to reboot. "It was okay a second ago."

Brady threw the mike down and plopped down into the driver's seat. "Stay out of the way, kid," he shouted. As the kid jumped back, both guards slammed their doors. Brady jammed the Pathfinder into reverse. "We'll have to warn them ourselves, Kyle!"

"But how, Brady? They'll never hear us."

Brady reached for the ignition and twisted the key. "We'll flag them down from the end of the jetty."

Nothing.

The rescue vehicle was as dead as the radio. Brady pounded the steering wheel as he watched, helplessly, the lines of giant swells coming toward the *Distant Galaxies.*

Following a string of profanities, the guards bolted from their seats, grabbed their orange rescue buoys, and raced down the beach. There was nothing else they could do.

Chapter Seven

DOES OVERBOARD

HARLOWE AND RIVERSTONE were treading water twenty feet from the bow of the yacht when they heard the engines and the music die. Harlowe yelled up to the long-haired, bleached blond, handsome young man in a black silk shirt and white pants who was at the wheel of the yacht, "Don't stop now, toad! Point the bow out. There's a wave comin'!" He pointed to the twenty-foot wall of destruction that was coming straight for the beautiful white yacht like an unstoppable locomotive.

Riverstone had first spotted the deck full of dancing babes when the yacht rounded the bend in the channel. When it came to eye candy, his radar could reach the farthest corners of the universe.

The day had turned vicious, and it was almost lunchtime when he and Harlowe had bodysurfed as far south as they could without sucking face with the jetty. They were ready to come in, but waiting a bit longer to see a boat full of 12s come up the channel was a no-brainer.

Riverstone's plan was simple. He knew the boat would turn around at the end of the channel before it could be eaten by the giants. He and Harlowe would swim up to the yacht and beg for crumbs, hoping to catch a glimpse of the hot babes as the party motored back to the safety of the harbor.

Harlowe couldn't believe that much silicone existed on the planet. Riverstone didn't care. He was beyond gawking. He was shooting for an invite to the party and a couple of phone numbers in the process.

"What's up with that, pard?" Riverstone argued.

"They're older than us, dummy," Harlowe pointed out.

Riverstone grinned slyly. "Yeah, and way more experienced."

Harlowe was in.

They were swimming toward the end of the channel when the boat, to their amazement, kept motoring on for the open water like it was a normal day in paradise. Sure, it looked flat, but it was only between sets. The lines were out there, taking a breather. No one could hear their warnings above the magnitude-ten music, though.

Then the worst thing in the world that could happen, happened.

The stupid idiot killed the engine!

All Harlowe received for his Good Samaritan advice was a stiff middle finger from the arrogant little toad at the wheel. Then the big black man at the bow of the boat waved them away, cussing at them that he would jump in the water and drown them if they didn't stop bothering the babes. Riverstone smiled kindly and waved back with a stiff middle finger of his own while Harlowe displayed his best I-gave-it-my-best-shot grin and said, "Okay, brah, have it your way," and pointed again at the wave-of-the-day that was about to slam home.

Harlowe didn't believe he had ever seen two people's eyes grow so fast and round as the toad's and the black man's when they saw the wave of death breaking over the top of the bridge. The destruction was total and the screams loud as the bodies went flying. The sixty-foot yacht turned over on its back as easily as a toy in a bathtub.

After the wave passed, Riverstone popped up through the swirling mass of white water and grabbed the first doe he found floating face down in the water. To keep her from swallowing any more water as the succeeding waves passed over them, he covered her mouth and nose before he pulled her down below the next incoming mass of white water. Between sets, he managed to lift her head above the churning foam several more times before he finally got her onto the beach.

At first the girl wasn't breathing. He laid his head between the two most beautifully shaped breasts he had ever seen and listened for the heartbeat. Her heart was thumping beautifully.

The sound of heaven, brah.

He then quickly cleared her airway and pushed on her naked stomach. The power of the wave had completely ripped her thong bikini off her body. It took all that he had to keep his mind focused on the task at hand. But after several lip-locks and soft rubs of the stomach, he got her to puke her guts out on the sand. After that, Wiz—who had been watching the capsized yacht through the guard's binocs—took over the rehabilitation while Riverstone headed back out for another set of breasts.

Harlowe brought in the black man, who appeared to be unconscious. The boat's captain had a girl with him, but it was all he could do to lift himself onto the beach. A couple of lifeguards were waiting and took over the task of carrying the rescued bodies higher up the incline of the beach. Both the girl and the captain were okay. Harlowe made sure the black man was breathing on his own before he went back out, determined to fish out another body.

Harlowe wanted the toad that was responsible for the carnage, even if he had to scrape him off the bottom of the ocean to do it. By the time he got back out in the morass, the toad was face down in the ocean, his legs tangled in the bowline of the sinking yacht.

Harlowe stroked wildly to snag his prize, but the wave claimed the toad first, and he was gone. Another wall was right behind that one. Harlowe had to act quickly before the sinking boat drifted too close to the rocks and the next set of waves crushed them both.

After sucking in a giant breath, Harlowe was about to dive under the wreck when something thumped his leg underwater. Reaching down, he yanked up a handful of thick blond hair and brought the head to the surface.

Go figure. It was the toad himself.

Harlowe tried to clear the toad's airway, but another wave forced them both under again. It was all he could do to hold on to the body while trying desperately to get his unconscious head back above the water line. Two more times he took the body under to avoid being smashed by the full force of a wave. And two more times their bodies twisted in the torrent of unyielding power, and two more times he had no idea what direction was up or down.

I should let him go.

Harlowe was so disoriented and exhausted he wanted to puke. He had already swallowed an ocean. But if he did, he promised himself he would do it down the toad's throat first.

The battle raged.

Then, just as he was about to let go of the toad's goldilocks hair, they broke the surface, and Harlowe found himself standing in waist-deep water.

A miracle.

Harlowe dragged the toad by his hair up the beach, where he found Riverstone, whose smiling face was lying across another silicone chest, acting like he was too exhausted to move. Ian came over to help Harlowe with his catch of the day. At that same moment the lights and sirens of bright orange lifeguard vehicles arrived in force, skidding to a stop at the top of the berm. The crew quickly jumped out of their Pathfinders carrying green oxygen bottles, and ran over to begin working on the survivors who needed it most.

Ian turned the toad over and wiped the caked-on sand from his face. "Do you know who this is?"

Harlowe coughed, puking up a ton of saltwater, and said between breaths, "A stupid toad."

"He's Simon Bolt. *The* Simon Bolt. The famous movie star who plays Captain Julian Starr in *Distant Galaxies.*"

Harlowe leaned over and retched on the star's legs. He was unimpressed.

Ian shook the star, trying to revive him. "He's not breathing, Harlowe."

Harlowe studied Simon's face with all the respect he would show a dog dropping. His remedy was simple. He lifted the star's head off the sand, slapped it twice, and then gave him two quick shots to the gut.

The cure worked. Simon erupted like Vesuvius, coughing and puking up a geyser of vomit ten feet into the air.

Harlowe deadpanned, "He's breathing now."

Just then the two guards from earlier in the day joined Harlowe and Riverstone on the beach, shouting, "You're both under arrest!"

Ian held his ground, not letting the guards get to Harlowe. "Hey, brah, if it wasn't for my friends here, all these people would be statistics. They were helping you out, dudes, so leave them alone."

For a long moment guards and lawbreakers faced each other off, no one backing down until a gray-haired man in his early fifties stepped in.

"It's alright, Brady. I've been watching. The young man's right. Without these two, many could have died."

The angry guard cooled his jets the moment he recognized the man. "Yes sir, Mr. Mars. Do you know them?"

"Yes, they are friends of mine." He turned to Ian. "You've been busy, Wiz."

"Thanks, Harry."

A small creature with big ears bounced over to Harlowe and began licking his face with its slick green tongue. "What is it, Wiz?" Harlowe asked, staring at the pet with wrinkled cheeks.

"Keeper of the land," Ian informed him.

Harlowe stared at the keeper like he was trying to understand what made it tick. "You're soooo ugly, dude."

The keeper sat back on his haunches and yipped, wanting attention.

"I'd be nice to him," Ian advised.

Harlowe tried to sit up. As he did, Mr. Mars offered him a bottle of a clear blue liquid.

Harlowe took it gladly, flipping up the cap. It wasn't like water or any kind of juice he had ever tasted, but it was really good. Almost instantly Harlowe's arms and body felt like they were gathering strength. He quickly emptied the flask in three big gulps, burped, wiped his chin of the overflow, and handed back the empty bottle saying, "Thanks, mister."

"This is Harlowe, Harry. And that's Riverstone next to him," Ian said. "My stupid friends I was telling you about."

Harry nodded, studying the two rescuers. "Your friends, huh?"

Ian smiled. "By default."

Harlowe paid no attention. He was busy fending off the keeper's wet licks. Brady, who had been administering oxygen to the movie star, got the attention of the black man and asked him, "Is everyone accounted for?" The black man sat up and looked around at all the bodies.

"My daughter," Mr. Mars said with some assurance even before the count was complete. "She's still out there."

"That would be right, Mr. Mars," the black man replied. "I don't see her with us."

Ian helped one of the topless girls to a sitting position. She was so exhausted, however, she fell back onto Harlowe, who then laid her gently on her side. The two friends both searched the ocean where the boat was being slammed by another wave, pushing it closer toward the rock jetty where it would soon be reduced to kindling. At the same time, a twin-engine rescue inflatable had arrived on the scene and was darting in and out between the troughs, still looking for bodies.

Harlowe stood up. He was feeling much stronger. "Your daughter, huh?" he asked, feeling he owed the man something for giving him the blue quencher.

Harry reattached the empty bottle to his belt. "I don't see her here. She must still be in the boat or in the water."

Harlowe swallowed hard as he traded uneasy glances with Ian. He couldn't put a finger on it, but things seemed to be going from kind of awkward to way weird by the moment, and he didn't know why. Maybe it was the undog in his arms or the flask of sweet blue liquid that made him feel like he could climb Mount Everest in a single bound. Or maybe he had just been in the water way too long, but his gut was shouting loud and clear . . . *whatta day!*

Then an incredibly beautiful woman with model's legs and long flowing yellow hair came up to Harry and took his hand. She removed her sunglasses, revealing the most radiant green eyes Harlowe had ever seen. It was as if a jeweler had made them. She asked, simply, "Will you save my daughter?"

The undog yipped twice, pleading with his big yellow eyes. Harlowe didn't even realize he was holding the keeper in his arms and scratching behind his parabolics.

What? He was going to say no?

"What's her name?" Harlowe asked.

"Leucadia," the woman answered unemotionally.

Harlowe dumped the keeper on the sand as he kneeled down beside the groaning movie star and yanked the oxygen mask from his face. "Yo," Harlowe said, shaking him back to consciousness. Simon didn't answer right away. The guard tried to stop the aggressive interrogation, but Harlowe pushed the guard away like he was a small child. "Answer me, toad. What happened to Leucadia?" He shook him again and swore that he'd throw him back in the ocean if he didn't answer.

Simon must have gotten the message because his mouth started pumping out words almost immediately. "In the galley," he coughed. "Lu . . . She went to get ice . . ."

Harlowe threw Simon's head back into the sand and came back to the woman and Harry. "If she's there, I promise I'll get her," he told them as he reached for his fins and began making his way toward the water.

Harlowe brushed back his curly mop of hair. His sunken eyes told the story. Even with the injection of blue stuff, he was running on "E" and he was still on land. But he had no choice. No one else on the beach was willing to go out through that surf and risk his life for someone who may or may not be alive and trapped inside a sinking boat. Besides, the yacht was so close to the rocks, who in their right mind would dare risk it except him?

For a nanosecond Harlowe hesitated, stealing a quick glance back at Harry's wife as he slipped on his rocket fins. "Those eyes can't be real, Wiz."

Before Ian could reply, Harlowe's clear blue eyes suddenly went laser as the incoming roar headed straight at them. Wiz backed off as Harlowe faced the torrent alone. When the mass of whitewater reached the top of the incline, he dove into the receding shore break, gliding like a serpent out toward the doomed wreck. A rip current gave him an extra push that catapulted him swiftly through the ugly surf. He seemed to disappear after that, lost in a vicious surge behind huge troughs of incoming waves that defied all that was normal.

"She's the good witch from the north. They're real, pard," Ian finally shouted in reply to the two black fins as they popped above the swirling mass, Harlowe stroking for the wreck like a man possessed.

Chapter Eight

LU

BY THE TIME Harlowe made it out to the boat, the two guards in the rescue inflatable had managed to snag a nylon cable to the belly-up yacht's propeller shaft. While one guard held the line, the other was throttling the Ribcraft inflatable's twin Yamaha 60 jet outboards to the max. The engines screamed loudly, doing what they could just to stay even. It was a noble effort, but Harlowe knew it was a lost cause. It would take a 5,000-horsepower salvage tug to pull the sixty-foot yacht away from the rocks. The Ribcraft didn't have that kind of muscle. All they could hope to do was slide the sinking yacht over into a rip current eddy where it could hide between swells. The eddy was only temporary. When the next sets came rolling in, the guards would have no choice but to cut the line or end up on the rocks with Simon's boat.

"Are you crazy?" the guard on the line shouted from the stern when he saw Harlowe coming near the overturned boat. "Get out of there, you idiot!"

"My lady's in there, brah!" Harlowe shouted back.

"If there's someone inside, they're already dead!"

"Just keep the boat away from the jetty for as long as you can!" Harlowe shouted back.

The guard at the helm stared out over the bow, eyeing the incoming sets with a sense of futility. The other guard at the aft tow bar had a knife ready to cut the cable. Harlowe's stare was so intense the guard pulled his knife away from the rope and cried out, "She better be worth it!"

Harlowe thought so too, but he didn't have time to discuss it. Looking out at the lines building on the horizon, if he was going to buy it, he was hoping she was at least a nine or better. What else could he do? He had given his word. There was no turning back.

He inhaled a mass of air and dove under the boat. *Crazy?* The guard was being kind, he told himself. *He wasn't crazy. Crazy was for people with minds.* His mind was lost the moment the green eyes asked for help.

Fighting through tangled deck lines, broken bulkheads, and ripped-out chair cushions, Harlowe was swimming completely blind. He reached the side handrail in nothing flat. *No difficulty there.* He hung on to the wood rail while the boat swayed with the current. He didn't try to fight it or his arms would have been pulled out of their sockets. He just went with the flow. When the boat drifted back his way, he pulled himself under the rail, reminding himself that everything that should have been up was down and down was up.

The first thing he bumped into felt like the cockpit refrigerator. He grabbed the open door and crawled his way past some debris that tried to tangle itself around his legs as he made his way for the below deck's hatchway.

All around him the sounds of the boat strained to live, fighting against the churning sea, the crashing waves, and the rocks. The only thing keeping it alive was the whining of the twin outboards that, in all likelihood, couldn't last much longer.

Like his air.

Even now, it seemed like a lifetime ago that he had taken that last gulp of fresh air. His lungs should be exploding by now, he thought. He should be heading back to the surface, catching a second breath. But he was okay. His lungs weren't ready to burst yet. *The blue liquid again? Who knows!* Man, he would offer to buy a truckload the next time he saw the dude. Still, he would need a breath soon.

Then, with a quick flip of his fins, he slid out of the tangle, released his grip on the refrigerator door, and found by sheer luck the sliding-door handle that led to the stateroom inside the main cabin.

A sudden surge shoved him hard against the thin jamb of the stateroom entry. It felt like someone blind-sided him with a blow from a two-by-four. He lost a precious bubble of air as he gathered his wits and scratched his way through the opening, feeling the first hint of panic for air.

The heat inside his chest began to rise. He thought of an air pocket. *No, that would be lucky. Luck was for people with brains. And you ain't got any brains, remember, Pylott?* a voice shouted at him as he clawed his way forward, only to find the next obstacle—a heavy table made of thick wood and glass. He pushed it aside and spent priceless blinks of time hunting with outstretched arms, waving back and forth and up and down, hoping to touch something human instead of something that was expensive furniture, liquor bottles, or drug paraphernalia.

Or a floating body.

But it was one narly big room, as staterooms go. *Stay focused, foo!* He didn't have time to check out every nook and barstool in the place. *Where else could she be? She went to get ice. That's what the toad said. She went for ice. Stupid! You didn't hit the toad hard enough.* The next time he'd rearrange his face so he looked like a reject creature from *Star Wars*.

Did she go to the bar or to the galley? She's a doe, pard. She could have gone almost anywhere. Harlowe's mind raced through the options. He tried to think logically. His lungs were screaming now. Logic was not an option. Logic required time to think things through. He needed a breath for that, and he hadn't had a breath since the beginning of time. *And women aren't logical, you moron. Try to think like one. Okay. What's the one thing they never pass without using?*

The powder room!

Every stateroom had a toilet nearby, he figured. He just needed to feel his way along the deck forward to the hatchway that led to the lower berths. There, right off the hatchway, should be a guest bath.

Bingo!

Luck was with him. Harlowe tore through the opening and felt along the wall. The problem was that there were too many doors. He swallowed water. And now he was out of air. His lungs were on fire and tearing up his insides. He turned over, his mind a jellied mess, and floated up. Just when his world was about to go dark, his face broke the surface of an air pocket.

Well, ain't that a twist.

He still couldn't see squat, though. Everywhere was black, but as he bobbed his hands felt the top of the pocket. He seemed to have about six inches of beautiful trapped air nestled between the walls of the ship's main corridor. His chest pumped in and out like bellows over a blacksmith's fire, sucking in as much as he could in a few short seconds. He took one more valuable gulp and was about to duck down to pursue his quest when he heard a thumping sound hitting a nearby wall.

Diving down, he clawed his way toward the thumping, which didn't seem far away. It took him only a moment and he was there. He knocked back just to make sure his mind wasn't playing tricks on him.

The thump replied. It was real!

It appeared that whoever it was on the other side couldn't get the door open. With a powerful forearm slam, Harlowe broke the hinge right off the door. A surge of water came into the small bathroom and quickly filled the compartment. He still couldn't see his nose in front of his face, but suddenly he was feeling a familiar shape: the body of a slender doe. And the best part about it was, she wasn't dead.

He lifted her up into what was left of the air pocket.

"How'd you find me?" she asked. Her voice was incredibly cool and unafraid.

"It was awkward," Harlowe replied. He smelled her breath. It was clean and sensual. He wanted to kiss her. But that wasn't cool. He reached out for her and brought her toward him. She had lost the top of her bikini.

"Do you always examine your damsels in distress?" she asked.

The darkness covered his sly smile but not her eyes. They were glowing faintly in the dark. Not bright or evil like in *The Village of the Damned.* They were emerald green and beautiful and intelligent and intense like her mother's. "Well, yeah," he said to her.

Suddenly the whine of the twin jet engines changed. The pitch went from one of stress and resistance to one of high-pitched revolutions and speed. The sound then faded into nothing and was gone. The guards in the rescue boat had left the scene.

"What's that mean?" the damsel asked.

"We swim or we're dead."

They took one last gulp of air as Harlowe felt the sudden lull in the surge.

Uh oh!

He quickly grabbed her in his arms and braced himself, his legs and back against the wall of the powder room, the instant the wave struck. The sudden jolt lifted the boat, then slammed it back brutally against the ocean bottom. Bulkheads cracked. Glass shattered. Metal bent under the immense pressure. Through it all Harlowe held onto Leucadia. And she held on to him like she was just as determined. Although he had never seen her face, he knew, even if she was coyote ugly, he would never let her go. In the short few moments he had been with her, there was a closeness that stretched a lifetime, even if that lifetime had only a few precious moments left. Someone this cool under stress was a keeper, he told himself.

The air pocket evaporated the instant the swell struck the boat. And with it, Harlowe knew, went every air pocket within the boat as well. What they had in their lungs was all they had between life and death.

The yacht suddenly settled as Harlowe felt the swell recede. Frantically, they both kicked in an effort to break free. Harlowe figured they had about eight or nine seconds before the next wave would send them into the rock jetty. Nine seconds after that another wave would crush them into toothpicks. Nine seconds after that he was done counting forever. They had to get out now!

Leucadia felt the urgency in his movements. She tried to help Harlowe, but she was weakening rapidly. It was all she could do to hold on to him while he pushed and clawed their way out. He moved a beam away, and then a cot or mattress thudded against his face. There was so much debris and blackness he had no idea if they were making progress or if they were heading toward the bottom when they should be going up. It was all a wild guess. Leucadia lost her grip once, and Harlowe reached out and miraculously found her forearm and yanked her to his side. He swore to himself that he would never lose her again.

Then he saw it.

Light!

Maybe it was a hole. Maybe he was hallucinating. But if it was real, it was their way out.

He stroked with one arm, kicking with all that was in him, the powerful thrusts of his black rocket fins driving them upward. The light became brighter and brighter until suddenly they broke the surface.

His first breath could have filled a dirigible. But they had only a heartbeat before he dove them deep again to avoid the next wave that struck. Down they went, Harlowe holding on to the damsel with both arms as they tumbled inside the swirling mass. He felt the rough edge of a granite rock rub against his back. He was that close. All that was left was to kick and hope.

He opened his eyes and watched a surge of bubbles going sideways. His mind told him that was wrong. Up was ninety degrees the other way. But bubbles didn't lie. Neither did gravity. His mind was playing tricks on him. It was being coy and deceitful. He went ninety degrees right and found the surface again. As he did, he lifted her face—the face of a goddess—out of the water.

He shook her. She wasn't breathing. Inside the channel, as they were, the rocks were only a few yards away. Harlowe winced. The yacht had been shattered into a billion pieces. He knew they were headed for the same fate if he didn't get him and his goddess outside the breakers in the next few moments.

He kicked again with all that he had.

He kicked to save *her* life.

Up the steep wall of a giant they went. Up. Up. Way up the wall. The top of the crest broke over their heads but he managed to push them through, out the back side, and into the next trough before they were sucked back over the curl. Between the troughs he fed her air. By the time he had kicked them over the worst of it, they were far enough outside where he could give her a steady, rhythmic flow of air in the open water without getting pummeled again by a breaking wave. After a couple of quick pumps to her stomach, she coughed up an ocean and opened her eyes. She kept staring up at the sky, wondering if she was among the living.

"You're okay now," Harlowe said to the goddess calmly.

She touched the side of his face tentatively, testing to see if he was real or not. His dark, sun-tipped hair was a glistening mass of clinging strands that gracefully framed his boyish face. From there her hands slid along his strong neck and powerful broad shoulders to his chiseled arms that held her steady in the choppy waters where they floated together, touching and feeling each other's warmth.

"Thank you," she said.

Harlowe said nothing. His focus was only on her. He checked her eyes to make sure they were lucid and clear.

Then she asked, "Are you taken?"

Harlowe replied with a boyish smile, mesmerized by her deep green, faceted eyes. They were the most extraordinary eyes he had ever seen. Clear, intelligent, yet fearless and steady. He brushed back her long blond hair with a gentle hand so he could see her better. Her face was beautiful and flawless. He wondered if he were stuck in a dream and she would vaporize in his arms the moment he awakened.

As if she felt the same wonder, Leucadia drifted closer to him, their bodies touching as they rose and fell over the rolling troughs. For the moment they were the only ones in the ocean. Alone. No need to talk. No need to rush. Make every moment count. Make every moment theirs with hands held securely onto each other . . . forever.

She took in his strong warmth and the scent of the sea and musk, and laid her head comfortably against his broad chest as though they were one, like they had always been and always would be. Resting peacefully, she cooed, "Gamadin . . ."

Chapter Nine

UNEARTHED

"IT IS DONE," Sook said to her husband as she returned to its gilded box the handheld device she had used to cut the power to Simon Bolt's yacht. Lying next to the box was a beautiful flower with deep blue petals and a dark red stem that secreted a curious sweet scent. They were alone upstairs in the second-story study with its tall windows that overlooked the beach and the Pacific for endless miles in all directions.

Harry, her lover, her companion, her soul for the past half-century, came up from behind and held her. "They could have both died, Sook," he said worriedly.

Her eyes closed as his slight scent of sandalwood and ocean air caressed her shoulders and neck under her long golden hair. Together they watched the young man who had saved their daughter's life carry Leucadia in his arms toward their beach house. Unlike Harry, Sook had remained youthful over the years. She was still strikingly beautiful for a woman seventy-three years of age. Her long flowing hair was natural. No dyes or bleach masked a single strand of her golden hair. Her face displayed only gentle lines around her large, jewel-like green eyes. And if one looked hard enough, there was a quality about them that did not quite belong to anyone born on this planet.

"It was necessary," she replied. She shut the lid and latched the clasp of the simple box. Her pensive, green stare watched the young man wrap her daughter in a white beach towel. Next to them, Mowgi panted, wanting to play. Behind them, the young man's two friends were just coming away from the crowd of onlookers and media that surrounded the guards and the other victims of the waves.

Harry came around to Sook and stared at her in disbelief. "Why? To lose our daughter and someone we do not know. How can that be necessary?"

Sook picked up the flower beside the box. "Because the search has ended, Dorrity. I have found Millawanda." There was never holding anything back from him; in many ways, he was stronger than she was. And two people who have lived together for so long a period of time cannot hide their innermost thoughts behind a silent wall. From the night they met when they escaped from the soldiers who swarmed over Sook's crashed spaceship, they had built an empire of wealth and power for one reason only: to find the Gamadin.

For a very long moment he stared at his wife in silent dismay. No being he had ever known had such courage as hers. Harry knew the richest of the rich and the most powerful beings on Earth, including presidents, prime ministers, popes, generals, bankers, and CEOs of the world's most powerful corporations. Not one of them could stand in the room with her. She was a giant among beings, alien or earthling. He was so proud of her. For who among them was ready to stand against a galactic empire that would crush them to comic dust at the blink of an eye?

At times he wondered if his alien wife had ever felt amazement. Such a *human trait,* she would say, kiddingly, to him in their private moments. Her alien oddities were a fair trade-off, he often told himself. For all the layers he had not touched—and there were many that would always remain hidden—one had always been his since the day they first met—her heart. It was as big as the ocean and as warm as the sun. They had searched the entire planet together and spent billions of dollars over many decades to find Millawanda. During all this time, not once had they found any clue to the Gamadin existence. In recent years, they had even begun to cut back their expeditions to the distant regions of the planet because they had simply run out of places to look. Yet, in all this time, where he had wavered, she had remained steadfast, never giving up her hope that someday she would have the means to save her planet, Neeja.

"You're sure?" Harry asked.

Sook met his questioning eyes with confidence. "Yes. In Utah."

"Utah? There's not an inch of ground we haven't covered there."

She gave him the blue flower.

"From the yellow pathway?" he asked her.

"From Utah."

Harry examined the flower and breathed its sweetness. "It's sweeter, more pungent than the ones we have here. How did we miss her?"

"It wasn't yet time," Sook replied, looking again at the beach. Their daughter stopped to kiss the young man and then they resumed walking toward the house. "Millawanda is summoning us."

"Why now?"

Sook thought for a long moment before she turned to her husband. "She may sense danger."

Harry tried to follow her thoughts. "The government?"

"No. The government is no threat to her. Millawanda would not react unless the madness now threatens the planet, my love. The waiting is over. She calls to us."

"The Fhaal?"

"Perhaps. I don't know. But it seems she is telling us it is time to begin her . . ." Sook's deep green eyes met his. "Resurrection."

"You are certain?" he asked. "It is Millawanda?"

"Yes. I am sure of it. The flowers cover the gorge where she lies hidden. This is her calling to us. She waits."

"How can we be certain she is alive? After so long, Sook, she may be dead," Harry said soberly.

"The flowers live. She also lives. It is her sign, like the one on the map."

Harry nodded toward the beach. "But why the young man and our daughter? Why must we involve them? Surely you can't mean they are—"

Sook finished his statement for him. "Yes, they are the future, Dorrity." She called him by his old family name when they were alone, in their most private moments together.

Harry stared at his wife with disbelief. "They might not want to be a part of this future."

Sook's face was solemn with worry, almost regretful. "It is unavoidable."

Lines of uneasiness ran deeper along Harry's face. "They should have a choice."

Sook stared coldly into Harry's eyes. "Fate has already made that choice. They are the ones who will carry on our fight."

"But they're so young," Harry said. "They have not lived."

"Your friends. Have you forgotten them?" Sook asked.

"No. You know that."

"They were also young, Dorrity, before they perished. They had not lived either. And if we do not stop the enemies of Gamadin, how many after that will not live, my love?"

Harry's eyes filled with pain. It was hard to reconcile the facts of life and death on a galactic scale when there seemed to be no immediate threat. "But Neeja is so distant. Even if we have indeed found this Gamadin technology, how could it matter now?"

"Because even Earth is not safe, Dorrity. One day the Fhaal will find us here. Their coming is not a maybe, not a possibly; they will find us. They will come, and they *will* destroy this beautiful planet of ours. After that, many others will die. Neejan forces were thousands of times more powerful than Earth's, and the Fhaal killed that great star. Neeja is lost, my love, but Earth still lives free. We must save Earth, Harry. Our sacrifice is not what we surrender, but what we must do to save our planet from the evil Fhaal."

Harry could say nothing. He remained silent as he struggled to accept the inevitable truth that lay before them.

"Earth is our home too, Dorrity. It is our daughter's home and the home of all that is important to us now, my love. We cannot allow this home to suffer the same fate as Neeja."

"And you believe this Gamadin technology will protect Earth?"

"It must. When Xancor entrusted me with the Gamadin artifacts, he had already seen the future. He knew without the Gamadin there would be no future. That is what he died for. That is what my family on Neeja died for and your friends died for. That is what we will die for, my love. The future of Earth and ultimately the galaxy, for the wrath of the Gamadin will be felt throughout the stars to bring peace again to the quadrant, and beyond."

Harry's gaze returned to the beach. "The young man has courage. I'll grant you that, Sook. But what is it you saw in him?" he asked.

In that moment, Simon Bolt's big bodyguard came pounding up the beach behind Leucadia and the young bodysurfer. There was rage in his eyes and great destruction in his tense muscles and cocked fists. Obviously, he had been sent to do Simon's dirty work in defending his honor. First the movie star had lost his boat and now his girl was being led away by the conquering hero. It was an insult too great to go unavenged.

The black bodyguard was the type that looked like he ate galvanized tenpenny nails for breakfast. He was six foot six, 255 pounds of solid gristle. They said he was an ex-Navy Seal with a black belt and three degrees in an oriental martial art that no one could pronounce. His hair was black and long and tied in a ponytail down the middle of his back. He had round dark eyes and a small mouth that was centered in a square handsome face that was clean shaven and mean. The young man would never survive the assault.

Leucadia seemed to see it coming. She let go of the young man's hand just before the bodyguard's powerful fist came exploding toward her young hero's head. Harry glanced at Sook for her reaction. But in that briefest moment what should have happened, didn't. Harry wasn't sure if his eyes were playing tricks on him, but somehow in that instant, the black man's body was lying face down on the sand, a twitchless mass of inertness.

Sook's eyes remained on the scene below. She had seen it all. For the first time since their discussion began, her grave mood tempered. Her mouth turned up slightly. One could believe it was a grin. Down on the beach her big-eared little chinner was jumping playfully beside Leucadia as the young man held his black fins in one hand and took their daughter's hand in the other. This was the happiest Sook had seen Mowgi since her daughter was born. For he sensed as well as she that Millawanda had awakened and that walking on the beach with Leucadia was a sign of the resurrection. It had begun.

Sook took Harry's hand. "That is what I saw, my love. Our future is there."

Chapter Ten

TINY POINTS OF LIGHT

With unhurried ease, Dr. Thomas Shaffer danced his fingers along the keyboard to bring the two-hundred-inch Hale telescope into perfect alignment. He was sitting in the high lookout cage on top of the giant scope. The astrophysicist announced with a calm voice over the intercom, "Moving the primary to one second right ascension, Ed." He stretched his six feet four inches and read the digital readouts on the display as the thousand-ton telescope glided on its thin film of oil. The south pedestal pivoted, the north pedestal swung around, and the massive horseshoe bearing rotated around the polar axis ever so smoothly until the east-west celestial meridian was found. The giant Hale was in perfect sync with Earth as it turned from east to west. The primary mirror held rock steady, focused at 13h 18m 25s, +0° 21.6' in central Virgo.

"All go here, Tom," the friendly voice over the intercom speaker replied.

When Shaffer looked into the eyepiece and felt satisfied that everything was as it should be, he flicked the intercom switch again and said, "Let her rip, Ed."

"Commencing exposure, Tom," the same voice replied.

It was chilly; a good night for observation, Shaffer thought. Because of a freak storm off the coast, this was the first night in two days he had had a chance to follow up on last Sunday's observations. Many nights in his twenty-four years of observing the sky, since his father gave him a pair of binoculars on his eighth birthday, had been exciting. This night was no exception. Shaffer felt like a kid waiting for Christmas morning. If his theory proved correct, he would have two more potential "Earthgrazers" added to the six he had discovered the week before. This would never make him famous, he knew, unless they became a problem.

He grinned inwardly, reflecting almost fondly on what astrophysicists like himself called "grazers." Out of the hundred thousand or so asteroids large enough to cause great damage, a few regularly passed moderately close to Earth's orbit. If these floating pieces of rock remained in a stable orbit around the sun, then no one worried. But some, like the ones he had recently plotted, had slightly changed their orbits. Where they would wander was anyone's guess. Still, there was no cause for alarm. Grazer orbits were forever being slightly altered by Earth itself, or by the sun, or by other planets in the solar system. Only once every ten to twenty million years or so did one come close enough to worry about.

After a couple of routine checks of his console instruments, Shaffer climbed out of the cage and made his way to the elevator still wearing his parka zipped up tight. It was cold that high up in the dome. He figured he could get a quick cup of hot coffee to warm his insides before Ed had the photographic plates ready for his preliminary examination.

Shaffer stepped into the tiny cubicle and pressed the switch with the arrow pointing down. As the elevator drifted along the curve of the dome, he could almost taste the crisp pine air of the Ponderosas as he watched their needle-like tops pointing unerringly up at the heavens. In a grand sort of way, he envied their ability to stand watch over this peaceful setting for an eternity.

A winged shadow flapped across the starry hush of the night. It touched a splinter of light, then another, and another, traveling the stars faster than light. Shaffer sighed. If there was one thing he had always dreamed of doing one day, it was traveling to other worlds, touching stars. A part of him left the confines of the dome and reached out. Hello, he called to them. Is anyone out there? Can you hear me? When you're ready to answer, you'll find us here, waiting to welcome you.

* * *

"Coffee, Tom?" asked a familiar voice, disturbing his dream.

For a short moment, Shaffer was stuck somewhere on a distant doorstep. He hadn't realized the elevator had already stopped on the control deck. He blinked. The toucher of stars had flown away and in its place his devoted associate's round happy face greeted him beside the elevator with two mugs of steaming hot coffee.

"Earth to Tom," Dr. Edward McCarty said, smiling. He handed Shaffer his mug that read: "Hello . . . is anyone out there?" Below the inscription, a gangly, happy-faced alien cupped his purple three-fingered hand over his dish-shaped ear, listening intently.

Shaffer stepped from the platform and graciously took the mug. "Do you ever wonder what's out there, Ed?" he asked as they both turned like wide-eyed kids toward the night.

McCarty chuckled. "How many times are you going to ask me that?"

Shaffer shrugged. "Until they land."

McCarty's eyes widened. "What makes you say that?"

Shaffer took a loud sip. A small cloud drifted lightly around his face as the cold night mixed with the hot vapors. "I don't know. I was just thinking how I will react when I first meet someone from another world," he said, pointing the mug skyward.

McCarty snorted. "Like every other schmuck, you'll probably pee in your pants the moment you shake hands with one."

They laughed together and began walking toward the developing room.

"Do you think we're typical? I mean, do you think they look like we do?" Shaffer asked, genuinely thoughtful.

McCarty rubbed his face and yawned. "Gosh, I hope not. Not after the sleep I've gotten the last three nights."

"Kitty keeping you up?"

McCarty shook his head with a look of disbelief and exhaustion. "You'd think the woman drank Viagra like tea. We've been married for, what?" He thought a moment as he counted the time with his fingers. "Twelve, no, it's fourteen glorious years and she still thinks we're on our honeymoon."

"And after three kids too."

"Yeah. The woman's insatiable. I swear I have to make sure she's got a fully charged debt card before I leave or I'm in deep doo-doo when I get back."

"Whatever Kitty's drinking, I'll take some for Julie."

While Shaffer laughed, McCarty's eyes turned fearful. "Don't even joke about it, Tom. Trust me. Feel fortunate she's normal."

"You knew she was a wild one when you married her. Remember what you said? And let me get your exact words right. You wanted 'someone to bounce off the walls with' after the lonely business of stargazing."

"That's right, I said that," McCarty said, pointing a finger at Shaffer. "So be careful what you wish for, Tom. You might wake up one day and find aliens knocking at your door."

Shaffer laughed. "As long as they're not horny aliens, we should be safe."

"Amen, brother."

Shaffer's face cringed as he took another hot sip of his coffee. "You know, Ed, I'm sure glad you have photometric skills to make up for your coffee."

"Kitty says the same thing. But she has a different take."

Shaffer held up his hand. "Spare me the details. I've heard enough already."

They walked into the constant-temperature photo room together.

"So how'd we do last night, Ed?"

"Well, you may want a new associate after you see these," McCarty commented, making his way toward an elongated rectangular table. Above their heads, a series of eight-foot-long fluorescent tubes hummed with white radiance. "I think the secondary mirror is out of alignment."

"Not a chance. I checked everything twice before the run."

"Yeah? Well, take a look. See what you think."

Shaffer unzipped his parka. It was a pleasant seventy-two degrees in the photo room. He bent over the layout table and began studying the reversed negative photographic plates McCarty had already laid out. "I thought everything went pretty smoothly."

"I thought so too. I checked everything three times. But something peculiar's going on that I can't explain yet."

"Maybe it's the new software."

"Software checks out, Tom."

"Well, let's see what we have." After draping his parka over a chair, Shaffer picked up a large magnifying glass. "This is our boy here, isn't it?"

"Yeah, uh-huh," McCarty replied as if there was something more he was waiting for Shaffer to find.

To an untrained eye, looking at a white plate of black dots was like looking at spilled pepper on a white tablecloth. Tom Shaffer didn't see pepper, however; he saw doors. As an astrophysicist, he could readily distinguish an asteroid from a planet or even a meteorite. They all move at different, but predictable, speeds. Shaffer knew what the one small line was in the middle of the plate. He also knew what the length of the line meant in terms of the object's speed. But what he didn't know was the meaning of the streaks his sharp eyes quietly spotted in the lower-right corner of the photographic plate. "These three are uninvited, aren't they?"

"Looks like it," Ed replied dryly.

"And they're all moving in the same direction too." He glanced at McCarty. "What do you think the chances of that occurring are?"

McCarty allowed himself a brief moment of calculation before he volunteered an observation. "How about zero?" Then he added, "They look like they're in squad formation."

Shaffer hadn't looked at the plate with that kind of eye. It was an intriguing idea, however, and he took a thoughtful moment of his own before he suggested, "We'd better check the mirror alignment before we take another exposure." His eyes moved carefully to another plate. "The mirror could have a fluctuation. Better check the software again too. You know Zagorsky. He'll want every detail covered and double-checked before we submit a report."

McCarty nodded agreement.

"After that, and if everything checks out, we'll center these puppies," Shaffer ordered, instantly losing his boyish tone. "Try another one degree west, two minutes, ten seconds north, this time. Whatever they are, they're moving fast." He reached for a small ruler and placed it on the plate. "What moves two millimeters in ten minutes?" he asked after making the calculation.

The answer was simple: nothing.

Chapter Eleven

42ND STREET

BAD HAIR DAYS have a way of starting out like normal days. But when the shot ripped through Baby, grazing Harlowe's scalp and putting a gaping hole through the vintage VW's roof, it wasn't just a bad hair day. It was war!

As bullets whizzed past his head, all Harlowe could think about was revenge. He bolted out the car door, bullets be damned, and sprinted across the wide-open field at Mae Boyar Park off Del Amo, leaving Riverstone and Ian with their mouths stuck open, wondering what kind of death wish Harlowe had in mind this time.

"He's totally whack!" Ian cried out from the backseat. Running after the assassins unarmed meant nothing to Harlowe, though. When he was angry, even the ocean parted to get out of his way.

All Ian and Riverstone saw was Harlowe's backside as he took off across the park toward the track homes where the toads that shot at them were fleeing in two cars. Harlowe couldn't have been an easier target. But it didn't appear the snipers cared. They weren't sticking around for Harlowe to catch them, even if he was on foot. The two cars split up and Harlowe had to pick one. The old brown Chevy sedan got the better jump, so Harlowe set his sights on the low-riding, yellow Cougar that was trying to do a quick U-turn on Loomis Street.

Riverstone traded futile glances with Ian as he took over the driver's seat. "Let's go pick up the parts," he said, turning Baby around. They went back to Palos Verde and began searching the neighborhood streets, expecting to find Harlowe's bullet-riddled body somewhere under a bush. After thirty minutes of going up and down streets, they finally located Harlowe, lying face up on a bus-stop bench at Palos Verde and Arbor. They saw blood all right. All over his face and hands. They thought for sure the homeboys had won this time. But they hadn't. *Harlowe doesn't lose,* Riverstone reminded himself. To his chagrin, when he and Ian drove up alongside the bench, Harlowe rolled over, his bright blue eyes very much alive, and began reaming out his pals for taking so long to find him.

"You're so whacked, Pylott," Riverstone countered, staring at Harlowe's bloodstained face. "Look at you. You're a mess. How are we going to get into Farnducky's class with you looking like that? I can't miss that test, pard."

Riverstone wanted to say a lot more, but he cut Harlowe some slack because he'd been the one with the bullet-parted hairline, not him. From the look of things, Harlowe should have been dead. Across the service street, four homeboys were laid out on the front lawn of a track house. One moved painfully but the three others were still as death. The Cougar's front windshield was shattered in a million pieces where Harlowe had bodily crashed through the window. When Harlowe was in payback mode, no one was spared, not even souped-up old Cougars.

His friends asked him for more details on what had happened but got only grunts as an answer. Harlowe wasn't in the mood for conversation. He grabbed a smelly gym shirt Ian handed to him and pointed south. "Forty-Second Street, pard." Forget school, waves were his painkillers.

Harlowe made a nod to show that he was going to drive, but Riverstone pointed at the shotgun seat. "No way, toad. You're sitting there. Sullivan sees you driving like this and he'll have your whacked up head in jail tonight. The test, remember? Stay focused on that. I promised my parents this morning I would go to Farnducky's class so I can go to the game on Friday. I intend to keep it."

Harlowe didn't argue. He was too tired to do otherwise. He dabbed the smelly gym shirt over the wound where the bullet had grazed his scalp and obediently took his seat. As he made himself comfortable, he eyed with dull relief the exit hole through the roof. He winced as he thought, *Fresh . . .* His knuckles were bloody and swollen, and they stung from the faces he had smashed. Harlowe flexed his fingers in and out; no bones were broken. A small price for justice, he figured, as he wiped them with the rag.

He looked at the digital clock he had stuck on the dashboard with Velcro. It read: 7:02 a.m. He'd been awake for just an hour and thirty-two minutes.

The day can't get any worse.

The air was cold and it felt like a storm was approaching. In the east, a pink sun was just coming up along a cloudless horizon, while in the west, an offshore squall of dark clouds was threatening the peace off the coast. It seemed to Harlowe like a perfect standoff between good and evil.

Riverstone guided Baby toward the 605 freeway entrance off Carson Street and reminded Harlowe again that if he didn't pass the physics test in Farnducky's class, he couldn't go to the game Friday.

"Wiz will take it for you," Harlowe said.

"No way. The last time brainiac took the test," Riverstone said, pointing an accusing thumb at Ian, who was sleeping in the backseat, "he didn't miss a single question. Farnducky thought I stole the test."

Harlowe leaned back and nudged Ian. "Hey, pard, miss a couple this time, okay?"

Ian yawned, readjusting the large black flipper he was using for a pillow. It was way too early for a night owl like him. "I couldn't miss a Farnducky question if I tried," he mumbled without opening his eyes behind his thick lenses.

Riverstone turned toward Harlowe. "See, I'm screwed." Harlowe didn't care. He just stared westward, out the window, while his pal continued to rant. "Nothing's going to work this time. No football game, no date, no life. It's all coming to an end, foo. I can see it now. I might as well be enslaved on some lifeless planet."

Ian muttered, "Be careful what you wish for."

Harlowe put his finger through the bullethole. "Yeah, you're screwed."

Yeah, well, screw them both, Riverstone thought as he turned right onto the 605 onramp. Baby was rat-tat-tating along nicely up the small incline when a giant shadow flew over them. He nearly lost it trying to keep Baby steady in the buffeting wind created by the creature's draft. Although Riverstone couldn't see exactly what it was in the dim morning light, he could tell that it had a great wingspan and its silhouette was like that of some medieval dragon. It glided along the treetops and then headed southwest toward the ocean. Riverstone swore its big yellow eyes stared at him as if thinking he was a juicy steak when it flew by.

Ian's mouth still hung open in awe as he commented, "That was awkward."

Harlowe didn't seem to care what it was. "Just get to the beach," he ordered.

It took a long moment for Riverstone's lungs to fill and give him enough air to finally say, "Aye, aye, captain."

* * *

Little more was said about the creature. No one wanted to be labeled a kook for his opinion. They made one more stop after that to pick up a bag of ice at the nearest 7-Eleven for Harlowe's bruised knuckles. Then they continued south until they hit Pacific Coast Highway off of Bellflower. PCH welcomed them like an old friend. They all needed the salty air and the damp mist to help clear their minds and put the early-morning war behind them.

Riverstone shivered from a sudden blast of cold, moist air. The chill found its way through the cracks in Baby's weather-stripping, the fresh-air vents that never closed, and the hole in the floorboard at the base of the clutch. He shook again. *Where'd that come from?* This was not the first time they had faced danger. So why was he so scared? Why now? He reached down between the seats, next to the stick, and stretched an elastic bungee cord to one side to hold it in fourth gear while he pushed the hot-air levers to full blast. He nearly ripped off his pinky performing the maneuver.

That's stupid, he swore, *Baby's a piece of junk. Nothing's been right since Lu dumped Harlowe for that toad-faced movie star.*

Riverstone watched but did not see the road. For the first time in his life he really felt frightened about where they were headed. The future looked grim.

Riverstone wished they could all go back in time. Three years ago, before they met Lu and Sook and Harry and their freaky pet. *No! Make it longer than that. I don't care. Yes, I do care. Make it before the gangs tried to take over. Before it all became so frickin' confusing. Make it when we were kids making flying saucers out of sand at the beach. When we were starship captains flying to distant worlds, protecting good from evil and saving planets from destruction. Yeah, make it the good times when it was all just pretend. Oh man, take us back to the beginning when it was all make-believe.*

As Riverstone finessed the old bug up to the light at Newport Boulevard and 32nd Street, he made a careful stop, mindful of the two police cars across the intersection. No use drawing attention to themselves. Everything by the book. Knowing Sullivan, he just might have the cops out looking for them because of what had happened earlier. Harlowe was always at the top of his hit list.

Suckwad . . .

Riverstone looked both ways. They had a choice. They could turn left and head down to the peninsula, or they could turn right and go to their old haunt at 42nd Street. He glanced at Harlowe, who looked gloomy. He wasn't the old Harlowe since Lu got wise. He had become a tough read.

When his dad was killed the year before, Harlowe became focused on one thing: revenge. He was obsessed with finding the killer. But when Lu stepped out of his life, he turned numb. Riverstone knew how much the consecutive blows hurt. Not even Harlowe could withstand such pain. The beach seemed to be the only place where they could chill out. Harlowe was down, but he would work it out. He didn't lose. And someday he would have his revenge.

So, even if the swells were pumping at the Wedge, there were too many old wounds that still hadn't healed to allow Harlowe to go there. No, the peninsula was off-limits. It was turn right, onto 42nd Street, and forget about the past. As Baby sputtered into action, Riverstone breathed a sigh of relief because the officers appeared to be more interested in the shiny black Hummer they had pulled over.

"Step on it," Harlowe demanded. His gaze kept looking off past Riverstone, to the west, trying to get a short glimpse of the breakers among the multimillion-dollar beachfront homes that blocked most of his view.

"Didn't you see those cops?" Riverstone shot back. "They were eyeing us, toad. Ya think Sullivan called ahead?"

Harlowe dropped the towel between his legs. "They shot at us, remember?"

"You think Sullivan cares? I'll bet anything he called ahead. Maybe we should have waited around to give him an explanation."

Harlowe lifted his blooded middle figure from the ice and stinky shirt. That was all he had to say.

Riverstone's stomach tightened by another notch, however, when the black Hummer they had passed earlier rounded the corner and began following them. Normally, he would never have given the Hummer a second thought, but it was the second one he had seen that morning. The big car had done nothing out of the ordinary, but why didn't it pass them? A powerful car like that could speed by them in a heartbeat. Riverstone asked Wiz to keep an eye on it while he drove. But Wiz was clueless and cared more about his sleep. As long as it wasn't Sullivan, he didn't want to be bothered, and neither did Harlowe.

Riverstone considered the idea that the Hummer was taking tourists on a leisurely drive along the coast. It was that time of year, right? So what was the big deal? *Don't go getting so bent. Chill out!*

They crossed the Santa Ana River Bridge and cruised into Newport Beach with Coldplay's "Clocks" blaring on the radio, and soon after that, they passed by the Pine Knot Motel. At Cappy's, Riverstone flipped the turn indicator, devoured a quick mouthful of chocolate perfections, and downshifted into third while screeching right onto Balboa . . . a flawless execution.

After a short half-block, they passed under the River Avenue that-a-way arrow and then made a quick right onto the one-way 46th Street running parallel to the beach. It was routine from here. Riverstone could have done it blindfolded. They took a left onto Newport Drive and then a right onto Seashore Drive going north. The narrow street was nearly deserted except for a scant few cars that no one cared about protecting from the ruinous sun and salt.

The backs of tall, multilevel dream homes lined the beach side of Seashore Drive, while across the street sat two-story apartments that were dull and uninspiring. Their low-pitched roofs were in disrepair, their fences were crooked, their sidewalks needed sweeping, their gardens needed tending, and their windows needed washing. Except for the loud tinny sputters of Baby's muffler that resonated off garage doors and neglected cars, all seemed unpleasantly quiet, like Death had somehow moved into the neighborhood.

Riverstone downshifted into second, passing the 37th Street sign; there were no cross-streets, just numbered signs that marked the entries to the beach between the beachfront estates. "Road to Nowhere," by the Talking Heads, had thankfully replaced an ad on the radio for new carbon laser surgery for hemorrhoids.

At the blue and white 42nd Street sign, Riverstone parked Baby. He zipped up his jacket tighter and gazed at the dark clouds amassing on the horizon. "There's a storm comin', pard. We'd better bag it for today or we'll never make it back for Farnducky's stupid physics test."

Harlowe didn't care about the test or the approaching darkness. His priorities were simple. Waves. "We'll make it," he said with his usual self-assured brevity. Riverstone wanted to object, but Harlowe's eyes flared, cutting off any thought of debate.

Riverstone expelled a hot breath of disgust. *Why did Harlowe need to see the waves? He knew what they looked like. He'd seen them countless times before. Why not see them from inside the bug, where it was nice and warm? The water had to be freezing. It was the common-sense thing to do. Why punish ourselves?*

Harlowe reached in back and grabbed his fins from under Ian's sleepy head.

"You're whacked. You know that!" Riverstone exclaimed. "It's just stupid to go out there, brah."

Harlowe opened the door and got out. "Stay here then," he said, tossing the bloodied rag on the front seat. He took his wet suit and towel from under the seat and headed out to the beach.

Toadhead! Riverstone got out too, hurling a phalanx of four-letter insults toward Harlowe. He couldn't let him go alone. He might do something even more stupid! As his two friends headed out onto the sand, Wizzixs slept in the backseat and kept Baby company.

With heads down, Harlowe and Riverstone forced their way through the buffeting gale that fought to hold them back. Before they had gone too far, Riverstone glanced back to take a concerned look at Baby. It was then that he spotted the black Hummer he had seen on the highway. It came to a slow stop at the corner of 36th Street and Seashore Drive. A sudden chill straightened his neck hairs for no apparent reason. Riverstone tried to ignore it by turning back to the deserted beach.

The waves were hidden from view below the high sandy berm, waiting for them. Riverstone could easily hear their thunderous power crashing against the shore. Farther out on the horizon, the dark clouds of the squall were gathering strength. Black and foreboding, they came toward the shore, ready to crush them—like the snipers back in Lakewood had tried to do—the moment he and Harlowe ventured out onto the sand, unprotected.

I see ya, Riverstone shouted to the clouds. *I know you're there.*

The storm laughed. It had no peers.

As the teens continued on across the soft sand together, the salty spray dampened their faces. The roar of wind and surf was deafening. Seventy yards out to sea, they saw the tops of the waves spitting their frothy-white spray into the air. The chaotic lines of wind-driven waves broke out above the horizon, coming angrily toward the shore. Smiles broke wide across both their faces. It didn't matter how bad the day had turned out; just being here, at this moment, challenging all that was powerful and mighty against them, had been worth the effort.

When they made their way over the berm, they sat down on the moist sand and used the windward side of the slope for a backrest. From where they were sitting, they looked due west along the shoreline of wrathful waves. The tide was coming in. Soon it would reach them, and they would have to move or get wet.

Riverstone shivered again and wiped the corner of his eye for the umpteenth time. *Must be the salty air affecting my vision,* he rationalized. He wanted to forget all that had happened this morning. He wanted to be in class and be plain old Riverstone again, walking through Hartwell Park on a warm summer evening, listening to the sycamores sing in the breeze with a girl he hadn't yet met. Yeah, that's what he wanted. A girl to walk in the park with. Someone to hold. Someone to talk with about the silly things that were important only to them.

A sudden chill made him rub his arms together. "Harlowe . . . I feel so cold."

Harlowe crossed his arms and gave Riverstone a long stare. After a long moment, he announced, "I'm going in."

A seagull plucked a sand crab from the receding shorebreak.

"Don't be a foo; it's blown out," Riverstone objected.

Harlowe started taking off his clothes and changing into his wet suit. "I have to, pard," Harlowe replied, his voice poignant. "I promised myself I'd do it."

Riverstone turned toward the angry waves, away from Harlowe's sullen face. In many ways, they were easier to fight. The cold spray, much colder than before, blurred his vision. He didn't care if he could see or not. The squall, nearly on them now, was darker. It had picked up power. He could see that. The predator was coming into shore to get them.

Riverstone looked south toward the short stubby breakwater that held the drifting sands in check. Coming toward them, a tall woman in dark clothes strutted through the sand, fighting the wind, as a small dog with big ears ran to keep up with her long graceful strides.

"You staying here?" Harlowe asked.

"For a while." But as Harlowe turned to leave, Riverstone grabbed one of his long black fins. "Listen, toad, don't stay out long. The test, remember? I want to go to the game, Harlowe. It's important. Lakewood's going to annihilate Wilson and I want to see it. Understand?"

Harlowe winked. "I'm down with that, pard."

Riverstone let go of the fin. "Hurry up, then."

Harlowe reached the water's edge and waited for the surge to run up the side of the sandy berm. In one clean motion, he put on his fins and dove in. The roiling water swept him away in much the same way it had a year ago when they faced the giant swells that destroyed Simon Bolt's yacht and nearly killed them both.

On shore, Riverstone swallowed hard as his focus returned to the woman and her pet. He knew that stride, that long flowing hair. The undog had vanished like a ghost. Riverstone twisted around, searching for a place to hide, a place where he could make himself unnoticeable in the sand.

Still searching for a way out, Riverstone spied two men down the beach in long black overcoats making their way toward the water from the opposite direction. He snickered inside, thinking that someone else was as stupid as they were to be out in this weather. Were they the same dudes he had seen stepping out of the Hummer? He thought so. Their gait was stiff and deliberate. Strong, Riverstone thought, by the way they pushed themselves through the wind like it was nothing at all. Yeah, they were very strong.

"Hey, Matthew," the woman said.

Too late, toad, there's no place to hide.

Chapter Twelve

UNDOG

RIVERSTONE'S LOUSY DAY had no intention of redeeming itself, especially when the undog bounded up and smacked him with a wet one on the side of the face. He pushed the goopy weirdness away with a disgusting straight arm. "Stop it, Mowgi, you slimeball!"

He hadn't seen the undog for six months. Not since the infamous breakup between Harlowe and Leucadia Mars that made all the tabloids around the world. Of course, Mowgi hadn't changed. How could he? He was like no other dog on the planet. Calling Mowgi a dog had always been a stretch for Riverstone anyway. Four legs and a thin whippy tail were about the only features the critter had in common with your average Spot or Rover. Harlowe said Mowgi was clear proof that aliens did exist. But not even Wizzixs bought that one.

Even so, Harlowe may have had a point. The bodily proportions of the messed-up mutt were way out of whack with the rest of the body. Its pointy teeth, green tongue, and parabolic ears—which Harlowe figured could hear a fly fart a thousand yards away—could only be attributed to some sort of alien dog pile. Yeah, Harlowe may have been right. Mowgi was a confirmed alien, but he wasn't about to concede the point.

The undog shifted into a soft purr when Riverstone began scratching the chinner behind one of his radar dishes. "Keeping the fire hydrants well marked, huh, Mowg?" Then he swallowed hard, waiting for the other shoe to drop as the tall form of Leucadia Mars came to a slow stop inside his space and waited for his response.

He couldn't look at her eye to eye. Not yet, anyway. She was just too hot. "S'up, Lu," Riverstone finally said, acknowledging her presence. He kinked his head up at the overcast sky, trying to swallow his lecherous cravings while staying cool at the same time. "A little dim for you today, isn't it?" he added.

"It's been awhile, Matthew," she began.

He noted a sadness in her tone, maybe even regret. He wasn't sure it was decipherable. Trying to read behind those sparkling green eyes was like trying to untie the Gordian knot. Harlowe was the only one who could see through those eyes. Regardless, Riverstone's gut was telling him that her being here at this moment wasn't just happenstance.

"Yeah," Riverstone acknowledged, "a lot of waves, Lu."

She looked out at the surf and asked, "Where is he?"

"I don't know. I haven't seen him. He could be anywhere. You know Harlowe, a tough guy to keep track of. A mind of his own and all that."

She pointed. "That's him out there, isn't it?" Riverstone figured she was guessing.

"Yeah, ah, mayb–," he caught himself. "No, no. It's not Harlowe."

"He's the only one thick-headed enough to be out there on a day like this."

"Yeah, ya got that righ–," Riverstone caught himself again. That's not what he meant to say, but she had a way about her that threw him off balance, especially when she pressed for answers he was reluctant to give.

"Ah, that's not him. I told you, it's someone else. Even if it was, he won't be in for a long time."

She nodded. "Why would you be sitting here if Harlowe hadn't come with you? And in that case, why aren't you out there with him? That's not like you, Matthew."

"Don't call me Matthew, Lu. I don't like it. Your mom can call me that, but not you. You're not my mother."

"Alright," she apologized. She waited a moment longer before she went on. "So where is he, Matt?"

He didn't like Matt either. Riverstone was his name. But plus-tens had privileges. "I told you, I don't know."

"You used to be a much better liar."

"Come on, Lu, don't bother him. You're bad luck for him, and he's had a ton of bad luck today already. Trust me. He doesn't need any more, especially from you."

"I miss him."

Riverstone's eyes shot skyward again. How could he handle her? "He doesn't miss you. He's got a new doe and she's a real find, Lu. She loves him."

"Much more than me, huh, Matt?"

Riverstone saw he was losing the battle. *Man, she was tough.* "Whatta ya want, Lu?"

"I need to see him."

"I told ya he doesn't want to see you. Stay away from him. He's got his head back on straight again. Took him some downtime, but he did it. So let 'im be, Lu."

"It's important, Matt. More important than you could imagine."

He stood and looked into her brilliant green eyes. "Listen, I can imagine a lot. But there's only one important thing I'm imagining right now, and that's the test in Farnducky's physics class. Nothing is more important than that. If you can imagine that, Ms. Mars, I'd die a happy man."

"Don't hate me, Matt," Leucadia said. "There were reasons. I—"

"There are always reasons. A ton of them," he said, cutting her off. "You hurt him bad, Lu. Kicked him right between the legs when he needed you. That's no way to treat anyone. Not even a toad-head like Harlowe. You didn't have to take off with Simon Bolt like that just when . . . Well, you know."

"I . . . It couldn't be helped, Matt."

"We saw the papers, Lu. You're not easy to hide. You made your choice. You chose toad face over Harlowe."

"I didn't—"

"That's whack, Lu. We saw the papers. You were buzzing around in Bolt's chopper outside Vegas, whoopin' it up. That was you, right?"

Her gorgeous green eyes turned glassy. "That was me," she admitted.

"The paparazzi had a field day with that one, girl."

"We weren't 'whoopin' it up,' Matt. It was business. I needed a ride to my mother's archeological site in Utah. Simon's chopper was available."

"Available, huh? Like your dad doesn't own a fleet of choppers around the world."

"Simon was going my way. His movie set was nearby."

"That's fresh. I like that one. What was it your mom found again? The Lost Dutchman mine?"

"Something out of this world she's spent her whole life looking for. I couldn't let her down. I had to go."

"Sweet. The news guys had you and Re-run spending the night in a Navajo Hogan smoking peyote. I bet that was fun."

She bent over like she was going to rearrange his good looks. Riverstone gritted his teeth. He was one nanosecond from a Martian launch when she looked him straight in the eye, leaving no doubt in her reply. "That was a lie. I love Harlowe. I would never do anything to betray his trust. If you don't believe anything, believe that."

"This your doing?" Harlowe asked, appearing out of nowhere. One minute he was catching a blown-out wave and the next he was standing alongside them, like he had suddenly been transported between the mothership and Earth. He stood there dripping wet, staring angrily at both Riverstone and Leucadia like he had been set up.

Harlowe stripped off his wet suit and reached down for his towel. He tried being cool, but from the way he was dabbing himself off, one could see he was a boiling pot about to explode.

"No, stupid," Riverstone replied defensively. "She just appeared out of thin air like your bony head. It's a free country, you know."

Harlowe only grunted as he began putting on his clothes. But before he could get his second leg in his pants, Mowgi took one leap and landed in Harlowe's arms. "Hey, mutthead, still ugly as ever, I see." Mowgi lapped up the attention with a yelp and a howl. After a couple of sloppy wet ones and an ear rub, Harlowe let the undog drop to the sand and finished pulling up his pants.

Leucadia spoke first. "Riverstone didn't know."

"Doesn't matter," Harlowe said.

"I need to talk to you, Pylott," Leucadia continued.

"Nothing to talk about," Harlowe said. "It's over. We had a good time and now it's over. So buzz off."

"I'm sorry, Harlowe."

"I feel better now."

To Riverstone, Leucadia's expression of regret sounded heartfelt. If he were Harlowe, he would have made up with her on the spot. But Harlowe wasn't going down that road. He wasn't buying her act. He had seen those green doe eyes too many times. Although he had never known her to lie, he was in no mood to figure out if she was starting to now.

Leucadia then noticed Harlowe's head. "What happened?"

Harlowe dabbed it with his shirt. A little blood came off on the sleeve. "An accident."

"Someone tried to part his hair with a bullet this morning," Riverstone chimed in.

Harlowe pointed a finger at his friend's face. "Stay out of this."

"Is that the bad luck you were talking about?" Leucadia asked Riverstone.

Riverstone held up his hands. He wasn't saying any more. He knew he was in a no-win spot, regardless of what he said.

Leucadia had to walk fast to keep up with Harlowe as he headed back to Baby, but her long legs didn't have trouble maintaining the pace. "How many times does this make, Pylott?" she asked, using his last name again to show she was in a no-nonsense mood. He didn't answer her. "Do you know who it was?" she persisted, returning to Riverstone.

Riverstone nodded yes.

"I took care of them," Harlowe said sharply.

She shot a hard look at Riverstone. "Did he kill anyone?"

Riverstone gritted his teeth and shrugged. He mouthed silently, *Maybe two.*

"Don't tell me, Pylott, the gangs again?" she asked.

She got barely a grunt from Harlowe, but when she glared at Riverstone, his eyes and smirk betrayed him. "It wasn't a random shot, was it? They were waiting for you again, weren't they? Someday your luck might run out, Harlowe."

Harlowe stopped in his tracks, his face displaying its typical resolute confidence. "It's not going to run out . . . ever!" But in the next breath, he added, "How would you know about anything?"

"Harry," Leucadia confessed.

Harlowe stared at her cockeyed. "Harry? He wasn't there. How would he know?"

"It's his business to know things," she said. "And he's concerned about you, Harlowe. You too, Matt. He wants to see you both. Is Ian in the car?" She turned and glanced in Baby's direction. "Of course he is. The three musketeers are always together," she said, answering her own question. "Harry wants to see all of you right now. My mother does as well."

"Mrs. M, too?" Riverstone blurted out involuntarily. In his mind, Leucadia's mom was his real true love. No one could say anything immoral or harmful about her that he wouldn't have gone to war over. They all called her Mrs. M. And it was through her that Riverstone finally understood the reason behind the Trojan War. He plotted nightly about landing a fleet of ten thousand ships off the coast of Newport and stealing her away to some far-off land where they could live happily ever after. He sighed, his chest full of lustful dreams that would never see the light of day. *Man, why did Harry have to be so cool?*

Harlowe kept his eyes level on Leucadia. "What's the rush? How about tomorrow? Next week is even better. Riverstone has a physics test today. I promised his parents I would have him there or he doesn't go to the game on Friday."

"There are things more important than a stupid football game," Leucadia said.

Harlowe's jaw set like a granite block. The instant she spoke the words, she wanted them back. She closed her green eyes, knowing she had stepped over the line. Her comment was blasphemy.

Harlowe's veins popped out along his neck. "Maybe to you that's not important. But to us it is! So you tell Harry to chill. Nothing's so important it can't wait until the weekend . . . AFTER THE UNIMPORTANT FOOTBALL GAME!"

Harlowe dismissed her, and then started toward Baby again.

"It's the world we're talking about, Pylott!" she yelled at him.

Leucadia wouldn't let him go. She jumped in front of him, chest out, defiant. Harlowe moved to go around her, but she moved with him, blocking his way. He faked right and then went left. She blocked him again. Frustrated, he picked her up bodily and placed her behind him. "Being a little dramatic, aren't we, Ms. Mars?" Harlowe stated.

That didn't work either. She tackled him like a middle linebacker. Harlowe looked around at her in wide-eyed surprise and spit grits of sand out of his mouth. *Man, she was tough.* No wonder his gut ached. He was still in love.

"Now, Pylott!" Her brilliant green eyes flared bright with fire. He tried to struggle to get away. Maybe not as hard as he could have, but enough to make it appear he wanted to get away. She held fast. Then they were rolling face to face together in the sand.

Just then a lifeguard vehicle drove up to check out the commotion. Riverstone did the only thing a loyal friend could do under the circumstances. He spread the beach towel as wide as his arms could hold it.

"Trouble, Riverstone?" the guard asked.

Smiling sheepishly with the towel flapping in the breeze, he replied. "Nah, everything's cool, Brady. Hey, Kyle," grinning big at them both.

In the background the sounds of heated smacking, moaning, and canoodling were loud and uncontrollable.

"That's disgusting, Riverstone. This is a public beach, bro."

Riverstone looked around, acknowledging the guard's point. "So it is."

The two guards started to get out of their Pathfinder. "We'll have to stop them."

"If you want to disturb Harlowe and Leucadia Mars, go right ahead. It's your funeral, brah," Riverstone warned.

Both guards hesitated when they heard the names.

"Harlowe?" Brady repeated.

"And Leucadia Mars."

"I thought they were—" Brady tried to ask, nervously.

"They're making up."

The two guards slid quietly back into their seats. "I guess there's no trouble, huh?" Brady asked.

Riverstone adjusted the towel a little better. "None that I see."

The guards gave him a two-finger salute. "Alright. Have a nice day, bro."

Riverstone nodded his good-bye as the lip-locked spooners continued. Twenty minutes later, a miracle happened. The reconciliation rested. Harlowe's deep voice mumbled something that Riverstone didn't quite catch. But Leucadia's answer was clear: "Harry knows who killed your father, Harlowe . . ."

Chapter Thirteen

THE BEACH HOUSE

RIVERSTONE RAT-TA-TAT-TATTED BABY down the narrow streets and alleyways of the Newport peninsula, following Leucadia's showroom-new Ferrari Modena. With its brilliant red paint job and throaty, tuned exhaust, the handmade Italian sports car looked like a rocket ship with wheels and driving lights. The back window was small, but when the angle was right, Mowgi was seen panting happily on Harlowe's lap. The chinneroth's big ears stuck above Harlowe's bushy head, making Riverstone wonder whose silhouette was more freakish, Harlowe's or the frightening-looking dudes' he saw walking on the beach earlier.

"Did you get a load of those Dakadudes?" Riverstone asked Ian, who was riding shotgun with him in Baby.

Ian grinned fondly, remembering their childhood term for anything big and ugly. "They were gnarly," Ian replied.

"Whatever they were doing couldn't be good."

"It's a free country."

"Not when you're the walking dead."

The rocket's right-turn indicator flashed on two hundred feet from the next turn. Riverstone tried to do the same but the lever was missing. He faked it, made a clacking sound like a turn indicator, then asked, "You really think Harry knows who did it?" Riverstone didn't want to say the "K" word concerning Harlowe's dad as he made the turn. The thought of Buster's murder was still too painful.

"It doesn't matter. Harlowe knows," Ian replied, all hunched down and bundled up inside his heavy jacket.

"So why are you and I driving to the beach house when we should be driving back to Lakewood? This is *his* deal. Lu can drive him home," Riverstone said, nodding at the rocket.

"Baby's getting a facelift."

Riverstone eyed Ian a moment to make sure he wasn't yanking his chain. "Does Harlowe know?"

"Nada."

A hot stream of protesting air left Riverstone's lips as he stared straight ahead and grumbled, "Maybe I should call the school and tell them to leave a note for Farnducky. You know, say we might be a little late."

"I don't have my cell," Ian replied.

"You left it at home?"

"No, when you called me during physics class yesterday, Farnducky nabbed it."

Riverstone tilted his head, a little embarrassed. "Hand me Pylott's then."

Ian removed Harlowe's cell phone from the sun visor and peered through the bullethole through its center with his thick spectacles. "It needs fixing," he quipped before tossing it in the back like it was a used Kleenex.

Riverstone's eyes stared at the Marses' massive beachfront home coming into view. "We're not staying long," he said with finality.

At that moment a black helicopter thundered over their heads and landed on the rooftop at the south end of the Marses' beach house. As the thumping chopper settled on the rooftop helipad, three black-uniformed soldiers popped out of the cargo bay, wielding stubby military assault weapons. A fourth soldier in black followed a split second later. After removing a helmet, the soldier's hair fell down past her shoulders in long golden waves.

"Mrs. M looks hot in black," Riverstone drooled.

"She would look hot in a gunnysack," Ian countered.

"No doubt," Riverstone agreed.

The red rocket then slid into one of the seven garages while River-stone found Baby's special off-street parking space just on the other side of them.

Chapter Fourteen

JUSTICE

Harry was staring at the overhead surveillance monitor that was located in the second-story study when Sook entered the room still dressed in her black combat fatigues. She was the only woman he knew who could transpose herself from a living weapon to a *Glamour* magazine goddess within the span of a few short moments, but she had remained ready for battle. Why, he wondered?

Sook laid a large manila envelope on the desk before she slipped an arm around his waist and asked, "What do you see, Dorrity?"

"They're parking now," Harry replied. Something was amiss, he knew. She had that battle-ready focus in her eyes that only he would notice.

Sook's bright green eyes studied the screen as a surgeon would and then switched almost instantly to a widened surprise. "Leucadia found Harlowe?"

Harry knew her mild astonishment was for his benefit. If Sook was ever surprised about anything, it was self-induced. "At the beach," he replied.

"Of course."

Harry looked at her, worried. "While you were in Utah the boys were shot at again this morning. That's twice this week. We must put an end to this."

Sook removed a large color photo from a manila envelope on the desk and showed it to Harry. Two bodies were lying on the ground in front of an old brown Chevy sedan. It appeared that the two men had been dragged from their seats and ripped apart by some wild animal. Harry's mouth twisted with revulsion at the grisly scene.

"Justice is done," Sook stated unemotionally. "Sullivan and his partner are no longer a factor. It will give Harlowe peace to know his father's killers have met their fate."

Harry sighed heavily, laying the photo back on the table. "The authorities could have handled this. We have all the information right here that would have convicted them both."

"This could not wait. Harlowe must have closure before he can join us."

"But he's young and undisciplined. He's—"

"He is the future," she said, finishing his statement. She stood defiantly at his side. "He will make a good soldier, as will Matthew and Ian."

Harry watched Harlowe and Leucadia standing together by the garage. There was a certain pride in his gaze. "Yes, Harlowe is better than we had hoped. But we agreed they would not join us until they were ready."

"I know. But Fate has intervened. They must join us in Utah today."

An intense shock tore through his spine. He understood at that instant what the urgency in her eyes really meant. It was the one moment they had devoted their lives to preparing for. "They're here?"

"Yes, the Fhaal have landed on the planet, my love. The waiting is over," she stated.

In many ways it was almost a relief that the empire that had conquered Sook's home world had reached Earth. The decades of waiting were over. Sook came to Harry's side and held him closer. She knew he needed her touch—another human trait—to help calm his fears.

Sook then told him how Millawanda's deep sensors had detected a small force of Fhaal battle cruisers entering the solar system. The Fhaal advance squads had already arrived on the planet, and their search for the Gamadin technology would begin with her. With their advanced sensor capabilities, her discovery was imminent.

"You're sure it is the Fhaal?" Harry asked.

"Yes."

He nodded. "I prayed they had forgotten about you."

Sook sighed with a heavy heart. This was the moment she had been waiting for since coming to Earth so long ago. Her gaze shifted to the approaching storm, and she watched a bolt of lightning strike the water miles out at sea. "They are Fhaal. Their search will never end until they find the Gamadin power they seek. Once the Gamadin ship is secure, they will destroy this planet. It is their way of cleansing the defeated."

Harry was always amazed at how calmly Sook spoke of such evil beings. He worshiped her strength to stand against such mighty odds. His love and awe of her had no boundary. "Are the soldiers ready?" he asked.

"Nearly," she replied, explaining that the soldiers had been arriving at the Utah location since early that morning.

"Let's hope we are not too late."

"There is no time to lose. We must stop the draking Voids before their battle cruisers reach the planet. It is a small but powerful fleet of ships, modified with long-distance capability. It is imperative we kill them with the Gamadin ship before Earth's location is revealed and our beautiful blue planet is destroyed."

"But if the Voids' ships don't return, the Fhaal will send an even bigger force," Harry stated prophetically.

"By then we will be many light-years away. They will search and find nothing. Earth will no longer be a target because Millawanda will be gone."

"They will find us again."

Sook's face turned cold and hard. It was a face that had not been so focused since she left Amerloi. "Yes. But they will not stop us. With Millawanda's blessing, we will raise a new generation of Gamadin before we are discovered. And when we meet again, it will be too late. Millawanda will be strong and ready for battle. Her power will kill the mightiest empire in the quadrant. My Neeja will once again be free."

Her plan would work, Sook thought with every living ounce of confidence in her body as she watched Harlowe and Leucadia in front of the garage bays. "She picked well."

Chapter Fifteen

THE UNINVITED

Leucadia held on to Harlowe's hand while she redirected River-stone to back Baby out of her normal space and put the old VW into the far garage bay. After switching off the engine, Baby continued to idle for several seconds longer. The car then backfired twice, as the pistons slowly rumbled to an exhaustive stop. After making sure Her Highness had no more lingering discharges, Riverstone glanced back at Leucadia and commented, "She's on her last leg."

Leucadia looked at Baby not like she was a car that needed to be junked but like an old lady with a glorious past. Harlowe was staring at her too, but not in the same way. He seemed more like a doting father watching over his one and only.

"I'll have maintenance patch the roof and replace the side glass," Leucadia said, seeing his troubled frown. "And while they're doing that, the engine will be replaced."

Harlowe went rigid. "No way!"

"It's necessary, Harlowe. Baby will be okay," she told him.

Before things went totally south, Ian stepped forward and sided with Leucadia. "Let her do it, Harlowe. Baby's motor is about to blow. Didn't you hear her? That's not good, pard. I know these guys. They're cool. They'll extend her life by years, before she really gets sick and stuck in the middle of nowhere."

If there was anyone on the planet Harlowe trusted about cars, it was Ian. Harlowe shook his head and grumbled, but after a long internal battle, he reluctantly gave his approval. Leucadia then led them to a rear doorway where Jewels was standing patiently holding the door open. They were all about to go into the beach house when the throaty roar of a finely tuned sports car motoring toward them got their attention.

* * *

Harry and Sook watched the sleek Aston Martin Vantage stop alongside the garage bays behind Leucadia's red Ferrari. "Did you invite Simon?" she asked.

Harry nodded. "We have a meeting with Braxton to go over his new movie contract. But it wasn't until this afternoon."

Sook's eyes grew cold turning back to the screen. The movie star was an unwanted kink in her plan.

* * *

Simon Bolt killed the engine of his new titanium-gray Aston Martin Vantage black-top convertible. Unlike Harlowe's Baby, the throaty purr of its six-figure motor quit instantly with no loud pop or extended rumblings. Simon opened the driver's-side door of the flawless car and stepped out with his bodyguard, Monday Platter, who swept the immediate vicinity for anyone, or anything, that might harm his employer. They were both dressed to a tee. The new-car leather interior smelled overdone and pungent, like its owner.

The way Simon Bolt stood with his forced grin, his selfish eyes, and his cocky presence, you thought he would stick to your clothes if he got too close. He wore a blousy soft green silk shirt with long sleeves that were rolled up perfectly just below his elbows. His dark khaki pants were tied at the top with a string knot. On his feet he wore lambskin Uggs on top of three-inch high heels. They made him feel tall. Everything from head to toe was custom made from the best clothiers in London, New York, or Milan. He had one-karat flawless round diamond studs in each ear. His long, blond streaked hair hung gracefully down to his shoulders.

But unlike Harlowe and Riverstone, the orangey lines of sun came from a lavish tanning salon on Rodeo Drive in Beverly Hills. His twenty-one-year-old face looked much older than their seventeen-year-old faces. He had manicured eyebrows, a narrow mouth, and a stylish beard that added a manly ruggedness to his face. His light blue eyes oozed a hot, sultry charm. As much as they disliked the guy, they had to admit he was a woman's dream of what a hunk should be.

"Mornin', gents," Simon said with an easy-to-read, made-up grin that went with the rest of his deception. He bowed toward Leucadia. "Hello, Leucadia. You look so hot this morning, but then you always do."

"Your meeting with my father is at four o'clock," Leucadia pointed out, visibly irritated.

"You didn't return my calls. I was worried." He tried to move near her, but she stopped him with a straight arm.

"My father wants to talk with Harlowe, not with you, Simon," she told him straight out.

But Simon wasn't listening. He cared more about his new ride. "I just got her this morning," he said, nodding with pride at his handmade sports car. "Like it?" It was like he wasn't hearing a word she said. But then, nothing was as important as he was.

"Nice paint job, Si Baby," Riverstone commented first. Since that day on the beach when they rescued him, Monday Platter, and the rest of his entourage, they never gave Simon much respect. They knew who he was and even enjoyed his movies. Riverstone was his biggest fan, but no one cared for Simon the man. On the few occasions they did meet, they would address him by many names, but never his own. "Lines are clean. Did you pay for it yet?"

Simon's eyes narrowed, wiping away his cocky grin. "Of course. I paid cash. Got a problem with that?"

Riverstone glanced back at Harlowe and Ian with a sly grin, and he was about to add a few more tongue-in-cheek remarks when Leucadia put an end to it. "Enough!" She glared at Simon with her green eyes at full luminosity. "Simon. Go to the game room, out to the beach, or drive around all day in your new car. I don't care. But keep yourself busy until my father calls you."

Simon leaned forward like he was about to protest.

"Do it, Simon, or kiss your next movie contract good-bye."

Ian let out a small giggle as he turned toward the garage bay where Baby was parked. He had better things to do than listen to a whiny, self-centered movie star. Monday made a move like he was going to harm Ian as he walked by Simon's new car. Ian knew it was coming too, but he also knew Harlowe was watching.

"How's she drive, Platter?" Harlowe asked.

Monday looked up and caught Harlowe's unflinching eyes looking right at him. "Real fast, Harlowe. Sweet."

"Take a ride later?"

Monday glanced at Simon for approval. But the movie star was boiling in his own juices too much to speak. "Sure, Harlowe. After you're done."

* * *

Leucadia led Harlowe into the great steel and glass foyer of the beach mansion, leaving the others behind to fend for themselves. Jewels was waiting there to greet them. Along the marble walls, Harlowe took note of a blue Picasso, a Jackson Pollack, and Van Gogh's *Starry Night*. All originals. "Your father and mother are expecting you," Jewels announced. "They're in your mother's upstairs study, Ms. Leucadia."

"Thank you, Jewels," Leucadia replied.

"Mr. Harlowe, nice to see you again," Jewels said with genuine affection and a wink.

They traded a soft high-five and a thumb slap and then touched elbows.

Leucadia thought that was juvenile. "Men . . .," she said under her breath.

Harry showed himself at the top of the stairs. "Good day, Harlowe," he said, looking down. "Thank you for coming on such short notice." To his side stood Sook, her unsmiling face conveying her serious thoughts.

"Harry, Mrs. M," Harlowe replied with a forced grin.

Harry turned and said, "Jewels, I believe you know what Harlowe drinks."

With an all-knowing grin, Jewels nodded confidently. "Indeed I do, sir. I'll see to it directly."

Harlowe and Leucadia then proceeded up the wide blond oak stairway as Mowgi climbed the curving banister like a surefooted cat, jumping into Mrs. M's arms before they all retreated to the study.

Chapter Sixteen

SMARTER THAN PREY

Ed McCarty's photo plates were enlarged a hundred times and projected on a wall screen. On the display were what looked like fuzzy black balls on a field of white. Two of the largest balls measured a foot across. The "balls" were actually stars, however, hundreds of light-years away.

Dr. Robert Zagorsky stood at the podium in front of the projector screen. His unruly white hair surrounded a face that held bright, inquisitive blue eyes behind gold wire-rimmed glasses. Doctor Zagorsky had more political clout in the world of science than many politicians did. Presidents confided in him; senators who sought reductions in the space budget feared him. He had appeared on the covers of *Time* and *Newsweek*. He was famous and powerful, and to mistake his round, pink face for that of a kind, gentle scientist at the head of the JPL was a mistake.

Three other astrophysicists sat around a large redwood table in the special high-security conference room at the end of the astrophysics hall. Layers of concrete, steel, high-absorption fabrics, and wire mesh encapsulated the entire room. The wire mesh, when switched on, canceled out any stray sound waves the layers failed to stop.

Among Doctor Zagorsky's guests were Dr. Tom Shaffer, looking like he needed ten more hours of sleep, Dr. Ed McCarty, who needed twelve, and Dr. Carole Rodale, JPL's extraterrestrial specialist and one of the best theoretical minds in the business. None of the scientists appeared to be interested in the black fuzzy balls. What they were captivated by were three needle-shaped objects in formation that spread out along the center of the projection between the two largest black spheres. Zagorsky had just finished thanking them all for getting to Pasadena on such short notice. Rodale had been briefed in transit.

"Getting straight to the point, I assert that an off-world approach to the planet is a certainty," Zagorsky said. "Does everyone agree?"

A blend of worried, cautious, yet anxiously eager faces nodded their unanimous agreement. Yes, it was a certainty.

Zagorsky kept his expression solemn. If the discovery had been a newfound comet, asteroid, or some other spatial body, it would have been common practice among the scientific community to name discoveries after the finder. But this was no ordinary find. It might be the greatest in human history, with global implications. There would be no names associated with the group of alien spacecraft headed their way. Earth had been visited in the past, but thus far governments had been able to pass off the extraterrestrial visitations as visual anomalies or lunatic hysteria. Not so, here. The alien ships racing toward Earth were brazen. They didn't care whether they were seen or not. The U.S. government was in a quandary. If they couldn't stop the visitors from coming, how would they control the worldwide turmoil that was sure to follow their arrival?

"Based on our latest projections," Zagorsky resumed, "the alien spacecraft should enter Earth's atmosphere within a few days if they continue on their present course."

"Have you determined their mass, doctor?" Rodale asked, studying the projection.

Zagorsky's expression remained composed. "Best estimates put them at better than two thousand feet long and another seven hundred feet wide."

Rodale let out a low whistle. "That's incredible, doctor."

McCarty leaned over. One of his pet hobbies was the study of spacecraft: the kind that traveled between stars, not the shuttle launch into orbit/return to Earth kind. "An incredible size to us, Carole, but not for interstellar travel. I believe these ships are too small for any long journey. No, they got here in a hurry. I think we're talking light speed, people."

Rodale nodded slowly. "Interesting. You believe that's possible, Ed?"

McCarty faced Rodale with matter-of-fact confidence. "How else could they have gotten here so quickly? Even at five thousand kilometers per second, it would take them something in the order of 250 years to get here from our closest neighbor, Alpha Centauri. That's just not practical, Carole." His eyes didn't blink. "No, it's light speed and beyond. With some type of star drive, or wormhole entry, or—"

"Something we've never dreamed of," Rodale interrupted.

"That's right," McCarty agreed, "and however they did it, it was fast."

No one disputed the point as Zagorsky took back control of the discussion. "Let's save this discourse for later. What I need from you now is some speculation as to what and why they're coming to us so boldly."

"That's easy," McCarty replied. "They want something."

Zagorsky glanced anxiously at the large wall clock. "Okay then, what is it they want? I have a conference call with the president and the joint chiefs in less than an hour. I need a strategy on how to deal with these visitors, not radical theories or speculation." He turned to Shaffer first. "Alright, Tom, you're up."

Brimming with pride, Shaffer gazed at the projection on the wall. "I just can't believe it's true, doctor. After all these years of pounding on doors, someone has finally answered our knock. My feeling is that unless they do this every day, they're as excited as we are about finding intelligent life."

Zagorsky found Shaffer's observations too naive for his liking. "Tom, I can assure you the president and the joint chiefs do not believe these are new neighbors bringing housewarming gifts. They're frightened like everyone else. They're frightened because they don't have control of the situation. Even if these visitors are friendly, how will the world perceive this visit? Will there be mass hysteria in the streets? Are they here to stay? What is their intent? If it's hostile, how will we deal with them? We need answers, Tom, not fanciful romantic hopes."

Shaffer quickly lost his starry-eyed gaze. "Okay, doctor. But until proven otherwise, I'm holding on to the belief that no one travels to a tiny, unassuming planet like ours to kill us."

"Let's hope so, Tom. For the planet's sake," Zagorsky replied.

"If they're so excited about coming here, why haven't they tried to communicate with us?" Rodale asked, putting herself in the middle of the discussion. "That bothers me, gentlemen. For anything traveling star distances to get here, failure to communicate seems mighty unneighborly to me. I'm sorry, Tom. I fall on the side of caution on this one. I don't believe we can assume these are nice guys just here to say hello."

"And why not?" Shaffer countered. He had always felt that anyone advanced enough to travel between the stars was like him—wise, gracious, benevolent, and curious. "Just because they haven't communicated with us doesn't mean they've come here with an intent to harm. There could be dozens of reasons. One very likely possibility is that they can't communicate because we're too primitive to hear them. If they can travel between the stars, you can bet their communication systems are far more advanced than ours. Could we have communicated with anyone coming from as far away as the moon even fifty years ago?"

Zagorsky felt like he was getting nowhere. "We have to know their intent, doctors. The president is interested in only one thing:

control. So, back to Ed's earlier point: Why are they coming to our little world at the fringe of the galaxy?"

"And why three ships? Why not one?" McCarty added.

"Columbus had three ships," Shaffer pointed out. "He was an explorer."

"Yes, at first. But ultimately, the native Indians became the explorers' slaves," Rodalc pointed out. "The intent of this group bothers me a great deal, gentlemen. Predators are always smarter then their prey."

Chapter Seventeen

BLUE POWER

With Harlowe busy with Harry and Mrs. M, Riverstone felt like a potted plant. He tried to get Jewels to come along with him to see how Baby was doing in the far garage. "Wiz is there. You two can talk shop," he said, knowing the butler's love for cars was as passionate as Ian's. But Jewels's face was that of a loyal soldier falling on a grenade for his pals. "You go ahead, Mr. Riverstone," he said, handing him a blue juice to quench his thirst. "I must take care of Mr. Bolt."

Stepping out into the narrow street with drink in hand, Riverstone immediately heard troubling sounds coming from the garage bay where Baby was parked. The closer he came to the bay, the more concerned he became that taking Farnducky's test—along with his having a social life—was becoming a pipe dream. This was not the time for Harry's mechanics to be doing anything rad with Her Highness, he thought.

He tossed the empty juice can into a nearby receptacle and entered the bay, joining Ian. His jaw sank three feet down his chest when he saw Baby's engine lying off to the side of the garage like it was ready for the junkyard. And that was only the start. Baby's engine compartment had been stripped clean of wires, cables, and air filters. The entire housing was empty except for a curious metal ball about the size of his fist attached to the firewall. Extending out from the ball were four thin tubes that curled around and disappeared under the housing, presumably going to the drivetrain. The tubes were filled with a blue fluid that was practically the same color as Harry's special blue juice he had just downed.

Baby's engine transformation accounted for only one foot of Riverstone's jaw drop. What accounted for the remaining two were Harry's mechanics. They weren't human at all. They were three stick-like mechanical beings. The stickmen stood about five feet tall and resembled a tinker-toy man with a skeletal framework of long, thin tubes. At their joints were tiny spheres that allowed their arms to swivel and move and bend with ease. Their heads were made of a blue crystalline material and were shaped like a Chinaman's hat, while a blue light glowed around the brim of their heads. Adding to their simple deftness, three flexible fingers went clickity-clack, clickity-clack when they moved.

"Robobs?" Riverstone uttered, aghast, under his breath.

Ian, on the other hand, took it all in as though the stickmen were old buddies. He recalled seeing similar robobs along the yellow brick pathway that had held the signs that showed him the way to the beach. He was delighted and amused at the same time. "Cool."

Riverstone made a move forward like he was going to stop them. "What are they doing to Baby?"

But Ian held him back before he could cause any trouble. "It's alright, Matt. They're fixing Baby."

"Fixing? That's whack. They've just killed her!" he cried, staring at the oil-crusted black motor on the floor.

Ian pointed at the fist-size sphere where the engine used to be. "It looks like she has a new power drive. Knowing Harry, it will be tight."

"That's because she's not moving out of the garage. She's parked forever."

Ian turned Riverstone around and looked him straight in the eye. "Trust me, Baby will run better than ever. No more rat-ta-tat-tat."

"Right now I'd settle for rat-ta-tat-tat. Especially now that I've seen what's installing it. Where did the robobs come from?"

"Robobs?" Ian wondered.

"Dude! Don't you remember when we were in the third grade and building starships on the beach? After the Dakadudes attacked the ship, Harlowe would say to me, 'Mobilize the robobs and make repairs, Mr. Riverstone' because he couldn't say robots. His tongue always tripped up on the letter T. How many times did we try to correct him on that?"

"Lots," Ian admitted.

"That's right. And then I said to you, 'You heard the captain, Mr. Wizzixs, mobilize the robobs.' Bingo! Robobs were forever a part of the crew."

Ian's eyes smiled behind his thick glass lenses. "Yeah, you two would always take the next wave and leave me with the robobs to clean up the mess."

Riverstone leaned into Ian's face. "Nothing's changed, toad. Now, mobilize the robobs, Mr. Wizzixs." He stuck a finger in Ian's chest and continued barking more orders. "Make the repairs to Baby pronto, toadhead, so I can get to Farnducky's class and take the toad's physics test!"

With fire exhausting out of every facial orifice, Riverstone stomped out of the garage bay for parts unknown, leaving a grinning Ian behind to clean up the mess. Seeing what had happened to Baby had put the final nail in Riverstone's social coffin. He would be a pariah on campus. The chance of him going to the football game on Friday night was about as likely as running away with Mrs. M; it was all nothing but a dream.

Chapter Eighteen

THE PROMISE

MONDAY WAS POLISHING the Vantage's hood to a glass finish when Riverstone steamed by and asked, "How 'bout a lift to City College, brah? I gotta test to take."

An amused twist shot across Monday's mouth; he enjoyed seeing Simon's nemesis in pain for once. "Not a chance, kid."

"It's important."

"Not my problem."

It seemed eerily quiet now that they were the only two left outside in the driveway.

Riverstone felt like telling him to jam a crowbar where the sun didn't shine but thought differently when he figured the big black bodyguard didn't like being here on a cold overcast morning either. "Thanks, brah. You're a dear."

Monday glanced back toward the garage as he removed a cigarette from the packet in his shirt pocket. "Car problems?"

"If you only knew."

Monday offered a cigarette to Riverstone, but he refused. "Suit yourself." Monday struck a match and lit the end before he added, "Did someone try to kill him again?"

Riverstone took a long cool breath, and when he breathed out again, he could see the frosty mist shooting out of his mouth like jet exhaust. "It wasn't a good morning."

"Some day his luck will run out."

"Not Harlowe's."

"How can you be so sure?"

Riverstone let out a small chuckle. "Because I know Harlowe, dude. He doesn't lose. I don't care how big and bad they are. Harlowe will take them down."

Monday rubbed his reassembled jaw before he pointed his cigarette at Riverstone's hands. "You're shaking."

Riverstone turned his palms up. His fingers were trembling uncontrollably. "It's cold out" was his excuse.

Monday nodded slightly with the wise eyes of someone with first-hand experience of the shakes. "When I was in Afghanistan, my squad was in a firefight. It lasted only thirty seconds. We killed six Taliban. But I couldn't stop shaking for days."

Riverstone stared at Monday, surprised. "You were in Afghanistan?"

"Yeah, for six months. Never really get used to it," Monday replied, "being shot at, I mean." He then looked up at the low-hanging soup. "Take a walk?" he asked Riverstone.

Riverstone zipped up the front of his jacket and looked down the alley. A dismal thick fog hovered just over the rooftops along the partially lit street. The mist seemed to suck the warmth right out of his bones. *Maybe Platter wasn't such a suckwad after all. Just his boss.* Regardless, walking seemed like the right thing to do. "Yeah, sure," he finally agreed.

Without any more discussion, they headed down the narrow street to the vault gate, where they could take the shortcut to the beach along the yellow brick pathway. At the side of the gate, Riverstone pressed the activator button on the side of the wall and said, "Neeja." The vault door's heavy bolts slid back with their usual distinct clank. The massive door then opened onto the yellow brick pathway and the overgrown forest of tropical trees and blue flowers that lined the path.

He hesitated before stepping through, briefly glancing south at a black Hummer that was creeping to a slow stop behind a parked car. It was like the one he had seen on the highway earlier that morning and then again at 42nd Street. A sudden chill rose up the back of his neck. Dakadudes always gave him the shakes, he remembered.

Moving fast onto the yellow path, they meandered together through chinner country without seeing the keeper, and past the Emerald City fountain a short distance later. It was as though the eerie silence of the alley was the third one in their party. When they came out onto the deserted beach and marched out onto the sand away from the beach house compound, he thought the sounds of the waves that were hidden below the high sandy berm would help calm his dread. But not even the sound of breaking waves could help his shakes.

Riverstone glanced up at Monday, smelling his rich musk and woody aftershave as they lumbered across the mushy sand together. The bodyguard was a good head taller than him and seemed not to care about ruining his Italian leather shoes on the beach. They were polar opposites, Riverstone thought.

Riverstone then looked back at the Mars estate. Most of its massive futuristic form was barely visible through the mist. The lights were out on the first level. Only the study upstairs had activity, where the Mars family was having their private conversation with Harlowe. The rest of the house seemed cold and vacant.

A big hand tapped Riverstone on the shoulder, bringing him out of his malaise. "Are we going or stayin'?" Monday asked, nodding toward the beach.

The wind was biting. Riverstone's body ached. His head boiled from the inside out while his feet grew numb from the cold. To stop now and go back without seeing the waves would be like slapping an old friend in the face, he thought. He had to make an appearance, if only to nod a simple hello. Before giving Monday the green light, though, Riverstone looked southward and caught sight of two dark figures strolling out onto the footpath that ran along the Newport harbor channel. He wondered if they were the same Dakadudes he had seen earlier on the beach at 42nd Street. On a day like this they hadn't come for the waves. Only Harlowe was that stupid, he told himself.

A sudden chill made him turn to the north. Two more Daks were coming their way. He wondered what their purpose was. They all seemed to have the same powerful stride as they pushed through the soft beach sand like fast-moving tanks.

Riverstone shivered. Despite the dreariness, the beach had suddenly become very popular. He shook again and wiped the corner of his eye for the umpteenth time. The salty air was affecting his vision. "They don't look friendly," he finally said to Monday.

Monday was concerned as well. "I saw them earlier."

Riverstone turned back toward the south. "The same dudes were in the alley too."

Monday reached into his coat pocket. "We should tell Mr. Mars."

A wave rolled up on the shore, drenching the two dark figures to the south. The water didn't appear to affect them at all. They kept coming, doing nothing to veer away from the shorebreak.

Riverstone's eyes collided with Monday's. "That's whack, Platter."

Suddenly, the exploding sound of glass breaking ripped through the mist. Immediately afterward, a brilliant flash of orange light struck the second story of the Mars beach house.

* * *

Mowgi didn't wait for someone to open the door. The instant he heard the faint click of the alien weapon being removed from the Void's coat, he went crashing through the patio door like it was Hollywood stunt glass to protect the mansion. Sook was right behind the chinner, charging through the broken glass with a weapon in each hand, firing intense bolts of blue light at the dark figures coming from both directions along the beach. Harlowe couldn't believe his eyes. The speed at which Mrs. M reacted to the assault and the way she plucked off the dark figures in the distance was mind-boggling.

He had thought his dad was the best he had ever seen with a pistol, but Mrs. M was in a league all her own. She didn't miss.

Harlowe tried to help. What the Marses had told him a moment ago was no surprise. He had known for months who the killers were. The police force was rife with corruption. The death of Sullivan was only the beginning, he told Mrs. M. Then the whole world exploded before he had the chance to tell her he had volunteered at the department to get the rest of his father's killers.

Harry grabbed Harlowe by the waist and pulled him back away from the patio doorway. "No, son. Sook will handle them. You and Lu get to the chopper on the roof."

Harlowe fought back. "Riverstone and Ian are still out there," he shouted over the incendiary explosions. "I'm not going anywhere without them!"

"I'll find them and bring them there," Harry said, glancing at Leucadia for help with Harlowe.

Leucadia grabbed Harlowe's hand and tried to pull him toward the doorway that led to the helipad on the roof. "Harlowe, please," she pleaded.

But he wasn't going anywhere without knowing his friends were safe in the chopper first. "I'll find them," he shouted above the noise of more exploding glass.

There was no time to argue. Harry pointed toward the stairway. "Hurry, then! They're in the far garage."

Harlowe bolted for the stairway, but before he could take a step, Leucadia pushed him out of the way, taking an orange plas-round to the chest, catapulting her over the banister.

* * *

Monday fired his 9-millimeter Beretta at the two Daks coming from the south. "Move, kid!" he cried out, pushing Riverstone forward as they both ran for the beach house.

Out of the corner of his eye, Riverstone watched the Dakadude from the north remove something large and black from under his coat. He didn't need to see the long slender object clearly to know its intent. He jerked Monday's head down just as a bright flash of intense orange heat whizzed past their heads.

"That wasn't a bullet, Platter!" Riverstone cried out as Monday ripped off a few quick bursts. Riverstone thought he saw a Dakadude go down but he wasn't sure. A split second later another bolt from the opposite direction incinerated a two-inch hole clean through the steel garbage can.

They were caught in a cross fire.

So they ran, their legs churning as more charged bolts of hot plasma exploded around them.

Monday kept firing back, but his pistol was only a minor irritant compared to the more powerful and deadly Dakadude weapons.

Then a hot blast of plasma exploded at their feet, making River-stone lose all sense of direction. His face hit the sand just as another orange bolt of sizzling heat flashed over their heads and struck the second-story windows. When he looked up, he was staring down the barrel of the Dakadude's weapon. Just as he was thinking his life was over, a winged shadow swooped out of the mist and severed the Dakadude's head. The Dak hovered for a split moment before it dropped where it stood. The body of the second Dak was lifted from the beach as though a bird of prey was snatching a rodent.

Riverstone couldn't believe his eyes. For the second time today, the same evil-looking creature had dropped out of the sky. Where did it come from? Would the beast kill them next?

The other Daks turned their attention on the creature, sending a trail of hot orange bolts after the screaming dragon as it flew into the low-hanging clouds. And as fast as the creature had appeared, it then disappeared into the frosty mist. Before Riverstone and Mon-day could digest what had just happened, Mrs. M came out onto the second-story balcony wielding two wickedly lethal weapons in her hands. They watched in jaw-dropping awe as she dropped three Dakadudes from the north with searing blue bolts of heat. Like a trained killer, she was deadly accurate. Three shots, and three Daks were lying dead on the beach.

Before they could say anything, she yelled down to them from the balcony. "Get to the cars, Platter!"

Monday quickly hoisted Riverstone to his feet and they both dashed for the yellow pathway. Their thighs burned as they dug and pushed their way through the sand. More Dakadudes came out of nowhere. Monday shot at them as best he could, unable to aim at anything but tall dark shadows in the mist.

When they were within yards of reaching the yellow path, the southern end of the beach house exploded, sending fiery sections of the black helicopter skyward. Chunks of falling debris rained down on them like fireworks as Monday and Riverstone ran. Then two more shots exploded nearby, sending them both to the blue flower beds along the pathway. Between explosions and bright orange flashes, they managed to crawl to the thick forest of trees that would cover their flight to safety.

Fighting the urge to look back, Riverstone and Monday rounded a corner of the path and saw the Emerald City fountain engulfed in steamy clouds from the hot pieces of metal and debris that had landed in its outer pool. It was another fifty yards to the vault door to the outside alley. They stumbled to the vault gate at the same moment a loud explosion ripped out another long section of the beach house. Their faces were plastered against the trunk of an overhanging tree as blue bolts from the second story sizzled down the narrow street on the other side of the wall. It seemed the war zone had shifted from the front of the beach house to the back streets.

Watching the blue and orange streaks crisscross over their heads, Riverstone wondered what had happened to Harlowe and Ian. Would they all meet up at the garages?

Monday shouted, "NOW!" and together they slammed the vault door open with their shoulders. On the street side of the wall, they saw that the garages were still intact. The fire hadn't damaged the Vantage yet. It was still parked in the same open space next to the garages. Then, unbelievably, Baby came backing out of the far bay where the robobs had been dissecting her. Wiz's silhouette was unmistakable. Riverstone was aghast. Baby was moving on her own power, and she was humming.

Riverstone and Monday bolted for their respective cars while someone from the beach house gave them cover. There was no time to huddle and wait for the outcome. Riverstone's only thought now was getting to Baby.

They had gone only a few yards when another loud crack exploded above their heads, taking out a section of the back wall. The Dakadudes were on them again. Down the alley a black Hummer screeched sideways, blocking any northern escape. Another blue bolt shot out from somewhere above them. A second and third Hummer slid sideways, blocking any southern escape. Now everyone was cut off at both ends of the narrow street.

More black-coated Dakadudes jumped out of their Hummers, blasting away with their long thin weapons. Monday charged past the Vantage and into the first garage bay, screaming at the top of his lungs for "MR. BOLT!"

Riverstone was a step behind Monday, but he didn't follow the bodyguard. He ran to Baby and asked Ian where Harlowe was. There was no time for conversation as a burning bolt of flame-colored death tore through the top of Baby's roof. Riverstone felt the heat from the blast singe the hairs on the top of his head.

Monday was gone for an eternity. Two, three, five times Baby took glancing hits before Riverstone figured Her Highness couldn't withstand another hit against those types of weapons. He shouted at Ian to get Baby back inside the first garage bay before she was toast.

Then a door inside the first garage flew open, and Harlowe came running out from among the flames. He had Leucadia in his arms. She appeared to be unconscious. Harry was right behind him carrying a weapon that could only be a prop from Simon's *Distant Galaxies* thriller.

"GET OUT OF THE DRIVER'S SEAT, WIZ!" Harlowe shouted at the top of his lungs.

Ian didn't argue. He leaped out of the driver's seat while Riverstone held the door open for Harlowe, who laid Leucadia's lifeless form in the backseat.

Riverstone stared at Leucadia's inert face, wondering if she was alive. "She took one in the chest saving me," Harlowe replied, reading his mind.

Next came Mrs. M, running through the doorway. She spotted the Hummer at the north end of the street and handed off one of her wicked pistols to Harry. In the same breath, she grabbed his long rifle-like weapon, and with deadly precision, she twisted an actuator to full on the side of the weapon. Facing the Hummer, she shot from the hip without taking the slightest aim. An intense bolt of blue plasma shot out from the weapon's muzzle and BLAM! The Hummer exploded into a billion pieces.

Wow! That was sick!!

"Riverstone!" Harlowe cried. "Stop gawking and help Platter!"

Right at that moment, Monday exploded from the flames, dragging Simon's unconscious body with him. Above their heads, on the upstairs balcony, Jewels was wielding one of the heavy weapons like a pro, plucking off Dakadudes like rabbits in a shooting gallery.

With deadly orange bolts flying past their heads, Mrs. M turned to Harlowe and handed him a small square piece of folded paper. "Take this. It's a map. It will lead you to a box canyon in southern Utah where my soldiers are waiting. They will need this to find Millawanda."

Harlowe's mind battled against the nightmare that was raining down upon them. Soldiers? Utah? He didn't understand what she was talking about, nor did he care about himself. "What about you and Harry? You're going with us."

"No. The Voids must be dealt with first. They have found me. I can't lead them there. But you can deliver the map to our soldiers. They will know what to do with the Gamadin artifacts." Before Harlowe could respond, Sook whirled around and dropped three Dakadudes bolting toward them with weapons blazing. He was grateful she was on their side. When Sook came back to Harlowe, she was cold as ice, as if killing was routine for her. "Don't ask questions, Harlowe. Just listen. You don't have time to drak around. It's Leucadia's only chance. You saw the hole in her chest. If she doesn't get help, she will die."

"But doctors—"

"They don't have the skill to save her. Her heart is punctured, Harlowe. Only Millawanda can save her." She came closer to him, nose to nose. "It's her existence, Harlowe, and ours too. Your home, Lakewood, this planet, and far beyond. The Omni quadrant will die without the Gamadin power to destroy the coming madness."

More bolts whizzed past their heads as Harlowe stayed low. Mrs. M remained cool and unaffected by the searing discharges that could have easily fried her head at any moment.

"Listen to me, Harlowe. Failure is no option. Many billions of lives depend on you. Do you understand?"

Harlowe stood as though frozen. "I'm trying, Mrs. M. But the planet? Everyone? What's a quadrant?"

"There's no time to explain. I'm afraid Fate has chosen you to begin this mission prematurely. But promise me that one day, when you have the power of the Gamadin, you will take my world back from the Fhaal. Neeja must be freed, Harlowe. Promise me that much, Harlowe, before I die."

"You're not going to die, Mrs. M. We can stay here to help you. I won't let you die."

"No, Harlowe. There are things more important than you or I. The madness. You must stop it before it spreads and reaches Earth. Now go!" she ordered, pushing him down into the driver's seat.

"But Mrs. M—"

"Promise me you will destroy the madness and free Neeja! Promise me, Harlowe. Promise me now!"

Her bright green eyes were hard and forceful. He would not deny her anything. Not at this moment, when it seemed the whole world was trying to kill them all. "I will, Mrs. M. I promise." He didn't know what he was promising, but his word seemed to be the only thing left that he owned and that he could give her.

Harlowe lifted up the small square in his hand and said, "I won't let her die, Mrs. M."

Then she kissed him on the forehead like the Good Witch of the North bestowing her magical spell of protection upon him.

Sook shut the driver's-side door. "Godspeed, Harlowe Pylott."

In that moment her strength of will seemed to pass to him. If it took a million years, he would carry out her charge. That was his quest, his mandate, to fulfill the promise until it was completed or he was dead.

"Don't stop for anyone. Not the police, the highway patrol, the military, anything or anyone. Nothing gets in your way. Understand? Nothing!"

"Yes, ma'am."

Sook showed Harlowe two lethal-looking weapons. "Do you know how to use these?" The large black pistols were like nothing Harlowe had ever seen, but they had a trigger and a barrel and something deadly came out the end. That was all he needed to know.

"I think so."

Sook handed one weapon to Harlowe and the other one to Monday, who had come up beside her after he had laid Simon in the backseat of the Vantage. "Did you hear what I told Harlowe?" she asked. Her green eyes were vivid with intensity.

"Most of it, ma'am."

"Do I need to repeat anything?"

"No, ma'am."

Sook then grabbed Monday and pulled him over toward Harlowe. "Use these weapons if you have to. Kill if necessary. Don't think. Find Millawanda. The soldiers I have gathered there must get her off the planet. She is weak. She needs to be regenerated before the Fhaal find her and kill her. Clear?"

"But—," Harlowe tried to say.

"CLEAR?"

"YES, MA'AM!" Harlowe and Monday shouted back like new recruits.

"Go then!" And just as they were about to take off, Sook handed three foot-long, two-inch-thick cylinders over to Ian in the passenger seat. "Don't lose them. Keep them with you at all times. They are as important as the weapons in your hands and the map you carry. They will help you find Millawanda." Harlowe tried to ask another question but Sook cut him off. "That's all you have to know. Millawanda will guide your path."

Sook led Monday back to the Vantage and shut his door. He stared up at her with frightened eyes. "Stay strong, Platter. Don't deviate, don't pull off the road, and whatever you do, don't let Harlowe out of your sight. That's an order, you understand?"

With no room left in Baby, Riverstone climbed in the passenger seat of the Vantage as Monday pressed a button on the dash and the Vantage's V12 roared to life. "Yes, ma'am!"

Harlowe had already jammed the stick shift into full reverse, spinning Baby around like a top. After that, a great cloud ejected from under Baby's wheels as she burned rubber down the narrow street. Monday followed with screeching wheels, blowing through the rubbery smoke. But only for a short distance. Inexplicably, Harlowe slammed on his brakes and came to a four-wheel slide in the middle of the street. It was only a miracle that Monday was able to keep the Vantage from plowing into Baby's back end. With bright orange bolts blazing all around them, Monday and Riverstone couldn't believe their eyes. What was Harlowe doing stopping in the middle of the road? It was suicide.

Then the undog thumped down on Baby's roof like he'd dropped out of the sky. Harlowe grabbed Mowgi by the nape of his neck and tossed him into Ian's lap. Jamming the stick forward, Baby burned rubber again, her potent new power source blowing a dim blue glow out her exhaust pipe. The two cars raced down the alley heading north and disappeared into the blaze-colored mist, leaving the orange and blue streaks to carve up the multimillion-dollar real estate.

Chapter Nineteen

BOX CANYON

THE SUN WAS nearly gone when the two cars slowed to a stop at a fork in the middle of a no-name canyon road. The bumpy dirt road they were traveling over was mainly used by off-road vehicles. It had turned bad the moment they left the highway ten miles back. The Vantage's low ride was especially vulnerable to bottoming out on the unseen ruts.

After what they had been through to get this far, Harlowe had found a new respect for Monday's driving ability. Across four states they had outraced patrol cars, shooting out their tires or killing their engines with a blue bolt of light shot through the engine block. Through it all, Monday had miraculously kept up with Baby's new power plant that made the Vantage's quarter-million-dollar, hand-built job seem pathetic.

Baby's dashboard digital clock read 4:05 p.m. They had driven more than five hours straight. But that wasn't the right time either, Harlowe thought. After traveling through the day across the deserts of California, Nevada, Arizona, and now Utah, he figured they must have passed a time zone or two. There should be plenty of daylight left. But looking at the sky through his dust-caked windshield, he could tell it wouldn't be long before it was dark.

Flanking both sides of the road were red vertical cliffs nearly three thousand feet high. Where they were exactly, and which canyon they were in, no one had a clue. The matrix map Mrs. M had given them was hardly an updated AAA road map. It had no names associated with the canyons and mesas in the holographic topo projections. So if Wiz's readings of the map were anywhere close to correct, they were somewhere south of Hanksville and west of Highway 276. It was a long circuitous route, but according to Mowgi's twangy yips, they were still on the right course. That was good enough for Harlowe.

Throughout the hair-raising escape from Newport and the hundred-plus-miles-per-hour speeds, Harlowe did his best to keep Baby as steady as he could without jerking Lu around too much in the backseat. Harlowe had one eye on her the whole way. If she had moved or made some indication she needed him, he would have pulled over to see to her needs. But she had been in the same comatose state since leaving Newport. She hadn't moved once. Whenever they stopped to fill up the Vantage, Harlowe would wipe her face with a damp towel and talk to her like she understood what he was saying. He would tell her where they were and how she had to hang in there because they were on their way to meet up with the soldiers and someone called Millawanda who would make her better.

* * *

"Which way, Mowg?" Harlowe asked the undog, who sat between him and Ian looking out over Baby's dash. So far Mowgi's ability to guide them had been flawless. As far as Harlowe was concerned, he was better than the matrix map, and much easier to understand.

Mowgi's parabolics twisted around like they were attached to a turret before he pointed right and yipped once.

Harlowe didn't need confirmation from Wiz to know which way to turn. The undog was still batting a thousand, so Harlowe took the right fork without a second thought.

"He's right again," Ian confirmed.

Harlowe scratched behind the parabolics. "You da man, Mowg." The undog yipped once, keeping his keen yellow eyes on the road ahead as Harlowe glanced back at the Vantage through the cracked side mirror and asked, "How much farther?"

"You sound like my little sister," Ian moaned.

Harlowe was in no mood for games. He was tired of driving and wanted to be there a hundred miles ago. "Just answer the question," he snapped.

"Not far now" was Wiz's usual answer.

Shortly after turning, the VW bug scraped against a dry tumbleweed under its carriage and struck another rain-gutted hole. Thump!

"Stupid road!" Harlowe cringed, hitting his head on the roof. Worn shocks squeaked as he wrestled back control of the wheel. "Sorry, girl," he said to Baby and affectionately patted her dust-covered dash as he listened to the whirr of the motor. Although he missed the old rat-ta-tat-tat, Baby's new purring voice was beginning to grow on him. He looked back again at Leucadia. *Would they make it in time to save her? What was it they were looking for anyway? Millawanda? Who was she? Gamadin? Was that a place? A hospital? An office? What was he looking for? Mrs. M said Millawanda would take care of Lu. Out here, in the middle of this godforsaken wasteland? Get real.* Harlowe kept repeating the words Mrs. M said to him. *There's no time to explain. I'm afraid Fate has chosen you to begin this mission. But promise me that one day, when you have the power of the Gamadin, you will take my world back from the Fhaal. Neeja must be freed, Harlowe. Promise me that much before I die.*

Harlowe didn't understand a word of what Mrs. M had been saying. Especially why the Dakadudes were trying to kill them. *Freaks! Who were they? Where did they come from? Man, they were freakin-ugly. And what about this saving the planet thing? What's up with that?*

"Turn right here," Ian cried out, which shook Harlowe from his musing. "A mile that way . . . right after this dry wash, that's it," he said. "Look for a big oak, Harlowe. Up there, see it? Stay to the right of it."

The matrix map was another oddity of confusion. It was like no map they had ever seen before. At first Ian thought it was some type of microfilm sandwiched between high-tech 3M film until he began to unfold it on the freeway, speeding down the back side of the Cajon Pass. From a one-inch square it became a two-inch square, then a four-, an eight-, and finally a sixteen-inch square. Harlowe's eyes grew as the paper grew.

"How did you do that?" Harlowe asked, more than a little awed by Ian's sleight of hand.

"Got me. I fiddled with it and it just got bigger," Ian replied, searching for an explanation. He was as surprised as Harlowe. Ian's brown eyes went wide with fascination as he pushed up his thick glasses and scrutinized the micro-thin sheet on his lap. Then his brow wrinkled, confused. "Mrs. M did say this was a map of southern Utah, right?"

Harlowe looked at the surface of the paper. "Does it say that anywhere, Wiz?"

"Just keep your eyes on the road, Harlowe."

At first the map appeared to be useless. Lines for roads were nonexistent. There were no state lines, no highways or markings to follow, and no shaded areas of topography. Nothing. The entire surface of the so-called map was the color of faded, yellowed old rice paper. It was like someone had found it in an old attic squirreled away in some suitcase or something. It was entirely blank except for an unusual sapphire blue flower in the lower-right corner.

With one eye on the road, Harlowe pointed at the three cylinders on the floor at Ian's feet. "What do you think they're for?"

Ian hadn't a clue. He picked one up and held it an inch from his face, eyeing it carefully. "Maybe if I rub it, it will give us three wishes."

Harlowe nodded agreeably. "Try it."

Ian took an end of the matrix cloth and began rubbing it up and down along the cylinder. Fast or slow, nothing happened.

Getting nowhere, Ian placed the cylinder back on the floor and refocused his attention on the weird cloth. After poring over every square inch for the gazillionth time, he did the only logical thing left. He lightly touched the flower at the bottom of the paper with his finger. Instantly, somber hues of blue light began to dance across the paper before it suddenly coalesced into a three-dimensional projection, like someone had slapped it awake. When the projection stopped completely, they saw what appeared to be a moving view of the solar system, what someone might see traveling from another star toward Earth. It was totally mind-boggling.

Harlowe tried to touch the surface of the matrix again, mesmerized by its holographic qualities. But Ian slapped his hand away like he was keeping a mischievous child away from a valuable heirloom. "Quit screwing around, will ya? You could wreck it."

Ian studied the projection again. It was definitely high-tech. But it wasn't something anyone could make without sophisticated equipment, which he knew didn't yet exist.

The blue glow of the matrix reflected off Ian's face as he turned to Harlowe and asked, "So who do you think this Millawanda is?"

Harlowe looked in the backseat. Leucadia still hadn't moved since Harlowe had put her there. "She'd better be a surgeon," he stated flatly.

Ian understood his concern. "Mrs. M is always right, Harlowe. I've never known her not to be. When we find Millawanda, everything will become clear."

Harlowe thanked Ian for his confidence and turned back to the road with a sudden revelation. Thus far they had seen only one way in and no way out. If the Dakadudes or the law were hot on their tail, he didn't see any way out of the canyon. They were trapped.

Ian agreed but pointed out that there was an exit on the matrix map. It was a small crack in the canyon walls. "There's a gap here that the trail climbs through. After we get up that, we'll be on top of this mesa here. It should be clear sailing from there until we get to this small canyon, here. Then we're messed up again."

Ian touched the flower and the scene zoomed in on the narrow gorge until it stretched out across the entire matrix. On both sides of the gorge were sheer cliffs several thousand feet high. And all around the rim and inside the gorge was a curious blue sheen. As Ian zoomed in closer, the sheen became tiny dots of wildflowers that were identical to the one in the lower corner that Ian had touched to change the scenes. The flowers seemed to grow rampantly everywhere. Curiously, though, the blue flowers grew only in the small canyon.

"They look like the same flowers planted along Lu's yellow pathway," Harlowe pointed out.

"They are," Wiz confirmed.

"How far again?" Harlowe just wanted to get there.

Ian adjusted the matrix back to the canyon road they were traveling on. "We cross this dry riverbed, and then we turn left through that narrow canyon up ahead. See? We're almost there! The box canyon's after that."

"Well, we'd better find whoever we're supposed to quick. Leucadia won't make it through the night. I don't care what Mrs. M and the planet are going through," Harlowe said.

"I don't see a lot of doctors out here, Harlowe," Ian said, stating the obvious.

Harlowe was about to express another worry when the undog let out another throaty yip as they whirred around a blind twist in the canyon. "There!" Ian blurted out. He pointed at a narrow gap in the cliff wall that apparently led to another spur off the main canyon. "That's it. That's the box canyon." He glanced at Harlowe. "Feel better?"

Harlowe rolled the VW bug to an easy stop to take a better look at their situation before going in. "My gut aches." Like the projection had foretold, there was no way except through the narrow crack in the cliff face. "If anyone catches us in there, we're screwed, Wiz."

Just then Ian pointed above the ridgeline of the canyon at the columns of smoke rising into the cloudless evening sky. "What's up with that?"

Harlow reached under his seat for the sidearm Mrs. M had given him, looking for some small morsel of comfort. He exhaled a whispering breath of futility. If the law caught them, the sidearm was no match against officers who knew how to use their pistols. If the Daks caught them, they were simply dead. He then glanced at the rearview mirror. The dust was so thick that the Vantage was practically invisible. The smooth sound of the car's throaty exhaust pipes, however, was a clear signal they were still right behind them.

Harlowe shifted into first and eased Baby into the entrance of the box canyon. They hadn't gone but a few hundred feet when Ian smelled it first. From the moment they entered the box canyon, the foul air from outside began rapidly seeping through the cracks of Baby's nonexistent weather-stripping, cutting right through the desert sage, cactus, and dust. A moment after that the story unfolded before them as Harlowe and Ian motored through the killing field of dead corpses.

"Death," Harlowe said.

Chapter Twenty

CLICKITY-CLACK

LARGE BLACK BIRDS were picking at the carcasses lying between the small pockets of fires left over from a recent battle. The low-hanging smoke stung Harlowe's and Ian's eyes and the odor from the decaying bodies made them gag.

Harlowe brought Baby to a stop just before an old timber bridge that crossed over a small creek meandering through the canyon. That was as far as they could go. Minivans, pickups, and a black Hummer H2 were charred and burning, blocking their way. It appeared the vehicles had jammed the entrance to the bridge as their occupants tried to escape their attackers.

"I've seen that blue Porsche Carrera before," Ian said, pointing at a car flipped over on its side and smoldering in a melting lump of fire.

"One of Harry's?" Harlowe asked.

"Yeah," Ian replied. "I know the plates."

They all got out and met between the cars while Mowgi made a beeline for the nearest cottonwood. Harlowe thought the undog had a year's supply stored in his bladder the way he washed the tree trunk with his mark. After that, he began searching among the dozens of uniformed bodies strewn on the ground. If anyone was still alive, Harlowe knew Mowgi would find them.

Monday came up to Harlowe and Ian immediately. Like everyone, he was tired and distraught from the hours of fast driving. "We didn't sign up for this."

"I did," Harlowe snapped back as he scanned the killing field.

"Mr. Bolt is angry."

"Too bad."

"He wants to leave."

Harlowe didn't care. "Let 'im."

Monday glanced back up the canyon road. "They could be behind us."

"Count on it," Harlowe replied, feeling the gnawing ache in his gut that wouldn't go away. The box canyon was anything but safe.

At the base of the talus slope that extended down from the cliff wall was a green meadow of tall grasses, yellow poppies, and hundred-foot-tall cottonwoods. Their glossy, triangular-shaped leaves flickered quietly in the early evening breeze. The patch of greenery followed the stream through the interior of the canyon until it was stopped by an ancient rock slide that cut off its escape to the outside world. The stream, however, was unaffected. Over time, it had simply carved itself a new path around the obstruction and went on its way out the canyon. It was there, just beyond the rock slide, that Ian said the trail began.

They had to move on in a hurry. Whoever had killed the soldiers would return, or Daks from the beach house could have followed them here. That was a given. And the two pistols between them were hardly enough protection to fight a force that had already wiped out Mrs. M's elite soldiers.

Mowgi, however, was their ultimate alarm. If there was anyone or anything lurking in the canyon that could do them harm, Harlowe knew the undog wouldn't allow them to come this far into the canyon. With that in mind, Harlowe turned his attention to getting his small group and Leucadia onto the trail that led out of the canyon.

Leaving Leucadia momentarily in the safety of the car, Harlowe and Ian walked back to the Vantage, where Simon, Monday, and Riverstone were standing. The instant Simon saw Harlowe coming his way, he launched a frontal attack. "My car's totaled, Pylott. You'll pay for this. I need a phone right now. Mine doesn't work. I have to call my agent—"

Bam!

Simon's jaw went sideways. His body followed, landing motionless on the Vantage's hood. Harlowe, rubbing his sore knuckles, immediately turned and faced Monday, who had the big alien weapon Mrs. M gave them pointed right at his head.

"Do you want to join those dudes or listen to your boss?"

"This wasn't the plan."

"I know, but there's nothing we can do, Platter. We're in it. We try to go back, we're dead. We stay here, we're dead. Our only chance is for all of us to find the trail up there," Harlowe said, nodding toward the cliffs, "and find Millawanda. Do you understand that? That's our *only* choice. If you want to stay here with Bolt, go ahead. But if he comes with us, you keep him quiet, or so help me I'll shut him up permanently."

Harlowe boldly took a step closer to Monday. "So make up your mind what you want to do, because we don't have the time to screw around."

After a long deep breath, Monday dropped the weapon. "Leave him to me next time."

"Gladly."

Harlowe then turned to Riverstone, who had been relieving himself on the Vantage's back tire during the tense exchange. "I need a Big Gulp, pard," he said, zipping up his fly.

"I'll order you two when we get there," Harlowe promised him.

Riverstone gazed out over the killing field with Harlowe. "Where is there?"

Harlowe kept a watchful eye on Mowgi. The undog had not found a single soldier alive and was snooping around the rocks. "I haven't a clue."

"We're looking for a gorge with blue flowers," Ian added.

Riverstone's mouth twisted. "Now *that* makes sense."

While Monday tried to revive Simon enough that he could walk, the other three stepped onto the bridge. Riverstone looked thirstily at the stream running below, but the water was dark, almost black.

"That's blood, toad," Ian pointed out.

Gagging, Riverstone turned toward Harlowe and asked, "What happened?"

"Looks like Daks," Harlowe replied.

"Now what?"

Harlowe shrugged. "We wait for Mowg to give us the all-clear."

"Didn't Mrs. M tell you anything?"

"She told me Sullivan killed my dad."

"That's not news, pard."

"Yeah, well, he's sprouting wings now. That's news," Harlowe said.

"How do you know?"

Harlowe spit at the bloodstained stream. "I saw the pictures. Marvin got it too." He glanced at Monday. "Platter's phone working?"

"Nada. It's whack. It's a black hole here," Riverstone explained.

Harlowe spit again. "Let's think about something else. Like finding Millawanda."

Riverstone looked at Harlowe sideways. "Did I just land here from a different planet, 'cause you and I aren't talking the same language. Who's Millawanda?"

"She's going to save Lu's life."

Riverstone pointed at the killing field. "What if she's one of them?"

"She's not, or Mowgi would have found her," Harlowe replied, irritated with the possibility. They were wasting time. They had to get moving before it got too dark to see or they would be in bigger trouble than they already were.

Ian turned around as though something had caught his attention. "Do you hear that?"

Neither Harlowe nor Riverstone heard anything beyond the stream and the crackle of the nearby fires. But Ian was sure he heard someone moving through the fires, along the creek bed. He went to the end of the bridge and tried to see through the dirty smoke. "There!" He pointed out across the killing field, toward the slopes. "I swear I saw something moving up there."

"You're sure?" Harlowe asked, joining Ian at the end of the bridge.

"Where?" Riverstone asked.

Ian wiped his glasses with the back of his jacket sleeve. "Up there. It was moving fast."

"And it went click?" Harlowe asked.

"Yeah. Clickity clack. Clickity clack. Real faint. I can't believe you didn't hear it."

Harlowe tried to see what Ian was pointing at, but the haze was too thick to see very far up the slope. Whatever it was, it was gone. Riverstone didn't see it either. Harlowe then nodded toward the hairline crack in the cliffs. "Isn't the trail up there?"

Ian nodded. "According to the map."

Riverstone looked at them both with concerned eyes. "Could be a trap."

Harlowe looked over at Mowgi sitting on the rock for confirmation. The undog seemed unaffected. He was as calm as could be, like nothing had happened. That wouldn't make sense if he had seen anything out of the ordinary. At the same time, he knew Ian wasn't a Gomer. Whether it was real or not, at least in his mind Ian had heard something.

Regardless, Harlowe didn't have time to figure out who was right and who wasn't. The canyon was a death trap. He had to get Lu to Millawanda, and they had to find the trail that led out of the canyon before the Daks found them. "Forget it," Harlowe said, moving back toward the cars.

But Ian wasn't giving up. "Harlowe, I heard something."

Harlowe kept walking. "I believe you, Wiz."

* * *

When they got back to the cars, Monday had Simon propped up against the Vantage. The movie star was conscious and standing, but his legs were wobbly. Harlowe let Ian fill in the details while he went to get Lu from Baby's backseat. There was no way around it. He would have to carry her until they found Millawanda. He wasn't going to leave her behind for the Daks.

Ian pointed to the rock slide on the other side of the bridge and explained that they were all heading for the trail that would lead them to the open crack in the cliff wall. Riverstone wiped the smoke from his eyes and thought he found the separation. "Only a toad would crawl through that, Wiz."

"It's bigger than it looks," Ian replied, and then he added, "After that, the trail leads to the top of the mesa where there's a gorge with blue flowers in it. We should find Millawanda there."

Monday was as skeptical of the plan as Riverstone was, but for different reasons. If he was going to risk his boss's life on any trail, regardless of the size of the crack in the canyon wall, he needed a better description about where they were going than some ditch in the desert with blue flowers. But when Harlowe came back without Leucadia, looking confused and dumbfounded, the conversation ended.

Ian immediately knew something was wrong. "Where's Lu?"

Harlowe looked around the canyon in a befuddled gaze like someone had just stolen Baby from under his nose. "She's gone."

Chapter Twenty-One

THE TRAIL

"THAT'S AWKWARD," RIVERSTONE stated. "Maybe she wasn't that hurt after all."

"She was in a coma, stupid," Harlowe pointed out.

"I've heard stories where people have snapped out of comas," Riverstone replied.

"That's right, Harlowe. I've heard of that too," Ian said.

"Not with a hole in their chest that I could put my fist through, foo," Harlowe shot back. He didn't know how Leucadia could have disappeared without anyone seeing her leave the car. But one thing was certain: she didn't get up and walk off on her own. She had help.

"Harlowe," Ian called out, and motioned for Harlowe to come back to Baby. When Harlowe joined him, he was kneeling beside the driver's-side door, pointing at the ground.

"What are they?" Harlowe asked.

"Tracks."

Harlowe studied the imprints. "Those aren't footprints."

Both Harlowe and Ian looked over at Mowgi, confused. They had never known the undog to be inattentive over anything. His big parabolics were on duty 24/7. The circular imprints in the dirt didn't make sense either. How could whoever took Lu get past the undog without him going ballistic, Harlowe wondered, before he asked out loud, "Why didn't Mowgi yip?"

"Maybe he was cool with it," Ian suggested, touching the edge of the prints with his fingers. "I've seen something like these before."

Harlowe nodded. So had he. "Along the yellow brick path."

"Bingo."

Like a light had suddenly switched on in his head, Harlowe jumped across the seat and grabbed one of the gold cylinders, showing it to Ian. "Two are missing."

"What are you thinking?"

He handed the cylinder to Ian before retrieving the alien weapon from under the seat. After shutting Baby's door, he said, "Those clicks you heard were something taking her to the gorge." Then, leaving everyone behind, he and Ian hurriedly struck off for the bridge, following the circular tracks.

Ian had to practically sprint to keep up with Harlowe's fast pace. "To Millawanda?"

"Yeah."

"But why did they wait until now to take her?"

"You're asking me like I know something, Wiz. I don't know squat."

"There has to be a reason."

"I can't think of one."

Harlowe was done talking. He was on a mission to catch up with whoever had stolen his girl.

* * *

No one wanted to be left behind, not even Simon. Once they saw Harlowe marching across the bridge like he knew where he was going, they all sprinted to catch up with him. They found a few more bodies along the creek bed before the round prints turned up a narrow wash that snaked up an incline toward the cliff wall. Along the way lizards scampered through the tall grasses of the meadow, and the fresh scents of wild thistle, poppies, sage, and cottonwoods gradually overtook the ever-present stench of death. A short distance up the slope, Mowgi crawled to the top of a boulder and yipped.

He had found an unexpected surprise. It wasn't a human body this time. It was a full-blown Dakadude, dead as stone, lodged between a couple of jagged rocks alongside the trail.

The instant Harlowe and Monday lifted the Dak from between the cracks and turned him over, they recoiled. They had never seen one up close and personal before. He was the ugliest being they had ever seen. His head was oversized and boney. His hair was cord-like and black like his polished leather knee-high boots. His skin tone was a mixture of black, white, red, and yellow. His features didn't belong to the human race at all.

One thing was apparent: his death had been caused by the thumb-sized hole through the center of his brain. Ian figured it was done with a beam weapon like the one Harlowe was carrying.

Monday and Harlowe looked around for more bodies. Even though the darkness would soon cover them, it was not a good place to be. Simon was no help. It was all too vile for him.

"Someone nailed him good," Riverstone stated.

"He hasn't been dead that long. The ants haven't eaten too much yet," Monday pointed out.

Riverstone looked away. Up until then he had been feeling better. The idea of ants dining on a freak was way too much information for him to process. He was glad his stomach was empty.

They left the Dak and continued on, finding more Dakadudes along the way—all very dead. The group was almost to the trailhead, having counted a total of twelve freaks, when Mowgi yipped twice. Harlowe followed the undog's line of sight and immediately spotted the glint of a car's windshield in the distance driving fast into the canyon.

"Everyone up the trail, quick," Harlowe ordered.

No one needed to ask why. The black Hummer was easy to spot. Mowgi leaped from the boulder and led the way up the trail ahead of Harlowe.

Riverstone squinted. Two more black Hummers and a gray Cadillac Seville were right behind the first Hummer. It was becoming a Dak convention.

The group struggled up the trail, mindful of the rocky footing. A short distance away, the path continued its ascent behind a wall of large rocks. If anyone looked up from below, they would not see Harlowe and the others running up the path. It was as if the boulders had been arranged that way for a purpose.

They had gone merely a few hundred feet when Harlowe stopped between two boulders and looked down at the canyon floor. He zeroed in on the loud throaty sounds of the fast-moving cars barreling down the road on the opposite side of the canyon. There was little question about their zeal. The way the cloud of dirt was rooster-tailing behind them, they had to be doing ninety when they entered the gap. When the Seville got within a hundred yards of the bridge, it did a four-wheel police stop, blowing one of its tires in the process.

"Those dudes are serious," Riverstone quipped.

Both front doors flew open at the same instant and two Dakadudes hit the ground. They rolled once, recovered, and proceeded to pump hot orange flashes into Baby and the Vantage. A half-breath later, the cars exploded into flames.

Harlowe's eyes welled up like he was going to cry. Riverstone came to his side as the explosion shook the ground under their feet. The resulting flash was so bright that they had to cover their eyes. When the brightness faded, Baby and the Vantage were smoldering cinders of molten metal.

After that the Daks wasted no time rushing toward the bridge. Before the smoke had cleared, they were rummaging through the debris searching for bodies. Finding no one, they set out for the meadow. As they stepped heavily in long pounding gaits, they kept their weapons leveled, weaving back and forth, ready to cut down anything that twitched or moved.

Riverstone and Harlowe exchanged glances. The enemy was very good.

Seeing the Daks again, Harlowe felt the gnawing ache in his stomach return. He wondered whether Harry and Mrs. M had survived the attack at the beach house. They were supposed to meet them here. He couldn't imagine anyone, alien or otherwise, killing them. Yet, as Monday rightly pointed out, whatever Mrs. M's plan was, it had been compromised. The special forces team Harlowe and the others were supposed to meet here at the canyon had been wiped out—to a man. There was no one alive to meet. They were on their own against the alien killing machines. Their only chance of survival rested with finding the gorge with blue flowers, wherever that was, and Millawanda.

They wouldn't be safe for long behind the wall of rocks. It was as good a time as any to put distance between them and the black-booted Daks. Harlowe motioned for Monday to take off up the trail. "I'll catch up." He pointed at Mowgi. "Keep them on the trail, Mowg." The undog yipped once, understanding the order.

"Come on, Harlowe," Riverstone said, tugging on his friend's shirt. "They know we're here."

Harlowe held fast. "Not yet." He then turned to Ian. "You too, Wiz. Go with Platter." Simon didn't need coaxing. He was already making a fast exit up the path.

Ian followed orders, but he added before leaving, "They're out of our league, Harlowe. You can't fight these guys with pistols and a cylinder."

"I'm not that whack, Wiz. I'll be right behind you."

Ian and Monday then took off, leaving Riverstone and Harlowe behind.

"Get yourself out of here," Harlowe demanded.

Riverstone nodded at the Daks scrutinizing the ground with handheld devices, trying to find their trail. "They're not looking for lost children, Pylott."

"You don't have to stay."

"Someone has to cover your back side."

Rather than argue, Harlowe let Riverstone stay. "Mrs. M said something about these dudes."

Riverstone eyed Harlowe like his head was full of saltwater. "Let's introduce ourselves. Maybe we can negotiate."

"They want her dead. Why?" Harlowe asked bitterly.

Riverstone had another question. "More importantly, how'd they get here so fast?"

Then one of the Dakadudes suddenly called out to the other.

"They found their buddies," Riverstone stated.

The second freak quickly joined the first. He examined the body while the first kept watch, his head rotating like a search beacon. The Dakadudes talked together briefly, then they started back to the Hummers in soldierly double time.

"You think they're calling it a night?" Riverstone asked, seeking a glimmer of hope to help ease some of his anxiety. "Maybe their union doesn't allow them to work after dark."

It was a short wait. As the Daks made their way back through the smoldering wreckage toward their cars, a low muffled sound began to resonate above the canyon entrance. A half-second later the source of the sound was identified. A low-flying shuttle craft drifted down from the sky. In the dim light it was difficult to see any detail, but it was at least fifty feet long, silvery, and as aerodynamic as a stub-nosed bullet. It had short wings and no apparent engine or exhaust. It seemed to be powered through the air as if by magic.

"I'm not going to like this, am I?" Riverstone commented.

Chapter Twenty-Two

BLACK BEASTS

HARLOWE POINTED AT the side of the small craft coming into the canyon. "Look at that marking." On the side of the shuttle was a large black dot with nothing around it or inside it. It looked as if anything that came in contact with or even near it would be sucked inside its powerful event horizon, lost forever.

"Who are they?" Harlowe whispered in Riverstone's hear.

Riverstone didn't care. He just wanted to get out of the canyon alive while they still could.

The shuttle covered the two miles at an unbelievable speed, coming to an abrupt stop a few yards from the bridge, where it set down near the group of Hummers and the Seville. An instant later, a large door on the side of the craft swished back in a blink. Then, just when Riverstone thought nothing more could frighten him, a loud, horrifying scream bellowed from the bowels of the black interior. Two hideous black beasts were led out of the shuttle by their keeper. Around each one's neck was a thick chain. Compared to its body, each beast's head was huge. It was as though some perverted scientist had attached a raptor's head to the body of an enormous hairless dog. The sound of the pair's crushing jaws and snapping teeth echoed off the canyon cliffs like sharp, slashing steel blades scraping together.

Riverstone grabbed Harlowe's arm. He wasn't taking no for an answer this time. "Not in my worst nightmare . . .," he said, tugging on Harlowe's sleeve. "Do you want to suck face with them?"

Harlowe held fast; he needed to see more. Then the biggest Dakadude they had yet seen stepped out the shuttle door, making him reconsider Riverstone's plea. The other Dakadudes all dropped to one knee and saluted the instant this giant stepped out into the earthly air with power and authority. This Dak was twice the size of his underlings. He stood nearly eight feet tall and had scales for skin and claws for hands. A coyote-ugly black snout stuck outward, and his mouth was filled with razored, discolored teeth.

The leader's silvery eyes didn't blink or move, which led Harlowe to believe the Dak could see everywhere all at once without turning his head. His mere presence sent waves of chills down the back of Harlowe's neck, especially when the creature stood with his boney claws on his hips and looked up as though he knew exactly where he and Riverstone were hiding.

"Ugly, isn't he?" Harlowe said, studying the giant Dak's movements.

"Makes Sullivan look like a cute puppy dog," Riverstone whispered back.

The giant freak strutted out onto the canyon floor, flanked by his beastly pets. The Dakadudes led him to the bodies of the other aliens. It was all the handler could do to hold the beasts away from the corpses.

Riverstone grabbed Harlowe's shoulder this time. "Let's go, brah."

Suddenly, loud, shrill screams erupted from the beasts, sending apocalyptic shock waves through their bodies.

"Now?" Riverstone urged.

"Wait—"

"Pylott!"

When the Dakadude finished examining the corpse, he stood up again and searched the towering cliffs like he saw through objects.

Riverstone ducked behind the rock, taking Harlowe with him. "Are you nuts? The guy knows we're here."

"Stay quiet," Harlowe said, not breathing.

Riverstone was shaking in his Nikes. "He saw us, Harlowe. He looked right at me."

A long silence followed. Even the throbbing hum of the shuttle seemed to fade against the hush of the canyon.

Riverstone couldn't stand the stillness. He thought it was better to be seen and know than to be unseen and ignorant. He cased over the rock for a peek and saw evil in its darkest form glaring straight into his fear-struck eyes. He wanted to crawl in a hole and die.

The keeper let the beasts go. The wild carnivores bolted for the corpses. With its gaping mouth dripping ravenous, thick drool, one of the beasts bit off the head of the first body it came to.

Riverstone lost it. His stomach lurched like it wanted to run away on its own. He'd had enough. The three Daks stood by and watched as the crunching sound of bone reverberated off the canyon walls.

Harlowe finally saw the light. "We're done here."

Riverstone spit out a wad of foulness. He didn't need to be told which direction to go. Up was the only way out of the canyon. He bolted up the trail, turning every few steps to watch the scene below.

"Did they see us? No, they didn't! Did they see us?" Riverstone cried as they ran.

The keeper slugged the beast that had eaten the head to get its attention. The two pets apparently knew what their master wanted because they began to sniff the ground in a fiendish frenzy.

"He didn't see us," Riverstone stated, hoping that if he said it enough times it would be true. "He didn't see us, right? He's not sending them after us, is he, Harlowe?" Harlowe pushed Riverstone ahead. "Are they coming, Harlowe?" Riverstone repeated. "Tell me I'm right, pard."

Suddenly the earsplitting howls changed pitch.

With head down and legs chugging, digging hard for more speed, Harlowe concluded, "Yeah, they saw us." And they ran.

The beasts didn't need a holographic map. They had found the scent.

Chapter Twenty-Three

TRAPPED

Harlowe and Riverstone sprinted for the entrance of the chute where the trail cut back into the canyon wall and went steeply upward toward the top of the mesa. The slit was already dark, and they could barely see the trail at their feet. If it weren't for a riot of stars and the glow of the bright moon somewhere out of sight, they would never have seen the path at all.

"Where's Ian and Platter?" Harlowe wondered nervously. He strained to see farther up the incline that went along the southern edge of the vertical chute. "We should have caught up with them by now."

They couldn't run as fast as they wanted to because one slip and they might fall into the chute's deep crack. Riverstone leaped over a large rock on the path. "If they're hearing what we're hearing, they're in Vegas by now."

The chilling howls were unrelenting. The pair ran harder, but their efforts seemed fruitless; the beasts were rapidly closing the gap. The vision of the beast biting off the dead freak's head stuck in Riverstone's mind like a bad dream. It was a bad dream. If he was going to die, there were a thousand other ways he wanted to go. But his head . . . He grabbed his neck and swallowed hard, stumbling on another rock and nearly twisting his ankle.

On they ran.

With impediments nagging their every step, Riverstone prayed the beasts were having as difficult a time as he and Harlowe were.

He hoped their legs were stiff and unsure like a real dog's would be, not like the sticky-footed undog's.

They put aside the misery of a burning chest and a dry, dusty mouth and climbed. They climbed together, pushing, lifting, pulling, dragging each other. If one stumbled, the other picked him up. Climbing! Climbing! Always climbing to save their lives. Climbing to save their heads!

After another five hundred feet, the footpath changed again. The chute opened up, but as Harlowe and Riverstone looked down the vertical cliffs, they saw nothing but blackness, a bottomless void. One misstep and the outcome was obvious death.

From the moment the path had left the canyon, they had felt a hot, downward wind in their faces. The beasts' high-pitched cries remained constant but softer, giving credibility to Riverstone's theory that their pursuers' sure-footedness, or lack of it, was in their favor.

Farther up the trail, they sidestepped a sharp outcropping in the cliff wall, and for a short distance it was easygoing. The trail leveled out and was wide enough for the two of them to run comfortably abreast, with few obstacles in their path. That ended abruptly when they came upon a section of the trail that had broken away in a recent slide. For thirty feet or so, the trail was no wider than Riverstone's size-twelve shoe was long.

Harlowe looked down in the direction of the slide.

"See anything?" Riverstone asked, peering over the edge beside him.

"Nothing," Harlowe replied. Neither of them could see squat, and each was concerned that the slide could have been caused by one of the others.

Riverstone ventured a guess. "Maybe it was Simon."

"No time to fantasize," Harlowe replied. He turned back to the problem at hand. They couldn't go back. That was a given. They had to risk crossing the narrow ledge here or taking on the beasts. They chose the ledge. It was an easy choice.

In the low-level starlight they could see where the path opened out wider on the other side. They figured if they could make it across the ledge, the beasts, no matter where they came from, would think twice about leaping across the gap.

Riverstone scooted out first along the ledge, his fingers grasping a horizontal crack about chest high as he pulled himself forward. Harlowe shuffled next to him, holding Riverstone's belt in case he slipped. Both their faces were pressed flat against the rock face of the cliff as they made their way toward the opposite end without a word between them . . . without looking down.

Halfway across, Riverstone's foot searched for a stronghold and he stumbled. A portion of the ledge broke off into the abyss. Harlowe's strong hand pushed Riverstone back against the rock wall, allowing him to regain his balance. While this was happening, Harlowe's hand accidentally brushed against the side of his pants leg and knocked the alien weapon off his belt. Harlowe tried to catch it, but missed. Riverstone had to grab him before he went with it. Together they watched it sink into the blackness. After a long, protracted moment of silence, they heard the cheerless bang, bang, clank of the pistol striking against the rocks below, then silence returned.

Riverstone swallowed hard. "Perfect," he said, his face slack with futility.

Harlowe pushed him along. "Forget it."

Riverstone was about to take another step when another loud outcry broke the silence. "I can't," Riverstone replied. "I keep thinking of my head."

The howls continued. The beasts were drawing so close that their barks were amplified, echoing off the rock walls of the chute.

Then suddenly, for no apparent reason, the barking stopped. It was as if someone had shut the door on the beasts' snouts.

Unadulterated fear crawled up Riverstone's backbone and his neck hairs stuck out like sixteen-penny nails. He wiped the cold sweat from his face and asked, "What's that mean?"

He wasn't expecting an answer. Without hesitation, he and Harlowe scuttled across the final ten feet of the narrow path without thinking, and sprinted on.

The path continued another hundred yards before it came to a large crack in the side of the cliff that was wide enough for them to walk through single file. The black outline of a rope bridge appeared ahead of them against a soft glowing night. Three silhouettes were just making it to the other side of the bridge.

"There they are," Harlowe cried out. He shouted for them to stay put, then he turned back to Riverstone and added, "We can cut the bridge once we get to the other side."

"Then what?" Riverstone asked despondently. "That shuttle craft could be anywhere." He looked up at the stars that were so clear and close they looked like they could be picked out of the heavens and added, "With more cujos."

"No doubt," Harlowe agreed, following Riverstone's gaze up at the night.

"Well, how far after that?" Riverstone asked.

Harlowe didn't know. "I didn't think we would get even this far," he confessed.

Inside the tunnel it was so dark they couldn't see their hands in front of their faces. To their relief, however, it was not long, and soon a canopy of stars and the open air greeted them. Their sense of security was an illusion, however. Not a second after they emerged from the tunnel, they heard the low-pitched growls of the beasts from two different directions. It felt like they were surrounded.

All they could think about was reaching the bridge. Riverstone stumbled slightly. Harlowe steadied him and on they ran. Riverstone looked over his shoulder and saw two glowing dots of fire swaying unhurriedly through the tunnel.

Burping up sour bile, he felt like screaming for mercy. The panting seemed to grow closer, and Riverstone thought he could feel the heat from the beast's hot breath. It could pounce on them at any second.

They rounded a smooth boulder on the trail and saw the frayed ends of aged rope and wooden bridge supports that spanned the chasm. "Move!" they heard Ian shout from across the bridge. "They're right behind you."

They looked back. The red glowing eyes were still coming toward them. A dark silhouette emerged from the edge of the crack. It was darker than the night around it, its mouth drooling, snapping open and shut in a feeding lust.

The bridge . . . Could they make it?

Riverstone looked. Not far. Just a few more steps.

But then the other beast was standing directly in front of the bridge, blocking them with its twelve-foot hairless body. Its massive, odious head swayed left and right as it hissed and snapped its six-inch incisors, all the while dripping hot, sticky drool on the ground. Riverstone knew what both beasts wanted . . . his head.

The two friends stopped cold. Riverstone didn't have to look behind him; he could smell the other beast's putrid breath as it sprayed the back of his head with hot death. His stomach lurched, but his gut was empty.

In desperation, Harlowe reached for his pistol.

"Good idea, Pylott," Riverstone groaned. "*If* you had a gun, you'd make a real cowboy."

At that moment heavy footsteps came stomping across the bridge. It was Monday and Wiz. Monday had his pistol out, shooting bolts of blue plasma. Wiz was a step behind him, shouting and holding the gold cylinder above his head like he was going to use it for a club. Momentarily the sentinel beast was stunned by the audacity of their assault. But Monday's first shot missed. The beast ducked under the blast. A second shot scored, though, hitting the beast's shoulder. It tumbled sideways. For two heartbeats, it lay in the dirt before it sprang back up on its feet, madder than ever. It turned as if to charge across the bridge.

Monday leapt off the end of the bridge and had the beast dead in his sights, but the pistol failed to shoot another round. Ian, thinking fast, did the only thing that saved Monday's head from being sheared off by the charging beast. He launched the cylinder and struck the beast in the side of the head. It wasn't a lethal blow, but it was enough to throw the beast off kilter. Its deadly claw tore into Monday's arm like a butcher knife. The pistol flew into the air and landed on the ground near Harlowe. Monday went down hard, grabbing his bloodied arm as he fell. Ian stopped at the end of the rope bridge, unsure of what to do next.

Meanwhile, the ink-black bodies hovered momentarily. The beasts seemed to have no immediate reason to finish the kill, preferring to savor watching their prey squirm with fear before the hunt was ended.

Then, it was time.

Chapter Twenty-four

THE GUARDIAN

As THE BEAST that had severed his arm moved in for the kill, Monday had no idea that he was its next meal. He was delirious and twisting in pain on the ground. Harlowe grabbed the weapon from the dirt and challenged the beast in a desperate attempt to draw its attention away from the bodyguard.

"Come on, ugly!" Harlowe jeered, pointing the pistol like he was going to shoot. "Take a bite!" He pulled the trigger and nothing happened. Frantic, he tried twice again. Nothing!

The pistol was dead. Used up.

The beast turned on him and so did the second one.

"That's it, Harlowe," Riverstone said out the corner of his mouth, "you've made *two* friends now."

Suddenly, the cylinder came alive under the beast closest to Monday. It began to glow blue in the darkness. It vibrated like there was something inside it that wanted to get out. The beast jumped back and cried out. It was as bewildered as they were.

They were all struck dumb as they watched with curious amazement the cylinder divide in two, then separate, expand, and unfold again and again. When the transformation was complete, the robob charged with fearlessness toward the beast.

"Sweet!" was the only word Riverstone could say.

The beast at the bridge charged. It could wait no longer and was unimpressed by the stickman's gall.

Riverstone and Harlowe watched with stunned amazement as the robob slammed head-on into the beast like a charging fullback.

"DUDE!" Riverstone cried out, cheering the stickman on.

The beast was shaken. It was as surprised as they were at the ferocity of the attack.

Then the other beast charged. Riverstone braced himself as Harlowe let fly the pistol in his hand. There was a hard thud and a blue light erupted from the muzzle, striking the beast from its neck all the way down to its underbelly. But the grotesque creature kept coming. Harlowe caught it full force by the jowls, holding its massive jaws away from his face. The beast's claws dug through his shirt, cutting into his chest.

Riverstone was on the beast instantly, jumping on its back and pulling the giant head away from Harlowe with all his might. The beast was incredibly strong, maybe too strong for the both of them. Harlowe's mouth twisted in pain as he battled to keep the attacker's snapping jaws from biting his face off.

Riverstone managed to yank the head backward, and the beast howled as if it was in great pain. Now he saw why. Black ooze kept squirting from the side of its neck and belly. The beast jumped and kicked, trying to break free, but Riverstone had a death grip on its neck and wouldn't let go. He pressed on the wound, hoping to aggravate it more. He twisted the head one way, then the other, searching for a weak spot so he could snap the neck bone backward and kill it. The effort was futile. The beast was too powerful.

Then Riverstone lost his hold. He fell off sideways, bringing the beast down on top of him. Harlowe rolled away, clutching his chest. The beast's blood was splattering all over Riverstone's face, blinding his vision. He couldn't hold it off much longer. He was one nanosecond from collapsing when he felt a heavy thump. Again and again the blows recoiled against his outstretched arms. It felt like someone was standing over him with a sledgehammer, breaking rocks. Gradually, with each succeeding blow, the beast grew weaker and weaker until the last decisive blow shattered the contents of its skull.

Riverstone struggled to push the massive carcass off him. His arms were wrought with blood and pain. The overpowering smell was sour and rotten, like puke that had fermented in the sun all day. He blinked the vile substance from his eyelids and saw Harlowe's face above him, breathing hard and twisted with exhaustive pain. He was covered with dark blood, his bloody chest heaving. Then Riverstone saw the jagged rock Harlowe had used to bludgeon the beast to death. Exhausted beyond their limits, the pards collapsed, but their attention was soon drawn to another howl that broke the air.

It was the other beast! The battle with the robob was still raging on.

The beast howled at the heavens as it found its legs and lifted itself. Mouth agape with dark spit, the beast bit down on the robob's mechanical leg and snapped an incisor in the process. In a frenzied panic, the robob lifted the beast bodily in the air. Its flexible fingers dug into the beast's hideous neck and tried to choke the life out of it.

Riverstone wished he had a gallon of blue stuff to drink so he could help the little guy out. His own strength was too far gone. If nothing else, he wanted to shout volumes of encouragement, but even that was too much. He couldn't lift his head off the ground.

Harlowe tried to do the same. He saw a rock but hadn't the strength to lift it. His arms were lead weights. All he could do was grunt, "Kill it . . ." to the stickman.

From where Riverstone was lying, the robob looked like he was about to do just that.

Man, he was winning!

The beast shivered wildly, sensing its own doom. But then the robob's foot was in the beast's mouth and . . .

Snap!

A sudden gush of bright blue fluid spurted out onto the ground. The robob fell down, its severed right foot still in the beast's mouth. The beast found the foot too tough to chew and so swallowed it whole.

The robob faltered, trying to get up. It looked like a tired drunk as it tried to steady itself against a large rock. The beast seized the opportunity. With a massive chomp, it grabbed the robob around the midsection and smashed its crystalline head against the boulder again and again, trying to break it into a thousand pieces. Although the robob's hat didn't crack, it began to flicker and fade, and then it lost its blue glow altogether just before its stick frame went completely limp.

The beast pawed at the robob cautiously, checking for life. When it got no response, it cracked the stickman hard against a boulder one last time before turning back toward Harlowe and Riverstone. With renewed lust, it let out a loud, heart-stopping scream.

Ian started coming farther across the bridge to help out, but Harlowe stopped him. "No, Ian! Find Lu." Ian wasn't listening. Harlowe turned almost hostile. "Cut the bridge, Wiz, and find her." Ian tried one last time to protest. "Do it!"

With tears in his eyes, Ian turned and ran back across the bridge.

Harlowe crawled beside Riverstone, the deep cuts in his chest bleeding profusely as he tried to hide the troubled look on his face. Rough sand stuck to the blood-soaked pieces of stringy meat on Harlowe's side where the first beast had sliced it open. Although together they couldn't even lift a pebble, they were able to help one another turn around and brace their backs against a rock to meet the beast. Riverstone wondered what kept them both from passing out.

The beast opened its mouth. Its gullet expanded like a cavernous void. It would easily swallow them whole. Its red glowing eyes scanned back and forth, sizing them up for the kill. It was taking its time. It, too, was tired and had to gather its strength to make the final charge.

Riverstone pulled himself closer alongside Harlowe, catching his friend's face before it fell in the dirt.

"You can't sleep now, pard," Riverstone said, propping Harlowe back up with his body.

Harlowe squinted. "Where is it?"

"Can't you smell it?" Riverstone asked as he turned Harlowe's head toward the beast.

Harlowe tried to spit but couldn't find enough saliva. "Looks like Sullivan's mother."

Riverstone laughed at their old joke.

"You know, I've been thinking," continued Harlowe deliriously.

"You've picked a good time to start," Riverstone griped. There was a long moment of silence that made him uneasy, so he added, "Okay, *what* have you been thinking?" He blinked his eyes, trying to stay focused.

"Where's Mowg?" Harlowe looked around. "Must be with Lu . . ."

Riverstone bent over Harlowe, apologized for touching the deep gash in his chest, then glanced in the bridge's direction. "Just like him to miss a fight."

The beast snapped like it was irritated with their conversation.

Harlowe paid no attention and smacked his dry lips together. "I need a drink." His eyes found Riverstone's. "Give me the flask—"

"I drank the last drop."

"You liar. You're saving it all for yourself."

The beast charged.

In that next pulsating moment, when the beast was airborne and would soon come down on top of them, something huge dropped out of the night and overpowered the beast, smashing it to the ground in a single devastating blow.

The force of the impact was so hard the collision thumped in their stomachs like a bass drum. Riverstone winced, holding his gut. He tried clearing his bloodied eyes so he could see the distorted creature that was trying to save their lives. Clearly it wasn't a robob or anything mechanical. It was at least twice the size of either beast, with clawed wings that spread twelve feet out like a dragon's. It stood erect on strong sinewy legs and had long talons that curved like long Arabian daggers. When its snapping jaws opened, a long green tongue stuck out between razor-sharp teeth, dripping dark drool out the sides of its extended snout.

But what shocked Riverstone the most were the huge, round eyes that glowed yellow and were fractured by bright red squiggly veins. The black dot the size of a golf ball in their center completed the venomous stare. As frightening as the creature looked, however, Riverstone felt as if he had seen those bestial eyes before. The soul behind them seemed familiar.

He shivered, bringing back his sense of reason. How could that be? He had never seen this creature before. Not even in his worst nightmares. The dragon was off-world, just like the beasts. The beach house? How could that be?

The black beast twisted around on its haunches, trying desperately to right itself and counter the attack. But before it could balance itself well enough to spring, the dragon bit off its head and swallowed it whole. The action was so swift and precise, the beast's headless form lingered momentarily in its crouched position before it fell back like a chopped log, kicking up dust as it hit.

Riverstone's mouth dropped open. The winged dragon was looking straight at them. His heart froze as the dragon let out the loudest bloodcurdling scream he had ever heard in his life. He started to pray.

Please don't eat my head . . .

Then the world went dark.

Chapter Twenty-Five

FOLLOW THE STICKMAN

Harlowe felt something wet and smelly wash up the side of his cheek. Then something cooed somewhere in the distance, making the dull ache in his brain a reality. He pushed the irritant away. The cooing, however, wouldn't go away. "Shut up!" he groaned. Adding insult to injury, the wet licks returned with a vengeance, drenching his nose and mouth with a nasty goo. If he could only see what it was, he'd kill it!

"Stop!" he called out.

The cooing went on as the odorous slime continued to plaster his face.

It was an attack!

"You're toast, toad!" he cried out. In a desperate effort, he tried in vain to push the annoyance away. With his eyes still closed, and the irritant hopefully subdued, his mind drifted back to his heart. "We'll get you to Millawanda and you'll be alright, Lu," Harlowe muttered. He reached out and gathered her into his arms. He held her like he would never let her go for fear he would lose her again. He puckered his lips trying to kiss her and got a mouthful of gooey spit.

Yuck!

Leucadia's worried green eyes looked up at him but they were fading fast, turning into something large and yellow. He tried to hold on to her, but she was losing substance and slipping away from him. "Lu, what's happening to you?" She shook her head helplessly. There was nothing she could do to stop her evaporation.

"LU!" Harlowe screamed in desperation.

Then he woke with a start. He had no idea where he was or why he was sleeping on the sandy ground. He rubbed his face, feeling the wet mixture of spit and sand. The same dirty concoction was stuck to his hair, the back of his shoulders, his arms and neck; everywhere he touched, tiny nuggets of grit were embedded in his skin.

The attack began again, and Harlowe looked up to see two large yellow eyes staring him in the face. "Mowgi!" he cried upon recognizing the little critter. He pushed him away with a mixture of relief and disgust. "Where'd you last stick that nose?"

Harlowe did his best to scrub the grime from his face with his shirt. The little undog twirled around in gyrating fits, happy to see him coming to life. Mowgi held a rock in his mouth, acting like he wanted Harlowe to throw it for him to fetch. But playing games was the last thing on his mind. Harlowe brushed him off. "Not now, Mowg. We've got business to do." Mowgi yelped, letting the rock drop before he leaped to a small nearby boulder waiting for the next command.

With his slimy irritant under control for the moment, Harlowe could think about other things. He sat up, rubbing his arms together for warmth in the predawn chill he felt deep down in his bones. There wasn't a cloud in the sky. Somehow he hadn't pictured himself awakening under a blue sky. He hadn't pictured any sky, really. After last night, he was thinking more along the lines of an afterlife. So it didn't matter how cold he was, or how achy his joints felt, or how numb his mind was, he was just grateful to be alive. Thinking about himself was one thing; thinking about Leucadia Mars was another, and it jolted him to action.

"LU!" Harlowe shouted and looked around. She wasn't there. Then he remembered she had been taken from Baby and carried away. But by whom, or what, and where was she now?

Just then Harlowe spotted Riverstone next to him, out cold. He was alive. His mouth hung open, and he exhaled in loud, heavy breaths. Then Harlowe saw the rope bridge. *Ian hadn't cut it.* But where were the others? No one seemed to be around except

Riverstone, Mowgi, and him. The rustling of dry twigs just a few feet away made his heart jump. Harlowe jerked around in the direction of the sound as a lizard darted from the shadows into the sunlight to warm itself.

Sighing heavily, Harlowe stretched his neck, feeling grateful it was still attached to his head. He then reached over and, with the aid of the large, round boulder next to him, creaked to his knees. Although his mind was working, if he spent any more time thinking about last night, it would seize up like a rusted cog. Harlowe stowed any recollections of the previous day into some isolated crevice in the back of his mind. He didn't need to think about yesterday. He needed to think about the here and now and what to do next. Where were they, where would they go from here, and most importantly, where was Lu?

From his higher elevation, he surveyed his situation carefully with a different, more rational eye. The path they obviously needed to follow was across the rope bridge.

Harlowe kicked Riverstone in the side of the leg. "Hey, get up."

Riverstone bolted upright like someone had jerked him on a puppet string. He flung himself at anything that moved and would have rolled off into the abyss if Harlowe hadn't grabbed him.

"Hold on, pard," Harlowe said, holding on to the back of Riverstone's Levi's.

Riverstone turned around, confused. "Harlowe?"

Harlowe bodily pulled him back from the edge. "Yeah."

"Are we sprouting wings?"

Harlowe let go and dusted himself off. "Nearly."

Riverstone groaned as though he had just awakened from a three-day hangover. He spit out grits of sand that had stuck to his teeth and replied hoarsely, "What smells?"

Harlowe helped him to stand. "Your breath."

Riverstone spat out a large wad of something green and yellow that appeared to be alive for his response.

Harlowe's face recoiled. "That's rank, brah!"

Riverstone shrugged. He didn't care. The last thing he remembered was hot drool from the beast's gaping jaws dripping onto his face. His heart jolted with a start. He whirled around in the direction the beast had charged from. There was nothing there.

"What happened to everyone?" Riverstone asked. "Platter was right over there," he added, pointing at the area near the bridge.

Harlowe agreed. Monday should have been there. "His arm was shredded like lettuce. If he's alive, he couldn't have gone far," Harlowe observed. Yet he was nowhere to be found, and they could both see pretty far across the mesa.

Riverstone came to a waist-high boulder and looked over the top. A putrid, deathly odor slapped him square in the face like a wet mop. He quickly covered his mouth and nose with his hand.

Harlowe took his cue from Riverstone, covering his mouth and nose before he peered over the top of the rock. A few feet away lay a black beast, very still and very dead. Half of its head was gone, and the rest of its body was spread all over the ground.

"Tight shot, Pylott!" Riverstone said, impressed.

Harlowe was bewildered. "I didn't do it. The pistol jammed."

Riverstone canvassed the immediate area, looking for any other sign that would account for the beast's migraine. After a moment, he simply shrugged. "Sweet . . ."

He then stiffly, and very grudgingly, wandered a few more steps away, where he stumbled upon another black carcass. "Here's the other one," he announced, looking down. This one had no head at all. He shivered, bending over, his arms folded across his belly, as he tried to stifle his shakes.

He turned to Harlowe with a revelation. "The dragon—"

"It saved us."

"Where'd it come from?"

The image of their winged savior jolted Harlowe's imagination. "Straight out of Harry Potter."

"I thought it was going to kill us next."

Harlowe spat bits of alien matter from his teeth. "No doubt. So what happened to it?"

"I was eating sand like you, remember?"

Then both sets of eyes landed on Mowgi at the same time. The innocuous little creature leaned back on its haunches and yelped like he was waiting for a biscuit.

Riverstone grinned. "Our ace in the hole?"

Harlowe smirked. "I'd stay on her good side."

Riverstone pointed at Harlowe in an almost panicked state. "You! Your chest was ripped open like a beef taco. Look at your shirt."

Harlowe stared down at his bloodstained, shredded T-shirt in disbelief as Riverstone edged over and motioned for him to pull it up so he could see his stomach. The massive tear in his skin where the beast had clawed him was covered with a strange translucent substance that appeared to be some kind of artificial skin. The outline of the injuries was clearly visible under the new skin. The deep cuts were clean and sterile. There seemed to be no infection anywhere. His broken ribs looked as though they had been welded together and put back into place.

Riverstone touched the edge of the rubbery substance that was fused to the skin. "What's it feel like?" he asked, pushing on the weird stuff with his finger.

Harlowe rotated his torso laterally. "Like it never happened."

Something was going on that neither of them could explain. "This is dope, Pylott," Riverstone uttered in a low, guttural breath.

A soft clickity-clack sounded somewhere close by. Harlowe heard it too. They stepped around the boulder and looked up the trail toward the rope bridge they had tried to cross the night before. Twenty yards away a robob, its blue-lit China hat glowing bright again, was be-bopping across the bridge like it was on a Sunday walk in the park. They glanced at each other. The beast hadn't beaten the stickman after all . . . or had it? Then their eyes caught sight of a cylinder attached to the robob's tubular frame. It was dull and partially bent, not smooth and bright like the one Mrs. M had given them back at the beach house. Another robob, maybe? If so, where did it come from?

They limped and creaked after the mechanical stickman as fast as their tired, sore legs would take them. Without ever thinking the bridge might collapse under their feet and they'd fall three thousand feet into the abyss, they quickly crossed the rickety hundred-foot span.

Harlowe was the first to catch up to the robob on the other side of the bridge. "Hey, hold on, pard," Harlowe pleaded with the nimble stickman. "Have you seen our friends? There was a girl. Where is she?" The robob didn't stop or make any kind of sign that anyone was talking to it. It simply kept moving at a respectable clickity-clack pace like it was on a mission. "Hey, come on, pard. Do you understand English?" Harlowe persisted.

Seeing the futility of getting an answer from the robob to any of his questions, Harlowe mentally turned back to the problem at hand. What to do next? They could go back the way they came, or they could follow the robob down the trail. But that was hardly a choice. Renegotiating the path down the chute was not an option, he thought. The Dakadudes could still be in the box canyon with a herd of cujos. They had beaten the odds so far. The only reason they were alive now was the timely appearance of the neighborhood's friendly dragon. Would it show up again the next time?

Harlowe tried again for another thirty yards to get answers to his questions. When the robob didn't answer, Harlowe stopped on the path, obviously frustrated. Riverstone caught up with him and asked if the robob had found his tongue. It seemed that Harlowe had picked up some of the robob's bad habits. He wanted answers, not conversation. Both Riverstone and Harlowe were sweating from the heat and unrelenting pace of their forced march across the mesa. The hot sun was higher in the cloudless sky, and there was nothing but mesquite and prickly bushes for shade for as far as they could see.

As the robob continued on without them, Riverstone persisted with questions. "What's the map say?"

Harlowe reached into his Levi's pocket and came up empty-handed, remembering only then that Ian had it.

"Fine. So we're lost, right?"

Harlowe looked at the robob. "He knows where he's going."

"But you memorized it, didn't you?"

Harlowe's lips thinned as he shook his head. "The bridge . . ." His eyes drifted across the mesa until they spotted the tall snowcapped mountain rising monolithically out of the desert floor. "And that," he said, pointing. "That's all I remember."

Riverstone grunted pathetically. "Even I remember that. I remember the desert too. And those Dakadudes that tried to kill us yesterday and the cujos last night. I remember them all, Pylott. It's been a kill fest, and we've been the stars. You do remember them, don't you, Pylott? And those ugly godzilla-breaths back there that wanted to swallow us whole. It's all fresh in my mind. So tell me something, toad-brain, why can't you remember the map and how to get us outta here?"

"Chill out!" Harlowe shot back, getting into Riverstone's face. "I suppose you're going to blame me for everything that's happened so far?"

"That's a splendid idea, Pylott. I will. I don't see any reason why we had to come on this . . . this . . ." He looked around. There was nothing but desert twigs and salmon-colored dust in every direction. "Why are we here again?"

"We're looking for Millawanda," Harlowe replied.

"Millawanda? Oh yeah, she's got a hot-dog stand right over there and the doctor's office should be right next door if I'm not mistaken. You remember that, don't you?"

Just then he spotted two big ears moving behind a scraggly mesquite bush. "Hey," Riverstone said to Harlowe, nodding toward the tree. "What's the little mutt-head doing now? Looks like he's found something to splatter behind the rock over there."

Harlowe's eyes rolled skyward as if to say "what now?" He glanced at the robob pulling away on its unstoppable course. "We should follow the stickman. Mowgi will catch up."

"You think you're ticked off now. What if you're leaving behind Lu or Ian or even Monday?" Riverstone asked.

That was all Riverstone had to say; Harlowe crossed the fifty or so yards on a dead run. He didn't seem to care if it was another beast, or even a dragon, he was going to check out what the undog was curiously sniffing out behind the rock. By the time Riverstone caught up with Harlowe, Mowgi was dragging a kicking and screaming body out from behind the rocks.

"The toad was digging a hole to China, trying to hide," Harlowe said as he helped Mowgi drag Simon Bolt's dirt-encrusted carcass out onto the open mesa.

Harlowe tried to pry Simon apart. Every time Harlowe let go of one of his arms, Simon retracted into a fetal ball, sobbing and shaking like he was about to be eaten alive.

"Some hero," Harlowe said, letting him spring back.

"Captain Julian Starr has had a little meltdown, I'd say," Riverstone added, his face registering disgust at the star's lack of control. "What do we do with him?"

The compassionate side of Harlowe was on empty as he saw that the stickman was already a good hundred yards from their present position. He crowbarred Simon's hands away from his head before he slapped the movie star hard across the face.

"Snap out of it!" Harlowe demanded. He scolded him with more choice phrases before he lifted him on his feet and kicked him toward the robob like a soccer ball. "Start walking, toad, or we'll leave you here for the cujos."

Every time Simon stumbled, Harlowe or Riverstone was right there to pick him up again. Each time Simon tried to fall back to a fetal position, Harlowe kicked him down the trail again. It wasn't pretty, but after a dozen or so up-and-down thumps on his backside, Simon began to understand that life would be less punishing if he cooperated. Soon he was moving in front of Harlowe and River-stone on his own.

"So you think the robob knows where it's going?" Riverstone asked Harlowe.

"I trust him."

Riverstone glanced at the round prints in the sand, then he wearily looked up, shading his eyes from the sun. "That's just grand, Harlowe. I feel a whole lot better knowing you trust someone that can't speak a word."

Chapter Twenty-Six

BLUE FLOWERS

After another hour of trudging across the desert, Riverstone's mouth was beyond parched. It was dust. The world about him was shadowless and hot. The sun was heating his dust-covered Nikes to intolerable levels, and his body felt like he was roasting in his own juices. Although he had been thirsty the moment they entered the box canyon yesterday, running from alien beasts had kept his mind off his thirst. Now that his mind was less occupied, water had returned with a vengeance as his number-one concern.

"That robob better be headed for water, Pylott," Riverstone said to Harlowe's back. His raspy voice was hardly audible as he fell out of step and let Simon pass him. Simon didn't need as much prodding lately. The fear of being left alone with the enemy kept him close.

"If we don't find a 7-Eleven quick, you'll be carrying me, pard," Riverstone complained again.

Harlowe said nothing, marching on as automated as the robob.

"Listen to me," Riverstone kept on. "I need a Big Gulp. Even that skanky wheatgrass juice that Ian drinks would be fine. Anything wet . . . *except* Mowgi's slobber. I can't handle that. Don't give me any of his spit, Pylott, even if I'm half a breath away from dying, understand? Just let me die, okay, pard?"

No one stopped or cared about Riverstone's thirst. "I don't know how much longer I can go on, Harlowe. You hear me, toad? How 'bout a short rest, then? Can't we stop for a second? Man, if I was . . ."

Riverstone collapsed along the side of the path. His rubbery legs simply gave out. How far they had traveled, he didn't know. Miles, for sure, with no Millawanda-that-way sign in sight. He had reached the limit of his endurance. The salty taste of blood trickled onto his tongue from his sun-cracked lips. Maybe with some rest he could make it a little farther, but not without water, and not with the blazing sun beating down on him like a vengeful demon.

"More, Silvia," Riverstone pleaded to an old flame in his delirium. He felt the moisture hitting his lips and sighed with relief. "Thanks, babe," he told her. The cool sweetness continued dripping into his mouth. The rate was slow. He wanted more. Much more. He cuffed his hands over his mouth to catch the splatter, not wanting to miss a drop. He had never tasted anything so good. *More, Silvia, more . . .*

The drops stopped and he opened his eyes. A thin band of blue light was hovering over him. For an instant he was baffled. He expected his first childhood girlfriend's sympathetic brown eyes to be peering down on him, not a robob's glowing rimmed head.

When he realized it was a stickman standing over him squeezing fluids out of a handful of bright blue petals, he began to choke. "You're not Silvia!" he gagged. He grabbed his throat and coughed. "What are they?" he asked the robob, pointing at the flowers. The robob said nothing as it remained standing patiently in front of him.

Harlowe took a handful and stuffed a few petals in his mouth. "Tastes like the blue stuff Harry gave us a time or two. Take some more."

Following Harlowe's example, Riverstone took the flowers the robob was offering him. Harlowe then took a handful and squeezed some drops into Simon's mouth. The drops beaded up on his lips and rolled off. Harlowe then forced Simon's lips apart and squeezed the juices into his mouth. "Chew or I'll stuff them down your throat," he threatened.

Reluctantly, Simon's jaw began to munch the blue petals.

"These flowers must mean we're getting close," Harlowe said.

"You think Ian and the others will turn up there?" Riverstone asked, hopeful.

Harlowe pointed down at a big footprint. Beside it was another round impression in the dirt. "These have to be Platter's and the other robob's. We're on the right track."

Riverstone stepped over to another print. "That's Ian's waffle mark, alright. I'd recognize it even with his lousy eyesight."

The three trekkers picked as many blue petals as they could stuff in their pockets in case this was the only batch they would find. Then Harlowe motioned for the robob to continue. It turned and began to roll southward, leading them along the same path the others had apparently taken.

Harlowe was confident that following the robob was the right choice, and until the trail ended or they ran out of petals, they were sticking with the mechanical guide. Leucadia was at the other end of the trail, and that's all he really cared about at this point. If that's what it took, he was prepared to walk to the ends of the earth to find her.

The snowcapped mountain was directly ahead of them by the time they came to a high overlook at the edge of a narrow gorge.

"Look at all the flowers, brah," Riverstone cried out, excited that they had come upon an endless supply of the energy-rich blue plants. "That's sick!"

"This is it," Harlowe announced with certainty. Coming upon the flowers inside the narrow, steep gorge was like finding the "X" on a treasure map. All around the rim of the gorge and into the ravine the blue flowers grew abundantly. Except for the flowers and a small grove of cottonwoods at the bottom of the ravine, however, the gorge was as dry and desolate a place as he had ever seen. The sheer vertical cliffs into the gorge were made up of stratified layers of purple and brown and salmon-colored rock.

Although no river twined along the bottom of the gorge, there were isolated signs of life nevertheless. He saw clumps of beavertail cactus, the twiggy stems of withered ocotillo, mesquite, and purple sage, and everywhere, of course, the abundant blue flowers.

Riverstone tugged on Harlowe's shirt. It was then that Harlowe realized the robob's clacks were fading. He didn't want to lose sight of the stickman now, not after being with it all day. Harlowe, Riverstone, and Simon went along the ridge for another hundred yards before the robob stepped onto a path that led down into the gorge. Although it was barely a body-width wide, Harlowe was unafraid as he looked down the side of the two-thousand-foot sheer wall of the ravine. Maybe he was too tired to think about falling, he thought. Or maybe he was just too worried about Lu to be scared of anything. Down they went.

"This better be the place, Pylott," Riverstone nagged, "'cause I can't walk out of here on my own." Every now and then he caught Harlowe staring on ahead. "What are you looking for?" he asked.

Harlowe shrugged. "A big, fat sign."

"Like Millawanda's Bar and Grill that way?" Riverstone joked.

"Something like that," Harlowe agreed.

At that moment, Riverstone lost his footing on some loose gravel. He fell forward and hit his head on the side of a jagged rock.

"You stupid toad!" Harlowe said, catching him before he fell over the side. "Why don't you just throw yourself off the cliff, pard? It'll save me time worrying about your stupid head," he said, his voice betraying the mixture of relief, worry, and anger that he felt.

"You'd like that, wouldn't you?" Riverstone shot back. His head throbbed with excruciating pain.

"You're not hurt," Harlowe replied as he took a moment to examine the growing egg on his friend's head. "It's just a little ouchy. You were more hurt kissing the cujos last night."

"It hurts just the same."

Riverstone sucked in a deep breath as he braced himself against the vertical rock wall. "I don't like this, Harlowe. I'm fed up with all of this hero stuff. As soon as I can, I'm going home. No more desert for me. No more sand. No more prickly cactuses *or* freakin' black beasts trying to eat my head like it was a peanut-butter cup! I'm going back to Lakewood, understand, toad?"

Riverstone looked down the path. "Okay, I'm ready, but where's the robob?" he asked, squinting through his bloodshot swollen eyes. "It was right there."

Harlowe searched the path and the surrounding rocks. "The Mowg's gone too."

"Oh, great. If he's gone, we're really screwed," Riverstone stated flatly.

They descended another few hundred feet before they realized they had been left behind. The robob, Mowgi, and Simon had all disappeared off the trail completely. Riverstone and Harlowe were still a third of the way from the bottom of the gorge. They could see a hundred yards up the trail behind them and in front of them, but there was nothing to see of their companions.

Gathering their wits, they mulled over the problem, trying to act like reasonable men would in a similar situation. There was a sensible explanation for this. "If we weren't so tired and lost, we could see the solution," Riverstone said.

Harlowe tried to keep himself from pre-ignition launch. "Alright, think back on what happened," he said. "You fell and hit your head. You were out a few seconds, that's all, right?"

"Tops," Riverstone chimed in.

"So where did they go?"

Riverstone peered over the side of the path. "Maybe you got your wish about Simon."

Harlowe looked too, but neither saw any body lying on the rocks below. The only logical direction the robob or Mowgi or Simon could have gone was down, since the two stragglers were blocking the uphill direction of the trail. They hadn't traveled far when Riverstone found a fresh round print in the dirt off the right side of the path.

"The stickman's been here," Harlowe agreed. "No one else could make a print like that." He pointed toward a pile of large boulders straight ahead that was under the shade of a massive overhang a thousand feet above their heads.

Trailing a few steps behind, Riverstone wondered why they had left the path here. It didn't seem to make sense. There were no openings or gates or doors in the cliff, just a jagged wall of bruise-colored rocks.

After a short distance of climbing over small boulders, the two found themselves tripping through a thick patch of blue flowers. Riverstone closed his eyes briefly, drinking in the sweet alluring fragrance. A moment later Harlowe was lifting his friend's face out of the flower bed and saying, "Don't whack out now, toad. I need you thinking straight."

Riverstone thought he had closed his eyes for only a second. Confused, he turned around and said, "I saw something between the stems." He reached down between the long shoots and pulled out an empty Three Musketeers candy wrapper for Harlowe's inspection. "We know this litterbug."

Just then they both heard a faint clickity-clack from beyond the boulders, which led them to an opening hidden behind an outcropping of rocks. The slit in the rocks was barely large enough to squeeze a head through.

"Through there?" Riverstone questioned.

"Looks like it," Harlowe said, moving toward the slit. On the ground in front of the opening were more familiar tracks. "Here are Platter's and Wiz's treads. There's a round one too."

Harlowe flattened himself sideways and entered the darkness. If the stickman and the Mowg went this way, so would he. Reluctantly, Riverstone followed. It was a little more difficult for his larger frame, but he was able to squeeze himself through easily enough after he got his head and shoulders past the slit. Once through, they heard the familiar clickity-clack of the robob echoing as if inside a cavernous space. Almost immediately upon entering the cavern, its strong musty odor mixed with the sweetness of the flowers. It reminded Riverstone of his grandparents' attic. That meant only one thing to him.

Something very old was waiting inside.

Chapter Twenty-Seven

THE PORTAL

BEFORE HE WENT from the light into the blackness of the cave, Riverstone glanced back over his shoulder one last time, not at all convinced that sliding through was a good idea. Above the entrance, the massive overhanging rocks loomed menacingly as though they were ready to slam down on him the moment he squeezed through the opening. He swallowed hard, tasting the sweet bile of the fermenting flower juice in his stomach, fighting with himself to go on. The thought of being trapped underground forever sent a violent shiver through his spine. The war in his gut ended in a stalemate, Riverstone resigned to the fact that there was really nothing he could do to change his reality. He slid behind the outcropping of rocks and into the cave to catch up with Harlowe.

At first they could see no farther than their noses. Gradually, as they went deeper into the cave, their eyes adjusted to a faint blue light that was coming from some unknown source in the ceiling. The dim blue glow seemed to be everywhere. The cave walls had also fallen away to an underground chamber that felt incredibly vast. When they spoke, their voices echoed as though Harlowe and Riverstone were in some empty auditorium. It was also cooler inside and less dry than the hot desert heat they had just come from.

After a short distance, the light from the small cave opening was totally lost from view, making Riverstone even more anxious about whether they could find their way back through the eeriness of the blue glowing light. Losing sight of the opening didn't seem to bother Harlowe, though. For him, it was a one-way road. He forged ahead, never losing sight of the robob's familiar headband of thin blue light.

There was no way of telling which direction they were headed. Their vision was limited to almost nothing. The only thing that kept Riverstone from losing it altogether was the presence of the blue light and the faint sound of the robob's clicks that seemed impossible to overtake no matter how hard they tried. Then, just when he was about to demand that they turn back for fear of being lost forever, the undog let out a glad-to-see-you yelp.

Riverstone sighed with relief. Never in his life had Mowgi's weird little yip sounded so comforting to his ears.

Harlowe called out to the undog, and within moments, Mowgi leaped into his arms. After a couple of quick licks and a rub behind the ears, Harlowe put the undog down and the three of them continued on through the blue fog.

Moving more quickly now that they had found a reliable guide, they caught a glimpse of the robob's lighted head as it passed by a massive cylindrical structure that was extremely wide and curved out of sight toward the nebulous ceiling. The stickman looked like a tiny ant as it moseyed past the structure carrying in its spindly arms a droopy form that had the size and shape of Simon's unconscious body. They didn't really care whether the actor was alive or dead. They were just grateful the robob—not the two of them—was transporting his worthless hide.

As Harlowe and Riverstone moved past the structure, it was even more massive than they had imagined from a distance. Like a structural pillar of a tall building, it seemed to come down from the blue glow above their heads and disappear into the dusty floor of the cavern. Riverstone had the distinct impression that it had been there a very long time. He touched the surface and was amazed at how smooth and warm it felt. He swallowed, wondering mystically if there was something inside that wanted to get out.

"I'm scared, Pylott."

"Of what?"

"I don't know. I just am."

Harlowe bent down and touched Mowgi on the tip of his parabolics. "Mowg seems okay with things."

"I don't care if he thinks it's a giant fire hydrant. This place is dope."

The faint clickity-clack of the robob stopped, drawing their attention away from the column to the tiny mechanical form in the distance. The knot in Riverstone's stomach tightened several notches. As long as he heard the familiar clacks or an occasional yelp, he felt secure in the darkness. But when the clacking stopped and Mowgi suddenly took off, leaving them behind, it signaled to Riverstone that something was wrong. The silence was hair-raising. To him it meant trouble, and he'd had enough of that. He wanted to get this nightmare over with and get home in time for a stack of his mom's blueberry pancakes for breakfast back in Lakewood.

"There," Harlowe cried out.

Riverstone edged himself behind Harlowe as he watched Mowgi and the stickman line up next to each other like they were waiting for a bus. A second later something switched on from somewhere inside the cavern. While the high-pitched whine resonated throughout the grotto, they tried in vain to find its source in the muted darkness. All they could hear was a highly sophisticated servomotor working fine machinery.

Harlowe was about to move toward the robob when a ray of light projected down from a hole in the multistory high ceiling. As the hole expanded, two sets of long thin tubes projected out and down at a forty-five-degree angle from the hole to within a foot of the waiting bystanders and touched the floor. When that step was complete, an intense blue light connected the long thin tubes and they solidified.

"Cool," Riverstone muttered unconsciously in a whispery breath.

To their amazement, Mowgi bounded up the lighted ramp like he was home, the robob clacking up the ramp behind him.

Harlowe placed his foot on the ramp. "Seems solid enough," he commented, bouncing up and down and testing it with his full weight. Then, without further hesitation, he began to climb up, waving to Riverstone to follow. Harlowe was in a hurry and didn't want to lose sight of the stickman. Riverstone stepped forward, wishing he had a pair of ruby-red Nikes for a shortcut back to Lakewood. The new explosion of light didn't help him resolve the dilemma of where they were or where they were headed. He wasn't even sure he wanted to know. Making his usual nervous glance over his shoulder, and seeing zilch that would change his mind, Riverstone climbed up after them.

* * *

The climb was like running up ten flights of football bleachers, but Riverstone made it without falling backwards. At the top, Harlowe patted the undog on the head. "Good work, Mowg." The undog yipped with excitement as Harlowe looked through the opening and saw the robob making its way across a large open space that was the size of a huge arena. Everything about the place was built on a grand scale.

When Riverstone caught up, he was panting heavily and sweating. "That's a workout."

Harlowe pointed through the opening. "The robob went down that corridor over there."

Stepping through the large opening together, they saw golden ceilings above and great, tall archways.

"Sweet," Riverstone said in awe as he stepped onto the plush blue-carpeted floor.

Inside, the musty odor of age dissipated and was replaced by the sweet aroma of a bouquet of flowers that seemed to welcome them.

Wide-eyed with fascination, they fast-stepped across the open space to the corridor Harlowe had pointed to earlier. The corridor was so long, they couldn't see its end.

"What if a Dakadude jumps us?" Riverstone cautioned.

Harlowe walked on without a reply.

Riverstone persisted. "Maybe it's a trap. You know, like a spider or something."

Harlowe shrugged with indifference. Until he found Leucadia, nothing else mattered.

By the time they arrived at the corridor where the robob had entered, the stickman was gone and so were the familiar clickity-clacks.

"Are you sure it went this way?" Riverstone asked.

There was no doubt in Harlowe's mind. "Yeah, I'm sure."

But he wasn't sure which door the stickman had entered. The corridor went on forever and had an uncountable number of arched doorways on each side of the passageway. Interestingly, none of the doors had a handle or a hinge or any type of hardware one would normally see on a door. To one side of each entry, however, was a pad with strange cuneiform markings written on it.

Riverstone was about to touch one of these pads when Harlowe grabbed him. "Not yet," he warned.

"He had to go through one of these," Riverstone stated.

Harlowe looked down at the undog, which had remained strangely silent the entire time they had been in the structure. "Which way, Mowg?"

Mowgi yipped twice and trotted away, leading them to another intersection of corridors. The corridor to their left ended abruptly some fifty feet away. They made a quick inspection of the short passage and discovered a large circular platform in the center of the blue-carpeted floor, not unlike smaller ones they had seen randomly along the first corridor. Directly above the platform was a wide hole in the ceiling several stories above their heads. But unlike the first opening through which they came into the structure, this hole in the ceiling was dark and had no apparent ramp leading up to it.

"Any ideas?" Riverstone asked, still looking up.

Harlowe scowled. "Not a one."

He turned around, looking for the undog, when the familiar clacking of the robob sounded again, drawing their attention to the intersection of the giant corridors. The robob seemed to be standing there waiting as though it wanted Harlowe and Riverstone to go with it. So as not to disappoint the little guy, they hustled toward it before it took off again.

"Where's the Mowg?" Riverstone asked.

Harlowe didn't know.

"Maybe we should look for him. He could find the way out for us."

"We're not going anywhere without Lu and Wiz," Harlowe replied determinedly as he marched away.

Further down the endless corridor, the robob with Simon in its arms stopped in front of one of the arched doors, and an instant later, the door swished open and the robob disappeared through the doorway.

Harlowe never took his eyes off the doorway as they both ran down the corridor. They stopped at the open entryway and looked in. Inside it was dark. Tiny flickerings of red and blue and yellow lights winked here and there in the darkness. Nothing more. Then a dim blue glow from the ceiling was switched on, casting an eerie chill over the entire area. As the robob with Simon moved across the room, several other robobs were busily working on the unconscious body of a naked woman.

"LU!" Harlowe cried out.

Chapter Twenty-Eight

CODE BLUE

*L*EUCADIA LAY FACE up on a long, flat table in the middle of the room. A single frail, yet graceful, column supported the table. As Simon's body was being placed on a similar table next to her, they saw Monday on a third table at the far end of the room. All three bodies were deathly still, as though lying in state. The shadowy lights only added to their corpse-like appearance. The instant the robob set Simon upon the table, another stickman injected a colorless fluid into his chest with a long hypodermic needle. Two more robobs popped out of nowhere, springing to life, and instantly began cutting away Simon's three-hundred-dollar silk shirt like it was toilet paper. The only one of their group unaccounted for was Ian.

Riverstone stepped across the threshold to Harlowe's side. "Can't we do anything?"

Harlowe didn't take his eyes off Leucadia, turning his head slowly, no.

"What if they're experimenting on them?" Riverstone asked.

"They're not."

"It's where they brought us," came Ian's voice from somewhere in the darkness. They turned toward his voice and saw him step tiredly toward them.

"Wiz!" Harlowe exclaimed. They came to their friend's side and hugged him, happy to see he was alive. "You're okay, pard?"

Ian looked like he would drop dead on the blue-carpeted floor at any moment, but he held himself up heroically and assured Harlowe he was okay. "You?"

"Don't ask. How did you get here?" Harlowe wondered.

For the next few minutes, Ian quickly explained how a bunch of stickmen had come out of nowhere and carried him and Monday across the mesa and down into the gorge to an underground place and then to the room they were standing in. They hadn't been here that long; Harlowe and Riverstone were only an hour or so behind them. Ian hadn't seen any other humans. Only robobs.

"Where's Mowgi?" Ian asked.

Harlowe turned back to Leucadia as Riverstone wisecracked, "Marking territory."

Harlowe came to Leucadia's side. One of the robobs politely stepped aside and allowed him room. Leucadia's face was stiff, her mouth open to one side. Seeing her so still, lifeless, he began to lose it. They were supposed to find Millawanda. That was why they came here, to save Lu's life. So where was this Millawanda? Where was anyone? What was happening to their world, and why did he feel so helpless?

Harlowe reached over and placed Leucadia's arms by her side so they would not dangle over the edge of the table. After that, he wiped a tiny speck of drool from her mouth with the back of his hand and straightened her long strands of blond hair that had a greenish hue under the blue light. He wanted to do more for her. Shaking from powerless frustration and clenching his fist at the ceiling, he looked up at the dim light and yelled, almost hysterically, "Don't let her die, Millawanda! Please, don't let her die!"

Almost instantaneously, as if Harlowe's emotional outburst had awakened the custodians of the room, Leucadia's body was completely covered with a wide beam of radiant blue light. Unlike the soft, dim light they'd seen before, this was an intense blue light full of energy, as though it was alive with some organic force. Riverstone pulled Harlowe back from the table as the light reached out, probing Leucadia with its luminary fingers.

Now the entire room was alive with dazzling medical displays of human forms on its walls. Incredible three-dimensional lifelike graphs, one after another, precisely exposed the real-time conditions of Lu and Monday and Simon. There were no loud noises or clicks or beeps or high-pitched whistles. Only the movement of color was heard. Not a kaleidoscope of color either, but gradient shades of yellow and orange and bright red showing the inner workings flow and move. Tiny cells bumped into each other; molecules bartered for elements; and massive armies, far greater than Alexander's or the Great Khan's, battled for position. If Harlowe, Riverstone, and Ian could have perceived the movement of troops, they would have understood the strategic direction the war was taking.

Unexpectedly, the blue light was shut off and a long narrow door across the room opened. They recognized right away the long cylindrical objects: they were more robobs unfolding, coming to life.

The first robob carried a crystalline ball in its pincers. It moved to Simon's side, and the instant the ball touched Simon's chest, it began to glow bright blue. Three more mechanical walking sticks—each with a different instrument in its hands—moved swiftly toward the bodies. The robotic teams looked like ER surgeons working "code blue" to save their patients.

Riverstone watched the robobs' long thin arms and crystalline heads move quietly over Leucadia's long, beautiful body, but suddenly he heard a strange thump coming from the table where Monday lay. Riverstone stared in awe at Monday's arm, which had been completely cut off just below the shoulder joint.

Dazed, Riverstone turned once more to see a mechanical pincer holding a probe cut open the middle of Leucadia's chest while other robobs spread her ribs, exposing her insides to the world. Breaking bones snapped the air, and blood flowed onto the table and dripped in heavy droplets to the floor.

Riverstone felt the splatterings hit his arm. He had seen enough; he had to leave the room. He stepped backwards out the door. The last thing he saw was a robob removing a large bloody hunk of throbbing tissue from the middle of Leucadia's chest. He turned away. Harlowe and Ian followed after him, their stomachs retching in dry heaves. Riverstone caught his own vomit in his hands before crashing into a corridor wall and collapsing onto the thick cushion of blue carpet.

Chapter Twenty-Nine

"STUDENT DRIVER"

"Hey, Matt!" A distant voice called out.

Riverstone's eyes shot open. Dazed and somewhat disoriented, he rolled over and found himself on the floor of the corridor where he had passed out. The voice cried out again, only this time it was louder. "Watch out!"

Riverstone jumped to his feet as a blurred object came barreling down the corridor toward him. He rubbed his eyes clear of sleep and blinked. It was Leucadia, driving some kind of bullet-shaped car with no wheels.

Cool! It's riding on air!

Then a thought struck him. Lu couldn't be driving; she should be dead. Even if she were alive, she wouldn't be up and around like this. *Just a few moments ago I saw her heart ripped out of her chest.*

"Where did she get *that?*" Riverstone asked aloud, referring to the sleek wheel-less car.

The car wavered from side to side. Twice, since he had been watching, Lu had bounced the car off the corridor wall like a misguided bumper car in a penny arcade.

Hey, take it easy, Lu!

Riverstone quickly glanced at the lush blue floor in front of the doorway where Harlowe and Ian had passed out. They were gone and the carpet was spotless. He whipped himself around and looked through the open door of the medical room. It was as clean as the carpet.

Riverstone was baffled. He was sure everything he remembered had actually happened: that Leucadia had been on that table with her guts exposed to the world, that Monday and Simon had been next to her, that Harlowe and Ian had vomited all over themselves right there. He couldn't have made that up. Yet, where was the evidence? Where were the robobs? And where had Harlowe and the others disappeared to?

"How do I stop this thing?" Riverstone heard Leucadia cry out in a panicky voice.

"Look out!" Riverstone shouted back.

She frantically waved her hand. "Get out of the way, Matt!" she screamed.

Riverstone froze. The bullet form kept coming, unstoppable. Lu wasn't kidding; she *was* out of control.

At the last possible second, Riverstone dove through the open medical room door, out of harm's way. Two seconds later, the sound of a loud crash came from the end of the corridor. When he poked his head out the door again, the car was angled up against the bulkhead and Leucadia was lying next to it on the carpet . . . out cold.

Riverstone ran down the corridor as fast as his legs could function. Leucadia was coming to by the time he got to the crash site. He quickly pulled her away, just in case the tilted vehicle were to fall back on top of them. At a safe distance he propped her up against a wall. Kneeling beside her he checked her limbs for fractures before he asked, "Are you okay?"

"I think so," she finally replied, still stunned.

"Man, what were you trying to do?" Riverstone asked. "You could have killed us both!"

"I was trying to find Harlowe."

Riverstone pointed to the car. It was teetering precariously against the wall. "In that?"

"It's all I could find. This place is huge."

Riverstone looked up and down the corridor. "No lie. They need a bus service." He turned back to Leucadia. "That was a stupid thing to do, though."

"I couldn't walk," she said, becoming more alert. "So I tried putting on the *gravs,* and I got all tangled up."

"Gravs?"

Lu held up the conglomeration of limp spaghetti-like cords that had been wrapped around her ankles. "Yeah, these things. When you strap them to your arms and legs, they make you stronger."

Riverstone figured that Lu was shy a few dots on the dice. "Sure they do."

"No, really, Matt. That's what the instructions said."

He took the grav cords but kept staring at her, making sure she wasn't some apparition or something other than who she really was. Convinced for the moment that she was indeed the Leucadia he knew, his eyes fell back on the cords, which were connected to either the one-inch-wide belt wrapped around her waist or the one around her chest. The cords ran along her long slender legs and arms to her satiny gold-colored shoes and matching gloves. Cords on both sides of her elbows and knees were connected to four other sets of smaller belts to add additional support to the joints.

"Do you cook this stuff first?" Riverstone commented wryly.

"No, silly. Get me out of this and I'll show you."

"How did you get them on in the first place?" he asked.

"I don't really know. I strapped myself into one leg, then the other. Before I knew it, though, I couldn't walk, so I had to take that car and find someone to help me."

She looked down the corridor in both directions. "Have you seen Harlowe?"

Riverstone shook his head. "No, but he's got to be around. He was right back there, sick as a dog, when I last saw him." He thought it best not to tell her everything yet. "Ah, well, he and Ian were with me, watching the robobs operate on you . . . I mean, taking care of you. And then we must have passed out. You haven't seen anyone either, huh?"

"What's a robob?"

"A stick guy about five feet high, with a funny head."

"Huh?"

"Don't worry, you'll see them soon enough. They're around here like flies."

Leucadia looked at Riverstone quizzically. "Soooo, what exactly is this place?"

"I don't know, Lu. I was hoping you could tell me. I mean, your mom's the one who sent us here to save you, right?"

Her mouth twisted into a funny smirk. "Did she? I don't even know how I got here," Lu replied.

Riverstone studied their predicament. "Perfect," he sighed.

He started to laugh, however, when he figured out what the problem was with the gravs. "Lu, you've got these cords on backwards," Riverstone chided as he noticed the tiny blue light pulsating through the back of her shirt. Riverstone touched the box with his finger and the belts relaxed like a hose being emptied of water. "That power box is supposed to be in the front."

"Oh." She tried to cover her embarrassment with an innocent smile.

Riverstone grinned, congratulating himself on how easily he had solved her dilemma. He unfastened one knotted cord, then another. When that was done, he helped her stand so he could work on the other tangles. As complicated as he thought it should be, after he understood how they worked, he untangled the cords easily. In less than a minute Lu was able to slip all her limbs out from under the apparatus. Except for one last big knot in front, he was done.

"Turn around, Lu," he directed, "and lift your shirt a bit so I can untie the front."

She started to turn around and as she did, she began to laugh in a slow, abnormal way. Riverstone thought she was demented. He heard something hit the floor, and when he looked down, heavy droplets of blood were seeping into the carpet. He looked at his hands, and they were covered with blood too.

Leucadia turned completely around, her face waxen and ghostly. Her insides were exposed as though she was still on the table. Her intestines glistened, oozing fluids that reeked of death. Her blue veins, pulsing and crooked, slithered like restless snakes. Her heart lurched out, beating thunderously, hurting Matt's ears. All the while Leucadia just stood there with her hands on her hips, laughinglouder and louder, and staring at him, shouting ridicule and abuse at his stupidity for believing nothing had happened.

Riverstone fell to his knees, burying his face in his hands. "No!" he cried, trying to crawl away.

She blocked his way. Bending to whisper in his ear she hissed, "What's the matter, Matthew? Are you afraid of the truth? You're never going home again, Gamadin . . ."

Chapter Thirty

NEW DUDS

Riverstone bolted upright in bed. "NOOOO!" he screamed, his chest heaving as his heart pounded and tried to break free. Something strong forced him back down on the bed.

"Chill, pard! You're okay," said a deep familiar voice.

Riverstone shut his eyes, concentrating on settling his terror. It took a few moments of deep breathing, but soon he was able to focus on Harlowe's intense blue eyes staring him right in the face.

Riverstone threw back his silky blue bedcovers. "Where am I?"

Harlowe looked around. "I think it's a bedroom."

"Did you put me here?" Riverstone asked.

"No."

"Well, how *did* I get here?"

"I haven't a clue."

"Someone put me here."

"Not me."

"Who torqued your brain?"

"A woman driver. That tell you anything?"

"Plenty."

Riverstone kept gulping sweet air while he looked around the room, trying to get his bearings. How he ended up in the bed buck naked he hadn't a clue. Surprisingly, he was clearheaded and alert, not groggy at all from his sleep. And if he hadn't been so whacked about the dream, he felt sharp-headed enough to take even one of Farnducky's physics tests.

Passing it was another matter.

The room's decor was tastefully done in gradient shades of blue. The walls were gently curved, not squared off. There were no corners. Even the bed was oval. The only other pieces of furniture were two padded chairs and a small table. Along the walls at each end of the room were three arched doors. A small graphic was pictured above each door's activator. At first blush Riverstone was unable to decipher what they meant. But as he studied them closer, he felt he had a pretty good idea of what lay behind them. He was unable to reason why he knew the factoid. He just did.

Directly above the bed was a skylight. The four-foot elliptical shape was the only window in the room. Strangely, it seemed to have no other purpose than just being there. It looked on to nothing or nowhere. It was completely opaque, with no light at all coming through the glass.

Riverstone climbed out of bed. "How long was I out?" he asked, walking across the room. The right arch door swished open and he went inside to relieve himself as if he had done it a thousand times before.

Harlowe shrugged. "I just woke up myself."

"Have you seen anyone . . . alive?" Riverstone continued through the open bathroom door.

"Just you and Ian and—," he glanced at the undog sitting patiently at the foot of the bed, "—the Mowg."

"Oh yeah? Where's Wiz now?"

"My guess, he's figuring out how this thing ticks."

"Good, maybe he'll find us a way out of here."

Riverstone came back into the bedroom and eyed Harlowe's new blue uniform with reserved interest. "Where'd you get those clothes? You look like one of Bolt's space toads from the movie set."

Harlowe pointed. "Behind the far door."

Riverstone headed in the indicated direction, his rear end lily white in contrast to the dark tan lines of his legs and back. "What happened to Lu and the other two nimrods?"

Harlowe's face went slack as he remembered the room where the robobs performed their incredible surgery on Lu's chest and Monday's arm. "I was going back to the medical room next."

Standing next to the door, Riverstone faced Harlowe with anxious eyes. "You sure you want to go back there?"

"I have to."

Riverstone struck the activator with a quick slap of his hand, as though it was second nature to him. The door slid swiftly back into its pocket, and he walked into the small room and disappeared from sight.

Harlowe's eyes fixed on a point a thousand light-years away. "You saw what the robobs did, right?"

"Yeah, I saw," Riverstone replied loudly from inside the room. "There were guts all over the place, Harlowe. Platter's arm dropped like a dumbbell on the floor and then . . . Oh, man! I'm sorry, pard, but Lu's got to be sprouting wings."

Then, as though Riverstone was talking to someone else, he said in a commanding tone, "Hey, this shirt is too small, brah. Give me something in a double X."

"Who are you talking to in there?" Harlowe wanted to know.

"My robob tailor. The China-hat thinks I'm a size small."

"He's looking at your lower half."

"That's cool, thanks," Riverstone said to his tailor.

"You're no doctor. There could have been something else going on. Lu could be alright," Harlowe said defensively.

"I don't have to be a doctor to know a corpse in the making when I see one. That wasn't surgery they were doing, Harlowe. That was *CSI,* robob style."

Harlowe remained undeterred. "She's alright."

"Hey, these China-hats are cool. They've got all kinds of stuff in here."

"She's not dead."

"You're living in a tree, dude. You saw what I saw."

"They were saving her."

"Believe what you want." Then to the unseen entity, Riverstone said, "I'll take a pair of those, too." A few minutes later he came back into the bedroom, dressed in a new blue outfit similar to what Harlowe was wearing.

In his right hand Riverstone carried a pair of dark blue slippers with gold bottoms. As he sat on the edge of the bed to try them on he said, "As Dr. Laura would say, you're in denial, pard. She's taking harp lessons." The slippers reminded Riverstone of soft reef-walkers. The soles were extremely rough, though, like a cat's tongue. He thought they were a little pretentious for his taste, but until he could find his red Nikes, they would do. He wiggled his toes. The fit was perfect.

"She's not dead!" Harlowe argued one last time, like he was trying to convince himself more than Riverstone.

Changing the subject to relieve the tension in the room, Riverstone asked, "Did you see a phone around here? We need to call our parents. My mom's got to be hysterical by now, and yours too. If they read the newspaper and see what happened at the Mars beach house yester—" His brain suddenly froze. "When *did* we leave Newport, Pylott?"

Harlowe motioned Riverstone toward another arched door. "No phones. No clocks. I barely know my name."

"Which means?"

"We need to find answers," Harlowe said.

Out the corner of his eye, Riverstone spotted his watch on the bed. "Hold on. At least we'll know the time." He went over and picked up his watch. "According to this, it's been just a few hours since we got here."

"It's off," Harlowe stated.

"It's quartz. It's off a zillionth of a second every billion years, toad." His face scrunched up tight. "No phones, huh?"

"None. Your watch is junk. No way it's been only a few hours." Harlowe's tone was beyond impatient. Mowgi seemed to be in a hurry too as he scratched at the door. "What's with him?"

"When's the last time you took him for a walk?" Riverstone asked.

"He walks himself."

"In a place like this there's got to be a ton of phones, Harlowe," Riverstone persisted as they both headed for the exit door.

Harlowe pressed the activator, and the door blew back into the wall in a blink. Instantly, Mowgi leaped up into a pair of waiting arms.

Harlowe and Riverstone practically leaped out of their cool, new slip-ons when they saw the tall, shapely goddess standing in the doorway.

"LU!"

Chapter Thirty-One

FULL DISCLOSURE

RIVERSTONE CAUGHT HARLOWE falling backwards as Leucadia, without a stitch of clothing on, held Mowgi in her arms. For the first time in his life, Riverstone wished he were the undog.

Lu seemed as surprised as they were, but for different reasons. "Harlowe? Matt?"

Riverstone stood Harlowe up, and cautiously he stepped through the doorway, gawking wide-eyed at her body like it was the first time he had ever seen her naked. "You're alright?" Harlowe's words posed a question rather than expressing his joy upon seeing her.

She didn't like his tone. "What do you mean by that?" Perplexed, Harlowe kept staring, not at her nakedness but at her apparent miraculous recovery. Riverstone, on the other hand, had an equal amount of lust to go along with his surprise.

After a long moment, Harlowe reached out for her and reiterated, "You're alive."

She saw the amazement on both their faces. Even Mowgi's head was cocked a little askew. "Yeah." She then added, "Should I be otherwise?"

"Well—" Harlowe elbowed Riverstone in the side before he could utter another word. He then gently held her out at arm's length to examine her more closely. Like the two of them, Leucadia was completely healed of her injuries and bore not a scratch. "You seem okay."

Leucadia's big green eyes began to burn in anger. "I am. Why the incredulity, Harlowe? You're looking at me strangely. Do you know something I don't?" Her eyes surveyed the surroundings. "Where are we? And how'd we get here?"

Harlowe glanced at Riverstone with a can-you-believe-it frown. "We're not sure. You don't feel weak or tired?"

"No."

Harlowe led Leucadia back into the bedroom. To Riverstone's drooling disappointment, Harlowe felt she needed to wear something. He opened the closet door and introduced her to Riverstone's tailor. Ten minutes later she came waltzing out in some dark blue, low-cut number that looked like it was sprayed on. It wasn't quite the conservative improvement Harlowe had in mind, but her new duds would have to work.

"Where are we?" Lu asked again, running her hands down her thighs, driving Riverstone's body heat to full boil.

"We're not sure," Harlowe replied.

"I'm confused. The last thing I remember is that the beach house was under attack."

Harlowe nodded. "That's right."

"Is this a hospital? Was someone hurt?"

Riverstone nodded at Harlowe. "We should tell her now."

Harlowe glared back. "Not now."

Leucadia studied Harlowe for a moment before she said, "I take it you know something that you're withholding from me." His eyes said there was. "Okay, but we're not finished with this conversation, Pylott."

Harlowe nodded, gritting his teeth. *Yes, dear.* He hated it when she called him by his last name. "I'm down with that." Then he tried changing the subject. "Time to find Ian and the movie star."

"Simon's here too?" Leucadia exclaimed.

Riverstone grunted his distaste. "Yeah, our movie star is here. So is Platter."

Leucadia turned to Harlowe. "I think now would be a good time to continue our conversation."

Harlowe turned away. "No. It's not a good time." Mowgi yelped twice. Harlowe glared down at the undog and pointed a finger at his snout. "You be quiet."

Riverstone leaned into Harlowe's face. "Tell her, Pylott. She should be dead and you know it."

"You're so smooth."

Leucadia recoiled. "Dead? Do I look dead to either of you?"

"A conundrum," Riverstone stated flatly.

Harlowe stuck his arms out to keep her from launching herself at Riverstone. "We've got bigger problems to consider, Lu. Like what happens next?"

"And how to deal with the Dakadudes," Riverstone added.

"What are Dakadudes?" Leucadia wanted to know.

"The big ugly guys who chased us here." Riverstone leaned toward her. "And guess what? They're not from this planet either."

"How do you know?" Leucadia asked.

"If you saw them, you'd know," Riverstone replied.

Leucadia turned to Harlowe for verification.

"He's right," Harlowe confirmed.

"They're already here, then," Leucadia stated quietly. Harlowe alone picked up on the subtlety of her reply.

The three of them wandered off to find the middle of the long corridors where they had entered the structure in the first place. As they walked, Harlowe reflected that now that Leucadia was alive, he had completed part of his mission for Mrs. M. Finding Milla-wanda and getting her off the planet was his next goal. How he would accomplish that was beyond his comprehension. Figuring out the square root of pi was an easier task than getting anyone off the planet. *Dude, he thought, NASA had a difficult enough time doing it even with the backing of the U.S. government!*

Harlowe explained as they went along that the corridor would come to a dead end, and if they went left, they would come to the huge foyer where all the corridors met. The exit hole with the lighted ramp should be there. It had to be there. It was their only way out.

"How do you know so much?" Leucadia asked.

"I don't know jack, Lu. Everything's a guess. But we have to start somewhere," Harlowe explained as he led them toward the hub.

They walked on in silence until they got to the open foyer. To their great relief, the massive hole in the floor was still open.

"Where is everyone?" Leucadia asked.

Harlowe turned his head around, looking for clues. "Except for Wiz, who went exploring, and you, we've seen no one since we woke up."

"Ya think it's some kind of underground military place?" Riverstone asked. He slammed his fist against the wall. "It's sure built like one," he commented.

Harlowe turned to Leucadia. It was time to come clean. He had seen in her eyes and heard in her voice that she knew. He stepped in front of her and asked, "Alright, you know what this is, don't you?"

"I've never been here before, Harlowe," she replied coolly.

"But you know all about it, right?"

She tried to act ignorant. "No, I don't know *all* about it."

"You're dancing."

"I know a little."

Harlowe knew better. "You're Harry's daughter. Your mom's got eyes like you. You know plenty."

Leucadia's bejeweled eyes darted back and forth between the impatient faces of the two young men. She nodded, accepting the inevitable. "I'm pretty sure *this* is Millawanda."

"What do you mean by this?" Riverstone asked, waiting for the other shoe to drop.

"This entire underground structure," Leucadia added.

Harlowe knew there was more. "And?"

"She's a spaceship from another world, Pylott."

Chapter Thirty-Two

NO RETURN

A LONG MOMENT OF suspended disbelief preceded Riverstone's next question. "As in flies through space?" he asked.

"As between the stars, Matt," Leucadia answered straight out.

"I was getting to that one," Riverstone added.

Harlowe's fuse was short. He felt like he was becoming the butt of a joke. "And how long were you going to let us play around in this place before you told us?"

Leucadia put her arms around Harlowe's neck and looked him in the eye. "About as long as you were going to wait to tell me what I want to know."

He pushed her arms away. "Not the same."

"It's close," Riverstone chimed in.

Harlowe pointed a hot finger at Riverstone's nose. "You keep your mouth shut, toad."

"Who put you in charge around here, Pylott?" Riverstone countered.

"I did. I'm captain, and he's my elite guard," asserted Harlowe, pointing at Mowgi.

Riverstone backed off as Leucadia cut off Harlowe's escape. "Just tell me, Pylott, then we can move on. How bad can it be?"

"Oh, it's bad," Riverstone added.

Leucadia glared at him. "Zip it, Matt."

"Yes, ma'am."

She turned back to Harlowe. She was waiting.

Harlowe locked eyes with Leucadia. *Oh man, she's gorgeous when she's angry. Yes, dear . . .*

"What do you remember?" Harlowe asked.

"Nothing, really. My mom's study, that's it."

Harlowe folded his arms and stood firm. "Alright, here it is. You were shot in the chest by a Dak beam weapon. Your mom stopped the hemorrhaging, but she couldn't save your life because the Dakadudes hit the beach house from all sides."

Leucadia looked frightened. "They found the beach house? But how?"

"I don't know how. They just did. Let me finish, Lu. You wanted it all, I'm going to give it to you."

Leucadia didn't need to know any more details. "Just tell me my family's okay, Harlowe."

Harlowe looked into her pleading green eyes. He had to tell her something. It had better be the truth, he told himself. "I don't know. The beach house was getting hit pretty hard. But they were all alive when we left." Leucadia swallowed. "Listen, Lu, your parents had some pretty rad weapons themselves and they were kicking some serious Dakadude booty. So I'm sure they're okay."

Harlowe turned to Riverstone for support. "Weren't they, pard? Tell the truth."

"A Dakadude wasteland."

"My mom's elite soldiers should be here by now," Leucadia said.

Both Harlowe and Riverstone's faces went long.

"We saw them," Riverstone said with a touch of sorrow in his voice.

Harlowe finished. "They're all dead, Lu."

"Dead? All of them?" Leucadia went numb when their sad expressions didn't change. "There were more than 140 men and women."

"We didn't have much time to check every body, but Mowg found no one alive. Do you want me to stop here?"

Leucadia wiped her eyes. She had recruited many and some had remained close friends. She took a deep breath before she said, "No, go on. I need to know."

Harlowe took the end of his sleeve and dabbed around her eyes a little before he went on. "Simon and Platter were still at the beach house when we arrived and they got caught up in it all. Simon turned chocolate. We had to knock him out. Platter handled himself well. He grabs the Vantage and I get in Baby. Your mom shoves two of these narly pistols in our hands and tells us we have to get out of Dodge. She believed Millawanda was the only thing in the world that could save your life which," he said, staring at her up and down, "looks true enough."

"So that's it?"

"No! There's plenty left."

Riverstone broke in. "Just cut to the chase, Harlowe. Like where the robobs cut her open."

Leucadia's eyes flared like she didn't understand.

"You know what a robob is," Harlowe informed her.

Leucadia gave him a puzzled look. "I do?"

"Yeah, your dad has a garage bay full of 'em," Harlowe said.

"They're robobs?"

"Yeah, that's what we call 'em. And when they walk they make a funny clickity-clack noise."

Riverstone defended Harlowe. "He's not messing with ya, Lu. That's what they do. They clickity-clack, clickity-clack. Really."

Harlowe continued. "So we drive all day, and we're in Utah. Only Wiz and Mowgi know where. Then a couple of robobs kidnap you. But before we can find you, the Dakadudes drive into this canyon like they have a GPS up Baby's tailpipe. The whole world goes bonkers after that."

Riverstone broke in, putting his own spin on the story. "Yeah, this spaceship drops out of nowhere, and out pops Freddie Krueger on steroids, who lets go two of the gnarliest cujos you've ever seen in your life. Well, just when we're about to become Happy Meals, this dragon flies in and saves us."

As they were both reliving the events of the day before, Harlowe kept reading Leucadia's face, looking for details in her demeanor that betrayed what she already knew.

"Well, after somehow surviving the night, we followed this robob across the desert, and who do we find?" Leucadia waited for Riverstone's answer. "Bolt, all curled up in a ball, wetting in his pants."

"Cut the details," Harlowe growled.

"So the robob leads us into this humongous cavern and the room where we find you about half a nanosecond from death. Then all kinds of other stick dudes are popping to life with weird instruments in their claws. Suddenly these lights and graphs come on and it's showtime, boys and girls."

Leucadia put a loving arm around Harlowe's shoulders as Riverstone continued his narrative. "Don't get all warm and fuzzy yet. The best is yet to come." He points up at the ceiling. "This big light snaps on and scans you, Lu. Bang! The robobs go into hyperdrive; their little hands and elbows are a blur. They slice open your chest, break your ribs, and cut out your heart and dump it on the floor like it's yesterday's news."

Leucadia turned pale as she grabbed her chest.

"After that we kinda lost it, you know. It was nasty in there."

Harlowe's face twisted into a knot, reliving the details as Riverstone continued. "Yeah. We stumbled back out the door and puked our guts out. After that the world went blank. The next thing we know, we're waking up in a strange bedroom and you're standing at our door in your birthday suit." He put his hand on his hips and glared at Harlowe. "How'd I do, captain?"

Harlowe just shook his head as he came back to Leucadia's side. "You wanted the truth. Satisfied?"

"I don't feel like I just had open heart surgery."

Riverstone concurred. "Yeah, you look pretty fresh."

"Yeah, a miracle," Harlowe agreed.

Leucadia stiffened. "I should believe you?"

Harlowe stared off toward some unknown galaxy, far away. Would he ever learn? "No. It's all a lie. You're a smart doe, Lu. Coming from Riverstone's brain, could he think of something that tight?" he said, as he knelt down to Mowgi and rubbed one of his parabolic dishes.

Leucadia went up directly to Riverstone and looked him in the eyes. "I can tell if you're lying, Matt. I can't with him." Suddenly she realized it was the truth because Riverstone's face wasn't changing under her intense scrutiny.

Harlowe stood up. He had to get the ball rolling or they would be stuck here for hours. He pointed at the long, thin streak between her breasts. "See that faint red line? You didn't have that before. And I know every square inch of that territory." He laid an ear against her chest. "And hear that?" In the silence they could hear a faint whirring sound coming from inside her chest. "That's your new engine, sweetheart. You've just given new meaning to the phrase heartless doe."

Harlowe wandered out into the center of the large open foyer and shouted for all creation to hear, "What a weekend!"

"Amen, pard," Riverstone echoed.

Harlowe nudged Mowgi out of his way. "Find your own space, Mowg," he said as he kept turning around inside the great domed chamber, hoping to see some sort of sign that would illuminate the reason for being there at that precise moment. "So why did we come here, anyway?"

Riverstone had an answer. "Because you promised Mrs. M you would save the galaxy."

"Not the galaxy," Harlowe countered.

Leucadia faced Harlowe. "What did you promise my mother?"

Harlowe acted like it was none of her business. Riverstone, on the other hand, felt it was everyone's business. "He said he would fly

Millawanda away and save the planet, the quadrant, and some hick place called Neeja from the Fhaal. Whoever they are."

Leucadia asked, "What did she say to you, Harlowe? Matt couldn't have known any of this."

"No doubt," Riverstone cracked, as he drifted over to the edge of the opening and found a seat while the other two hashed things out.

"She gave me this map—," Harlowe began.

"The map with the holographs?" Leucadia wondered.

Harlowe stepped into her space. "Yeah, that one."

"Where is it?"

"Lost."

"Lost?"

"Yeah, lost. After going through what we did the last day or two, you tend to lose things."

"I understand."

"No, you don't, because you keep asking me stupid questions like I know the answers and I'm trying to hide something. I'm not, Lu. I don't know a thing. There's a lot of weird crap going on around here, and you're not helping." His eyes were pleading with her to understand, but he didn't know how to express it. She just didn't get it. He was helpless.

Leucadia grabbed him and held him. He was trembling inside. Not from fear in the sense that he was scared but from the fear that the burden was on him to do "the right thing." That all their lives, and much more, depended on him. He just didn't know how to define the right thing and the course of action he needed to take to accomplish it. He wanted to break away—not to run but to fight the war himself. But she wouldn't let go. No matter how hard he fought, she kept holding him, letting her strength and caring warmth help him realize they should fight the war together.

Only when his trembling began to ease did Lu release him. She stayed close by and said, "I'm here, Harlowe. I'll be here with you all the way." She kissed him softly. "I love you, Pylott."

Harlowe put his arms around her. They kissed gently again and then guided each other over to where Riverstone was waiting for the conflict to run its course. There they sat down beside him and gazed down the long ramp of no return together.

Chapter Thirty-Three

UTILITY ROOM

For the next hour, the three of them sat with their feet dangling over the edge of the massive opening, sharing what they knew and filling in the gaps about the things they didn't. Harlowe recounted the promise he made to Mrs. M. Some parts were sketchy because of the many plas-rounds that whizzed past their heads as Mrs. M outlined his instructions. The part about taking Millawanda away from Earth particularly needed a lot more clarification. He wanted to know everything Lu knew about Millawanda, and why the space-ship was so important to her mother.

Unusual for Riverstone, he kept quiet and listened like someone who had come to the meeting late. His face was a mixture of disbelief and out-of-this-world wackiness when Leucadia spoke of her mother being from another world. This fact alone didn't surprise him; after all, his heart had known since the first time he saw her that she was an unearthly goddess. But the idea that she was also an elite Triadian soldier who was sent to Earth to find the Gamadin power that would save her planet? Two days ago, he would have thought that was a stretch. But after seeing how Mrs. M had plucked off Daks coming down the beach, he was now a true believer.

"So, with this one ship your mom was going to fight an empire?" Riverstone asked in wonder.

Leucadia's green eyes flashed his way. "She thought it was possible."

Riverstone pointed down at the ramp. "Have you noticed that we're buried inside a mountain?"

"My mother has a plan to release Millawanda from her tomb," Leucadia replied.

Riverstone burped up a small laugh, looking at Harlowe. "Oh, really?"

Harlowe turned to Leucadia. "How long has she been parked here?"

"About 150 centuries, give or take."

Harlowe and Riverstone traded cynical glances. "That's as old as the pyramids, Lu," Harlowe pointed out.

"Older."

"Did your mom tell you what the plan was?" Riverstone asked.

"No. She just said she had a plan and that Millawanda would take over once her crew was ready. It would all be automatic after that."

Riverstone returned to being his usual self. He was done listening with an understanding ear. "That's a great plan, Lu. Why didn't I think of that? Just press the 'auto' button and we all blast out of here freeeeeeee as a bird," he said, flapping his arms in the air like he had wings.

Mowgi jumped up and down like he wanted to go, too.

Ignoring Riverstone's sarcasm, Leucadia asked, "Where does it go?" as she nodded toward the ramp.

"Home," Riverstone replied.

Although it was good to know that a way out was available to them, the ramp was also a way for someone else to walk in just as easily. Riverstone looked around, and on a nearby wall he spied what he thought was an activator. Harlowe and Leucadia stood up when Riverstone slapped the wall switch with his open hand. As Mowgi quickly leaped back to the foyer floor, the ramp retracted into the structure. No one had any idea how, but it completely disappeared somewhere. The hole spiraled closed until nothing was left of the opening but the blue carpet.

"That works well enough," Leucadia said, walking out over the hole and tapping her foot on the carpet's soft fibers. "Not bad for 150 centuries."

"Get back," Riverstone said, motioning for her and Harlowe to step aside.

He tapped the activator again. The hole opened up and the ramp deployed, appearing to be unchanged.

Riverstone was relieved. "I had to be sure," he said as he slapped the activator one more time to close the opening.

Losing interest in the disappearing hole, Harlowe's attention focused on the shorter corridor. "I've felt like someone's been watching us since we came here."

"Duhhh!" Riverstone taunted. He was about to slap the activator one more time, but Harlowe interrupted him.

"Keep it closed, in case we have company."

"It will close itself after we leave," Riverstone replied emphatically.

"I'm not done looking around," Harlowe stated.

Riverstone confronted Harlowe nose to nose. "I knew you would say that. Don't you get it? I don't want any part of this. I want to go home. My parents are sick with worry right about now, wondering where I am. I'll be grounded until the next century as it is. I don't want to put them through any more agony, Harlowe. I'm hasta-la-bye-bye, Bucko. History!"

Harlowe stuck a finger in Riverstone's chest. "No, toad, it's you who doesn't get it. We're going to find out a little more. It ain't safe to go back out there, don't you remember? The cujos, the shuttle, the Dakadudes. They're still out there, dimwit. So why don't you just go back up that trail and see how long it takes to get your head fried, peabrain?"

Riverstone shoved Harlowe's finger out of the way. "I'll take my chances. It's your promise, not mine. I'm not in this game, pard. I'm outta here."

Harlowe set his jaw. "No way, toad. You're staying right here. They'll shoot you the moment you step outside and that will give us all away."

Riverstone slapped the activator to open the hole up again.

Harlowe lunged to close it and they fell to the carpet together. Fists flew, but none connected. They rolled and tumbled together down one of the corridors, swinging big roundhouses at each other's heads, missing wildly. They crashed against the bulkhead twice before Riverstone pinned Harlowe against a door that suddenly flew open. He was about to Fedex Harlowe's teeth to the next state when something caught his arm and held it fast. It was Leucadia. "No, Matt!" she cried out.

Riverstone looked at her with renewed respect. Her grip on his arm was incredibly strong. He couldn't move it an inch. He half-expected her face to turn into something evil like in his dream, but she didn't change. Although she was flush with exasperation, something else about her appearance was different. Something he couldn't quite grasp.

She pointed through the open doorway. "Look."

Riverstone twisted around and Harlowe released himself from the full Nelson and stood up. The chamber before them was double the size of the foyer. Leucadia helped Riverstone to his feet as he let out a low whistle and asked, "What is it?"

Harlowe cautiously strolled into the room and rotated slowly around to focus on all the new stuff that he saw.

Following Harlowe's lead, Riverstone and Leucadia entered the chamber, their eyes dancing with fascination. Along one entire wall, unidentified objects were stacked or hung in neat, organized rows. Some items were tools, they guessed, like welders' torches and cutting devices. Other items seemed to be bundled up, ready for use at a moment's notice for some unknown enterprise.

Walking up to an eye-level shelf, Harlowe removed one of the golden helmets stacked there in two rows of six. He examined it closely. It was light and seemed large enough for his head. He tried it on for size.

Riverstone gave him a thumbs-down. "Not your color, pard."

Harlowe removed the headpiece. "It lit up inside when I put it on," he said.

"Can I see it?" Leucadia asked.

Harlowe handed it to her. "It might be too big for you."

She put it on her head. After a brief second she said, "No, it fits fine. It seems to be adjusting to my head." She turned her head left, then right. "I see what you mean about the lights. They're pretty."

"They don't make any sense," Harlowe said.

"I've never seen symbols like them before," Leucadia agreed.

"Any ideas what it's used for?"

Leucadia passed her hand in front of the blue, mirrored faceplate. "The base looks like it attaches to something." She turned to the shelf. "Probably this suit here. It must be some sort of isolation suit." She fingered the suit material. "It's very pliable."

Harlowe offered up a guess. "Organic fiber?"

Leucadia thought that made sense. Riverstone was unimpressed. He was looking for something more useful as he ventured toward the opposite wall and gawked up at the many things hanging from the ceiling. Along the way, he tripped over the legs of what he thought was a dead body sitting in his path. Practically leaping out of his new blue duds, Riverstone jumped back. Then he figured out it was only something that *looked* like a human form. The overstuffed manikin sat by itself in the corner as though it was waiting for someone to play with. It had no ears or mouth or hair and two pea-size dots for eyes. Riverstone judged it to be at least a foot taller than he was. He gave it a slight nudge with his toe. It was solid. Not hard like metal; more like hitting a punching bag filled with sand.

"The Chargers could use you, dude," he joked at the manikin.

He was about to move on when he saw what appeared to be a pair of binoculars hanging within easy reach above the manikin's head.

If they were binoculars, they would be useful in helping them find their way back to civilization. He removed them from the hook and was surprised at how light they felt. These were golden like the cylinder Ian had thrown and like many of the other things in the room. Proud of his find, Riverstone moved along, studying the eyepiece. When he actually looked through the lenses, a short whirr sounded as the optics inside automatically adjusted to his eyes. What he saw made his heart skip a beat.

He lowered the field glasses and stared with incredulity at a wheelless bullet-shaped car parked across the room.

Mowgi was in the front seat, his slimy green tongue panting happily in anticipation of going on a ride. Riverstone suffered through a long, anxious moment, making sure the vehicle wasn't going to suddenly rise up and run him down.

It can't hurt you, toad. It's parked. The undog can't drive, either, so what's the problem?

After convincing himself it was indeed harmless, Riverstone let out a big sigh of exasperation before he walked over to give it a better look. What really twisted his insides was how the sleek blue car with the thin windshield wrapped around its front was the same as the one he remembered from his dream. But how did his subconscious know about the car before he did? *You know how to drive it, too, don't you?* "Yeah, maybe—" *No maybes, Riverstone, you do. From either side, okay?* "Yeah, but why would I know that?"

Riverstone's head was dizzy with the riddles when Harlowe called him away from his quandary. He clipped the binoculars to the side of his pants and nearly tripped again over the lifeless manikin's outstretched feet as he absentmindedly threaded his way back across the room.

Riverstone joined Harlowe and Leucadia, who were standing next to a tall slender door they had opened.

"You look like you've been hit by a car," Harlowe said with concern.

Riverstone swallowed. "Don't even joke about that."

"Well, check this out," Harlowe added. He pointed proudly to a rack where nine weapons hung. Three of them resembled small commando rifles and the six others looked like large pistols. No markings were etched on their surfaces to indicate where they had been made or who they belonged to, but they did look familiar.

"Recognize these?" Harlowe asked.

"Yeah, they're like the one you dropped in the crevasse and the one you threw at the beast." Riverstone turned toward Leucadia as he pointed at Harlowe. "Most people pull the trigger and shoot things. Our hero throws the pistol, the gun goes off, and the beast that's about to eat us gets killed. Go figure."

Riverstone removed one of the pistols and looked at the front of the barrel. "No hole in these either." The pistol had a fine golden sheen and felt quite solid in his hand. Like the robob cylinders, its apparent weight was deceptive. The grip was a little large for his hand, but he thought it was something he could get used to with some practice.

He then picked out a holster for himself, and with a couple of minor adjustments to the belt, it fit comfortably around his waist. When he reached down with his left hand, he found he could remove the pistol with surprising swiftness. The four-inch barrel was less than a third of its length.

Riverstone held the weapon up and stated, "Not bad for 150 centuries."

Harlowe took a holster from the rack and put it around his waist. After a few adjustments, he was satisfied with the feel of the device on his hip. He reached for a pistol like the one Riverstone had chosen.

"Watch where you're pointing that, cowboy," Riverstone quipped.

Harlowe stepped away, giving himself some room. He then looked out across the room, fixed on an unseen opponent, and drew. The pistol snagged on something and flipped out of his hand. It fell on the blue-carpeted floor with a muffled thud. Mowgi yelped. Leucadia laughed out loud and Riverstone rolled his eyes.

A little flushed, Harlowe picked up the pistol off the floor and pointed the butt end at Riverstone. "Shut up . . . or I'll throw it at you."

Figuring he could do Harlowe one better, Riverstone removed a rifle-like weapon from the rack. It was about thirty inches long and was light in his hands but very solid. "How can these work after so many centuries?" he wondered aloud as he brought the device up to his shoulder. He was about to pull the trigger when Leucadia stopped him.

"I think you should take your testosterone outside," Leucadia told them, grasping the barrel. "Maybe these weapons are harmless, but you shouldn't take a chance on finding out in here. You might damage something," she added, staring at Harlowe, who was holding his pistol awkwardly.

Harlowe nodded. "Yeah, it might upset Millawanda," he joked.

"But what if it's dark outside?" Riverstone whined.

Looking like a just-off-the-bus recruit, Harlowe headed for the exit doorway with a rifle in his hand. "Then it's dark, pard. Come on, Mowg."

He paused and looked at Leucadia. "You coming?"

"Why don't you make it a male thing?"

"Suit yourself. We won't be long. Why don't you make yourself useful and find us something to eat and drink?"

"You're so smooth," she replied sardonically.

Riverstone smiled and headed for the doorway. "A tall Big Gulp if you please, Ms. Mars."

Harlowe gave her a quick peck on the lips before he walked away. "Just do it."

Chapter Thirty-four

PRIORITIES

LEUCADIA STAYED BEHIND in the storage room while Harlowe and Riverstone left to check out the weapons. Walking toward the exit ramp, they were pleasantly surprised to find Ian heading in their direction down one of the long corridors a hundred yards away. Harlowe let out an ear-shattering whistle and waved him over. Ian quickly came running, like an excited kid who had found a cache of candy bars. His smelly body preceded him by ten feet. He still had on his own dirty, stinky clothes.

Harlowe confronted him first, his face wrinkling from the stench. "Where have you been, Wiz? We've been looking all over for you."

"I need to show you something, Harlowe," he said rather than answer the question. "You're not going to believe what I've found." Ian's thick glasses were so dirty it was a wonder he could see anything out of them.

"Dude, you're disgusting," Riverstone said, getting a sudden whiff of Ian's foul body odor.

Harlowe didn't care about Ian's personal hygiene right now. Their survival was the only thing on his mind. He held up the alien weapons for Ian to see.

"They look narly," Ian noted, eyeing the smaller weapon with interest.

"We need to check them out. Come with us," Harlowe urged.

Ian declined, but added, "I think I know what this place is."

"We know. It's a spaceship," Harlowe replied as if it was old news.

Ian deflated. "How do you know?"

"Lu told us."

"She's alive?"

"Humming right along," Riverstone replied.

Harlowe pointed across the foyer. "She's over there in the storage room. It's your kinda place, Wiz. Trust me, you'll feel like you've died and gone to heaven. Let me know what else you find," Harlowe said as he turned away.

But Ian was insistent. "Harlowe, this is important."

When Harlowe was on a mission, his focus was as intense as a laser beam. "It's all important, Wiz. What you have to say can wait." He held up the alien weapon again. "This is more important. Find Lu. She'll find you a bath and some fresh clothes. We won't be long. We'll meet you back here at the exit in half an hour."

"It will take us that long to get to the entrance," Riverstone pointed out.

Harlowe recalculated. "Yeah, double that. We'll play show-and-tell with you then." Ian was about to protest but Harlowe pointed emphatically. "Take a shower." He gave the undog a small nudge with his shoe. "Come on, Mowg, we'll need those ears."

Mowgi whirled around once and yelped twice.

Chapter Thirty-Five

NICE SHOT

At the bottom of the lighted ramp, Mowgi dutifully led Harlowe and Riverstone back across the long stretch of open space toward the slit in the rocks where they had first come into the cavern. They had gone merely a few dozen steps past the end of the ramp when Mowgi took off, leaving them disoriented in the soft, eerie glow of blue light under the ship. In the vast cavern the undog's yelps were a far less certain guide than the robob's glowing headband had been.

"We should have put a leash on Mowg," Harlowe said in a huff.

"You try putting it on him," Riverstone replied. He then suggested they return to the storage room and find some kind of light to take along before trying to go on. Harlowe reluctantly agreed. They really had no choice.

They were about to turn back when Harlowe accidentally brushed up against an object hanging along Riverstone's pants leg. "What's that?" Harlowe asked.

"Binocs. I found them in the big room when you and Lu were having one of your Doctor Phil moments," Riverstone explained.

Harlowe reached for the ocular device. "Let me see."

"You won't see squat," Riverstone warned.

As Riverstone was passing Harlowe the binoculars, they both heard a shuffling noise from somewhere inside the cavern. "Doesn't sound like the Mowg," Harlowe whispered.

"Sounds human," Riverstone replied softly.

Harlowe raised the binocs to his eyes. "Whoa!"

"Problem?"

"It's like daylight with these," Harlowe said. "I can see every-thing."

"Sweet, huh?" Riverstone said. Then, hearing the noise again, he asked, "Can you see who it is?"

Harlowe nodded. "Yeah, Heckle and Jeckle. Looks like they're lost."

Riverstone took the binocs back from Harlowe. He zeroed in on the two subjects and was immediately awed by the optics. "These are mine, Harlowe. You get your own. And that isn't Heckle and Jeckle, it's Tweety Bird and Foghorn," he laughed, referring to Simon Bolt and Monday Platter as they stumbled around in the dark.

"Now everyone's accounted for," Harlowe said, nudging River-stone toward them.

Riverstone suggested he and Harlowe would be better off if they left the two lost blind men on their own. Personally, Harlowe liked the idea, but he knew they'd need Platter. "If we run into more Daks, he knows how to handle a gun. Wasn't he a Navy Seal?"

"That's the rumor," Riverstone replied, unimpressed.

"Well, if that's true, he could teach us a lot," Harlowe pointed out.

"Maybe a rock will fall on Simon first," Riverstone joked.

Harlowe kept pushing Riverstone forward. "Be careful what you wish for."

When they came within a few yards of the two lost spelunkers, Harlowe thought it best to announce themselves.

"Hey, dudes, it's us. What's up? What are you two doing out here in the dark?"

"We're leaving this dump. Got a problem with that, Pylott?" Simon's voice replied indignantly.

"Shut up, Simon," Harlowe replied. "You're not going anywhere. Didn't you tell him what's out there, Platter?"

"I did," answered Monday's deep voice.

"Don't tell me to shut—" *Whack!* Simon's voice was suddenly cut off.

"Simon!" Monday called out. There was no immediate response, just the rustling of an undefinable movement. "Mr. Bolt, where are you?"

"Don't worry, I've got him, Platter," Harlowe replied.

Harlowe could feel Monday groping for Simon's body. "What happened to him? Did you hit him?"

"I didn't touch him," Harlowe said defensively. "He was talking, then he wasn't." He turned to Riverstone. "Did you see what happened to the movie star?"

Riverstone sighed with indifference. "Yeah, his head thumped against this curvy thing here." He rapped the post a couple of times with his knuckles to show them he wasn't kidding. "Stepped right into it and . . . *blammo.* Serious headache, brah."

"Bummer," Harlowe agreed. "I guess that's what did it then."

Monday was worried Simon might have a concussion. "We need to take him back inside."

Riverstone helped Harlowe maneuver Simon's unconscious body against the post. "Not just now. We do need your help, though," Harlowe said, and explained to the bodyguard why they wanted his expertise. "We're not sure what it is we have here. If we run into any more Dakadudes and their pets, we'll need something more than rocks to defend ourselves. You understand that, don't you, Platter? We shouldn't be long. Simon will be alright here, hugging the post, until we get back. He's not hurt that bad, is he, Riverstone?"

"Sleeping like a baby," Riverstone replied.

"Which way, pard?" Harlowe asked, groping for his friend.

Riverstone took a moment to scan. "Looks like there's a slight crack over that way. I can see light."

"Go for it," Harlowe said.

They heard a short yelp in the distance. "It's the Mowg," Riverstone said. "How'd he get there so fast?"

"He doesn't live in the same dimension we do," Harlowe said.

With surprising ease, Riverstone guided them through the low light to the crack where Mowgi was patiently waiting. He clipped the binocs to his pants leg again as they sidestepped around the projecting rock. To their relief, the warm glow of sun greeted them at the entrance.

Riverstone was about to step out as if he was on a Sunday afternoon stroll when Monday yanked him back inside the entrance. "Are you that stupid?"

Riverstone shot him a hard look, like they were about to come to blows, and Harlowe stepped between them. "He's right, pard. We don't know who's out there. We need to be careful. Give him the binocs," he told him as he pointed to Monday.

Riverstone hesitated. He didn't want to give up his prized new toy. Harlowe didn't have time for childish games, however. He snatched them from his friend's grasp and handed them to Monday. "Check for Daks, Platter."

One could see from his reaction that looking through the ancient lenses was an awe-inspiring experience for Monday. He looked back at Riverstone in disbelief.

"You're only borrowing them, pal. I want them back."

They could hear the clatter of rocks outside as Monday crawled through the opening. After a long moment he returned and announced, "Looks clear."

Harlowe glanced at Mowgi, who was vigilantly scanning the gorge with his dual radars. "How 'bout it, Mowg?" The undog yelped twice, his usual affirmative response.

As they crawled out into the open, Riverstone commented, "I wonder what they did with his arm."

Monday glared at them both. "What are you two talking about?"

Harlowe elbowed Riverstone in the side. "Nothing, Platter." He traded Riverstone's binocs for the alien rifle, shoving the weapon in Monday's hand. "Think about this."

Monday marveled at the weapon Harlowe handed to him.

"Where are you getting these cool toys?" Monday cooed.

"Don't worry. There's a big toy store full of them. Just give us an idea of what we have," Harlowe said.

Riverstone squinted into the late-afternoon sun. The air was chilly, but the sun's rays were soothing and warm on his face. It felt great to be outside again. It was the first time he had seen daylight since . . . He thought briefly. How many days ago was it? One, two, . . . six? He noticed that Monday was wearing a watch and asked him for the time.

"Four-thirty-four," Monday replied after glancing at his Rolex.

"And the day?" Riverstone added.

Monday shrugged. "Sunday."

Riverstone's mouth dropped open. He turned to Harlowe. "We've been out a week?"

"No, kid," Monday retorted. "It's Sunday. The day after yesterday."

Harlowe was in shock as well. "Check your watch again."

"This is a Rolex Submariner day-date chronograph. It keeps perfect time. Always. So why is that such a big deal to you two?" Monday asked.

Harlowe pointed at the alien rifle. "You're right. It isn't a big deal, Platter. Stay focused on the toy, and stay low," he cautioned.

Harlowe wondered if the time issue was worth pondering, or was it just one of the many parts of the puzzle in the bigger scheme of Mrs. M's ship and what he was supposed to do with it? How could he keep a promise that was way beyond his ability to keep?

Millawanda was massive. And she was all *inside* the mesa. It would take a hundred-ton thermonuclear device just to blow the side of the cliff wall away, he reckoned. Now where was he going to get that?

Sweet!

He breathed in a lungful of irksome air. Why was he even wasting brainpower on such a stupid idea? He sighed again, trying to rid his mind of such impossibilities. While Riverstone and Monday were busy with the device, he bent down and caressed a clump of blue flowers at his feet, grateful that Lu was healthy again. It was nice to revel in some happier thoughts than the promise he had made. For a brief interlude, he allowed the flowers' freshness to dispel his worry about their plight.

Monday rousted Harlowe from his reverie. Fairly confident that no one was around, Monday suggested they try the smaller pistol-like devices first instead of the rifle.

Harlowe removed his pistol from its holster and volunteered to take the first shot in case the weapon happened to explode. But when he took aim at a nearby rock and slowly squeezed the trigger, nothing happened. Disappointed, he looked the device over, trying to figure out the problem.

Monday quickly pushed the end of the gun away from his stomach. "Watch where you're aiming that," he warned, then reached over and pointed at a small button on the side of the frame. "You might want to turn it on first," he said with a smirk.

Riverstone kept shaking his head as Harlowe swallowed his pride and turned the switch to what he figured was "on." A dim blue light showed that indeed a charge was left in the power unit. Comfortable with that, he once again took careful aim at the rock and squeezed the trigger.

A tiny flash of blue light shot out from the end of the device and struck the rock, dead center. At first blush it appeared that nothing remarkable had taken place. The rock had not moved and it was still in one piece.

"Congratulations!" Riverstone said with a smirky grin. "You can hit a rock with a bolt of light."

"Check it out!" Harlowe directed, waving the end of the pistol. "It might have done something."

"You saw it. Nothing happened."

"Humor me," Harlowe ordered.

Riverstone stepped dubiously toward the rock. Before he had gone halfway, he saw something that completely wiped the doubt from his face: a small hole in the rock. When he bent down to look at it, it was like peering through the shiny barrel of a twenty-two-caliber pistol, without the grooves. The tiny flash of light had not only burned a hole in the rock but also clear through a foot of solid sandstone!

Wow! It was a real working weapon after all.

Harlowe nodded with cool satisfaction as he examined the rock Riverstone brought back. "One down, one to go."

"This?" Monday asked, holding up the alien rifle.

Harlowe motioned for him to go ahead and try the rifle. "Go for it, Platter."

Monday carefully checked the switch, making sure the small blue light was activated, before he brought the weapon to his shoulder. After a quick scan of the gorge to find a target, he said, "See that lone tree along the ridgeline there? Keep your eye on the third branch down."

"Oh, right, deadeye," Riverstone scoffed. "That's a thousand-yard shot. Way out of range, dude. Try something you know you can hit, Platter, like the side of that cliff," he suggested, pointing to a nearby rock wall.

Monday smiled with arrogant confidence as he turned back to the ridgeline. "I was the best shot in my squad. If this is any kind of weapon at all, that branch is history." He laid his cheek along the stock and sighted along the barrel. He pressed another small button on the side of the stock. A scope appeared from inside the body of the rifle and fixed itself into place. The scope itself was rather small and unimpressive, but like the binoculars, its optical abilities were superb. It worked equally well in shadow, compensating for light and darkness. Monday stated he could see a butterfly taking a leak on the branch and laughed at the thought of shooting the branch out from under him. "This should really surprise."

Monday pulled the trigger and fired. The bolt of intense blue light flashed across the gorge in the blink of an eye. The thundering sound of a tremendous explosion was just rolling back across the gorge when Harlowe found his voice. "Well . . ." he said, trying to breathe, "I think the butterfly's surprised, Platter."

Riverstone was beyond breathing. He lowered his binocs and just stared in stunned silence. The bolt of energy had not only vaporized the tree, it had continued on across the wide-open desert and completely blown off the top one hundred feet of the snow-covered mountain ten miles away . . . all in an instant!

Monday had pointed the muzzle of the rifle skyward after taking the first shot. Forgetting about what he held in his hand and how easily he had pulled the trigger before, he accidentally fired the weapon again. This time, the rifle's blast struck the stratified rock overhang directly above their heads, cutting through the cliff wall.

Overhead, a great slice began to tear away from the escarpment. They heard the breaking rock and froze. Suddenly, a small part of the cliff slammed next to them, jolting the earth and causing Monday to drop the rifle. The gorge felt like it was collapsing, folding in all around them.

Riverstone looked up and saw the slice pulling away from the cliff face. "COME ON!" he screamed above the roar of the crumbling earth. Monday reached for the rifle.

"FORGET IT!" Harlowe shouted. Mowgi blinked back inside the slit as more fragments thunderously dropped down three thousand feet, without resistance, to the dry riverbed below, breaking trees like matchsticks along the way.

But the slice . . .

Larger than a house, the slice kept coming—plummeting, racing downward. No power on Earth could stop it!

Harlowe grabbed the back of Monday's shirt as Riverstone dove for the crack. The three disappeared into the cavern as, a heartbeat later, a hundred thousand tons of rock slammed past the crack, sending a hurricane-force wind roaring to the other side of the gorge and leveling trees in its wake.

Chapter Thirty-Six

GENERAL GUNN

*P*OISED AND COMPETENT in his desert camouflage, Brigadier General Theodore "Ted" Gunn vaulted out of the open cargo bay of the UH-60L Black Hawk helicopter before it had completely touched down near the edge of a tall desert escarpment. He had no apparent fear of the deadly whirling blades thump-thump-thumping just inches above his head. He strode upright through the violent cloud of copper dust on a resolute path toward the massive cut in the cliff wall. Still seated in the bay, his assistants, Captain Ed Walker and Second Lieutenant Robert Poole, waited for the helicopter to fully settle before they followed in the general's footsteps.

When General Gunn was fifty yards from a bright yellow barrier, the three guards who were stationed at the edge of the barrier lifted their rifles and snapped rigidly to attention.

"At ease, men," the general's baritone voice resonated with absolute authority. In sharp, disciplined movements, the guards lowered their weapons, following the command. The way their commander held his swagger stick firmly in his right hand and positioned his knotted knuckles on his hips just above his white-handled Colt semiautomatic pistol left no doubt in their minds that he was a man well aware of his rank and the forces that had brought him to this place.

From behind his dark, gold-trimmed Ray-Bans, the general surveyed the high plateau that seemed to extend forever. The desert mountain in the distance caught his attention. It jutted upward at the edge of the plateau, and its stunted peak was shrouded by rising smoke and vapor. The general knew from the recent reconnaissance photographs that the top one hundred feet of its rocky peak had been inexplicably blown away like the scores of dead paramilitary he had witnessed earlier in the box canyon a few miles northeast of their position. *Slaughtered!* He winced. *What happened? Why? Sonava . . . How is this all connected?*

Gunn shifted his attention as a blast of heated wind blew against his face. The hot air was flowing upward from a fifty-feet-wide by two-hundred-feet-long vertical cut into the face of the cliff. Scientists and soldiers alike were calling this alteration the "slice." The glazed rock surface was still so hot it glowed in the dim morning light.

Marveling at the cut's mirror-like finish, the general glimpsed the sun's reflection on the polished surface. From the angle of the cut and the force he knew was necessary to make such a cut, he had little doubt that both unnatural alterations to the desert landscape were major threats to the nation's security.

The general tapped his swagger stick lightly on the yellow barrier, surveying all the activity going on within the contamination zones. Along the opposite ridge and in the gorge his men were busily combing the desert for any evidence that would explain the recent destruction. Widely dispersed among his troops were white-shirted scientists. They swept their handheld instruments back and forth, looking for objects human eyes could not see. When he finished his visual survey, Gunn straightened and said to the two aides who were just coming to his side, "Beautiful, gentlemen. Simply beautiful."

Captain Walker and Lieutenant Poole exchanged quick, questioning glances.

"General?" the captain responded, his heavy dark eyebrows knotting with confusion.

"The desert, captain; it's beautiful."

"Yes, sir. Very beautiful, general."

"Who's trying to kill it?"

"I don't know, sir," Walker responded. He checked his clipboard before he added, "It's a crying shame."

The general smelled the sweet dryness of the air. His large aquiline nose, with its bristled hairs sticking out of his nostrils, whistled faintly with the rush of incoming air. "You're right it's a shame. We're going to get the SOBs who did this."

"Yes, sir!" both officers snapped in unison.

General Gunn transferred his swagger stick to his left hand and pointed down. "What's that sweet smell coming from, lieutenant? Burned wildflowers? You were big on that stuff in college, weren't you?"

Lieutenant Poole had received his commission just three and a half months prior. He snapped to, eager to please. "Yes, sir. I minored in botany, general."

The general's stoic expression, however, told the lieutenant in no uncertain terms to cut to the chase. This was not a Boy Scout wilderness adventure they were on. "It appears to be a combination, sir." He bent down and picked a blue-petaled blossom. "The sweet odor is a mixture of glassified rock and these, general," he said, handing the general a radiant blue flower to inspect.

General Gunn took the bud and scrutinized it briefly. This particular specimen had a ten-inch-long midnight blue stem with brilliant royal blue petals. An unusual color, he thought, considering most plants were green. The three petals spread out around a bright inner whorl of a blue, scented receptacle. He stuck the petals under his nose. "What's it called? Smells like some fancy De La Renta bath oil."

"Unknown, sir. Reports show it as unclassified."

"Unclassified?" the general growled. "You mean to tell me that with as many campers and desert ATV'ers who come kicking up dust out here this is the first time anyone's set eyes on this plant?"

"According to the reports, that's correct, sir."

General Gunn tapped the top of the lieutenant's clipboard with his swagger stick. "That's BS! You send that frickin' plant to Flag, Tucson, UCLA's botanical gardens, frickin' Communist China, I don't care. But someone's got to know what that plant is. Is that understood, lieutenant? I want to know what this plant is, stat!" He stuck the flower under Poole's nose. "This flower may or may not have anything to do with why we're out here, but if we're going to start figuring out about the unknown havoc that's going on out here, we'd better start by classifying this sweet-smelling body wash. Understood, Poole?"

The lieutenant clicked to attention. "Yessir!"

Just then several hunks of rock caught the general's eye when they came loose, bounced on the mirrored finish of the slice, and fell into the gorge.

"Did you feel that, captain?"

"Yes, sir."

"Like someone dropped a heavy weight on the floor," Poole added.

General Gunn glanced at his Black Hawk. The chopper's blades were slowly coming to a stop. "Better warn the men below about the instability up here, captain."

"Yes, sir."

The general then ordered his entourage back to the Black Hawk. Halfway back, a sergeant from the chopper ran up to Captain Walker and handed him a small piece of paper. Not missing a step, the captain read the memo and informed the general that Charlie company had more info on two of the incinerated cars in the box canyon. "They're separate events, sir. The crime scene boys put them twelve hours apart."

"Any bodies?"

"No, sir. None in the kill zone connected to either vehicle."

General Gunn responded with a silent nod and stepped under the spinning blades of the chopper, giving a one-fingered whirl signal to the pilot.

"Put someone on those two vehicles, captain. Let's find out who they belong to."

"Yes, sir!"

Over the roar of the twin turbos, Captain Walker nodded at Lieutenant Poole, who acknowledged the command by putting on his radio headgear and relaying the general's orders to someone on the other end. He would have a preliminary report on the automobiles by the time they returned to base camp.

General Gunn directed his pilot to fly over to the leveled mountaintop for a closer look. Circling close to the peak, they realized it wasn't smoke they had seen rising from the peak so many miles away; it was steam from nearly thirteen feet of snowpack, rising like a hot thermal vent. Below the steam, water ran down the steep slopes in great sheets, creating waterfalls and rivers and flash floods where before there had been only the slow drips of normal runoff. Through the heated mist, the flattened peak appeared to be crystalline and slick like the slice.

Gunn concentrated on the many similarities between the slice and the peak, connecting the same sweet odor with both places. Neither location had the scent of cordite or any other kind of explosive he was familiar with. The flowery scent had a strange uniqueness all its own. He had never known any weapon or explosive that left such a provocative residue after its use.

"Take her down," the general ordered.

"Negative, sir. The recon team says the rock is too hot to walk on without special gear."

"Headquarters, then," shouted General Gunn to the pilot, and the chopper nosed down, taking off across the plateau.

Chapter Thirty-Seven

HEADACHES

At FIVE MINUTES past 1300 hours, ten miles west of the flattened mountain, Richard Spicer felt a sudden movement in the ground. The short, carefree reserve airman first class was on his way to the command tent with a packet of classified materials and photographs for General Gunn. The jolt was short and abrupt, like a heavy door slamming shut. Spicer knew it was the white-shirted scientists involved in another one of their tests. He waited momentarily, anticipating further unusual motions or sounds, before he moved on toward the general's tent. Along the way an officer complained loudly about his spilled coffee while another airman cussed about a phone that was out of order.

As soon as he stepped through the flap of the general's tent, Spicer handed the closed packet to Sergeant Raymond Gunderson. The sergeant checked the packet over, making sure the proper descriptions were clearly marked before he handed it to Lieutenant Poole. Poole then followed the proper military chain of command and gave the packet to Captain Walker. The captain briefly examined the contents, making sure they were in order, and then presented the packet to General Gunn.

The general opened the mustard-tinted envelope and removed six 8-by-10 colored photos from the packet. He carefully scrutinized the glossy photos of the slice and the sheered-off mountaintop, and then he took a magnifying glass from a drawer to get an even closer look. "Our suspicions appear correct, gentlemen. These cuts were caused by the same source. Look at how they match."

"It doesn't surprise me," the captain replied after examining the photos. "The white-shirts have said all along that it was some type of light amplification device."

"A laser?" the general responded, almost laughing. "Impossible, all the lasers on Earth couldn't cut through rock like that. Who are they trying to kid, captain?"

"I don't know, sir. Until they know otherwise, they're sticking with the laser theory." General Gunn laid the photos on the table and fingered his way through the rest of the packet's contents while the captain stood by watching silently. There was a folding spoon, a small box of matches, and a wafer-thin chrome metal circle with a slit down the center.

"Is this from that VW bug?" the general asked.

"Yes, sir. What's left of it."

"Anything on the other vehicle?"

"No, sir. Clean. But we got the plates. California tags on both the bug and the Aston Martin. The Martin belongs to that movie star, Simon Bolt."

"Bolt? Who's he?"

"A very big star, sir. You haven't seen any of his *Galaxy* movies?" the lieutenant asked, amazed.

"I don't have time for that trash, lieutenant." He studied the color photos of the burned-out automobiles. "Bolt's body in that?"

"No sir. No one was in either car," the captain replied.

"How much does a car like that cost?" the general asked, pointing at the Aston Martin.

Poole didn't know, but Captain Walker gave it his best guess. "I'd say a couple hundred thousand plus, general."

General Gunn whistled. "Mighty expensive to be tooling around in the desert, wouldn't you say?" They both nodded their agreement. "So why would a movie star's car be out in the desert?" he mused. "Is the star missing?"

"No reports, sir," Walker replied.

Gunn pressed his lips together. "I suppose we'll find out quick enough if he is."

The general began to examine the rest of the photographs from the packet. There were two close-ups of the most grotesque beasts she had seen: in one, a large animal head had been separated from its body. "By all that's holy! These are some ugly SOBs" he exclaimed, his face torqued with disgust. "This some kind of a practical joke, captain? Did you get this off the Internet dorking around last night?"

"Ah, no, sir," Captain Walker replied. "It's real. The men had a heck of a time finding body bags large enough to transport them."

"What are they?"

"Unidentified, general."

Gunn tossed the photos to the lieutenant. "More homework, Poole."

"Yessir."

The general turned to the packet contents once more. "What in the world is this, captain?" he said with frustration in his voice.

Captain Walker grinned. "It's one of those backpacking gizmos for drinking water, general." He picked up the round wafer and by pressing in the middle with his thumb, it popped open to form a small conical cup.

"What's it have to do with the rest of these things, captain?"

The captain searched the handwritten data sheets that came with the packet and found the answer. "It says here that it was found in a jacket."

"So where's the jacket, captain?" the general snarled. "Why don't I see it on my desk?"

Captain Walker quickly reached for his field phone to contact the sergeant on duty. After several attempts, it was clear that the phones were still unworkable. "General, the phones are out. All I get is static."

General Gunn grabbed the phone from the captain's hand. "I just talked to Nellis a minute ago. They were working fine." He adjusted several dials and checked the power pack before conceding, "You're right, captain." Then, for no apparent reason, the phone cleared.

"They've had phone issues all day, general," Lieutenant Poole remarked.

At that moment there was a nervous call at the tent flap. Airman Spicer was asking permission to enter.

"Come in, son," Gunn ordered, and took the bundle from Spicer's hand.

Spicer explained that the reason the general had not received the articles earlier was that they were in decontamination. Captain Walker dismissed Spicer while the general untied the bundle and began to scrutinize the two articles of burned clothing. Inside the jacket, he discovered the handwritten letters W I Z on the back of the label. Searching further, he pulled out a gooey blue wrapper that was stuck inside the breast pocket. The white letters on the wrapper read "Mars Bar," and the chocolate residue proved it.

The general then turned his attention to a pair of stonewashed denims as he cleaned his fingers with a paper towel. The denims were in better shape than the jacket. He saw nothing unusual about the pants other than the odd contrast in size: the small waist of a boy with the long legs of a grown man. He searched the pockets and found a quarter, three pennies, and a dime.

He put the crusty denims in a box below the table. "That's it?"

"That's all they've found thus far, general," Captain Walker replied, bending down to pick up a piece of paper from the floor. "The men will have the area between the car and the gorge covered completely by tomorrow. Standing orders, sir, anything found gets to your desk pronto."

"What is that?" Gunn asked, referring to the small square of folded paper.

"It must have fallen out of the jacket, sir."

General Gunn took the square and pulled it apart, noticing some writing on the end of it. He pulled it apart again, then again, and again. After the tenth unfolding, the general was beginning to think it was some kind of magician's silk handkerchief trick. Finally, when the square was completely unfolded and laid out on the table, the officers were awestruck by the precise contour lines and symbols they saw projecting up from the drawing.

"Impressive, captain. How's that done?" the general asked.

Captain Walker had no idea.

"It looks like a detailed photo map of this area," Gunn observed. He took a pair of scissors from his desk and continued talking. "A mighty good one too. Look at that detail. That's field HQ right there," he added, pointing to the flat, red sandstone canyon five miles from the slice.

While the general was trying to cut a piece of the fabric with his scissors, the captain studied the map with a magnifying glass.

"It's similar to a holograph, general. Somehow the projection is refracted off the fabric into a three-dimensional form. And if I'm not mistaken, it's done in real time. Amazing."

The general was only half-listening to his aide. "Interesting." As much as he tried to cut off a small piece of the material, he couldn't do it. The tissue-like fabric was much more durable than it appeared.

Lieutenant Poole pointed to the corner of the fabric that was draped over the table's edge. "Look at that, general. It's a drawing of the wildflower."

Gunn turned to him, amused. "Well now, Poole, your education is paying off." He slid the entire piece onto the table so that nothing was obscured. He touched the flower at the lower corner of the map with his finger. When he did, the image quickly faded and was replaced by another image.

The three officers exchanged glances of disbelief.

"Captain?"

The captain hesitated. Without his notes he was afraid to venture an opinion. "I'm not sure."

"Poole?"

The lieutenant studied the image briefly. "A map of a star system, I believe, sir."

"Ours?"

Poole admired the tiny detailed drawing of each of the twelve planets. "Well, that one looks like Saturn, and Jupiter, Earth, and Mars are in their proper placements as well. But the planet between Earth and Mars, well . . . I've never seen that one before. And I don't recognize the outer three planets. It's unlikely the diagram is correct; I see a lot of errors here, sir."

At that moment General Gunn's clerk stepped into the headquarters tent with more information on the abandoned Volkswagen. "We got the name on those California plates, general." Sergeant Gunderson looked down at the piece of paper in his hand to make sure he read the name properly. "A Harlowe Pylott, sir." He handed Gunn the paper and added, "He's a senior high school kid from Lakewood, California."

"Lakewood? Where in Sam Hell is Lakewood?" the general barked. He looked around the room at a group of blank faces. "Well, doesn't anyone know where that city is?"

Guesses ranged from a suburb of San Francisco to just across the border from Tijuana, Mexico. Gunn reread the memo his clerk had given him, and for the first time since he had arrived in southern Utah, it looked as though some clues were starting to fall into place.

"Alright," he said, turning to the captain, "I want to know a ton more about this kid, stat! Pinpoint Lakewood. If we go knocking on doors, I want us to be in the right neighborhood, for heaven's sake." Heads nodded. "Get a full bio on him. What he likes. What he doesn't like. The girl he's dating. In two hours, captain, I want to know even what kind of toilet paper he uses to wipe that skull full of mush."

"On it, general."

Gunn was fascinated by the holographic visions as he continued to bark orders. "Get the white-coats on this matrix. Find out how this thing works. And find out where the name Sook comes from."

Poole picked up the map but didn't bother to fold it. "Yessir!"

As Sergeant Gunderson was about to leave, the general stopped him. "Gunny, get me the supply sergeant here on the double. I want these field phones checked out, stat. I don't care if he has to walk back to Nellis in the frickin' heat, I want communications without interruptions! Is that understood?"

"Yes, sir, general!" Gunderson snapped, and bolted out the tent flap.

Chapter Thirty-Eight

BREAK OUT

THE LIGHTS INSIDE the general's tent flickered briefly, winked out, then came back on again for the umpteenth time.

"Frickin' lights!" General Gunn growled angrily. The phones were no better. Since 1330 hours, anything that had a power source was affected, giving everyone fits.

Gunn and his staff were discussing the results of the day's fact finding with Drs. Robert Zagorsky, Thomas Shaffer, Ed McCarty, and Carole Rodale. The four JPL astrophysicists had flown to the site in the late afternoon from California. All of them had the nation's highest Top Secret clearance. They had been in the field since their arrival, directing Gunn's men and other scientists in the search for collectable evidence.

The rock samples, photos, unusual cloth map, and a two-inch stack of reports on the readings were all spread out on a white table-cloth. None of the items could account for the cause of either incident under investigation, except for the map, which both Zagorsky and Shaffer spent two hours studying.

Despite the interruption, Zagorsky continued the discussion. "Three days ago, General Gunn, Doctor Shaffer and Doctor McCarty discovered an unusual formation one degree, five seconds of arc in Virgo—"

"Doctor, please," the general interrupted, "come back to Earth for us ignorant, blood-and-gut types. Five seconds into a virgin means only one thing to me, and that's something I'm not about to discuss with a JPL scientist."

Zagorsky scowled at the general's crudeness but apologized anyway. He pointed to the map while explaining, "Near Saturn's orbital plane they discovered a formation of incoming spacecraft." The general grunted with disbelief.

"Doctor Rodale, could you hand me the photo plates from my bag, please?" Zagorsky asked.

Rodale retrieved the photos from an old leather satchel and passed them across the table. "These plates, general, are the recent photo enhancements of our visitors. As you can see, they are indeed spacecraft from an unknown origin."

The general studied the black-on-white plates with the seasoned eye of a twenty-five-year veteran who knew every type of military and civilian aircraft in use. The three ships were flying together in a tight formation. Each was long and slender, with stubby wings and giant drive extensions jutting out from their center fuselage. It was impossible to tell without further close-up enhancements, but on the end of their stubby wings were platforms that Zagorsky considered to be sensory and data-recovery equipment. "Most likely navigational instrumentation as well," he added.

"Navigation? That's bull. Those are gun turrets, doctor!" the general stated, drawing on his years of experience. "Defcon Three is nonsense." Captain Walker stepped forward, taking the imperative nod from the general. "We're going full Defcon One alert status immediately."

Captain Walker's unspoken marching orders were clear: head straight to the communications room and inform the Pentagon and the Joint Chiefs of Staff that, for the first time in the nation's history, General Gunn was ordering the entire U.S. military to maximum readiness.

"I agree that we can't take a chance, general," Rodale broke in. "This is arguably the single most important event in human history. We must be absolutely careful to control all information. The moment the public discovers there is incontrovertible proof that we are not alone . . . Well, the truth is, we don't know how the public will take this. There could be worldwide panic."

"That's right, doctor," the general agreed. "Precautions of the highest order should be taken immediately."

"We are not prepared to make any factual statements at this time as to the aliens' intent," Zagorsky noted. "We should not assume that it is a hostile invasion."

General Gunn looked up. "Don't be naive, doctor. We must presume all alien contact is hostile until proven otherwise. To act in any other capacity is foolish. These beings have traveled a pretty fair piece to get here using a technology that arguably we won't have for centuries. The military goes to Defcon One and that's final."

Everyone in the room seemed to be on board except Tom Shaffer.

The general then picked up a glassified rock fragment and paced. "And this is why all of you scientists are here? You believe the events here in the desert could be related, am I correct?" he asked, holding up the specimen.

"It's a possibility, General Gunn," McCarty replied.

"A *possibility?*"

"Ah, I mean, not yet, sir. There's no evidence to support the relationship. But the activity here is so unusual and coincidental, we believe it is possible."

"You know what I feel like, gentlemen—and lady?" No one answered. "Like a dang ninety-pound weakling. These guys are wrecking my neighborhood and I can't do one thing about it."

The general strolled thoughtfully to the far end of the tent before he turned back slowly. "Do we have an ETA on their arrival?"

"We've lost them," McCarty volunteered. "There's been no sign of them for ten hours, general."

"Terrific. And what about contact? Have they tried to talk to us?"

"No contact as yet, General Gunn," Rodale replied.

The general held the glassified rock up to the light, studying it like a jeweler would a precious stone.

Shaffer finally spoke up. "I don't believe it's as bad as it seems. My findings show random events. There was nothing logical about the destruction here. Both events could have been mishaps."

"Maybe in your world there are mishaps, doctor, but in my world I can't take that chance," asserted the general. "My gut says you're wrong. Excuse my ignorance, but why would I want to contact you if I were going to blow you to kingdom come?"

Shaffer stood his ground. "For what purpose, general? Why travel light-years to invade a little blue planet on the outskirts of the galaxy? It doesn't make sense. Everything on this planet is abundant among the stars. Why risk such an enterprise?"

The general came back to the table and placed the rock near the unclassified blue flower. "That's obvious, isn't it? We've got something they want," he stated. "So what is it?" His concentration then drifted back to the flower. After going all day without water, the specimen had not withered. He picked it up and took a whiff of its sweet, alluring bouquet. "Maybe it's this, for all we know," he added.

No one in the room took the general seriously except Carole Rodale. She wasn't laughing.

Momentarily lost in strategic thought, the general then turned to Captain Walker and asked, "What did you find on that word *Sook*, captain? Does it have a meaning?"

The captain shuffled through his notes. "Well, general, the only connection we've been able to come up with is that Sook is the name of a Korean Medal of Honor soldier's wife . . . Harold Mars, sir."

"Mars? Harold Mars the billionaire?" The general's face twisted with surprise, recalling with vivid admiration the name of the Korean War's most decorated hero. "He was a one-man army."

"Yes, sir."

General Gunn picked up the matrix. "He's still alive?"

"It seems so, general. Owns a lot of property around here. We're on his land right now. He even owns a number of the big hotels in the world. Harry's in Las Vegas is his most famous."

General Gunn's eyebrows rose. "He's *that* Harry?"

"That's him, sir."

"Where is he now?"

"Not sure, general. It seems there was a shootout at his beachside mansion in Newport Beach. Destroyed most of the house, but no one was found on the property. The police can't explain it, sir."

"Swell." The general's voice was heavy with sarcasm. "That clears up a lot of mishaps for me." He then picked up the map, addressing Doctor Zagorsky. "Any of your people come up with an explanation for this?"

Zagorsky took the matrix and laid it flat on the table. "We have reason to believe this device was produced on another planet."

The general's eyes locked on Zagorsky's. The meaning was clear. He'd better have solid evidence to go down this path or he'd find himself baiting fishing hooks in Nome, Alaska.

Zagorsky lightly touched the flower on the matrix and changed the topography holographs of canyons to the spheroid shapes orbiting around a bright yellow sun. "First, these outer satellites have yet to be discovered. From the way they are depicted here, I would say it was made, not by someone observing these bodies from Earth, but by someone coming into our system. An extraterrestrial navigator, let's say. And, I might add, general, all that we know about the inner planets is shown exactly as it should be, except for the planet here between Earth and Mars. That planet doesn't belong there. Other than that, there are no discrepancies."

He guided the discussion by drawing his finger along the matrix. "Many of these asteroids have yet to be found. And look here, general," he said, pointing to the far edge of the map beyond what Lieutenant Poole had speculated was the twelfth planet. "This sphere is not a planet. We think this map is showing us Nemesis."

"Nemesis?" General Gunn repeated.

"Simply stated, it's our sun's companion star. Many believe it is responsible for major catastrophic destruction throughout Earth's history. Take the dinosaurs' extinction, for example—"

The general held up his hand. "I don't want a history lesson, doctor. Just tell me what we're dealing with right now. If this is legit, then we're dealing with aliens already living on Earth?"

"Yes. That would be a fair conclusion, general," Zagorsky replied.

"That's unbelievable, doctor—"

"There is no other explanation, General Gunn. This kind of technology does not exist today." Zagorsky nodded. "Look at the image." He traced his finger along the thin blue line that went horizontally across the flat symbol at the top. "This is the power source. What you see is a display of low-current superconductivity that has been achieved only through supercooling metal-oxide ceramics when they are immersed in liquid nitrogen. Minus 273 degrees Kelvin, general, and they've done it at room temperature. Not only that, they've put it into a form that is so tough and malleable . . ."

The doctor stopped, realizing a picture was worth a thousand words. "Let me show you the result of a little experiment we did this afternoon, general." Zagorsky placed a flat piece of shiny metal the size of a dollar on the table. "This *was* a forty-five-caliber bullet that was shot at the projection. The fabric never even fluttered when the bullet struck. Impressive, eh, general?"

General Gunn was indeed impressed, and stared at the cloth with renewed respect. Maybe he couldn't understand how it worked, but he could understand what it would mean for one of his airmen going into battle wearing a uniform lined with this material. He may glow like a Christmas tree, he thought with a tinge of flippancy, but he would be indestructible.

"Can we reverse engineer it?" the general asked.

"No, sir," McCarty replied, touching the cloth. "It has properties we couldn't begin to explain because we don't know ourselves. But from our analysis thus far, we do know its elemental makeup has no earthly origin."

In order to relieve some of the confusion in the room, Shaffer thought of another way to further clarify some of their findings. "If you would allow me, Ed," he said politely, "I'd like to show the general something else."

Shaffer selected two photographs and placed them in front of the general just as the lights above the table began to flicker. After a short moment, the lights returned to a steady glow. Then a tray of empty water glasses on the table clanked together for no apparent reason. Heedless of the distractions, Shaffer went on with his explanation. "General, the first photograph here is—"

"Yes, yes, I understand these two photos are similar. I can see that," General Gunn interrupted, wanting to get to the bottom of things. "But what I want to know is, what kind of power are we dealing with here? Can we fight it if we have to?"

Shaffer's lips pursed as he shook his head, staring at the photos. "No."

Gunn's face grew flushed as he stared out beyond the small crowd. The lights flickered again. Two seconds later, the predictable small tremor was felt, and then all was normal again.

"A weapon of this power could vaporize tanks, aircraft, entire ships at sea, whole armies for that matter," Shaffer said to the room, "and from as far away as the moon."

Just then, Sergeant Gunderson requested permission to enter the general's tent.

"Alright, Gunny, come in," the general ordered.

Gunderson came into the tent and handed Doctor Zagorsky a slip of notepaper, which he read with a wrinkled brow. "It appears, General Gunn, that it's not your equipment that has been causing the electrical interruptions. Our instruments are picking up unexplained energy fluctuations in the area."

"Powell is a hundred miles away," Lieutenant Poole pointed out.

"No, it's not the dam, lieutenant. It's here. Our Las Vegas and Flagstaff stations have triangulated the source to . . .," the doctor rechecked his figures, "three-point-seven miles southwest of field headquarters, general."

"The gorge," someone mumbled.

"Here?" Gunn repeated. "Why wasn't I told about this, doctor?"

"Readings were not confirmed until now, general," Zagorsky answered, laying the note on the table.

"You mean whatever it is, is still out there?"

"Appears so, general. And it's quite active too."

General Gunn turned to Captain Walker. "Better get General Owens at the Pentagon, captain. Stat!"

The captain snapped to attention and double-timed it out the door.

"The energy appears to be constantly increasing, like a power source coming alive," Zagorsky added.

"Coming alive?"

"Yes, and exponentially, I might add."

"Frickin' mishaps," the general groaned.

The lights went off, cutting short Gunn's response. After a moment the table shook and the lights came back on.

"The power fluctuations are becoming more frequent, general." The lights flickered again and the tent shook. Zagorsky tried to continue. "As I was saying . . ." The lights went out again and the shaking became stronger. Everyone in the room grew anxious when the lights failed to come back on.

Suddenly, a gigantic explosion erupted from a long distance away. Like slow-moving thunder, the sound rolled across the plateau, jolting five hundred soldiers and scientists out of their tents and into the night. Orders rang out that the base camp was under attack.

In the general's headquarters tent the table with the rocks and papers collapsed. Support wires strained to keep the tent from falling in on itself and then snapped. As General Gunn and the rest of the meeting participants struggled out from beneath the collapsing tent, a powerful gust of wind slammed it. The force was so strong that it blew down what was left of the unstable rigging and dislodged the lighter equipment that was loose on the ground. Everyone hit the deck. They covered their faces to protect themselves from the flying debris, but as suddenly as the wind appeared, it stopped.

"Where did that come from?" the general barked. Then, before he started to shout orders and make more commands, an airman came running toward the group of bewildered officers and scientists.

"General, sir!" Airman Spicer yelled above the confusion. Holding his rifle in one hand, he tried desperately to keep his helmet on his head with the other. Terrified and out of breath, he cried out again, "Sir! I saw it, sir!"

General Gunn looked him straight in the eye and said, "Hold on, son, calm down and tell me what you saw."

Still out of breath, Spicer gulped and said, pointing his rifle skyward, "Sir, something overhead, sir!"

"At ease, airman. What was it?"

"I don't know exactly, sir. It was an object just drifting through," Spicer said.

The general turned quickly to Captain Walker. "I didn't hear any aircraft, did you, captain?"

Spicer was too upset to wait for Captain Walker's response. He quickly defended his sighting. "I know, sir, but I saw it. It went right over us." General Gunn and Captain Walker glanced at each other in disbelief. "The wind, sir, the wind. You must have felt it. Right after the craft went by."

Zagorsky broke in with a composed voice. "Which direction was it headed, son?"

Spicer pointed his rifle westward, toward the flattened mountain-top still glowing faintly on the dark horizon. "That way, sir!"

They all turned at once and saw an immense gold and bluish object flying slow and low away from the camp in an almost drunken manner. It was round and very flat, as though Hercules had tossed a golden discus into the night. Then someone pointed toward the east at a bright fiery glow on the horizon.

At that moment an excited Lieutenant Poole ran up to General Gunn and said he had a report from the guards above the escarp-ment. The lieutenant was so out of breath and spoke so fast, it took the general's commanding voice to calm him down long enough for him to string together a clear phrase. When the lieutenant found his composure, he said that the round flat object had exploded out of the escarpment wall. During the entire time, Gunn never took his eyes off the slow-moving object as it headed toward what looked like a collision course with the flattened peak.

Before the general could order any countermeasures, someone yelled above all the commotion, "LOOK! IT'S GOING TO HIT THE MOUNTAIN!"

Chapter Thirty-Nine

FIRST SOLO FLIGHT

"PULL UP, HARLOWE!" Riverstone shouted. He remembered a flash of blue light, a sudden vibration, a muffled explosion, and then fire everywhere. After that, all was chaos. When he opened his eyes again, the fire was gone. But in its place a mountaintop seemed to pop up out of nowhere.

"PULL UP!" he shouted again.

"Left, Harlowe," Ian instructed calmly. "Slide your finger left and slightly down, just like we did in the simulation."

"I AM!" Harlowe shouted back.

Harlowe wrenched his back into a tremendous arch, as though he alone was trying to lift the ship above the peak with one Herculean effort. The alien guidance controls, however, did not respond that easily.

The alien ship had two side panels on either side of the center control chair—Harlowe's chair—that flipped into place when he sat down. On each of these panels were three stationary crystalline bars. When Harlowe touched them in a certain way, he could direct the craft to go right or left, to go up or down, or to turn around on its axis while still going forward. Ian thought Harlowe could even make the ship come to a dead stop while floating in the air if he touched the bars in the proper way, the way the ship had shown them.

But three hours of intensive training hadn't been enough time to completely learn what it took to fly a fifteen-thousand-year-old ship built for the stars. So no matter how much Harlowe used body English to lift the ship above the oncoming mountain, the ship refused to raise one inch until Harlowe's fingers touched the bars correctly and in such a manner as to *make* it pull up!

"Come on," Harlowe pleaded with the ship. "Up, Millie, up!"

* * *

Their introduction to Millie had come when the three of them woke up in the ship's dispensary just hours after the cave-in. Robob attendants moved around the medical tables with their crystalline balls, taking readings, administering painless injections, and then disappearing back into the wall when everyone was awake and functioning.

No one could believe they had actually survived.

Harlowe stared at Monday. "You okay?"

"Yeah," wheezed Monday. He was still disoriented and confused.

"What happened?" Riverstone asked. "The last thing I remember was Platter going nuclear with the rifle." Turning to Monday, he added, "Great shooting, toad. Did you get your freakin' butterfly, dude?"

"Listen," Monday said defensively, "I didn't pull the trigger."

"Someone did," Riverstone sneered. He wasn't in a good frame of mind. "You were the only one holding the rifle, Platter. I thought you knew all about military weapons." Riverstone didn't let up. "You just filleted a mountaintop and sealed the entrance to the cave, all in ten seconds. Nice work, brah."

"Knock it off, Riverstone. What's done is done," Harlowe said. "We have to think of what to do next."

Ian, Leucadia, and Simon Bolt came into the room. Simon had a large, purple goose egg over his left eye.

Riverstone looked at Simon and sighed heavily, turning away. "Just when I thought things were getting better, he walks in right on cue."

Leucadia came to Harlowe's side and kissed him. "We thought you were . . ." She trailed off, looking him over for injuries.

Harlowe stopped her. "We had problems."

She looked at Monday, then Riverstone, with her bright questioning eyes. Riverstone understood her curiosity and replied without being asked, "The weapons worked."

"I don't understand," Leucadia said, turning to Harlowe.

Harlowe replied with extreme seriousness. "The power in those weapons could destroy armies, Lu." He saw in her face that she was unmoved by his statement. "That doesn't surprise you, does it?"

Leucadia held him with her stare. "Listen, Ian has something to show you. And when you see it, you will understand why those weapons are only a tiny part of what this ship is."

Harlowe's forehead wrinkled tight. "Sweet . . ."

She pulled him off the table. "Come on, it's the main attraction, Pylott. Can you walk?"

Harlowe fell back against the floating table. "I could a second ago," he said, holding on to the side of the table.

"Which one of you two hit me?" Simon asked, holding his cue ball.

Riverstone stepped right up. "Trust me, it's an improvement."

Simon started to go for Riverstone, but Monday held him in check. "Your stupid face is mine when we get out of here, Riverstone," Simon threatened. "My lawyers will see that you never have another nickel as long as you live for what you did to my face."

Leucadia silenced the bickering and took charge. "Like the weapons, Millawanda is no toy. She's real, and very, very powerful." She pointed at Simon. "Help Monday. Ian, you help Matt. After they're cleaned up, we meet back here in the corridor. Then you're on, Wiz." This wasn't a request.

A short while later the whole group gathered in the corridor where Ian was waiting to guide them as if he was their tour guide in some famous museum. There was some mumbling along the way, but mostly there was uneasy silence. Mowgi trotted along beside Harlowe like he was on an invisible leash. When they came to the center foyer where the outside ramp was still deployed, Ian led them to the short corridor Harlowe and Riverstone had discovered earlier in their exploration of the ship. Harlowe saw nothing out of the ordinary and simply shrugged when they came to the end. Ian pointed up to the ceiling a hundred feet up. There was a dark hole approximately twenty feet across above them. Then, for no apparent reason, the dark hole lit up.

"An invitation?" Riverstone guessed.

Ian smiled. "Big time."

Harlowe stepped directly under the lighted hole and tilted his head up. The upper level appeared as lifeless as the level they were standing on. Beyond the opening was another ceiling where curious, faint blue hues of light were interspersed with flecks of red, yellow, and white lights that appeared to dance off the far ceiling.

"Let's crash the party. How do we get there?" Harlowe wanted to know.

Riverstone focused his deep blue eyes on the hole. "Yeah, where's the elevator?" he asked Ian.

Harlowe looked around and was about to strike the device on the nearby wall when Ian stopped him. "Wait!" He pulled Harlowe off the three-foot-diameter disk embedded in the floor and stepped on the disk himself. "Watch me first." He then pressed the small, crystalline activator on the wall. It was within easy reach. "Going up," he pointed.

And suddenly he blinked out of existence.

It was like some magician's disappearing act. "Wiz?" Harlowe called out, waving his hand over the space where Ian had stood an instant before.

Riverstone blinked. "That was cool. One second he's standing on the platform, then the next second *poof!* no Ian."

"Hey, pards," Ian's voice called from above. The group looked up. Ian was looking down at them from the edge of the hole in the ceiling. "The pad takes you up," he added.

Oh man, was he ever going to wake up? Riverstone wondered. He stared at Harlowe, who had the same look of disbelief on his face. The logical explanation was that they had fallen asleep and somehow during that brief period of time Ian had simply run up a flight of hidden stairs. It was that simple.

Leucadia guided Harlowe to the center of the disk and held him close. "Go for it, baby," she directed. "It's showtime."

Harlowe reached over and pressed the activator on the wall. "I can hardly . . .," he began, "wait," he said, finishing his reply a hundred feet above the place where they started.

Riverstone was next up, but he looked at the disk skeptically, wondering if it was a painful experience to break his molecules into subatomic bits of transport matter.

"Just do it, pard," Harlowe called down from above. "It doesn't hurt, wussie."

Riverstone followed directions and positioned himself in the middle of the disk. As Harlowe edged back from view, like he was moving out of the way, Riverstone took a deep breath, shut his eyes, and touched the button hesitantly with his finger. After feeling a slight tingle at the end of his fingertips, he waited for some jolting sensation telling him the trip was over. But he felt nothing odd. The force of the disk did not push against his feet to lift him upward toward the ceiling. He had obviously missed the button, he concluded, or maybe he just struck it wrong. Thinking his effort had failed, he opened his eyes and was about to make another swipe at the activator when Harlowe asked, "Cool, huh?"

Riverstone almost stumbled backwards *back down* the hole when he saw Harlowe's face staring at him, eye to eye, about two inches from his nose. Before Riverstone embarrassed himself further, Harlowe caught him by the arm. "You don't want to go back that way," he said, pulling him to safety.

Instead of looking up at the opening in the ceiling, Riverstone found himself looking down through the opening at Monday and Simon, who had been standing next to him a moment before.

Riverstone moved away from the hole, temporarily losing his voice. Ian led him away and turned him around toward the center of the room. "You think that's sick, check this out."

The moment his head turned away from the opening, Riverstone forgot about the transport disk. A new radiating power surrounded him and sent apoplectic shock waves rushing through his body. He knew without asking, without anyone's guidance, that this was the heart, the nucleus of the ship. This room was the source of all that was.

Harlowe slapped the speechless Riverstone on the back. "This is cool."

"Incredible, isn't it?" Leucadia chimed in.

Next to the opening in the floor was a wall filled with a million points of luminescence. It was as if they were prancing to a silent symphony all their own. The wall ran along the entire back width of the room. From the top of the wall the ceiling arched gracefully down to three massive, concave sections of glass that wrapped around the outer perimeter of the room. But like the window in Riverstone's room, they were completely opaque.

Below the center section of glass, a long console of crystalline knobs and bars and more dancing lights was positioned in front of three heavily padded chairs. The chairs matched the carpet in color but were much softer in appearance. Below the outer curving windows were two long comfortable couches, one on each side of the room, with the same color and feel as the chairs.

Harlowe pointed above the arched door in the middle wall of lights at the flat golden object crossing a starburst. "That symbol is everywhere. It's just like the one we saw on the matrix map, remember?" He turned to Leucadia and wondered aloud, "So we're here. Now what? We're underground with a million tons of rock covering the one entrance to this place, and that was only a crack to begin with."

Riverstone remained anxiously quiet as he cautiously stepped to the center of the room to join his companions. Leucadia was touching the chairs with great interest as Simon and Monday materialized on the main level.

"I have some ideas," Ian said, speaking so softly to Harlowe that no one else heard their conversation.

Above the large center section of opaque glass, a large, clear rectangle angled down toward them and darkened. A half-breath later, turquoise letters appeared on its surface. The letters or words—it was impossible to tell—had a cuneiform shape to them. They made no sense at all to anyone.

"That's the same alphabet that was used inside the helmet," Leucadia pointed out.

Riverstone made himself comfortable in the right-hand chair. "I wonder what it's saying."

"It's telling us to leave, that's what," Simon replied, stepping forward to join the others.

Harlowe wasn't going to take another outburst of Simon's fatalism. He faced Monday directly. "He makes another sound and I'll toss him back down the shaft. Clear?" Monday nodded.

Simon protested angrily. "Don't listen to him, Platter. You answer to me."

Leucadia grabbed Simon by the arm and hustled him off to one of the side couches in the giant room before a war erupted. His toes barely touched the floor as she sat him down and began reading him the riot act like a stern mother does to her misbehaving child.

With Simon out of the way, Harlowe, who had taken the center chair next to Riverstone, could concentrate on the problem at hand. "Go ahead, Wiz."

"Millawanda knows English," said Ian, sitting in the left-hand chair.

Someone had to be listening, Riverstone thought, because just as Ian spoke, the projection changed instantly from unintelligible symbols of an unknown language to very readable English.

"Do you prefer English, Ian?" the screen asked in large, bright blue letters.

They traded hesitant looks before Harlowe urged Ian to continue. "Go ahead. It's addressing you, Wiz."

"Ask it where the nearest phone is," Simon interjected from across the room.

Simon's question had Riverstone's attention. It was the first time he had heard any intelligence out of the movie star's mouth. "That bump on your head has done wonders for your brain, Bolt." He turned to Ian. "Go ahead. Ask it where the phone is," Riverstone urged.

Ian didn't ask that question, though. He focused on the bigger picture of what this all meant to them. "Listen, everyone, Millie—"

"Millie?" Riverstone asked, cutting him short.

Harlowe slapped Riverstone on the shoulder. "Let Wiz talk, or you'll be sitting in 'time out' with your pal over there."

Ian got the go-ahead nod from Harlowe and went on. "Okay, yeah, Millie. It's short for Millawanda. Millie's what I call her," he explained. "She already knew me the second I found her, Harlowe. I told her nothing. She already knew. So it stands to reason she already knows us all. It was like she was expecting us. Mrs. M must have gotten through to her that we were coming. What other answer is there?"

Riverstone looked up at the screen. "I don't care. There's only one answer I want to hear. Where's the phone, Millie?"

"Hear, hear," Simon echoed.

"No mentioned devices on board," the screen read.

"That's not good," Riverstone said. Simon concurred.

"Can you get us out of this underground tomb, Millie?" Harlowe asked simply.

"Oh, that's a good one," Riverstone chuckled.

"Yes," the screen read.

Everyone's face brightened. That got their attention. Harlowe pointed at the screen. "Good answer, Millie."

* * *

"What's up with that?" Riverstone exclaimed a short while later. "Are you whack?"

With resolute firmness, Harlowe stated clearly, "We're going to explode ourselves out of the mesa."

After that they argued for the next hour on how to proceed. If their own survival had not depended on Ian and Millie's plan of exploding the spaceship out of its tomb, no one would have thought in a million years it was even possible. Except for Harlowe and Leucadia, they would have taken their chances on the desert before flying one foot in a seventeen-thousand-year-old alien vessel. That's how long, Millawanda told them, she had been parked on Earth. Seventeen thousand was just a rounded-off number; she was precise to the second.

It didn't matter to Riverstone; this was lunacy to him. Suicide. *That's whack! He and Harlowe were just two toads from Lakewood.* They didn't belong in this contraption. It was for astronauts—Skywalker and Solo, other aliens from outer space, even E.T, man.

Riverstone started to protest. He pointed at Simon. "Even toad-head knows more than we do, Pylott. At least he played an astronaut in the movies. We're just a couple of surfer dudes from Lakewood, pard. Our names don't even make us sound like we're from a galaxy far, far away. What do you know about flying?"

"Not much," Harlowe had to admit.

"That's right, Ramjet. You don't know one thing about flying. So how about taking a few lessons first before we go taking off in a spaceship that's a billion years old?"

"We don't have time" was Harlowe's only reply.

* * *

Through the massive and filthy forward window, the flat-topped mountain bounced and turned sideways. It drifted back to an upright position, and bounced again. But as much as Harlowe tried to adjust the controls, the mountaintop refused to move out of their way.

"HARLOWE, MAKE THIS SPACESHIP GO UP, PLEASE!" someone shouted from the back.

Everyone but Harlowe and Leucadia dove for cover behind over-stuffed chairs or instrument consoles in a futile effort to protect themselves from the crash they knew was coming. A sharp jolt suddenly strained the seat fasteners, followed immediately by a jarring lurch forward. Without his seat fasteners Harlowe would have smashed against the console in front of him.

A long moment passed. More than enough time to crash into a mountain, Harlowe told himself.

"We're over it," Leucadia's voice announced, relieved.

Riverstone uncovered his eyes and saw stars swirling through the giant window. Somehow the ship had missed the mountain. He couldn't believe it.

The ship was spinning round and round, however, out of control. It did two more 360-degree flip-overs before Harlowe could steady the yaw and fly upright again.

Riverstone forced himself to talk. "Did you have to cut it so close?" he criticized, watching the stars wobble and bounce and drift from side to side.

"You're making me sick," Simon added.

"Shut up, everyone!" Leucadia snapped back at the small crowd of frightened onlookers. "He's doing the best he can."

Harlowe could say nothing. He was too busy trying to keep them all alive.

Simon backed off while grabbing a chair to steady himself for the bumpy ride.

Harlowe was piloting the alien craft because he was the only one stupid enough to try. Riverstone had wanted nothing to do with it. Monday didn't like flying and wouldn't attempt anything so foolish even if his life depended on it. Simon, of course, only flew on movie sets. Ian and Leucadia would have, though, if Harlowe had declined, but Leucadia told him she knew without a doubt he was the best man for the job. On this point, considering the choices at hand, Harlowe wholeheartedly agreed.

Nevertheless, Harlowe was a shaking mass of bones upon accepting his assignment. After all, piloting an alien ship that was larger than the new Houston Astrodome was going to require job skills that were far and above his abilities. Leucadia, seeing his anxiety and being an astute observer of the male psyche, led Harlowe to a suite of rooms off the bridge to help prepare him for his big moment. For the cause, one might say.

The suite was obviously set aside for the commander in charge of the Gamadin vessel. The fore rooms were the office areas. A large modernistic desk sat next to a wall of curving windows. On the opposite wall, a large oval table of rich blue stone that could seat more than a dozen waited patiently for its next meeting. What interested Leucadia, however, was the master suite beyond. It was sizable and grand enough for any ship's commander. They might have taken more time to gawk and touch all the fine appointments and royal blue furnishings if she weren't on a mission. Thirty minutes later, Harlowe was mentally ready for his first solo flight in the ancient alien craft.

"You're up, Pylott," she had said, slapping his backside toward the center command chair. "Show 'em what you got, Captain."

The relaxed and ready Harlowe had returned a confident wink and stepped forward to his center command chair. "Let's do it, Wiz," he had said to Ian.

* * *

"Harlowe!" Leucadia yelled as she stared, wide-eyed, at the guidance readouts on the console. What they didn't know about the ship's guidance controls they were picking up on the fly. The ship's altitude and speed indicators were changing so rapidly they were a blur. In a matter of seconds the ship had vaulted from one thousand to twenty thousand feet in altitude, and had raced from 150 to 2,300 miles per hour—and the speed was increasing.

"Slow down, Harlowe!" Leucadia warned. She was calm but firm.

"Just maneuvering thrusters, pard, remember?" Ian reminded him.

Harlowe's eyes danced over the different controls. "How?"

Ian bolted from his chair and pointed to the buttons on the side of Harlowe's center chair. "Touch those." Harlowe followed his instructions. "Yeah, that one," Ian instructed, staying cool like Leucadia. Harlowe couldn't have asked for a better backup team. "Not too fast. We don't want to drop like a stone. It needs just a little tweak. Yeah, that's it."

"Okay! I think I'm getting it." Harlowe responded, concentrating more than he had ever had to in his life. He slid his right index finger down the middle bar, and the ship immediately flipped over.

"WHOOOOA!"

More shouts of discontent came from everyone's mouth, but Harlowe was too busy struggling to right the ship to offer a worthy response to the criticisms. With his left little finger, he touched the right outer bar (the one he meant to touch the first time) and slowed their screw-like spin to a steadying wobble. After a couple of fine adjustments, he brought them even with the horizon again.

The ship stabilized, and Harlowe concentrated on slowing their speed. To the passengers, the night lights of small cities and towns below appeared to drift by slowly, but in reality the spacecraft was cruising toward the southwestern horizon at three times the speed of sound. When the captain did slow things down a bit, passing under Mach 2, he eased Millie to a lower altitude.

All on board figured someone had to be watching them on a radar screen somewhere. But even more troublesome was the fact that they were flying around at thousands of miles per hour and they didn't know how or what they were doing. In a word, they were dangerous—not only to themselves but to others as well. A commercial airliner could have easily appeared in front of their view screen and they wouldn't know how to get out of its way. A ship this large would crush any airliner in the sky in a heartbeat. That possibility scared them as much as the flying did.

As they got within a thousand feet above ground, Harlowe reduced their speed to a manageable one hundred knots. A few minutes after that, they came to a complete stop, hovering precisely 253 feet above the desert floor. Feeling comfortable with the craft at last, Harlowe floated the ship down until they could clearly make out the flat, beavertail cactus patches on the dim moonlit ground under them. A black jagged ridgeline divided the horizon from the glow of a bright city many miles away. "That's Vegas," Simon stated confidently, having seen that glow so many times from his private jet.

While everyone was looking outside at the scenery, Leucadia came over to Harlowe and put her arms around his sweat-soaked body and held him close and tight. "Ya did good, Pylott." His arms were as listless as a rag doll's and his mouth hung open, parched as sand.

Riverstone thought about what they had just gone through: exploding through the escarpment wall, just missing the mountain, flipping round and round at two thousand miles per hour! *Man, and they were still alive?* He wanted to faint, but couldn't, so he simply sat in the right chair, stone cold, his nerves and muscles too spent to try to move.

Leucadia, on the other hand, appeared to be taking it all in stride. She and Ian were Millie's twin anchors. She calmly kissed Harlowe as Ian announced: "Speed zero. Altitude a rock-steady 1253.21 feet."

Around the console, blue lights danced about in their usual silent way, seemingly unaffected by the recent events.

"Everyone okay?" Leucadia asked as she looked at the mentally and physically exhausted crew.

Harlowe sat silently, collecting his thoughts, as Riverstone broke the silence. "Do you have ice in your veins, Lu?" he asked her.

She twisted around in her chair. "All of us have to get it together, Matt. We don't have long to sit here before someone out there finds us. We've got to move Millie to a safe spot until we can figure out what to do next."

Harlowe mustered enough energy to lean forward in his chair. "Lu's right, pard. We can't stay here." He took Riverstone's arm and helped him to stand. "Come on." They helped each other in slow deliberate steps toward the bedroom. As they stepped through the door, two cylinders popped out of nowhere and grabbed them before they collapsed. From there the mechanical servants helped them to the bathroom, where they reenergized themselves with refreshing showers of warm, blue water. Whether it was the blue-water showers or the pukey chalk-like cubes the stickmen offered them to eat, they didn't know, but an hour later the dos amigos were good to go for their next death wish.

"And I thought women were bad," Leucadia quipped sarcastically, eager to get on with the relocation. "You two took forever."

Leucadia had already marked their exact location with a blinking blue light on the overhead screen. They were 96.73 miles north of Las Vegas, near the Utah-Nevada state line.

"Any ideas?" Harlowe asked his crew.

Riverstone's expression stayed vacant. Thinking of a place to go after they left the cavern never crossed his mind. He didn't have a clue about any next step.

All Simon cared about was Simon. The quicker they parked the ship, the quicker he could call his agent to have a chopper fly out and pick him and Monday up. "Just land it" was his only reply.

When Harlowe's gaze fell upon Leucadia, she had no problem coming up with an answer. "Las Vegas," she stated without equivocation. "There's an area north of the city that we own."

Simon grinned for the first time since the morning he drove into Harry's garage in his new Vantage. "Yeah, the *Distant Galaxies* set," he said, elated. "Nice choice, Leucadia. We can use the Harry's casino penthouse instead of this outdated rat trap." He looked around the control room with disgust. "That's the first place we met, remember?"

Leucadia smiled coldly. "No, I don't." She then turned to Harlowe and continued her description. "It's a small depression not far from State Road 157. About ten miles west of the junction."

Harlowe nodded. He was anxious to get his solo flight over with. He was exhausted; every muscle in his body strained and ached. So, with Leucadia's guidance, he steered Millie on a spit-in-the-hand course southward.

They flew low to avoid radar detection; tall Saguaro cactuses and Joshua trees passed beneath them in a blur. In-flight instructions were given to them miles in advance. In this way they could rise above tall, jagged mountaintops and fall into valleys without destruction. If Harlowe made a miscalculation, Millawanda—like a patient teacher keeping a watchful eye on a student driver—would help Leucadia flash the necessary corrections on the screen for him to follow. And, like a student driver, Harlowe displayed on his face all the strains and pressures he was enduring.

After less than an hour, Harlowe slowed the craft to a gentle creep and took a 263-degree westerly heading that Ian had calculated.

Leucadia transferred the bearing to the overhead screen, putting them on their final approach to their isolated destination in the desert northwest of Las Vegas. Twice along the way they had to stop, pivot the ship around like a search beacon, and recheck their position. At last they found Simon's old movie location—a saddleback depression in the middle of nowhere. A place even the lizards called "the-other-side-of-the-tracks." They all hoped anyone looking for them felt the same way.

The pink pastels of morning were beginning to tint the edge of the horizon as Harlowe eased the ship over the last ridge and into the hidden depression.

The ship had no special landing requirements. Any old piece of real estate a little more than a thousand feet across would do. On uneven terrain the landing pods fully adjusted to the level of the ground, and if it was too rugged for pods, the ship could simply float effortlessly over an area for as long as anyone cared to imagine. But none of these problems hindered their touchdown since the saddle was quite level and large enough for two vessels the size of the alien ship.

Millie floated down and touched the ground so gently that it was hard to detect from inside the control room whether they were once again on terra firma. According to the outside views on the overhead screen, however, the ship had indeed landed safely.

Overwhelmed with joy, Harlowe bolted to the nearest observation window, staring at the scenery, congratulating Ian and Leucadia for making the accomplishment possible.

Leucadia caressed his bearded face in her hands and kissed him softly on the lips. "You were wonderful, Pylott."

He smiled. "I was, wasn't I?"

Riverstone wasn't so elated. He announced, along with Simon, that since they had their feet planted again on good old mother Earth, they were headed back home. "Well, folks, we're outta here," he said and headed toward the hole in the floor with Simon by his side.

"You're really leaving, Matt?" Leucadia asked.

"In a blink," he stated bluntly for all to hear. He saluted Harlowe at the same moment that Simon slapped the activator and they both winked away.

Chapter Forty

HOMEWARD BOUND

IT TOOK RIVERSTONE less than ten minutes to change into his now cleaned earthly denims. Although Las Vegas was a place where anything weird or offbeat was cool, he felt more comfortable in his denims and scruffy, but clean, bright blue T-shirt. Except for his alien slip-ons and blue eyes, he was his old self again.

His main focus was to locate a phone and call home. He knew his parents were worried sick about him by now. He couldn't let them suffer any longer. Once that was done, he'd catch the first jet to Long Beach and be done with it.

When he stepped out into the corridor, Riverstone thought for sure Harlowe or Ian would be in his face, urging him to reconsider. They had always been a team, the three of them. To separate now under these circumstances was not the way he wanted it. But these were unusual circumstances. This wasn't Lakewood. Whenever they had argued or taken care of business or gone to the beach, he had always been home by night. Alien spaceships, Dakadudes, and off-world beastly killers were not part of the job description he had signed up for the day he had met Harlowe so many years back. *But where was Harlowe? This wasn't like him to give in so easily. He's up to something. I know it.*

To Riverstone's chagrin, instead of Harlowe and Ian he met Simon and Monday at the foyer exit ahead of him. They had already deployed the ramp and were about to head down when they spotted him coming down the corridor. He was hoping if he acted fast enough he wouldn't have to run into anyone. He felt a little clumsy offering them a halfhearted greeting. "Gents," he said, stepping up.

"Where are *you* going?" Simon asked in his usual arrogant style.

"There's a question here?" Riverstone replied.

"It's a long walk," Simon pointed out. "Do you know which way to go?"

"I'll manage."

"We should stick together, Riverstone," Monday suggested.

Riverstone looked at Monday. For the first time he thought he saw something like a plea in the big guy's face. Maybe it was because they had all been through so much misery together the last three days. *Misery loves company, and all that,* he pondered. Well, Monday was welcome in his little club; his tone seemed genuine enough. But the thought of listening to the movie star bellyache for twenty miles across the desert almost made staying a better option.

"No thanks, Platter. By the time we got to the bottom of the ramp, I'd be hating myself for saying yes," Riverstone said. "Better we go our separate ways."

"You'll never make it," Simon interjected.

Control was the only thing Riverstone knew he had to maintain or he would never leave the ship. He took in a deep breath of don't-lose-it-now-pard and replied, "I'll make it, but not with you, suckwad."

"Don't be an arrogant geek, Riverstone. You'll be dead before noon," Simon said.

Riverstone locked eyes with Simon. "I carried your sorry face farther than that and survived," he pointed out. "I'll make it to town way before you do."

Monday quickly recognized the growing tension and stepped between them. "Mr. Bolt's staying here, Riverstone."

Riverstone's puzzlement showed in his face as he stared at Simon.

Simon thought it was pretty self-evident why he was opting out of the trek. "You don't think *I'd* walk twenty miles in the desert, do you? That's why I pay Platter the big bucks. That's his job. The first phone he finds, he calls Saul. Presto! The chopper lands out front of this big salad plate. Next thing you know I'm sittin' in a hot tub with one of the babes at Harry's Casino. Besides, Leucadia says she can use my help."

Riverstone gazed at Simon thoughtfully. He cracked a smile. *Leucadia needed his help like she needed a facelift. She wasn't stupid, though. Cagey like a cat. Played Harlowe like a fiddle and he didn't even know he was the instrument. So keeping Simon around was part of her plan, huh? Okay. She's up to something. I'm down with that.*

"You really are a good actor, Simon. Has anyone ever told you that? You can play starship captain Julian Starr, brave, tough, decisive leader of the interplanetary seventh space fleet, and no one ever knows how much of a toad you are. That is an incredible feat, Simon. I'm really impressed."

Riverstone didn't wait for a response. He turned his back on the star and started down the ramp. Monday called after him. "I've got water too." He held up a blue canvas flask for him to see.

Riverstone turned. He hadn't thought of water. Stomping through the desert without water *was* suicide. His face remained pensive. If he was going to appear halfway competent, he had better act like it, he thought. He didn't turn around. He just gave him a wave. "Come along, then."

Monday caught up with Riverstone, and together they made small talk as they began trekking through the prickly mesquite and sagebrush. Would the Dodgers remain in LA after their sale to a Boston millionaire? How 'bout those Raiders making it to the playoffs this year? The conversation kept their minds off more serious matters that made no sense anyway. The cool morning air was crisp and dry. It felt invigorating to be out in the open again with the blue sky above their heads. Free at last!

As they began to climb toward the ridgeline, however, a twinge of guilt about leaving Harlowe and Ian without at least a see-ya-around-pard nod hit Riverstone in the gut. *Harlowe would never understand, he kept telling himself. He would try and talk me out of it. He would make me feel worse than I already do that I'm leaving him all alone with the ship. Well, he isn't really alone. He has Leucadia and Wiz. They're more than capable. I won't be missed. So what's up with the guilt, toad?*

Riverstone let out a troubled sigh before adding once more to the sports talk. They were on the Yankees now, and the subject was whether it was right that they had more money than the government and could buy baseball's best.

"Harry owns them, by the way," Monday stated casually.

Riverstone stopped suddenly and gave Monday an empty stare. "What *doesn't* he own?"

The two plodded along. Already Riverstone was tired and thirsty, and they had gone only a few hundred yards. Millie had shown Las Vegas to be 20.7 miles southeast of the saddle. The way Monday described the trek, except for crossing a few dry washes and a low line of hills two miles away, all they had to do was head south until they found Route 157, a narrow two-lane state highway impossible for them to miss. Once they found the highway they would walk due east on it until they got to I-95. From there they could hitch a ride easily. Monday had money. He would drop the driver a C-note, and they would be dining in style at Harry's Hotel and Casino by noon. After that, he could get them front-row tickets for 3 Doors Down.

"Wow, Platter. You can do that?" Riverstone asked. He was impressed.

Monday patted him on the back as they trekked over the dry desert gravel. "All the time," he told him. "I'll have the limo pick us up in front of Harry's Casino and take us to the Palace."

As Riverstone high-stepped to the top of the ridge (he was feeling really good now), he was surprised (although once he thought about it, it didn't shock him) to find Harlowe and Leucadia already there ahead of him, sitting cross-legged together on a large rock. The undog was sitting below them, his parabolics searching the area for anything threatening. Behind them was the wheel-less rover they had come in. Ian was one rock over, checking the contents of a blue canvas bag. "Inspiring, isn't it?" Harlowe uttered as he pointed toward the pink and gold sunrise on the eastern horizon.

"Don't try and talk me out of it, Pylott," Riverstone said as he walked on by them.

"It's a good idea, pard," Harlowe replied, his tone unusually calm and relaxed.

Riverstone stopped. "Perfect. Then there will be no discussion about it?"

"We agree with you, Matt," Leucadia added, making eye contact with Harlowe like there was some humongous secret between them.

"You do?" Riverstone took two steps then stopped again. "I know what you're thinking." He came closer, peering into Harlowe's eyes. "You two are up to something."

"Not this time," Harlowe replied, almost too casually.

"Alright," Riverstone conceded, hands on hips, "let's have it. How are you going to try and screw me then?"

For a long moment Harlowe kept his silence, sitting there like some all-knowing guru who had found Nirvana.

"Isn't Millie the most gorgeous lady you ever laid eyes on?" he finally said.

Riverstone reluctantly turned around. "You're changing the sub . . . ject . . .," he growled, but as he did, his face went flush.

He knew it. Harlowe had tricked him . . . again! During the climb away from the ship, he was afraid of looking back for fear of seeing something that might make him stay. Now, for the first time, he *really* saw Millawanda. All of her! The bright morning sun was reflecting off her clean and smooth golden skin. Every bit of dirt that had shrouded her body for so many thousands of years was gone, scoured away by a three-thousand-knot wind. Millie was breathtakingly glorious.

Riverstone forced himself to breathe again. On a scale of hot babes, she was Mrs. M.

He could see under the ship's hull three massive landing pods fully and gracefully extended to nearly two hundred feet off the ground. To the top of her gentle sloping dome was another two hundred feet at least. From side to side she had to be wider than five football fields, he figured. That kind of distance he was familiar with. She had no hard angles anywhere—no seams, no rivets, no connecting lines, only gentle curves and perfect symmetry.

A thin blue line of light pulsated around her perimeter edge, slowly beating like a heart at rest. He easily recognized the three large curving windows that wrapped halfway around the smooth upper-level dome. The flat, frisbee-like symbol they'd seen everywhere inside the ship was centered just below the forward window.

His knees weakened. "Yeah, Harlowe, she's one sweet doe alright. I had no idea something that size could look so beautiful."

"And to think, she's ours," Harlowe said, gleaming with pride.

Riverstone shuttered, coming out of his stupor. "Forget it, Harlowe, there's no we in this for me. She's all yours, pard."

Harlowe stepped off the rock, pleading, "Hey, once we get the hang of it—"

"I said no we, Pylott. I'm hasta-la-bye-bye, brah. You're the worst pilot I've ever seen. I wouldn't get back into that thing if you had a zillion hours logged. We're lucky we didn't crash fifty times getting here. That ridge!" Riverstone threw up his arms. "I'll have nightmares for the rest of my life thinking of how we barely missed that thing. JERK!"

Harlowe grinned. "Millie lifted her dress and jumped it."

Riverstone's eyes rolled round in his head as he stared at Harlowe. "You know something? I believe that too." He pointed a finger first at Leucadia and then at Ian. "Everyone here would agree, you need to see a shrink because you were born without a brain, scarecrow. So end of discussion! I'm outta here."

Riverstone looked out across the desert, getting his bearings. He thought he could almost see the dirt road four miles south that would take him and Monday to Route 157 and the interstate south to Las Vegas.

"Come on, Riverstone, it wasn't that bad," Harlowe contended. "She got us here. We didn't die, and we're not going to either, toad. What's that saying? 'Any landing is a good landing.'"

"They never flew in that salad plate," Riverstone insisted.

"Millie deserves a little respect, Matt. She saved our lives. We can't just leave her here in the middle of nowhere," Leucadia added.

Riverstone glared at Leucadia. "You act like she's human or something."

"Not like you and me. But I do feel her soul. She does have feelings, you know," Leucadia said.

"Oh, puh-leez, Lu, spare the incense, okay?"

Riverstone turned back to Harlowe. "I'm not cut out for this, Harlowe. I'm not playing hero anymore. Lakewood was okay. I could go home after a night of knocking heads and sleep in my own bed." He gestured at the ship. "Not with that, though. With that we don't go home. We go bye-bye, as in not on this planet. With that we are in a big heap of trouble."

Harlowe faced the ship. "There's a reason for all this, pard. Remember what Mrs. M said? The planet depends on us. The *planet*. There might be no planet to come back to if we don't get Millie away from the Dakadudes in time."

"Listen to him, Matt," Leucadia begged. "He's telling the truth. My mother wanted to save her own planet, Neeja, for sure, but she wanted to save Earth too. Earth one day will be next if we don't stop the enemy here and now."

Riverstone wasn't buying the sob story. "Have you noticed, by the way, that we're only five here? That's about a hundred and something *less* than your mom was training to fly this thing. And we can't even fire a gun without blowing the top off a mountain," he blared, staring at Monday as he spoke. "Imagine what we could do if we really knew how to shoot. God help the Earth!"

"There's no turning back, Matt. Fate has given us our only choice," Leucadia said with finality.

Riverstone pointed a finger at his chest. "Screw Fate. I'm making my own choice."

Harlowe's eyes continued to focus on the ship's smooth, symmetrical lines. "The story's just begun, pard. We can't walk away. We're in it to the end. There's no turning back," he reiterated.

Riverstone nodded with a somber face. "For you, maybe. You've given your word. Not me. I'm leaving, Harlowe. My home's in Lakewood, not here."

Monday broke in. "Come on, Riverstone, enough of this. Harry's Casino is waiting."

Harlowe made one last try. "I need you, pard. We're a team. You make a big difference to me."

"And me," Leucadia added.

"And me," Ian piled on, stepping forward for emphasis. "We all need you. We're pards, right? You know that. You'll be back sooner than you know."

"Not this time, Wiz," Riverstone stated with finality.

Leucadia turned to Harlowe. "If he wants to leave, let him. Don't ask him to do anything. I'll go instead."

Riverstone frowned. "You were going to ask me to do something?"

"It wasn't much." Harlowe came around the boulder and motioned to Ian for the bag. "Wiz, the gizmos." Ian handed Harlowe the blue canvas bag. "We need someone to go into town and scan for us."

"Scan?" Riverstone wondered. "Scan what?"

"Food," Harlowe replied, pulling a device from the bag that resembled a remote for a garage door opener.

Riverstone and Monday traded puzzled glances as Ian opened his hand and showed them a palmful of chocolate balls. "I scanned a left-over Goober I found. After I zapped it with this, Millie made a bowl full of the stuff from that one Goob. Look. They're exact copies."

Riverstone picked one up and examined it. "They're fake?"

"Try it," Harlowe said.

Riverstone popped the chocolate round into his mouth and grinned with satisfaction. "Millie made a bowl of these?"

"Yeah," Ian replied, quite pleased with himself. "Pretty cool, huh?"

Riverstone took the rest. This was the first real food he'd had in days. "Got any more?"

Ian shook his head. "I ate the rest."

"Of all the stupid things . . ." Riverstone grabbed the remote from Harlowe's hand. "Gimme that."

"Then you'll do it?" Leucadia asked happily.

"Those dust cubes we've been eating are for wireheads," Harlowe added, sticking his tongue out like he wanted to gag.

Riverstone's nose wrinkled with revulsion as he recalled the nutrient cubes the robobs had fed them. Unless the stickmen were programmed otherwise, the cubes were the only items on the menu. For a guy whose survival depended on Quarter-Pounders, Goobers, and Big Gulps—any flavor—eating cubes that tasted like chalk was an abuse of his body he wasn't willing to go through again. "Yeah, they were dog, alright."

"Scan the aisles of a couple of supermarkets the first chance you get," Harlowe explained. "Walk through a shopping center with it on and the device will do the rest. It's all automatic. It will send the info back to Millie and she'll store it for later. Fast-food joints,

Harry's Casino buffet—you be the judge. But make it good, and plenty of it. Sky's the limit."

Riverstone placed the remote in his pocket. "Sure. I can do that."

"And find out who the Dodgers traded for Buckingham," Harlowe added. "If they got a couple of good relievers, they might have a chance in October. But if they went for another catcher—"

"Yeah, the season ends early," Riverstone concluded with a worried look on his face.

"One more thing," Harlowe said. He saw the impatience on Monday's face. "Don't worry, Platter. You'll like these. They'll get you to Harry's for breakfast instead of dinner."

If Monday cared less about replicated Goobers and scanning supermarkets, he was doubly uninspired about the spaghetti-like strands Harlowe removed from the bag.

"We're supposed to eat them and get superpowers?" Monday bantered, hardly amused.

"Chill out, Platter. You'll find it worth your while," Ian said, taking one set of strands from Harlowe. Ian was about to ask Riverstone to strip down to his underwear when he started undressing on his own like he understood the drill. "You know about these?" he asked, incredulous.

"They're called gravs," Riverstone said, removing his pants. Leucadia looked on, unfazed. A short time later he had hooked up the belts and was strapping the cables to his legs and arms without instruction. "I'm ready." He took the other set from Harlowe and gave them to Monday. "Put them on."

"This is stupid," Monday replied, holding the limp strands.

Riverstone took one relaxed ten-foot stride forward and landed easily, pivoting like a ballet dancer. "Any questions?" he said, looking back at the slack-jawed bodyguard.

Mowgi yelped his satisfaction as Harlowe trotted over to River-stone. "How do you know about them?"

Riverstone glanced at Leucadia. "It's a long story. Just don't let her drive the car," he said, nodding at the wheel-less form sitting on the ground.

Leucadia was caught off guard. "What?"

"Never mind. Just don't let her drive anything," Riverstone repeated.

"Don't forget the liquor store," Harlowe reminded him.

Riverstone's reply was a thumbs-up. "First stop," he said with a wide grin. He turned away, but then he came back to his best friend. "I've gotta do it, Harlowe. What's more, you know I have to. If they're after us, and there's no reason to think they've stopped, then they might go searching for us again in Lakewood. I've got to know Mom and Dad are alright. And Tinker and Petey . . . We've gotta know they're all okay."

Harlowe's face went sad. He wiped a tear from the side of his eye as he fought off the sniffles. "Yeah, I know. You're right. But be careful."

"I will."

"Do you have a plan?"

"Sort of." Riverstone nodded toward Monday. "Platter said he could get me a private jet. Now that we have the gravs, I could be back in Lakewood by noon. Dad will pick me up at Long Beach Airport."

"No babes," Harlowe chided.

Riverstone cracked a small smile. "No promises."

Harlowe glanced at Platter. "Keep him away from anything with breasts."

They embraced, holding each other a long moment. It was difficult to let go. Then Harlowe bent down and petted the small chin-neroth along the back. "Take the Mowg with you."

Monday was about to protest that having a dog along would slow them down, but Riverstone stepped in. "No, it's okay, Platter. Mowg is cool. Trust me on this, big guy, he's good to have around." He turned back to Harlowe. "Thanks, pard. Good idea."

"He'll find my mom on his own," Leucadia said.

"No doubt."

She gave them both a warm hug. "Just get there in one piece."

"We will," Riverstone replied, glassy-eyed. He then turned away and took a ten-foot stride with ease. Monday strode next and landed right beside him like he had done it a thousand times before. Riverstone wondered silently if he had had a dream like his in order to be so proficient on the first try.

Harlowe said to them both, "Don't strain 'em, thunder thighs. They're way past the warranty!"

They exchanged one last thumbs-up before Riverstone cupped his mouth and shouted back, "She really is beautiful . . ." Then he and Monday were loping away in twenty-foot strides toward the southeast while Mowgi, to Platter's utter astonishment, bounced along beside them without breaking a sweat.

As they watched Riverstone disappear over the ridgeline in giant, gazelle-like leaps, Leucadia turned to Harlowe. Only then did she see the worry in his eyes.

"He'll be okay," she assured him, putting a caring arm over his broad shoulders.

He nodded at the ridgeline. "I should have gone," he replied, trading troubled stares with Ian.

"There was nothing more you could have done, babe," she said, nuzzling closer. "He was determined to go home."

Harlowe sucked in a breath of dread as he turned around to face the ship, feeling the immense responsibility weighing heavily on his shoulders. It was his word he had given, not Riverstone's. It should have been him in harm's way, not his friend.

"My parents will help him home," Leucadia said.

"Yeah," Harlowe replied, observing the peace and serenity of the desert morning reflecting off the ship and her graceful lines. "If he doesn't meet a Dak first . . ."

Chapter Forty-One

DEEP IMPRESSIONS

Ed McCarty exhaled a low whistle of awe before he blurted out, "Get a load of that impression, will ya, general! You could lose an Abrams A1 tank in that hole." His voice echoed off the sides of the massive chamber he and the others were standing in. "And if we turned the ceiling over, we could make an exact copy of the outer hull," he added.

The blast chamber was a vast, elongated cavity inside the escarpment wall. When General Gunn's Black Hawk first approached the opening, someone remarked that it felt as though he were being swallowed up by the jaws of Jonah's giant whale. The opening's maw was more than fifteen hundred feet wide, but curiously, like the shape of a mouth, the top tapered from its five-hundred-foot-high center to a gradual two hundred feet at its sides. The entire bottom line was flat, which made an easy landing platform for the Black Hawk.

At the front lip of the chamber the chopper waited, its profile silhouetted against the bright morning sunlight. After the preliminary survey team had okayed the area (they had found no radiation and surprisingly no superheated rocks inside the cavity), the general had flown his assistants and the team of scientists immediately to the site. Down below, in the bottom of the gorge, the story was different. Large fragments of hot molten rock still smoldered, their heated vapor tails rising into the sky. It appeared that all the debris from the blast had exploded outward, leaving the chamber inside cool and unaffected.

"Very precise, General Gunn." From as far away as the length of a football field, Doctor Zagorsky's deep, monotonic voice sounded clear and sharp, as if he was standing a few feet away in an acoustically engineered amphitheater. "The same way a hot knife cuts butter, the alien flying saucer cut through a hundred feet of solid sandstone an instant before it left its tomb." Like Gunn, Zagorsky was awed but also intensely sober with worry. "This kind of power, general, is frightening indeed."

General Gunn smacked his swagger stick against his leg as he studied the great impression. He was seeing this problem on a global scale. A flying machine that could cut through a hundred feet of solid rock in the blink of an eye was something to be deeply concerned about, not elated. Could this event be related to the squadron coming toward Earth? What star did Shaffer say they likely traveled from? He couldn't remember, but did it matter?

"The size of this ship is unbelievable! What I wouldn't give to know what powers her star drive. It must be off the scale!" McCarty cackled in amazement, touching off the general's already short fuse.

"Listen up people. This isn't a day at an amusement park," the general shouted at them collectively, his baritone thundering off the cavern walls. "I have a frickin' frisbee out there I need to put a stop to before it blows up the whole bloody countryside. Along with it I've got the three unidentifieds coming down our throats. Now, do you mind putting your heads together and start earning your pay? I need answers!"

Doctor Zagorsky addressed the general. "We believe, General Gunn, that what you . . . what we," he corrected himself, "all saw the other night can only be construed as extraterrestrial."

"I got that on my own, doctor. Tell me something I don't know," Gunn insisted.

Zagorsky's wise, inquisitive eyes looked up at the ceiling as he continued. "From the impression it left, we can tell it is unbelievably massive. Half a dozen *Nimitz*-class aircraft carriers could easily fit inside the body. It has two basic sections: an upper section that's 320 feet across, which you see there," he said, pointing to the imprint of the dome with the wraparound windows, "which presumably holds the control center. The lower section has a diameter of 1,510 feet," he concluded, making a wide sweeping gesture with both his arms. "Its landing pads are each a hundred feet across. If the ship were to land on a 747, it would crush it like a bug. Doctor McCarty believes we're at least fifty centuries away from building anything like such a fascinating piece of technology."

"How does it fly? No one saw or heard an engine," the general said flatly. "It's got to push itself along somehow. I don't need Poole to tell me that either."

"Well," Doctor Shaffer said, stepping over and picking up the conversation, "let me put it another way, general. We just don't know where to look. We were unable to find anything that remotely looks like a propulsion system. However," he continued, pointing to the outer perimeter, "Ed, here, believes the blue perimeter edge we saw last night could possibly use some high form of electromagnetic impulse or antimatter drive. But that's all speculation, general, nothing to hang your hat on. In reality, a ship like this probably uses power we haven't even dreamed of yet."

"Antimatter?" the general questioned. "I've heard that a drop of that stuff would make an A-bomb look like a firecracker."

Shaffer deferred to his partner on this one, knowing Ed had more experience with subatomic physics.

"Maybe, general," McCarty picked up, "but the fact is, we're hundreds of years from producing any type of power from antimatter. Everything we know is speculation, and much of that is stuff science-fiction writers have dreamed up. We're not even sure antimatter really exists. It's just a guess. Like Tom said, this vessel could use a power source entirely unknown to us. But whatever form of power they are using, it's out of our league. The way it accelerated past a thousand miles per hour in a manner of seconds, then flipped, turning over in mid-flight and blinking away . . ."

McCarty scratched the side of his head, still unable to believe what his own eyes had witnessed the night before. "With all due respect, general, I would be thinking of ways to make friends with these beings instead of trying to stop them. Your weapons would have about as much effect as a kid's BB gun would against uranium tank plating."

General Gunn squeezed his swagger stick between his fingers. He didn't like the idea of the world's mightiest army being forced to concede to anyone, especially one that looked like a giant frisbee. His dust-covered boots stirred the ground. "You made a reference to a tomb, Doctor Zagorsky. Why?"

Zagorsky jotted down something in his notes before he replied. "Yes, general, I did. This depression is one of three pod prints." He stepped to the edge of the depression, which was ten feet deep. "This pod impression has given us some very valuable information. See, for example, how hard the surface is?" He scuffed the soles of his shoes to illustrate his point.

"At first, we thought it was the weight of the ship that made the print." He pointed to the high ridge around the impression's perimeter. "But as Doctor Rodale discovered, the edge is nearly vertical, which leads us to believe . . .," he bent over and tapped a large, car-sized chunk of rock-hard dust with the end of his clipboard, "that these jagged chunks of rock were lifted up by the saucer when it retracted its landing pads." He pointed across the chamber. "The other two impressions have the same characteristics. With the amount of layered accumulation we have measured, we estimate that this vessel was probably sitting in this same location—a tomb, as it were—for approximately, oh, fifteen or twenty thousand years."

McCarty stepped forward. In addition to his astrophotographic expertise, he was also their geological authority. "The way I see it, the ceiling impression was made the same way. Note the smooth surface; it has no stress lines or faults. It's simply accumulated dust that turned to stone over the centuries and stuck to the chamber's ceiling."

The general tapped the side of one of the chunks with his swagger stick. "Nothing could last that long and still fly. Even the pyramids are crumbling, and they're what, five thousand years old?"

"Well, general, it did have a shaky start," Zagorsky noted.

"I still don't believe it. Those unidentifieds? I'll bet the farm they have something to do with this frisbee's sudden awakening." General Gunn said. "They could be calling to one of their own. Or heaven knows what."

Shaffer let out a deep breath. "We have no idea, general. Since the dawn of time man has wondered what's out there. Now, all of a sudden, Earth is beginning to be quite the hot spot for alien visitation. Since we have nothing that can go out there to meet the incoming fleet of ships; since nothing on Earth can catch what we saw last night; and since neither party wishes to communicate with us yet, I think we're just going to have to stick it out until they make their next move."

Shaffer looked to his fellow scientists. Although they accepted his conclusion, it was unenthusiastic acceptance. "In my opinion, we have to welcome our visitors with open arms, General Gunn. We have no other choice," Shaffer concluded.

The general glared at the four scientists collectively. "That's your answer? That we sit on our keesters and sing *Kum Ba Yah*?" His glaring eyes came to rest on Carole Rodale. "What do you say, Doctor Rodale? You seem to be having quite a love affair with that pod print. What's your opinion? You getting any vibes you can share at the campfire?"

Rodale remained in what seemed to be a meditative trance as she held the rock fragments in the palms of her hands, absorbing their energy. Then, after a long moment of silence, she let her arms drop to her sides. She took in a deep breath and exhaled.

"Did the earth move for you, Miz Rodale?" General Gunn quipped. He didn't like waiting.

She took her time. "What I have to say is going to sound corny," she replied, still squeezing the fragments.

The general didn't care; he wanted answers, and he didn't care how he got them. "Three days ago, doctor, I wouldn't have agreed with you, but today is another world. I am an admitted convert. Yesterday I did not believe in aliens, but today I do. Yesterday I believed in facts, but today, under the circumstances, I believe the term *corniness* to be quite acceptable. By all means, Doctor Rodale, please enlighten us with corniness. I am all ears."

Rodale gazed across the footprint as she began her corny explanation. "From the very first moment I saw the photographic plates of the incoming alien group, I was terrified," she began. "Like my colleagues, I wanted to feel good about our distant visitors. But I could never get my subconscious to cross over. It was telling me to beware. These beings have a reason for coming to our little out-of-the-way planet. I don't know what they want, General Gunn, but peaceful contact is not on their agenda. I'm sure of it."

"So they're all out to kill us then?" the general asked.

Rodale held up a fragment of solidified dust. "Not necessarily, sir. When I picked up this remnant here, my anxiety eased considerably. I would say it even stopped." She raised her arms toward the ceiling. "The fragments here are warm, but not from the blast; their warmth is as from a blanket that someone has been wrapped up in for a length of time. To me, *this* ship is not hostile, gentlemen. There is a reason she has come out of her hiding place at this point in time. Contrary to what Tom thinks, I *do* believe this spaceship has something to do with the incoming squadron. I think she wants to protect us from them."

The silence that followed lasted fully a minute before Shaffer spoke up. "Carole, you can't be serious. There's no evidence for any of this. You're just as apprehensive as the rest of us over this first encounter."

"Yes I am, Tom. I'm terribly apprehensive," she replied, admitting her inner worry. She stepped away from the impression and continued. "And yes, I admit I have no scientific evidence to back my theory; it's based on my own subjective feelings. But I don't have a problem with this ship, Tom. I have a problem with the incoming squadron."

"Why, Carole?" Shaffer asked. "Why accept one and not the other? The saucer has sliced off a mountaintop and cut itself out of solid rock, displaying immeasurable power. By all that's definable, your intuition should be more frightened of the saucer than of the supposed attack group—which has yet to display any aggressive intent, I might add."

Rodale rotated as though she was standing on holy ground. "I can't explain it, Tom, but that's how I feel. Somehow I know this saucer is for us, that if it were not for the approaching spacecraft, she would have remained hidden until called."

"She, Carole?" McCarty asked, catching the personification. "You've used the female gender several times now in discussing the alien saucer."

"All ships are called she, doctor," General Gunn pointed out. "That's a common term used by everyone in the military."

"I'm aware of that, sir, but I thought I was picking up something more from Carole's usage. I believe she considers the saucer to have a feminine soul. Am I correct, Carole?"

"Quite right, Ed. I smell her femaleness, if you will. Her sweetness." Rodale took a deep breath and then she bent down and touched the side of the impression with her full, open hand. "And I feel her warmth. Call it what you want, irresponsible, flighty . . ."

"Corny," Captain Walker chimed in with a smirk.

Rodale wasn't smiling when she replied, "Yes, even corny, thank you, captain."

She turned back to the group. "I believe she's waited as long as she could. Why?" she shrugged, "I'm not sure. Perhaps she is to protect something. It feels right. I just don't know, exactly."

Rodale turned to address Shaffer directly. "But I do feel she was forced from her hiding place before she was ready, Tom. She doesn't want this exposure. Not yet. I don't think she left her lair willingly." Rodale turned to face the open gorge, holding out her hands in an almost pious pose. "May God be with you, Millawanda."

"Is that her name?" McCarty asked.

Rodale tossed the small fragments she had in her hand back into the impression as though she were making an offering to the gods. "Yes. That is her name," she replied solemnly.

Like a good soldier, a good leader, General Gunn had listened intently to Rodale's explanation. Was she right? Or was Shaffer's childlike reverence of the noncommunicative squadron correct? He blew hot air through pursed lips as he turned away and walked to the edge of the chamber, his footsteps stirring clouds of dust. *This is nuts!* When he got to the edge, he put on his sunglasses and looked out at the mid-morning sky feeling helpless. *There's a world of crap going on out here, Mary! Excuse my language, dear, but what am I to do?*

An airman leaped out of the Black Hawk and jogged over to Captain Walker and handed him a folded piece of paper. The captain read the radio communiqué and immediately interrupted the general's moment of silent meditation with his dead wife. His aide informed the general that a Starlight orbital spy satellite had just spotted the saucer's location. "About twenty miles north of Las Vegas, sir."

"How old is this intel, captain?"

"Thirty minutes, general. We have a Predator in the air now and will be transmitting real-time intelligence en route. Shall I alert the Pentagon, sir?"

General Gunn snapped his swagger stick as he started moving for the Black Hawk. "Gentlemen! Ms. Rodale!" he called out loud and clear. "If you please. I will need your immediate assistance. The saucer has been found and it is parked . . ."

Then he ordered, for the captain's ears only as they marched for the Black Hawk, "That's affirmative, captain. Tell Pentagon that my opinion has not changed. The military is to remain at full Defcon One. Understood?"

"Yessir! Defcon One!"

Chapter Forty-Two

MEATHEAD'S

An hour after they left the ship, Riverstone and Monday slowed their gazelle-like strides to a more sensible gait where the desert ended and the paved streets began. As desperate as they were for a cold one, they knew they couldn't be seen bouncing along in giant leaps faster than any normal human being should. About a mile down the street they spotted Meathead's Video, Poker Bar & Suds. They plunged through the door with one thought in mind: quaffing the tallest, coldest beers the bartender could pour in the shortest amount of time.

As they stepped through the door at Meathead's, a cleanup crew was busy picking up large sections of broken glass off the ground. The entire front of the saloon's bar had been damaged.

"What happened?" Monday asked the bartender as they came up to the bar.

"Those Nellis flyboys showing off," the crusty old man stated angrily. "The government's going to pay for this one."

"He old enough?" the bartender asked, concerned about Riverstone's legal age.

Monday glanced at Riverstone. "Old enough," he confirmed and threw a C-note down on the bar for emphasis. "That cover any questions?"

The bartender swiped the note into his apron pocket. "Yep." He then served up two sixteen-ounce glasses that were so cold the air condensed to water before he had a chance to set them down. Monday downed his in two long gulps. Riverstone took several more to finish, but the result was the same. Mowgi jumped up on the bar with an expression that said, "Where's mine?"

The old man's eyes bugged out. "*What* is that?"

"A mutt. Are you blind?" Riverstone shot back, defending Mowgi's honor.

"Dogs aren't allowed," the bartender said.

"He's an alien, disguised as a dog," Riverstone countered.

The old man thought that was hilarious. "*That* I believe. He can stay."

Monday held up three fingers and pointed at Mowgi. "Then another round, and put the alien's in a salad bowl."

The bartender did as instructed. He quickly replaced the two empties with two more cold ones, and wearing an absurd grin, he put a cheap laminated-wood bowl in front of Mowgi and filled it to the top with Bud. Mowgi stuck his nose down in the suds and, faster than Monday's record two gulps, the bowl was sucked dry.

Monday and the bartender both did a double take of the empty bowl. The bartender refilled the bowl and said, still stunned, "This one's on the house." Mowgi dispatched the second bowl as easily as the first.

The bartender stepped away, shaking his head and mumbling, "That's one impressive mutt."

Riverstone took a relaxed sip, enjoying every drop of the second beer. "You don't know the half of it."

Monday let out a long sigh and the world seemed right again. "I'll call the concierge at Harry's Casino and have them send a limo," he said, heading for the pay phone next to the restrooms.

"And tell them to hurry. I'm starved."

Watching Monday at the pay phone made Riverstone wonder what he would say to his parents. He had never lied to them before, but under the circumstances, he wondered if this wasn't one of those times where maybe the whole story could wait. Somehow he thought telling his parents the complete truth was a little too much for them to swallow on the first call. He still didn't believe it either. So a simple "I'm alright, don't worry, I'll be home soon" seemed like the right approach to follow.

His second call would be to Harlowe's mom. She would be a tougher sell than his parents. But a small fib was decidedly better than the whole truth for the moment. All he needed was a little common sense.

When Monday hung up, Riverstone lumbered over to the phone and made his call. He struck 0 and waited for the operator. He had enough money for the call, but not enough for that plus food, drink, the plane ticket, or any other small emergency that might arise. So under the circumstances, he would reverse the charges. No sweat.

When the operator answered, he told the pleasant foreign-accented man that he wanted to place a collect call to Lakewood, California. He heard the computer-generated tonal sounds as the number was punched. Two seconds later, the first ring vibrated in his ear. Then the second and third rings passed. That was unusual because someone always answered by the second ring. When the phone kept ringing and no one was answering, the knot in River-stone's stomach began to tighten.

"Come on, come on," he begged impatiently under his breath.

After the seventh ring, the operator came back on the line and said that apparently no one was home. Riverstone thought the answering machine should have picked up by the fourth ring. What was wrong? Was it broken? His dad had just bought a new one the month before.

Riverstone gave the operator his dad's cell phone number for him to dial instead. Not only was there no answer this time but the recording said the line had been disconnected, and there was no new number listed.

"No new number?" Riverstone barked. "The old one's still good! It's been good my whole life. You sure you've got the right area code, brah? It's 5-6-2!" The operator was patient and understanding. He tried again. He punched in the numbers three more times, and each time the computer voice repeated the same precise, unemotional message.

"Not home?" Riverstone exclaimed and slammed the receiver on the hook. He hadn't meant to be impolite. The operator was just doing his job. But where could they be? Why wasn't anyone home waiting for his call? Didn't anyone care? *Of course they do,* he thought, trying to calm himself. *They're my parents. They always care about me.* There were a million reasons why they might not answer, but Riverstone feared only one: the Dakadudes had been to Lakewood.

He tried to shake himself free of the dreaded thought that something bad had happened to his parents. It was the alien ship the bad guys were after, not some senior high school kids with skulls full of mush that didn't belong in this interstellar trash heap anyway.

Riverstone went back to the bar where Mowgi and Monday were waiting. Along the way, he glanced to his side and saw a young couple giggling happily together, kissing playfully over their icy drinks. He looked away, unable to watch their happiness. He stepped up to the bar and took another long pull on his draft.

"Problem?" Monday asked, seeing how distraught Riverstone was.

"No one's home," Riverstone replied.

"Out of town?"

Riverstone frowned. "Something's whack. Even my dad's cell's been disconnected."

"Did he pay his bill?"

Riverstone returned a sour look. "Are you kidding? My dad always pays it. He's so anal, he makes Harry's team of accountants seem incompetent."

"Maybe he's a little short," Monday said.

"My dad? He's got plenty. Not in the Mars stratosphere, but he can buy a mountain or two."

"Well, the limo will be here in a couple of minutes. It has three phones. You can make all the calls you want from there. Have you seen today's paper, bro?" Monday asked, pushing the local newspaper in front of him on the bar.

Riverstone's eyes flared with disbelief as he read the date of the local *Las Vegas Sun*'s street edition. *Three days! That's whack! Only three days!* It was the same year, too, and the same month, and . . . Monday's Rolex had been right after all. They had to have been gone longer than that. A couple of weeks at least, he argued to himself.

"That can't be right!" Riverstone exclaimed incredulously. "It's an old paper."

Monday couldn't believe it either. "Nope. The bartender confirmed it. It's today's paper, alright."

While Monday went to the front door to wait for the limo, Riverstone read the lead story:

> *A sonic boom shattered a million dollars' worth of windows in the Four Corners region early this morning, while thousands of people were shaken out of their beds, including this reporter. A call to the neighborhood police stations asking for an explanation yielded no answer. Nellis Air Force Base denied it was a military craft of theirs. It was a sonic disturbance of unknown origin and that was all that was being said about it—publicly, that is.*

Riverstone looked toward the blinking slot machines. Not possible, he thought, an eternity had gone by since all of them had been on that freeway going flat-out to Utah. But three days? How had the world changed so fast? He didn't know how or why, but the world *had* changed into a chilling alternate dimension.

When he came back to Earth, he read further down the page. Normally, he wouldn't have cared about an obscure science article concerning someone on the other side of the world. But when you're a part of the changing world, seemingly odd and disconnected events *do* have meaning.

Australian Jacob Que, a famous backyard astronomer credited with many outstanding discoveries over the years that include several comets, says that he has discovered three new moons in orbit around Mars. Mr. Que believes that the planet's gravitational pull may have grabbed the new companions from the nearby asteroid belt that lies between Mars and Earth. He said he discovered the satellites a week ago and sent his findings to the International Astronomical Society for confirmation.

Since that time, he says, one of the satellites has inexplicably disappeared while the other two moons have changed orbits several times. Asked how he would account for such erratic behavior, Mr. Que laughed and stated, "If I didn't have my reputation to consider, I'd say they were some kind of alien craft." It is all indeed perplexing to him, too, and he went on to say that "obviously we're looking at very unstable orbits . . ."

Dr. Robert Zagorsky (pictured right), head astrophysicist for the Jet Propulsion Laboratory in Pasadena, couldn't be reached to verify the Australian's findings. His secretary, however, stated that he had indeed received Mr. Que's remarkable photos. She said recent Hubble photographs show only Phobos and Deimos, the two known moons of Mars. No other moons have been sighted despite three days of intensive search.

Just then a white-haired old man came up to the bar and excused himself as he read the front page of the *Sun* over Riverstone's shoulder. His long, straight hair touched his collar. The smell of Bay Rum aftershave filled the air as he invaded Riverstone's space.

After reading the headlines, the old man expounded loudly, "I knew it!" He slapped the paper with the back of his hand. "The Aussie's going public. Can you believe it?" The old man then turned his angry, green eyes toward Riverstone and said straight out, "So, what's going to happen to our world, young man? Are you going to save it or sit on your hind end and watch it die?"

Riverstone sipped on his beer. "I just got here, mister. It's not my concern."

The man stepped closer, his piercing stare spitting fire. Somehow his eyes did not match his face. They were younger, more robust than his outward appearance showed him to be.

"Of course it's your concern!" the old man roared. Riverstone reeled backward at his tirade. "Soon it will be everyone's concern! It's our planet we're talking about, son. It *is* your concern. Wake up! Our home is in danger!"

Riverstone smiled defensively. Maybe the old man had a screw loose, he figured.

The old man's whiskey breath smacked Riverstone across the face as he grabbed him by the shirt and looked him in the eyes. "Wake up, son. If not you, then who?" He shook Riverstone gently before dusting some of the desert sand off his blue T-shirt. Saddened, then, the old man threw a handful of silver dollars on the bar. "The next round's on me." Mowgi yelped twice as the old man petted him. Riverstone thought it peculiar how the undog licked and snuggled up to the old man like a long lost pard. Then the old dude turned and strolled out the front door to his dust-covered blue Bronco.

Riverstone watched the car roll slowly out of the parking lot. "A stupid nut case," he mumbled, pushing the paper down the bar. He vacuumed the dregs of his beer, wishing he had a tongue like Mowgi's to lick the few extra drops at the bottom of the glass. He set the mug on the bar just as Monday hollered from the front door, "Limo's here."

Mowgi yelped twice again.

* * *

The dry, cool air inside the limo felt wonderful. Riverstone toyed with the fresh Dos Equis Monday had handed him as he gazed out the window, not really paying attention to the Las Vegas scenery passing by. Other things seemed more important now. The old man had gotten to him. The world outside felt like a dream and he was just along for the ride.

Asshole . . .

Monday reached over and was just about to pick up the phone when it rang. As Riverstone looked on, the bodyguard's face suddenly changed, as though he were talking to a ghost on the other end. "Yes, ma'am," Monday practically whispered, "I'm with Riverstone. No, they're with the ship north of Vegas at the old *Distant Galaxies* movie set. Yeah, Lu's fine. Millawanda pulled her through. She's like new."

He covered the mouthpiece, whispering, "It's Mrs. M."

Then, back on the phone, he said, "I'm talking to Riverstone, ma'am. Alright, Mrs. M, I'll tell him. Yes, we will. Understood. Okay. Sure, Mrs. M. I will. Don't worry. You can count on it, Mrs. M." He hung up the phone.

"They're okay?" Riverstone asked, surprised.

"Yeah."

"Harry too?"

"I heard him in the background talking. They're both alive and coming here. They want us to lay low at Harry's Casino until they arrive."

"When?"

"Tonight. They'll meet us at the penthouse. She said your parents are okay. They're safe." Riverstone was relieved to hear that. "Tinker and Petey are okay too. She's got all of them in Harry's new Dream-liner headed for Hawaii. He had to get them out of Lakewood."

"The Daks?"

"No. The government. They're all over the place. It seems we got out of the ship just in time. They have the *Distant Galaxies* area surrounded. There's no way in or out now."

"The ship's surrounded?" Riverstone was worried.

"With three battalions."

"What's up with that?"

"They're after you and Harlowe big-time too. She doesn't want you sticking your nose anywhere in public. There are orders to shoot you, Riverstone. On sight."

Riverstone went nuclear. "Me? What did I do? I wasn't even driving. It was Harlowe. He's the one they should be shooting at. Blame him. I just want to go back to Lakewood!" he fumed.

"Hey, let Harry and Mrs. M handle it. Just stay out of sight for a few days like she says. Enjoy the penthouse. Everything will be fine. You'll see."

But Riverstone wasn't okay as he watched a huge shopping mall drift by on his side of the limo. "Stop. Pull over there, Platter. I need to get out."

"Dude! Didn't you hear me? The cops are out to shoot you," Monday warned.

"I heard you. But we have a few hours to kill before Mrs. M and Harry get here. I promised Harlowe I'd do him a favor, and I have to do it." He pointed excitedly. "And look at that. An In-N-Out. I'm in need of a Double-Double Cheese right now, Platter, and I can scan it for Millie and her crew."

"Mrs. M's orders were to stay low. That's what we're doing."

Riverstone reached for the door handle and pulled it up while the limo was still moving. "Stop now or I'm jumping out."

Monday reached out to stop him, but Mowgi wasn't going for it. His incisors lowered below his upper lip as he let out a low, evil growl. Monday wisely backed off. "Alright, bro." He reached into a cubby and pulled out two baseball caps and two pairs of sunglasses. "But let's at least cover our faces with these." He had the driver pull over into the mall parking lot, and then he added, "But the Mowg stays. They might connect the dots if they see him."

Riverstone thought that made sense. His "uniqueness" would be like a homing beacon to the authorities. "Sorry, Mowg."

Mowgi yipped once, jumped to another cushion, and pouted.

Chapter Forty-Three

SURROUNDED

THE SUN HAD faded behind the mountains to the west of the saddle, and the stars were already twinkling brightly in the heavens. Inside the ship's control room, Harlowe and Leucadia watched with guarded interest the mightiest armada the world had ever seen dig in around the ship. They didn't even attempt to flee. Where in the world could they hide an alien craft bigger than Dodger Stadium anyway? The government had too many eyes in orbit to escape their scrutiny. Leucadia wondered aloud what had taken them so long in the first place.

Through the massive front windows, they watched as fully loaded Apache and Black Hawk military choppers, F-16s, Abrams M-1 tanks, and mechanized troop carriers scurried about in the desert night. Displayed on the ship's overhead screens, Millie's three-dimensional, real-time graphics clearly indicated every vehicle, plane, and foot soldier within a ten-mile radius of the ship.

Ian sat in the control room studying the various panels of lights, small screens, and indicators along the wide control console below the massive windows. Slightly unsure, he tentatively touched a section of a small screen above one particular 3-D graphic of the ship. The ship on the screen turned slightly blue as a corresponding wispy veil of blue light suddenly covered the ship like a delicate blanket.

"What did you do?" Harlowe asked, alarmed.

"I didn't do anything," Ian replied defensively. He pointed at the graphic on the console in front of him. "I saw this same graphic snap on before the explosion. My guess is that it's some kind of protective field around the ship."

"Good idea, Ian," Leucadia said.

"I didn't turn it on, Lu," Ian countered.

"Then who did?" Harlowe questioned.

Leucadia studied the console in front of Ian briefly. "It could be automatic."

"Can you override it?" Harlowe asked. He wasn't in the mood for games. "It's no time to be fooling around. We've got problems. Those guys are serious."

Leucadia studied the blue shimmer covering the ship's outer hull. "We should keep it on. It could buy us time."

Ian touched the screen again and the field disappeared on the graphic. "What did that do?"

"It's gone," she replied. The blue shimmer had disappeared.

Harlowe had had enough experimenting. "Alright, keep it on, Wiz."

"Roger that," Ian replied, touching the screen to reestablish the protective shield.

At that moment, Simon materialized from below. He looked sharp in his new ship attire, as if he belonged on the bridge and was in command. "I spotted a chopper flying overhead from a portal. Monday must have made it okay. He sure took his sweet time. Drop the stairway, Pylott."

"Shut up, Simon," Harlowe stated.

Simon ignored the cold edge of his reply. "I want the stairway down, Pylott. That's my ride. I wanna leave."

Leucadia stepped between Harlowe and Simon. "It's not your helicopter, Simon," she said, pushing him away from Harlowe. "It's all military. They've surrounded us."

Simon didn't see any problem with that. "That's even better."

"No, Simon," Leucadia stated sternly, "it's not."

"Why? You're going to turn the ship over to them anyway, right? Let's get it over with."

"No, we're not."

"What are we going to do with it? It's of no use to us. Let them figure out what makes this thing tick. Just walk out there with our hands up and be done with it. They get the ship and we go home. It's a no-brainer. Everybody's happy. I'll call my publicity man in New York and he'll have us on the front page of the *New York Times* and *Newsweek* by tomorrow. We'll all be heroes. Ticker-tape parade down Broadway, an appearance on the *Tonight Show,* guests on *Oprah.* We'll have the world eating out of our hands. Harlowe, you'll be so filthy rich you couldn't spend it all in five lifetimes."

"That's not what my mom wanted," Leucadia said sharply. "This ship is not something to exploit. We're in trouble, Simon, or haven't you been paying attention?"

Harlowe shot Leucadia a hard glance. She could see he was about to take care of Simon in his own way and it wouldn't be pretty. "No, Harlowe. Let me take care of this."

"Do."

"I thought you needed my help, Leucadia," Simon tried to say out of Harlowe's hearing.

Leucadia forced Simon back toward the control room entrance. He tried to struggle and stop her, but he was no match for her strength. After one too many protests, she pinched the back of his neck and he went down to his knees in agonizing pain. "Sorry, Simon, but this is no time to be a jerk." She rolled his twisted body onto a circular pad in the floor and slapped the activator that winked him out of existence to the floor below.

When Leucadia returned to the console, Harlowe and Ian were looking at photos of all of them except her on a screen.

"That was taken last year after Sullivan found out I was driving without my license," Harlowe said, pointing at his own mug shot.

"Where did you get this?" Leucadia asked.

"From the news broadcast," Ian replied nonchalantly, as though it was no big deal that he had already figured out how to tune into the local TV stations. "All military and police units have our photos." He pointed at his face on the screen. "That's my driver's license picture. There's Monday and his rerun employer, Simon."

Harlowe's brow wrinkled. "But they don't have you, Lu."

"Are you sure?" she asked.

Ian took a few moments to locate the information he needed to answer her. "No. Nothing."

"How 'bout the beach house?"

"No mention of that either," Ian replied.

She looked out the front window at all the activity. "The cars. They found Baby and Simon's Vantage. That's how they know."

Harlowe wanted to know what the capital letters "D-10, STK" meant at the end of his and Riverstone's names.

Ian didn't have a clue, but Leucadia did. She faced Harlowe. "If they find Riverstone or you on the streets, they will kill you and ask questions later. STK means shoot to kill, Harlowe. D-10 is the highest category of enemy against the state. If you leave the ship, you're a dead man walking, Pylott."

Harlowe turned to Ian. "What about Riverstone's location?"

Ian shook his head. "Nothing yet."

That didn't make Harlowe any less comfortable. "Can you reach him?"

"I can try. He's out scanning things as we speak. But I don't think he knows how to use it both ways."

"You didn't tell him?" Harlowe snapped.

"I didn't know anyone was going to shoot him," Ian defended. "Come on, Harlowe, you saw him. He was bent on flying back to Lakewood. How was I to know?"

"Monday will take him to the penthouse," Lu stated confidently.

Harlowe agreed. He and Leucadia had spent too many romantic nights in the Mars penthouse suite not to know that's where they were headed.

"How do you know that?" Ian asked.

"Because Monday knows he's got the family penthouse open to him there anytime he's in town," she replied.

"Knowing Riverstone like I do," Harlowe began, "he'll hustle a couple of does up there before catching his flight back to Lakewood. We may have time to warn him." Harlowe started for the pad.

"Where are you going?" Leucadia asked, worried, but her voice conveyed that she already knew the answer.

"I've gotta get him back," Harlowe said.

Leucadia quickly caught him. "No! They'll shoot you the moment you step foot out there."

"I can't let him die out there, Lu."

"No. Let me go. They don't know I'm a part of this."

"I want to keep it that way. You're staying." They struggled for a moment until Harlowe's eyes spoke the final answer.

"Let me go with you then. I can get us into Harry's without either of us being seen," she suggested.

Harlowe thought briefly. "No. I can't risk you getting hurt again. Stay with Ian. You need to protect his backside from that toadhead movie star. Wiz can't keep the ship safe alone. He'll need your help. You can't let the military have it, Lu. I promised your mom I'd save the ship and that's what I'm going to do."

"She didn't mean for you to kill yourself first."

"I can't let my pard die, Lu."

"I know, but—"

"No buts. Keep Wiz out of trouble until I get back."

With tears in her eyes, Leucadia conceded she had lost the battle. "Okay, Pylott."

Leucadia held his hand as they made their way to the pad. "Let me go with you to the storeroom. I remember seeing some things there that can help you get through the military blockade." She locked eyes with him. "I want you back in one piece."

"You don't think I'd let a woman fly this ship, do you?" he said with a sly smirk.

After surviving a sharp jab to the gut, Harlowe then turned to give Ian instructions. "Don't rebuild anything while I'm gone, Wiz. Lu's going to set me up with one of those com things so we can stay in touch."

Ian gave him a thumbs-up. "Roger that, captain."

Harlowe slapped the activator and he and Lu blinked down to the lower level.

Chapter Forty-Four

THE BARRIER

Simon had never been in so much pain. His neck ached as if he had been hung. And the only way he could walk without collapsing was to use the side of the corridor wall to help himself along toward the cavernous center foyer of the ship.

He wanted to stay curled up on the floor, but if he did, he knew he would be stuck inside the ship. Something bad was going to happen. He had seen the military hardware from the control room. There were serious weapons of mass destruction out there. It wouldn't be long before they would try to overtake the ship or bomb it out of existence. No way was he going down with the ship. *Screw that!* He just had to get out of the ship and tell the soldiers who he was. A few autographs and a promise to send them a wad of money and he was home free. He would be back at Harry's in a couple of hours and out of this screwed-up nightmare of a weekend once and for all.

Forget Leucadia! She's history. I don't need her in my life. I'm famous now. I can make it on my own. I'm Simon Bolt, the movie star. I write my own ticket and can have any chick I want with a snap of my fingers. She'll see.

When he came to the center foyer, he searched in vain for the opening in the floor. It was large enough to drive a truck through the last time he saw it. So where was it? He fell on his hands and knees and crawled around on the floor, looking for any cracks or lines in the blue carpet that would give him a clue to its location.

Nothing.

Looking around, he spied on a nearby wall an activator like the one in the control room. He crawled over to it and slapped the flat, round switch from his kneeling position. The strain of his effort made his head swirl. He closed his eyes, catching his breath as he fell against the wall and rested. He didn't know if his action worked, but as he rolled sideways, he fell through the opening and started tumbling down the open ramp. He might have broken his neck and every other bone in his body if a spindly-bodied China-hat hadn't stopped him first. After helping the movie star to his feet, the robob then assisted him the rest of the way down the ramp. Simon, the ever-grateful person that he was, pushed the mechanical Good Samaritan away. "Get away from me, stickman. I'm done with this place."

Simon steadied himself against the ramp as he stared at the robob's lighted brim head. "Get outta here, I said. Leave me alone." The robob waited another half-moment before it obediently followed the request and began clacking back up the ramp, defying gravity. Simon glanced around briefly to get his bearings. When he turned back to rant once more at the robob, the stickman was already gone.

"Good riddance," Simon grumbled as he turned back toward the open desert. It was nearly dark. Only a wisp of red light was left behind the western mountains. Even in the dark, however, he could see he had a hike ahead of him just to make it to the perimeter edge of the ship. It wasn't a great distance for a healthy person, but in his condition it seemed like a hundred-mile walk. He saw plenty of movement among the troops beyond a filmy blue light surrounding the ship. They were still scurrying around, digging in, and taking their positions all around the ship.

Simon brushed up his hair and straightened his stylish blue uniform to appear more presentable to his fans. Near the ridgeline a tank rolled into place, along with many other kinds of weaponry he could only guess at. "Good," he said to himself. "The more fire-power, the better." He'd give his next residual check to the first sol-dier who put a rocket grenade thorugh Harlowe's thick head, he mused, before he limped off toward what he believed was the closest gathering of troops near the perimeter.

When Simon finally arrived at the ship's edge, he saw the blue shimmer of light he had seen earlier cascading down to the ground in front of him. He wasn't quite sure what it was, nor did he care. Just then, however, someone outside the blue shimmer yelled, "HALT! Stop right where you are, sir!"

Simon tried to explain who he was but he didn't get two words out before several heavily armed soldiers came out from their hid-ing places with their weapons leveled right at his head and shouted at him again. "STOP RIGHT WHERE YOU ARE! ON THE GROUND! FEET SPREAD! HANDS ABOVE YOUR HEAD!"

Simon was fed up with lower-class ingrates, of being pushed around like a nobody. "Just a minute, soldier. Do you know who I—"

A burst of bullets erupted from several M16s. Simon curled up into a little ball, trying to duck the blazing rounds flying at him. Strangely, nothing hit him. He checked himself for blood. He was okay. More shots rang out. He twitched a few more times as the fusillade of exploding rounds struck the light just inches from his body. Still, nothing was hitting him. He stepped closer to watch as the rounds struck the membrane of hazy blue light. The bullets stopped dead in mid-flight, then fell harmlessly to the ground.

Simon couldn't believe his eyes. He touched the light with his finger and felt a harmless static tingle. By slowly pressing against its spongy resilience, he could almost push his hand through—but only an inch or so. He put his shoulder against it, but no matter how hard he pushed, he couldn't get through. The wall of light was impenetrable.

Three soldiers in full assault gear came up from out of the bushes and pointed their snub-nosed machine guns at Simon's face, telling him to drop to the ground or they'd put a bullet in his head.

He glared at them like they were dumb as rocks. "Listen, I would if it would make any difference." He kicked the barrier with his foot in frustration. "If you can get me out from behind this thing, I'll give you each a million bucks."

"What is it?" the soldier in the lead asked.

"How do I know? A barrier, numskull; can't you see that?" Simon shouted back.

"I can see that, dork," the soldier shouted back, coming up to the barrier. Now they were just inches from each other's faces, but it might as well have been a mile for the good it did them. "Now shut the barrier off!"

"I don't know how or I would have done it a long time ago."

"Do it now!"

"Aren't you listening to me? Do you see a switch around here any-where? If you see a switch, I'll turn it off just for you."

"Kiss your pretty face good-bye, butthead," and the soldier fired three shots at point-blank range into Simon's face.

Simon barely blinked. "Hah! You got any other bright ideas, sol-dier?" He looked at the soldier's lapel and read sergeant. "Listen, sarge, my name is Simon Bolt. Heard of me?"

The sergeant's face froze. "You're *that* Simon Bolt?"

"That's right. In the flesh." He turned his head back and forth so the soldiers could get a good look with their flashlights. "Well, I want to get out of here too. I don't want to be on this side; I want to be on *your* side. So anything you can do to make that happen will make me very happy, and I'll be very generous in thanking you and your men."

The sergeant nodded. "Yes, sir, but our orders are to kill you and anyone else that comes out of this ship if we so much as see you twitch."

Simon was about to go into another tirade when one of the soldiers to the right shouted out, "Sarge, there's something happening over there. Look!"

The sergeant removed a pair of binoculars from his hip belt and remarked, "Another section of the ship is opening up."

Simon turned around, shaking his head. "Now what?"

Chapter Forty-Five

NO CHOICE

LEUCADIA TOUCHED THE activator and watched the opening in the ship floor expand wide enough to allow the wheel-less vehicle to drop through the bottom hull of the ship. But first, she pulled Harlowe's unconscious body over to the nearby wall and leaned him next to the lifeless manikin they discovered the first time they visited the storeroom together with Riverstone.

"I'm sorry, Harlowe. It was the only way. I'll always love you . . . forever," she told him.

She had tricked Harlowe into holding the grav cords while she put a stun device to his side and pulled the trigger. Tears fell down the sides of her cheeks as she tried to make him comfortable. She couldn't let him go out there and be killed. This time was even more painful than the prom night when she flew to Simon's boat in the Mediterranean to help her mother find her future crew of Gamadin, which never came to pass. If only Harlowe knew why, back then. It never was Simon. He could never be what Harlowe was to her: the only love she had ever known.

She looked at Harlowe propped there so helpless, so peaceful. Together, he and the manikin looked like two old friends who were sleeping off a night of hard partying. She smiled a little, thinking how cute he was, so brave and fearless. Too fearless, she thought, except when it came to her. He made mistakes because of her. She couldn't allow her presence to interfere. He needed Matt.

That was something she hadn't expected. She never thought Harlowe would let him go, and when he did . . . Well, she made the mistake of thinking Matt would never leave Harlowe's side. But she should have known that Harlowe would never let his friend down when he needed him. Right now, Harlowe's place was here with Millie. That was his destiny. Leucadia knew that. Harlowe was the only one capable of saving Millawanda from the Fhaal.

"Harlowe, I'm so sorry. Forgive me," she told him. She heard gunfire coming from the outside, jolting her to action. She kissed him one last time on the lips before she hopped into the vehicle. She dropped down to the desert floor and took off in the direction opposite from the shots. The shimmering veil of blue didn't stop the wheel-less car as it moved swiftly through the perimeter rim of the ship accelerating past three hundred miles per hour, whizzing by stunned troops who could do nothing to stop the speeding bullet.

Chapter Forty-Six

NEANDERTHAL MINDS

GENERAL GUNN WATCHED over Ed McCarty's shoulder as he brought up the shape of the golden disk onto the computer screen. The digital image of the ship was as close to an exact model of the alien craft as McCarty could make for the general in order for him to visualize what they were up against. As the general requested, McCarty rotated the disk on its axis and zoomed in on the forward massive windows. It was like he was an eagle and could fly anywhere he wished to view the ship without actually being there.

"How close are the tolerances, Ed?" General Gunn asked.

"She's pretty darned close, sir," McCarty replied. "Within inches, I'd say. Her underside may have some peculiarities we don't know about, but the topside," he tapped the screen with his finger, "she's balls on."

Gunn nodded, impressed with McCarty's visuals. "Can you give me any idea of the ship's capabilities from this?" he asked.

"A little, general. From last night's radar contact, here's what I have so far." McCarty manipulated the image of the alien saucer with his portable toggle mouse, aligning the disk along the X and Y axes, emphasizing the ship's perfect symmetrical profile. "She's built for speed and maneuverability, that's for sure, general." His right index finger traced the outline of the perimeter edge of the saucer along the screen. "See those lines? They show that the ship's drag coefficient is so close to zero that it's insignificant."

He clicked in three more numbers, and the disk turned 45 degrees along the Z-axis. After that, he placed an image of a Boeing 747 on the screen next to the saucer. "This will give you an idea of her size. She makes that 747 look like a Cessna by comparison, doesn't she?"

"Something that large should have torn itself to pieces from the g-forces," the general commented, shaking his head.

Wide-eyed with childish enthusiasm, McCarty began punching in more numbers. "It gets better, sir. Keep your eye on the screen."

The display blinked and up popped another one of McCarty's whiz-bang graphics. "What you're seeing here is a comparison of how gravity affects an F-22 Raptor, the planet's most advanced jet fighter." He pointed to the decreasing spirals on the screen. At one end of the radial lines were tiny F-16 icons. "Each one of these circles represents the turning radius by g-forces. At two g's a Raptor can complete an eleven-thousand-foot circle, and at the other extreme, a nine-g turn can be done in less than sixteen hundred feet. That would be a remarkable feat for the hottest military jet on the planet. Anything above a nine-g turn, the jet breaks up, though, right, general? I believe that's its limit."

Gunn confirmed McCarty's conclusion. It was unclassified information any school kid could find on the Internet.

McCarty changed the screen again. "This graphic shows how far an F-16 Falcon can turn at different speeds. A jet traveling at two hundred knots, pulling four g's, has a turning radius of 912 feet, and will fully complete a turn in seventeen seconds. The best in the world. Now, with afterburners blazing so it can travel at a thousand knots," he said, tracing a wide, open arch with his finger, "the radius becomes 23,000 feet, and the pilot would have completed merely seventy-two degrees of the turn in the same amount of time."

"I hope this is leading to some conclusion?" the general queried.

"Keep your .45 holstered, general," McCarty joked, his face alive with discovery. "With the data we collected the other night on the saucer, this is what the computer simulations came up with."

As his fingers danced across the keys, the disk drives whirred, extracting scrambled information before it was sent to random memory where the central processing unit gathered it, reassembled it, and spit it out in brilliant color.

McCarty split the screen, separating the two scaled-down original graphics. After that, he superimposed the saucer's graphic in blue over them to contrast with the first graphics so the eye could easily tell the difference. The blue overlays were so far inside the turning radius of both the F-22 and the F-16 that they were almost unreadable.

"Look at that flight envelope, general," McCarty marveled. "If your jet jockeys tried to keep up with that saucer, their wing rivets would pop in the first turn."

Gunn moved back away from the screen, the tip of his nose touching the top of his upper lip as he stood deep in thought.

"That salad plate pulled 150 g's when they made that turn at fifteen hundred knots, general!" McCarty exclaimed. "And I don't think they were pushing it, either."

"How is that possible? No pilot could stand g-forces that strong."

"Some kind of inertia dampeners is my guess."

"Impossible. There's no such thing."

McCarty pointed at the computer screen. "Tell *them* that."

Unable to accept the facts, Gunn frowned. Then, snapping out of his malaise, he asked, "Well, what about speed? How much faster can it go?"

McCarty turned to the general, wearing a look of calm, dreamy wonder on his face. "General, I think you're working at the wrong end of the speed curve. The saucer was just putting along in idle. If they ever get their transmission fixed and stick the vessel in gear, that frisbee, as you call it, will be past the moon before you can smack your swagger stick. It's a star craft, sir. I'd bet the farm that she's capable of light speeds. It's a ship built for the stars, general."

Gunn came to full military attention. "That's nuts! Do you know what you're saying, doctor?"

"Uh, huh. And JPL confirmed it. Zagorsky thinks I've been smoking dope. Nothing is supposed to go faster than light, but that ship got here somehow. Just like the group that is coming toward us now. This ship's not built like a slow, sub-light ship that would house generation after generation of star travelers for a journey across the void, general." McCarty shook his head, convinced. "No, sir, this baby can move."

He replaced the performance graphics with the original image of the saucer, then he rotated the monitor around so they could both see the screen clearly. "Look at her. She's lean and mean, and I'll bet you she's a fighter too. You're staring fifty centuries into the future, General Gunn. You're looking at a real live fifty-fourth-century Raptor on steroids."

Gunn studied the screen as though he was looking for something he hadn't seen before.

McCarty came between the general and the screen. "With all due respect, sir, don't even think about it. I've seen that look before on people who think they're one up on what's good for the world. I know you think we're a bunch of purse toters, but listen to me on this one, general. There's not an air force on Earth that can stop this spaceship. Even if she would allow you to get close to her, which she obviously has, your sidewinders would be spitwads against her skin. She's made of metal far beyond our technology. Diamonds couldn't cut through her hide. She's as much above today's fighters as your fighters are above the cavemen of a hundred thousand years ago."

The general glared at McCarty, who glared right back. He wasn't backing down. The general had to know it was futile. "You may not like my ideas, general, but lives are at stake here. You're thinking, maybe she can be taken because you have her surrounded in this saddle with every weapon in your arsenal pointed right at her nose. There's no way she can take off without you blasting her to pieces before she lifts an inch off the ground. But that's not good, because you would lose all the technology.

"So, you're saying to yourself, maybe I can just wound her because I have at my disposal the world's mightiest air force, and they can do anything I tell them, given enough time and resources. Then with a little bit of reverse engineering, Uncle Sam could have its very own faster-than-light spaceship. Eureka! *Star Wars,* here we come. *Enterprise,* move over; you've got competition. You don't know how you're going to do it, but you'll find a way," Ed continued, his tone heavy with sarcasm, "because you think you're smarter than an alien that traveled light-years to get here and somehow survived thousands of years under a plateau, then blasted out of a hundred feet of solid rock and flew away at five times the speed of sound.

"Am I right, general? You think you can pull it off. You can figure out a way to capture this spaceship because she's worth all that technology you'll find. Yeah, baby! The world will be at our feet. They'll be begging the big bad U. S. of A. to give them mercy. Why, general, we'll have a hundred more states in the union before the month's out!"

McCarty stood up as Gunn looked out the command tent's open window at the ship. His mind was closed, and the scientist saw it. "You can't hear me, can you, general? Even if you could by some wild stretch of the imagination capture that ship, her technology would be useless to you."

The general turned away from the window, his mouth displaying a wry smirk. "Oh, really?"

McCarty let out a frustrated sigh. He knew his protest was falling on deaf ears, but he had to say it anyway. "Yes, really. You can't pick up a book and expect to understand it unless you know how to read first, general. Technology doesn't happen overnight. It's learned step by step, through trial and error. Oh sure, there are times when we stumble onto things, like penicillin, lasers, and eight-track tapes. Or we develop technology out of necessity, like rockets and bombs, that pushes us forward. But sooner or later we would have had them anyway. But to race fifty centuries ahead in 'one giant leap for mankind'?"

Ed scoffed. "Forget it! That's arrogance talking. Would a Neanderthal know what a car was? Would he know how to drive it if he could start it? And if by pure luck he could start the car and drive it, he would kill himself as sure as I'm standing here talking to you. And that's just what we would do. We'd kill ourselves, general, and the whole planet as well. Look at how close we've come to killing ourselves already with the atomic bomb, when we leaped ahead a few decades before we should have. The repercussions of that are still with us. The atomic war clock is five minutes from midnight. And you want more?"

General Gunn lost his smirk. "I want inside that ship, McCarty," he said coldly.

McCarty was about to open his mouth again when Drs. Zagorsky and Shaffer, each looking glum, entered General Gunn's tent. It took but a moment to explain the bad news.

"Are you telling me that suddenly two more unidentifieds just *appeared* on your photo plates, doctors?" the general thundered, waving the recent photographs taken at Palomar. "What were they before, camera shy?"

"I don't know, general," Zagorsky replied.

"I've been hearing that a lot lately, doctor," Gunn growled.

"And you'll be hearing it again until we make contact," Shaffer added.

The general searched his tent for his swagger stick. He needed something to hit with. "Where is the squadron now, Doctor Shaffer?"

"They've already moved past Mars," Shaffer replied.

"And no communications yet, I suppose?"

"That's correct, sir."

"I wonder how many more have an aversion to cameras," Gunn muttered half under his breath. "We don't have to guess where they're headed, do we, gentlemen?"

Shaffer's jaw set. "What would you have us do, general? Invent a ray gun to shoot them down?"

Gunn laid a fuzzy, black-and-white close-up photo of one of the alien ships on the table. "Yes, I'd like that very much. I'd feel better knowing I had something I could shoot back with." It was difficult to see exact detail, but one didn't need to be an expert astrophotographer to understand that the outer wings of each spacecraft were equipped with deadly weaponry. "Then you would agree that these ships aren't here to sing around the campfire and smoke pot?"

"Yes, sir, I would agree," Shaffer admitted reluctantly.

The general turned to McCarty with a rapier glance. "Now wouldn't you like to have that saucer in your arsenal?"

"Having that ship will not help us," Zagorsky answered for McCarty.

"I know, I know," the general interrupted, "McCarty here was kind enough to fill me in on our caveman mentalities. Well, we don't have a lot of choices now, do we? Those hostel aliens are out there, and no one's answered our calls, have they?"

Shaffer replied with a silent shake of his head. "So," continued the general, "they're not interested in working deals with us, huh, doctors? Then it's time to improvise. How long do we have?"

All eyes fell on Shaffer. "The main force should be here in eleven hours and thirty-two minutes at their present speed. But if my guess is correct, they were already slowing once they crossed the orbital plane of Mars. That might buy us a few more hours."

"Great. That's just great. I've got less than twenty hours to hijack an alien frisbee that may or may not have the capabilities to stop what looks to be an all-out invasion of this planet." He leaned forward. "This isn't an action movie, doctors. I'm not Arnold Schwarzenegger or Bruce Willis or even Captain Julian Starr. I'm just an ignorant grunt general. And I don't even know what the enemy wants!"

General Gunn stood erect again and took a long look at his group of brainiacs. "Gentleman," he lamented, "I hope you're right. She better be on our side. If we can't figure out what make this frisbee tick, or get inside that craft, we're in for a world of hurt. That ship is our only hope, wouldn't you agree?"

Suddenly, loud rifle fire from M16s exploded across the headquarters compound along the ridgeline. It sounded like World War III had started inside the saddle. Sergeant Gunderson busted through the tent flaps crying out, "General, sir, the men have someone pinned down along the ship's perimeter."

"Is the hostile returning fire?" Gunn asked, checking his white-handled .45 and grabbing his hat and coat.

"No sir, no word on that," Gunderson replied.

"Well, what's all the shooting about, Gunny?"

"They just said that they got one and they're trying to neutralize him, sir," Gunderson reported.

"Have they killed him?"

"No, sir."

"Alright, Gunny, contact the men down there. I want that hostile alive at all costs. McCarty! Captain Walker! You're with me."

"Yes, sir," McCarty snapped, putting on his coat.

Captain Walker, long used to the commanding officer's hasty exits, had his clipboard in hand.

On his way out of the command tent, the general faced Lieutenant Poole. "Keep Zagorsky and Shaffer company," he ordered. "If I need them, I'll let you know."

"Yes, sir, general," Poole replied and watched Gunn and the others jump into a desert-camouflaged Humvee and head toward the loud cracks of the M16s that were spitting bright red flashes into the saucer's misty blue perimeter.

Chapter Forty-Seven

THE PENTHOUSE

IT WAS NIGHTTIME, but as Riverstone and Monday looked outside the limo's tinted windows at the Las Vegas Strip, it was anything but dark. It was always daylight, 24/7, on the brightly lit avenues. Riverstone put his Oakley sunglasses back on to admire the two thousand brilliant hand-blown Chihuly glass flowers that decorated the entrance of Harry's Casino under the magnificent porte cochere.

Harry's famous hotel and casino was nestled on the shores of a ten-acre lake right in the heart of the strip. The ultimate in Las Vegas five-star luxury hotels, its three thousand rooms were spread out over thirty-six floors of lavish opulence. The moment the limo pulled up, they were surrounded by an entourage of bellhops, doormen, and managers, all catering to their every whim and need. Lobby doors opened before them as security bodyguards led them past botanical gardens, massive fish ponds, an indoor rain forest, waterfalls, a fine arts gallery, twenty restaurants and cafes, and a world-class shopping arcade where the rich could spend their money when they weren't at the tables.

"Real first cabin, Platter," Riverstone confessed, grinning from ear to ear as he bounced into the lush lobby, gawking in awe. Everywhere he looked there were bright lights and gold surfaces, not to mention the beautiful women on display.

In the reception area a floor manager approached them, practically tripping over his own feet as he tried to avoid Mowgi. He apologized and handed Monday a small white envelope. "The Mars family is waiting, sir," the manager informed him. The small entourage made their way past the check-in lobby to one of the private elevators. Monday absentmindedly put the note in his front pants pocket as he said to Riverstone, "Yeah, it's a cool place, and just wait 'til you see the penthouse."

The polished brass elevator doors opened before them. Mowgi jumped ahead first to stake out his claim. Riverstone continued blabbing away. "You've got that right. Not bad at all. Oops, sorry," he said, apologizing for bumping into the bellhop, his eyes focused on the dazzle instead of watching where he was going.

The bellhop apologized profusely. Riverstone felt sorry for the young man. He patted him on the shoulder and said, "No harm, no foul, brah."

"Penthouse, please, Sam."

"Yessir, Mr. Platter," the bellhop replied.

"They got food up there?" Riverstone asked.

"A full spread. Harry does it right. We got our own chefs and all the lobster and crab's legs you can eat."

"Steak?"

"Prime rib that thick, bro," Monday said, holding his index finger and thumb with a three-inch gap between them.

"You're alright, Platter. I don't care what the rest of the world says."

"All that walking through malls set us back a little. We missed 3 Doors Down's first show."

Riverstone didn't mind. He was one step from heaven. "As long as I make the last flight to Long Beach, I don't care."

"Doesn't matter. Harry always has a jet waiting."

"Cool. It'll be past midnight before I'm done with the crab's legs anyway." He touched the polished rosewood panels of the elevator walls as he leaned closer to Monday's ear. "I need a shower first, Platter."

"Sam will show you to your room."

"Sweet," Riverstone said, and they rode on to the top floor in silence.

* * *

As they arrived at the penthouse, Monday glanced at his watch twice and said, "Simon will have my hide. He wanted to be picked up two hours ago."

"Dude. The toad could have come with us if he wasn't such a wimp. Now he's stuck. Forget him."

"He writes the checks."

"Get another employer. Better to strike out on your own than kiss his bootie."

That idea made Monday nervous. He pushed the envelope deeper into his pocket. He stared at all the inlaid gold and extravagant fixtures. "And give up this?"

Riverstone's stomach growled. "Listen, brah, Harry won't let you hang after all the garbage we've been through. I know he'll be impressed with the way you handled yourself out there with the ship. It took a lot of balls to make it across that desert, Platter. You did good. You helped save Lu's life too. That's a biggie. I'm telling ya, Harry will make sure you're treated right. I'll put in a good word for you, too, just to make sure. You'll be pulling down six figures working for Harry instead of that pusshead."

Acting like he wanted to change the subject, Monday finally pulled the note out from his pocket. Immediately, his eyes widened when he saw who it was from. "Riverstone, it's from Ian."

Riverstone himself thought that was rather odd. "How did four-eyes find us here? You know, there are times when I think he would intimidate Einstein. What's it say?"

"It says Harry and Mrs. M are waiting for us in the penthouse."

"We know that."

"Yeah, but Harlowe is coming to pick us up because the police know who we are and will shoot us on sight if they find us."

Riverstone took the note and read it himself. "That idiot. He'll get himself shot. They're after him too." He crumbled up the note and tossed it. He didn't care where it landed. "It's Harlowe. He's screwing with me . . . again!"

"What if he isn't? Maybe we'd better stay here just to be sure."

"You can. I'm going to Lakewood right after I get something to eat."

At that moment the elevator dinged at the thirty-ninth-floor penthouse. The instant the doors opened, Mowgi jumped out with his parabolics at full tilt. Something was amiss. Monday sensed it too. With one hand he covered Riverstone's mouth so he wouldn't make another sound, and with the other, he pulled out a fully charged Gamadin pistol.

Riverstone was shocked. "Where'd you get that?" he asked in a whisper.

"Harlowe slapped it in my hand while you were talking with Lu," Monday replied softly as he eased out into the penthouse foyer.

"How come I didn't get one?"

"He didn't want you to shoot yourself in the foot."

"Some pard. What's the problem here, Monday?"

"Harry usually has a couple of behemoths standing by the doors."

"Maybe he doesn't want anyone else around but us," Riverstone explained.

"That's not like Harry."

They stepped into the outer atrium. The twenty-foot-wide fountain of black granite and bronze dolphins bursting out of a giant wave was still and silent.

"Fountain's out, too," Monday said in a hushed voice.

Monday motioned for Riverstone to keep quiet as they separated and shuffled quietly around opposite sides of the fountain. He caught Monday pointing down at the pool beneath the sculpture and mouthing the words *No fish*. Two steps later, Riverstone knew why. He motioned for Monday to come quickly over to his side. When Monday arrived, he pointed to the hundred-year-old koi fish bones spread around the base of the fountain.

What now? Riverstone mouthed.

Monday lifted the wall phone off the hook. Dead.

Riverstone turned back around, hoping that Sam was keeping the door open for them in case they had to make a fast exit. To his chagrin, the elevator had already closed. Riverstone tapped Monday on the shoulder, informing him Sam was gone. It looked like they had no choice but to check out what was behind the front double doors of the penthouse, which were ajar.

Monday signaled for Riverstone to push the door open and then step back. With arms extended straight out, he was ready to shoot anything threatening.

Riverstone pushed, and the ten-foot-high, hand-carved wooden doors swung open easily on their heavy golden hinges.

They waited a long, god-awful moment before they realized the room was unoccupied. It was in shambles. There was broken furniture everywhere, and shattered glass covered the thick exotic rugs all over the living areas. It looked like wild bulls had been let loose to romp inside the suite.

Mowgi waited for no one and bounced into the room like he was carrying his own Gamadin weapon. Monday followed next, his weapon out front, still cocked. As they stepped through the debris, Mowgi found something under a broken table almost immediately. Riverstone lifted the coffee table away with his foot and made the grisly discovery: a severed arm with a gold and emerald diamond-studded ring on the little finger.

"It doesn't look like Harry's," Riverstone said, hoping for confirmation.

"No, it's Danny's," Monday replied. "Harry's security guard. I gave him that ring."

Riverstone nodded his condolences before they moved on through more wreckage and the main hallway. Riverstone inquired about another large door on their right. It looked important. Monday took a deep breath. He didn't want to find any more bodies. "Master bedroom," he whispered.

They stared at each other, wondering who should go first. From a broken table nearby, Riverstone picked up a black wooden leg with a gnarled brass claw on the end of it. He pointed at himself and mouthed *Cover me.*

The way Mowgi went through the open door ahead of them led Riverstone to believe there wasn't a Dakadude or one of their beastly pets waiting to eat them alive. He gave Monday the ready nod and was half a breath away from charging into the bedroom when he heard a small whimper coming from behind the door. He turned back to Monday. *Hold on.* He eased the door open and saw Mowgi on the bed between the two corpses. Riverstone had never seen anything so gruesome. Both bodies had been skinned alive, their hides stuck on the far wall like trophies. There was no doubt in his mind who they were either.

It was Harry and Mrs. M.

Chapter Forty-Eight

DRAFTED

Harlowe was still out cold next to the lifeless manikin in the storage room when Ian shook him awake. It took Harlowe a while to pull himself together, but the instant he snapped out of his groggy fog, he saw the stun gun lying nearby. "Where is she?"

Ian looked around the room. "The rover's gone."

Harlowe searched for something to hit. The padded manikin was the unlucky target. *Wham!* His fist struck a punishing blow. "How long?"

"Maybe an hour ago," Ian replied.

Harlowe stared at the opening in the floor where the rover had been. "Why didn't you stop her, Wiz?"

"Like I'm going to stop Leucadia Mars from doing anything," he said defiantly.

Harlowe nodded sourly. "How'd she get past the military?"

Ian shrugged. He couldn't figure it out either. "That vehicle books, Harlowe. She blew out of here so fast I don't think they could get a bead on her. Millie didn't register any shots at all."

Harlowe struggled to his feet with the help of the manikin's thick shoulders and Ian's proffered hand. "She'll get her head shot off yet. Will serve her right too."

"Why did she do it?"

Harlowe glared back at Ian. "She's a woman. How would I know?"

Ian came to her defense. "She was just doing what she thought best. Take one step outside that barrier and you're a dead man. You know that. She made the only decision she could to help Riverstone. You would have done the same, so don't blame her."

Harlowe gazed at Ian like he didn't understand. "Stick to cars, Wiz, and . . ." He looked up, waving his hand, "And Millie here. Don't ever get involved with a doe. They're trouble. Always."

"Is that why you keep them around?"

Harlowe stopped mid-breath, chewing on his tongue. "Who are you, Doctor Laura?"

"Her stand-in."

"Don't tell her that. She'll quit her day job." Then he remembered Simon. "Where's the movie star?"

"He's outside trying to find a ride home."

Harlowe's face saw blood. "Did he get through?"

Ian smiled. "I saw the whole thing on the monitors. The soldiers were shouting at Simon to drop on the ground, but he couldn't get past the barrier to comply. Bullets started flying because Simon wasn't doing what he was told. They shouted back and forth, and Simon said he would gladly grant their wish if he could get past the barrier. He even offered them a million bucks apiece if they'd get him to the other side."

Visualizing Simon's frustration brought a smile to Harlowe's face, albeit a very small one. "He's still out there?"

"Yeah, trying to dig his way to China. He looks like a dog after a bone. The barrier exists even underground, though. He's not getting out," Ian explained.

"Bullets didn't stop it either, huh?"

"Not even a tank shell fazed it."

"Cool." Harlowe then reached over and slapped the activator on the wall to seal up the opening in the floor. "Time to fetch our star," he said, and he and Ian shuffled their way out the storeroom door and toward the open ramp. Harlowe still wasn't a hundred percent, but he was picking up strength as they went along.

Ian stopped at the top of the ramp. He knew his place was inside the ship at the control console where he could keep an eye on the monitors and readouts. Personal problems were Harlowe's worry. "He won't like it."

Harlowe's look of futility indicated he understood the problem all too well. "As much as I'd love to kick him right through the barrier, we're a little shorthanded just now, Wiz. We may need an extra hand if we have to take off again. The dumb star doesn't know it yet, but he's just been drafted."

Ian nodded his agreement as Harlowe waved a "see ya later" and plodded off down the lighted ramp to fetch his new conscript.

Chapter Forty-Nine

DAK ATTACK

RIVERSTONE WAS PUKING his guts out in the master bathroom by the time Monday joined him.

Monday's curiosity had gotten the best of him. He went into the master bedroom, and a moment later he was right beside Riverstone, throwing up like a broken sewer line.

"I told you . . .," Riverstone gasped between heaves.

"Who could have . . ."

"Daks."

"They're savages." Monday grabbed the toilet tank to keep himself from falling over and passing out.

"Worse." Riverstone came to Monday's side and led him to the tub to clean up. "We have to get out of here," he said, wiping Monday's face with a wet towel. From the bedroom came Mowgi's inconsolable howls of loss.

"You think they're coming back?" Monday wondered.

Riverstone did not have Monday's military experience, but he was streetwise when it came to thugs and heartless killers. "Count on it." He tossed the soiled towel into a hamper, and when he did so, the scanning device fell out of his pocket onto the floor. They both stared at the pulsing blue light and each suddenly had the same thought.

"LOSE IT!" they said in unison. Riverstone kicked the device away in a panic as they helped each other out of the bathroom and back to the foyer. Riverstone was no scholar—he and Harlowe were members in good standing on the dean's probation list—but he knew that alien technology draws aliens like a superconducting magnet. The Dakadudes were homing in on anything Gamadin. That's how they found the beach house, the soldiers in the canyon, and Harry and Sook here in the penthouse. The scanner was Riverstone and Monday's own worst enemy. It would lead the Daks right to them.

Monday stopped with a sudden thought. "The ship?"

"I know. It's a massive homing device on steroids," Riverstone said, pushing Monday toward the front door. "We have to warn Harlowe in a hurry."

They were almost to the twin doors when a dark shadow crossed in front of the giant atrium windows of the penthouse. Riverstone slammed Monday to the floor a half-second before one window exploded inward with such force that the glass shards smashed against the back wall of the living room. Dazed, Monday still had the presence to draw his weapon and shoot two Daks coming through the shattered glass. A third managed to hit the floor, but Riverstone still had his table-leg club with the claw and implanted it into his skull before he could unshoulder his long weapon. Outside, more shadows were cutting across the bright lights of the Strip. Squads of Dakadudes were descending out of the night sky.

Riverstone shouted, "MOWGIIIIII!" at the top of his lungs as Monday shot three more Daks. By that point, the Daks were ready. They started returning fire, blasting away before they drifted through the window. Orange streaks of plasma were sizzling all around them. Monday grabbed Riverstone by the arm and pulled him out the doors and toward the elevator. It was only sheer luck that they didn't get hit. But the elevator was shot full of holes. Monday pointed down the hallway. "The service elevator!"

Riverstone didn't see how they were going to make the twenty feet they needed to reach the safety of the service elevator. Just then, a raging winged beast, growing immensely as it found space in the open living room to expand, broke through the opened door of the bedroom, screaming wildly. Monday's face drained of color in sheer fright as the crazed yellow eyes and long razored teeth of the black dragon glared straight at him.

Before Monday could fire a shot at the demonic beast, Riverstone dove and yanked his arm down. "No!" he cried out. "He's with us, Platter!"

Mowgi was in full nuclear rage. With unbelievable swiftness, Dak heads tumbled from their shoulders, and other bodies were cut in half like rag dolls as they came swinging in through the broken glass.

Monday tried to help Mowgi out by shooting at more Daks as they came into view. But there were just too many of them. Riverstone pulled Monday toward the open elevator service door and shouted once more, "MOWGI! COME ON!"

There was a momentary break as the incoming Daks swerved away to regroup for another assault. "MOWGI!" Riverstone kept calling. Just when he thought he'd have to run back and grab the undog, Mowgi broke away and flew across the room toward the elevator. Riverstone slapped the down button while Monday held the door open with his new arm and fired bolts of hot plasma for Mowgi with the other. A bolt struck one of Mowgi's wings. It made him twist and fall just ten feet in front of the elevator door.

"Cover me!" Riverstone cried out as he charged into the melee of blazing plasma rounds and swept up the shrinking dragon/undog. In one heroic leap, Riverstone dove back across the white marble floor and through the open doorway with Mowgi firmly in his arms. Monday quickly moved his arm and the elevator began its descent just as a barrage of bolts struck the three-inch-thick steel doors.

Chapter Fifty

RESPECT

THE SHIMMERING BLUE veil surrounding the alien ship reflected eerily off General Gunn's desert-camouflage uniform. He stared with curious interest through his special fifth-generation night vision optics at the figure coming down the massive center ramp beyond the barrier. A moment earlier, lookouts had spotted the male figure and advised the general that he was coming his way.

At this distance, the figure was tiny against the backdrop of the immense incline, but he appeared to be strutting like he was on a mission. He wore a dark uniform, the color of which Gunn couldn't distinguish through the green-tinted lenses of his night vision goggles. Against their heated protests, he had ordered the civilian contingent of his entourage to remain behind the Hummer a hundred yards away from the perimeter until their safety could be secured.

As the figure approached the perimeter, the general mused over the connection the movie star Simon Bolt had with an alien ship in the first place. There was nothing in his file that would indicate he was part of any diabolical plot to undermine the nation's security, yet here he was. Was he really trying to get away? Was he acting the part of some weak-kneed, spineless wimp in some plot? Had aliens tortured him and then let him go? Lieutenant Poole had speculated that Bolt may have been kidnapped because the aliens thought his movie roles somehow gave him the expertise to fly the ship. Possible, thought Gunn, but he had other, more important matters to figure out. His sole concern was the capture of the alien ship. Nothing else mattered.

"Do we have an ID on this one coming toward us?" Gunn asked Captain Walker, who was overseeing the soldiers near the barrier.

Walker flipped up his night vision optics above his Kevlar helmet. He then flicked on his red penlight to read the notes from his clipboard. With his usual efficient speed, the captain lowered his goggles again and studied the figure for a moment before he answered the general. He pointed to the picture on his board. "It's the Pylott kid, sir."

"Understood, captain," Gunn replied. He didn't need any further information on the individual. He had read the reports on the seventeen-year-old boy earlier in the day. The general recalled in particular the long list of volunteer police work that Harlowe and his friends, Matthew T. Riverstone and Ian B. Wizzixs, had been involved in over the years. Riverstone and Pylott had been considered local heroes until this mayhem broke loose just three days prior. Now they were fugitives wanted in connection with the slaying of three gang members and two police officers. Was there a connection, Gunn wondered? How did these teenagers become a part of this alien ship? Had their minds been altered? Had they been kidnapped along with Bolt?

He squeezed his swagger. He needed answers. "Spread the word to all units, captain, that there may be an opportunity for penetration."

"Yes, sir, general." Walker quickly radioed HQ. After the order was carried out, the captain listened intently on the secured wireless handset before taking a deep breath and relaying the content of the message to the general. "Sir, Harry's hotel and casino in Vegas has just been blown up."

Gunn removed his optics and stared at the captain, knowing there was more to come.

"Our boys, general," the captain went on. "Looks like a couple of them left the ship before we got here. Matt Riverstone and the movie star's bodyguard, Monday Platter, were seen fleeing Harry's just before the explosions. Eyewitnesses say they were leaping across cars in twenty-foot strides. That's hard to believe, isn't it, sir?"

General Gunn listened with a poker face. "No, captain, right now I'd believe in the tooth fairy. What direction were they traveling, captain?"

Walker looked at the general incredulously. "Northwest, sir."

"They're headed back to the ship, then, captain," Gunn said flatly.

"Sir?" Walker questioned, not quite following the general's drift.

"Riverstone and Platter. They've finished whatever it is they went to do. They're headed back to the ship, so spread the word to expect a couple of human gazelles leaping across the desert from the southeast."

"Sir?" the captain repeated.

"You heard me, captain. I want them caught."

"Yessir." Walker took up the handset and began relaying instructions to Lieutenant Poole back at HQ.

Gunn then refocused on Pylott, who was nearing the perimeter of the ship. Bolt was still trying to dig his way under the barrier, with no luck. Pylott appeared to have no weapons or anything in his hands that looked threatening. He had a serious frown on his face and strode like he was mad about something, Gunn thought.

"Gunny," the general called, his focus always on the scene inside the protective shield.

Sergeant Gunderson came immediately to the general's side. "Yes, sir."

"Have Sergeant Defoe take Pylott out," he ordered.

"Beg your pardon, sir, but Defoe and his men tried that with Bolt. Their weapons were useless against the barrier, sir."

"Just do it, Gunny," General Gunn demanded.

"Yes, sir," Gunderson replied, and then he barked the order through his com mike for the snipers to open fire on Harlowe Pylott.

Within seconds, the muffled sounds of suppressed, automatic rifle fire thumped against the barrier. The general watched stoically as more than a hundred armor-piercing rounds struck the barrier and fell harmlessly to the desert sand.

On the other side of the barrier, Pylott didn't even flinch. He briefly glanced at the ineffectual rounds lighting up the barrier before he reached down and grabbed the actor by the back of his pants and yanked him to his feet. The actor tried to take a swing at Pylott. Pylott caught the flying fist an inch from his face, twisted the actor's arm around behind him, and kicked him in the posterior toward the ramp. Bolt fell and got up several times in his attempts to hit Pylott. Each time his fists missed the target by a wide margin. Pylott thumped the actor on the forehead, knocking him back down on his hind end. Bolt turned over and tried to get away on all fours before Pylott kicked him again. Bolt launched into the air and came down hard, spread-eagled, in the dirt.

This wasn't a fight, Gunn thought; it was more like watching a wayward kid being disciplined for breaking the rules. Once more, Pylott lifted Bolt by the seat of his pants and tossed him forward toward the center ramp. Bolt didn't put up any resistance. On the contrary, he ran for the ramp like his life depended on it.

The general turned to Captain Walker and said, "I like that kid." It was too bad he would have to kill him.

Chapter Fifty-One

L.V.P.D.

"HOLD IT!" OFFICER John McQue said, his eyes squinting at two suspicious men walking through the westside neighborhood on Vista Verde Drive between Charleston and Sahara streets. He quietly pulled the blue-and-white patrol car to the curb and extinguished its lights half a block behind the two suspects. "Those two aren't taking a workout stroll. Pull up the hot sheet on those guys the feds are after, Mick."

McQue and his partner, Mickey Roland, of the Las Vegas Police Department, had been on the night shift four hours past their normal duty hours. After the explosion at Harry's, the town was on its highest terror alert. Every off-duty officer had been called in early, and no one was allowed to go home.

Roland pulled out his Glock .357 magnum. "Of all the luck," he griped, pushing the patrol car flat screen around for McQue to see. The two suspects matched the mug shots front, back, and sideways. Their faces on the screen were bigger than life. "Can't we get a break?"

McQue burped up part of his hot pastrami with extra mustard and extra pickle before putting on his hat and reaching for the 12-gauge shotgun on the dash. "Look at that, Roland! They want the kids dead," he added, pointing again at the computer screen.

The two fugitives were breathing heavily and trying to keep themselves from falling over into the gutter. They almost looked drunk the way they were holding on to each other for support. They gave no indication they had noticed the patrol car behind them.

The bigger one let out a loud hacking cough and then spat out a glob of dark phlegm.

Roland grimaced. "That's disgusting. We don't get paid enough for this kind of work, McQue."

McQue grunted his agreement, studying the fugitives' movements. "What'd they do, Mick?" he asked.

"Killed a bunch of gang members," Roland replied, reading the report on the computer screen. "And a couple of cops, too, Mac. No wonder they want them dead."

McQue quickly grabbed his radio mike and called for immediate backup. He told dispatch they had two of the feds' most wanted fugitives in sight and they needed the entire area sealed off. Dispatch came back a half-minute later to inform McQue and Roland that every available officer was on-site at Harry's. Command could not send backup; the two policemen had to capture or kill the fugitives on their own by whatever means possible.

Roland stared at McQue. "So what do we do?"

Resigned, McQue pointed the tip of the rifle at the fugitives. "We take 'em down, Mick. Why get ourselves shot? The night's gone South in a hurry. No one will blame us for shooting first and asking questions later."

Roland agreed as he watched the fugitives stagger under a streetlight and lean against the post. "They haven't spotted us yet," he observed.

"They're not too smart either, standing there in the spotlight," McQue added, quietly opening his door.

Roland followed McQue's lead. They took cautious stances behind their open car doors. "Keep an eye out. There could be others around we haven't seen," McQue whispered.

* * *

Riverstone lifted Monday up by his armpit to help take the pressure off his wounded leg. One of the Dak plas-rounds had found his leg through the elevator door.

"You think we lost them?" Monday asked, his tone conveying his eagerness to hear a positive answer, even if it was a lie.

Riverstone took a quick look around. "Yeah, we're cool."

It was late. A few cars were moving along the big boulevards in the distance, but in the working-class neighborhood they found themselves in, the streets were quiet. The air was dry and cold. Riverstone was shivering and scared. He hoped he could get to Harlowe and the others in time to warn them about the Daks.

Monday then held Riverstone up against the pole. Riverstone had not escaped the penthouse unscathed either. He had two plasma wounds: one through the right shoulder and one in the fleshy part of his hip. Although none of the wounds was life threatening, they were nonetheless painful and had slowed Monday and Riverstone to a walk. Without the gravs giving them the boost they needed, they would never have made it out of Harry's underground parking lot before the Daks caught up with them.

Riverstone was also grateful that Platter knew Las Vegas better than Mapquest. He could get them back to the ship without being seen. All Riverstone knew was that the freeway was in front of them and that Harry's was in flames behind them.

After a short rest, Monday said, "Ready?"

"Yeah," Riverstone said, grimaced.

Just then they heard something behind them. Monday tried to blink his eyes clear in the direction Riverstone was looking. "Can't see very far. Can you?"

Riverstone glanced up at the yellow, high-pressure sodium streetlamp. He couldn't see a thing. "I hate these lights," he grumbled.

"Maybe it was the Mowg marking territory," he added after a moment of silence.

Riverstone turned then and looked at Monday's leg. He saw the blood-soaked pants leg and the dark drops staining the pavement. "That looks gnarly."

"As long as the gravs hold up, I can run, if that's what you mean," Monday said.

Riverstone sighed, leaning back on the post. He was tired, sure, but it was more than fatigue that was on his mind. He swallowed hard, trying to make sense of it all. He looked back from where they had come and saw billowing smoke clouds rising miles in the air from the burning center tower of Harry's hotel and casino. Tears welled up in his eyes as he thought about Harry and Mrs. M dying like animals. They had sacrificed their lives to save him, and for what? The answer kept echoing in his mind from the old man he met at Meathead's this morning. *Wake up, son. It is your concern. If not you, then who? Shut up, Old Man. Stop messin' with my head.*

Riverstone shook off his grief and gave Monday a boost. "Good. I had visions of carrying you back all the way to the ship." Riverstone opened his shirt, revealing the gold power box. "How much do you think is left in these?"

Monday looked at his. The tiny lights moved but didn't seem as bright. "Can't read alien. Can you?"

"I failed that last semester, too."

"What good are you?" Monday teased.

"Good enough to nail that Dak with the claw before he shot you, brah," Riverstone quipped. "So, which way, Platter?"

Monday squinted up at the street sign before he nodded northward. "That's Jones Boulevard over there. We follow it for a couple of blocks to Rancho. Rancho will take us out to the 157."

"Where's that limo of yours? We could use a ride about now."

There was a long moment of silence as Monday's gaze searched for something past the glare of the streetlight. "What happened to the mutt?"

"I wouldn't worry about him."

"Trust me, I don't. But I feel safer with him around. He can smell a freak for miles."

Riverstone wiped the sweat from his brow before he went on. "Ya still got the pistol, right?"

Monday patted his right hip. "Yeah, got it."

"How much does it have left?"

"How would I know? I pull the trigger, it shoots. That's all I care about."

"You clicked off a bunch of rounds back there. It has a limit, toad. Any moron knows that."

Monday stared at Riverstone with a twisted grin on his face. "Julian Starr *never* runs out of bullets."

This wasn't the time to be flip. Riverstone removed the Gamadin pistol from Monday's belt and held it up to the light. "Alright, where do you look? I know it doesn't shoot bullets . . .," he remarked, pointing the alien weapon at Monday's head.

Monday abruptly slapped the weapon away with the back of his hand. "Watch it. You could kill someone like that," he scolded just as the alien weapon fired indiscriminately into the night. At the same instant the loud crack of a shotgun shattered the chaos. Monday and Riverstone froze in their places.

* * *

Roland looked at McQue in extreme disbelief. Roland hadn't meant to fire; it was an uncontrolled reflex action. He was shaking so hard when he saw the one fugitive take the weapon from the other's belt that he thought it was meant for them.

McQue didn't take his eyes off the fugitives. Now that Roland had blown their surprise and the fugitives were staring at them, he had only one choice. He leveled his shotgun at their heads and shouted, "FREEZE! LAS VEGAS POLICE! DROP THE WEAPON, OR YOU'RE TOAST!"

The two fugitives remained still. They made no sudden moves toward them.

"DROP THE WEAPON, NOW!" McQue repeated.

Suddenly, out of nowhere, they heard a thump as though a heavy sack of dead weight had landed on the trunk of their patrol car. The two officers traded quick glances, wondering what it could be, when the loudest, most terrifying scream they had ever heard nearly shattered their eardrums.

Roland turned and froze solid. Seeing his partner's reaction, McQue also turned and saw something he was sure came from the deepest bowels of hell. Unless he could shoot it, they were going to die. But the dragon beast was too fast. It lunged, jaws wide open and wings spread wide. It kept coming right for them both.

Roland had already fainted on the spot. As the beast struck McQue, his shotgun fired into nothingness. The officer tumbled over several times from the blow. When he regained his composure, he couldn't believe he was still alive. He quickly checked Roland. He was breathing.

McQue looked past the streetlight and saw the fugitives running flat-out. Before he could unholster his Glock, the two retreating figures had already crossed to the other side of Jones Boulevard.

McQue felt the wind from the dragon's flapping wings slap his face as the beast flew off into the night, trailing behind the two fugitives.

A moment later, he kneeled on the ground and prayed.

Chapter Fifty-Two

BALLS

"Harlowe Pylott!" General Gunn called out. The young man turned. In the blue glow from the barrier, he looked like a ghost. He stood there, motionless, like he was wondering whether he should turn back to the ship or respond to the officer. The general dismissed Captain Walker and his Delta Force contingent of bodyguards. "It's just us now, son. Talk to me," the general urged in a fatherly voice.

Pylott didn't wait for everyone to leave before he began walking toward the officer in charge. Gunn was impressed by the way Harlowe carried himself. He walked upright, his shoulders straight, and his gait was unhurried, steady, and sure. His hair could stand a good GI trim, though, the general mused.

"You walk like a soldier," Gunn began.

"My mother was a drill instructor. If I didn't walk straight, I was cleaning the trashcan with a toothbrush," Pylott replied. Then he came right to the point. "Who are you?"

Gunn was taken aback by the young man's audacity. Spreading his feet wide apart, the general brought his swagger stick under his arm in a relaxed posture. "Brigadier General Theodore Gunn, United States Army Delta Force."

"Nice title," Pylott replied. "Make it quick, general, I'm in a hurry."

"You're in a lot of trouble, son," Gunn continued.

"We all are, sir."

"It would help matters considerably if you lowered this barrier."

"That's not going to happen. Get to your point."

The file on the young man had been misleading, Gunn thought. He was quite intelligent and quick-minded.

"We could force the issue," Gunn warned.

Pylott looked away briefly. "We both know, general, that we wouldn't be talking now if you could."

"I'm supposed to let you sit here in the desert like you don't exist? You tore up quite a bit of real estate the other night. What was that all about?"

"That was an accident."

"I'm supposed to *believe* that?"

"Believe what you want. It's the truth."

"Are there aliens inside controlling you, son?" Gunn asked. He wasn't joking.

Pylott thought that humorous. "No, general. I'm afraid you've been watching too many sci-fi flicks. We're all on our own here. The previous owners died thousands of years ago."

"If that's the case, drop the barrier. Let the government handle it from here."

That seemed to amuse Pylott even more. "I see," he scoffed. "You're from the government, and you're here to help."

"That's right, son. Let us help you."

"You can't help us, general," Pylott stated straight out.

"You don't know what you have here, do you, son?"

"It doesn't matter what I know," Pylott replied. "No one is getting past this barrier."

"If you don't lower the barrier, many people could die."

"If they do, it won't be by us. We're not here to hurt anyone, sir. You have to believe that."

"I want to, son, but you're not cooperating with me."

"The barrier stays," Pylott said firmly.

Gunn realized he wasn't making any headway. Maybe a different approach was necessary. "We can work out a deal, son. You won't go to jail, I promise you. If it's money you want, we can arrange that.

You can have a new identity too. Just drop this barrier and hand over the keys. If nothing else, do it for your country, son."

The young man's face became solemn and thoughtful. "I'm afraid the problem is bigger than you realize, General Gunn. I gave my word to someone and I intend to keep it," Harlowe said.

"Listen, son—"

"We're done here, general. Good night." Harlowe turned around and began walking back toward the center rampway.

"I'll nuke it before I let you move this ship one more inch," Gunn warned, but the Pylott kid didn't stop or hesitate. He kept on marching on, unmoved by the general's threat of annihilation. As though he had a larger mission on his mind than even his own self-preservation.

Captain Walker returned to the general's side and waited for him to speak.

"The boy has balls," Gunn conceded, slapping his leg with his swagger stick.

Walker had heard the entire conversation over the general's lapel com. "He acts like there's nothing on Earth that can harm him, sir."

As Gunn watched the boy's receding figure silhouetted against the dimly lit ramp in the distance, he thought, *Maybe Walker's right.*

Chapter Fifty-Three

SAND TRAPPED

For Riverstone and Monday, the safety of their friends was the only thing that concerned them at the moment. Seeing Harry and Sook hanging from the penthouse wall put it all into perspective. The Dakadudes were evil and they had to be stopped. Harlowe had to be told that the entire planet was at risk, and together they had to find a way to get the ship off the planet. Riverstone had no explanation why. His apocalyptic fear simply made it clear to him that if he didn't make it back to Harlowe and the ship before the Dak forces arrived, Millie would never leave the saddle alive, and there would never be a Lakewood to come back to again!

So they ran.

They ran for everyone's life on the planet.

Ignoring their pain, they moved on, always maintaining a north-westerly direction.

"Meathead's isn't far away," Monday said, striding along. "We should get something to drink there before we go any farther."

Riverstone breathed a sigh of relief. He was glad they were on the same page. If they could make it back to the first watering hole they had stopped at that day, it was a cakewalk to the open desert from there. After that, however, things would go downhill in a hurry. Traveling in the open desert at night was a whole new problem they hadn't counted on when they left the ship. And the synapses in his brain wouldn't let Riverstone compute how they would get through the five thousand troops surrounding the saddle. Still, Riverstone was confident that Harlowe would think of something. *Harlowe doesn't lose.*

They leaped over a fence to avoid the headlights of a car before cutting down an alley. Meathead's should have been visible when they emerged from the back end of the alley, but it wasn't there. Monday admitted he must have made a wrong turn somewhere. Desperate for water, they found a hose bib on the side of a house. It looked like a cold one at Meathead's was all but a dream. The water tasted brackish, but neither of them cared. At this point it was better than a Heineken. Drinking like dry camels, they sucked down as much as they could stand without feeling like they had swallowed a fish tank.

Monday offered the hose end to Mowgi, who had retracted to his normal self. The chinneroth just stared, making no attempt at even a lick. "I think he wants a beer," Monday said to Riverstone as he tossed the hose away.

Soon the three of them came to an open stretch of property that turned out to be the back entrance of a golf course. That made things safer. Out on the open course there were no lights, but the residual glow from the city that never slept cast plenty of light to travel by. The course was perfect for fast open running with the gravs. The fairways were flat and relatively obstacle free, and the white sand in the traps reflected even more light, making them easy to avoid.

For about a mile or so they would be hard to spot, so they bumped up their strides. Looking north they saw the deep darkness of the night and concluded that the open desert wasn't far away. They could make out the darker blackness of the hills beyond and knew that if they kept them to their left, eventually they should run back over the highway and into the saddle.

Three fairways later, Monday thought he saw a shadow moving alongside them at their speed. Mowgi was nowhere in sight. Maybe it was the undog, Monday speculated. Just to make sure they weren't being followed, he suggested to Riverstone that they stop and scan as far as they could see.

They saw nothing more threatening than high-pressure sprinklers shooting bursts of water over the fairways.

"Probably nothing, huh?" Riverstone said. But something didn't feel right.

Monday kept staring into the night, his large head turning like a turret. Then he realized something was definitely wrong. "The Mowg—"

"What about him?" Riverstone questioned.

"He's disappeared again," Monday pointed out.

A bush rustled to their left. It was so subtle, a moment ago they might have passed it off as an innocuous breeze rustling some leaves, but not anymore. They knew the sound was no wind or animal disturbing a bush; it was something foreboding hidden in the dark.

Riverstone stood ready, his legs slightly apart. "Come on, toads," he commanded. He glanced quickly back and forth between the trap and the row of bushes. No one showed himself. It was almost too quiet.

Then, from out of nowhere, something bushwhacked Monday from behind.

"Platter!" Riverstone shouted.

Monday whipped around just in time to fend off a Dakadude as it leaped at him with its lethal black heels extended. Although this Dak was smaller than the others, it was incredibly fast and agile. Monday was quick to respond. When the Dak sprung at his head, Monday ducked to one side and felt the pointed heel graze his chin. Monday nailed the Dak on the side of its neck with his new alien prosthetic arm. The Dak was dead by the time it hit the ground, his neck broken and his head unnaturally twisted around the back of his shoulders.

In the next half-instant, two more shadows broke from their lairs, attacking them from opposite directions. Riverstone could have waited for them to come to him, but instead instinct took over, and he moved forward to meet the one from the trap first. The assailant stopped short, not wanting to commit himself too soon. Out the corner of his eye, Riverstone saw Monday rush the other freak. If he could handle this one, he was sure Monday would do as well against the other.

Waiting for Riverstone to make his move was the Dak's undoing. He never expected Riverstone's shot to his chest to be so fast and powerful. He tried to fend it off, but he only partially deflected the blow away from the heart. The shot hit his mid-section instead, doubling him up and raising him three feet off the ground before Riverstone finished him with a dropkick to the chest. The sound of cracking bones reverberated from Riverstone's knee to the top of his head.

Riverstone turned in time to catch the last assailant somehow twist Monday around and slam him hard in the back with a hammering kick. Any other person would probably have been instantly paralyzed by the blow, but thanks to the gravs, Monday was only stunned as he flew forward, spread-eagled, and fell onto the wet lawn. Spitting out bits of grass, Monday flipped around in time to parry the Dak's next blow.

Then, like dueling titans, they tumbled over the course, matching their strengths, looking for an opening to finish the kill. As they fought, Riverstone caught a glimpse of the Dak's yellowed eyes. They glowed with hatred. The Dak was pure evil, and the more he saw the death in its eyes, the more Riverstone knew he and Monday and the others had to summon every ounce of strength to defeat the alien killers. Failure was not an option from this point on.

Then, from somewhere deep inside the Dak's eyes, Riverstone saw abject fear. The muscles in the Dak's body shook as the hideous being tried to tear itself away from Monday's grip. But for no apparent reason, Monday's grip slipped and the Dak had him by the throat and was crushing his windpipe. If Riverstone didn't do something quick, Monday would lose.

Somehow Monday threw the alien on its side and that's when Riverstone saw his chance. With a piercing scream, Riverstone broke the alien's neck with a powerful shot to the side of the head. Uttering a disgusted grunt, Monday kicked the alien Dak away into the nearby sand trap. The limp body rolled to the bottom of the pit.

Riverstone took in a painful lungful of air as he helped Monday to his knees.

"I had him," Monday said, breathing hard between his legs. He felt his windpipe as he spit out a few loose blades of grass from between his teeth.

They both knew that if the three Daks had found them, more couldn't be far away. As strange as it sounded to them, getting back to the ship now was the safest place to be. They checked each other for broken bones and found merely a few superficial cuts and bruises. But as they tried to run, they discovered the bounce in their step was missing. They could hardly walk, and every step was a heavy chore. Sensing that something was wrong, Monday opened his shirt. The blue light from his grav power pack barely glowed. Riverstone checked his and discovered he had no power at all. The last brawl with the Daks was their last hurrah.

Riverstone slapped the power pack strapped to his chest with disgust. "I want my money back." He didn't believe he had it in him to get back to the ship without the gravs. His back hurt, his legs hurt, and every twist and turn he made aggravated the pain. Monday was no better. Just when they thought their predicament was as bad as bottom-sucking fish at the end of a sewer drain, a black Hummer crawled onto the fairway and stopped. A side window slid down, revealing the ink-black darkness inside.

Riverstone grabbed Monday as they tried desperately to hobble away across the open fairway. They took two steps before a bolt of orange light flashed from the Hummer's window. The next thing they knew, they were tumbling headfirst into a sand trap, staring face-to-face at one of the Dakadudes they had just killed.

Chapter Fifty-Four

INVASION

HARLOWE TOSSED SIMON down onto the floor of the control room like he was a sack of cow pies. All of his digging at the perimeter force field had gotten the star nothing except a dirty face and broken fingernails. Simon rose to his knees and tried to reach up along the center chair with his grimy hands. Harlowe slapped his hand and said menacingly, "Don't touch my chair, toad."

Simon was about to protest, and would have died a quick death, if Ian hadn't grabbed him from behind and pinned his arms. "Don't even blink or he'll mess your face up so bad, a Dakadude will look sweet."

Simon shrugged himself free. "Bug off, four-eyes."

Ian pushed back his glasses, brushing off the insult. With an I-tried shrug, he stepped back to his chair in front of Harlowe at the console of dancing lights. He had already given the insolent star too much of his time.

Harlowe was reflecting on his conversation with the general when he reared up and slammed his fist on the edge of the console. "This is wack, Wiz!" He pointed at the console of dancing lights. "Look at these controls! If we press this, does it set off the self-destruct? If we press this, do the thousands of troops out there vaporize?"

Ian felt useless himself. Cars he could fix in a heartbeat. Space-ships from the distant past were another matter. He had yet to find one bolt he could turn. *Now, what's up with that?*

It was a long moment before Harlowe's fixated eyes blinked and he snapped out of his sour mood. He put a friendly hand on Ian's shoulder and said, "Harry and Mrs. M better get here quick, or we'll be forced to do some guessing." He looked out again over the console of lights. "All this power and no way to use it."

Ian agreed. The only reason they had made it this far was that Lu knew what buttons to push. Neither he nor Harlowe knew jack about what to do next. He also knew the worst thing that could happen to Harlowe was sitting. Waiting for Harlowe was slow death, and it made him even angrier when an irritant fly kept buzzing around his space.

Simon was about to offer a brain fart of his own when something from left field slammed against the side of his face. The blow was so fast and solid, Simon never saw what it was that cold-cocked him into oblivion. "Lights out, butthead," Harlowe said to the still form on the floor.

Ian stared pathetically at the cow pie. "I tried to warn him."

"Too late."

Passing the irritation from his mind, Harlowe returned to the console like it was time to move on to the business at hand. He would not allow any more problems to get in the way of his goal: to get Millawanda off the planet like he had promised Mrs. M he would do.

Ian stood up and nodded at Simon on the floor. "He won't be much help like that," he pointed out.

"He's helping now," Harlowe replied.

Just then, a massive fireball shot up in the sky on the horizon, catching Harlowe's attention. There was no sound, but through Millawanda's massive forward window, his sharp eyes easily made out the billowing columns of smoke and fire rising miles in the air over the bright city lights of Las Vegas. "What's going on out there, Wiz?" he asked, coming to the console where Ian was seated.

"That's in the middle of town," Ian pointed out.

"Harry's?"

Ian didn't want to speculate, but the location was right.

"Lu's in trouble, isn't she?" Harlowe speculated.

Ian turned to the panel of readouts and screens still labeled in undecipherable alien symbols. Then their eyes met as they both spoke at the same time with an answer that was itself another question. "Or Riverstone?"

Ian quickly turned to check the local TV coverage. His fingers danced across the holographic screen in front of him. Seconds later, a large overhead display materialized with a local broadcast. The news report had all the answers they were looking for. In the top half of the screen was a picture of a giant luxury hotel engulfed in flames. Below the picture was the headline: TERROR STRIKES HARRY'S HOTEL AND CASINO! Right below that were four mug shots, all very familiar to Harlowe and Ian. His worst fears were now true. The whole world was after them, and Riverstone was right in the thick of it. He closed his eyes, blaming himself. He should have foreseen the problems. When he opened his eyes again, the screen had changed to Monday's and Riverstone's faces in connection with the hotel inferno and the deaths of the hotel's billionaire owner, Harry Mars, and his wife, Sook.

Stunned with disbelief, Harlowe stumbled back into the center chair, his eyes filling with tears. What now? Mrs. M and Harry were gone. If the newscast was right . . . *If it was right,* he kept repeating to himself. They can't be right. The news is never right. They miss a lot. Mrs. M and Harry can't die. She needs to be here. Harry and Mrs. M could still be out there, making their way to the ship. They had a way of sidestepping death. *Man up, toad. Think positive. Don't go there. Things are bad enough without you going negative. Think like Mrs. M was right here in the control room, looking over your shoulders. What were the choices she would make? Work it out with Wiz. Above all, stay cool.*

The problem is what? You're surrounded by the United States military. They won't let you take off. General Gunn made that clear. But Millie's safe, pard, the suckwads can't get past the barrier. But how 'bout rockets, bunker-buster bombs, or—he slammed his fist—*a nuke?* He closed his eyes at the thought. *Surely, so close to Las Vegas, they wouldn't use the bomb. Not with all the troops around. If they start to pull out, start worrying, Pylott, but until then, the ship is safe. That's important to remember.*

He recalled the last conversation he had had with Mrs. M. *"Forget us,"* she had told him, *"just drive. Don't look back . . . You can't fail. Many lives depend on you. More than you'll know. Do you understand? It's the planet . . ."* Harlowe had been confused then, and he felt no different now. He wanted to act. He wanted to run outside and beat up bad guys. Life seemed so uncomplicated that way. The bad ones were always easy to spot and eliminate. But that had been in his own backyard, where he was comfortable and knew the rules of the game.

Now other-worldly events were taking place at light speed. He had no control over them. He felt lost and disconnected from all that he had known in the past. *"Neeja. Earth. There's no time to explain. They're all in danger. You'll find a way . . ."* Mrs. M's words kept ringing loudly in his ears over and over again until Ian brought him back to the here and now.

"Harlowe," Ian cried out, "look there." He pointed to the bottom of the screen. "In the corner. The picture of those ships was taken a couple of hours ago from Australia. A guest on Fox says they're alien. His reliable sources say the government scientists believe this is an invasion fleet and it's only a few hours away." Ian's eyes met Harlowe's. "That's what this is all about, isn't it? More Daks are coming to kill Millawanda."

Harlowe stared up at the screen, his face drawn and somber, and silently nodded his head. *Sweet . . .*

Chapter Fifty-Five

BLACK BOOTS

WET BITS OF grit stuck to Riverstone's cheeks and entered his nose and mouth as he lifted his face out of the sand and tried to struggle out of the trap. But it was no use. Without gravs, his legs were useless. Still, he fought vigorously to escape the trap. He kept crawling forward on his elbows, digging, pushing, crawling his way up to the edge of the sand pit. He had to get away. He had to get back to Harlowe and the ship!

Finally reaching the top of the trap, he lifted his head and peered over the lip. On the grass to his right was Monday. He was flat on his stomach, either dead or out cold. He saw a tiny movement of his eyes and prayed it meant he was only stunned like him. Two red lights glowed at him from the Hummer as a car door opened and someone with heavy black boots got out of the car. He had to act fast. He reached for his pistol but it wasn't there. He frantically searched the area and saw his weapon to his immediate left, lying in the grass.

Summoning all the reserves he had left, he reached out and grabbed it, but before he could use it, another orange flash surrounded him. He fought, but nothing he did could make his body move. Although he was paralyzed, his eyes still functioned. He could also taste the wet, stony grains of sand in his mouth, and he could breathe. Otherwise, he was helplessly inert.

The heavy footsteps of the Daks took their positions all around the trap. The crisp, ratcheting click of readied weapons added to his dread that he was about to die. When it was quiet again, the

Daks parted to allow a single being to stride through the line like an unhurried predator that is about to eat his helpless prey.

A deep, raspy voice bellowed an unintelligible command, and Daks scurried to the outer parts of the fairway in search of more humans.

Riverstone forced open his watery eyes as a giant black boot stepped into his line of sight. It was the same black boot he had seen from a distance in the box canyon in Utah. Never in a thousand lifetimes would he forget its owner's killer-of-worlds stare. Then a giant hand reached down and grabbed Riverstone as if he were on a low-gravity moon and tossed him toward the Hummer. The Dakadude's power was incredible. Riverstone's head slammed against the wet grass, twisting his neck, and air gushed from his lungs as he released an agonizing grunt. He rolled over and ended face up, staring at bright shiny eyes that were inhuman and brutal.

Face-to-face with the most evil being he had ever seen in his life, Riverstone tried to turn away, but a sharp kick to the side brought him instantly back to the Dakadude's glowing eyes.

"It is useless to fight, Gamadin."

Riverstone, consumed with hate, fought in great spasms to break free and kill the giant Dak. His jaw twisted and strained as he spat out, "You're dead, you ugly toad. You and your whole gang . . ."

The huge Dak reared back and laughed with the confidence of the unconquerable. "The Fhaal will rule the stars, Gamadin. It is our destiny!" His glowing eyes—demonic, fiendish—rested once more on Riverstone. "Sook tried to summon you, but the Triadian has failed." He laughed again, deeper and more bitter this time. "Now you will *all* die. The ship is the last of her kind and she will be stopped before she can rebuild. Millawanda is cunning, and she was hidden well. But she has exposed herself prematurely; she is vulnerable like you—defenseless, weak, and inexperienced.

"Our main force is only a few hours away. When it arrives, we will destroy her completely and forever. Then the Fhaal will destroy this planet. There will be no more Gamadin for all eternity. The Fhaal will rule its empire, unobstructed."

Riverstone's lips curled with loathing. He wasn't afraid anymore; he could face his destiny. "You can kill me, but others will follow," he warned.

The alien's eyes dulled. He could not match Riverstone's force of will. The Dak was unsure as to whether there were, indeed, other Gamadin or not.

"That's right, dirtball," Riverstone persisted, "we're not the only ones left. We've got a gang out there of our own, see, and we're coming after you. We'll put an end to you and your stupid Daks. We'll track you down, butthead, and you'll be the ones sprouting wings, chump!"

A Dak subordinate standing next to the giant Dak pointed his weapon at Riverstone's head and spoke words that sounded roughly like "Die, Gamadin."

Riverstone's eyes slammed shut.

Zzzzzz!

Something whizzed above his head. Powerless to do anything but wait for the end, Riverstone fully expected his brains to be scattered across the entire back nine. Instead, he felt a heavy thud fall beside him. When he opened his eyes again, to his bewilderment the Dak who had had a gun at his head was now facing him with a sizzling plas hole through his brain.

Well, frost my . . .

Then the whole world erupted around him as the other Dakadudes around the Humvee opened up at some unknown assailant. Brilliant flashes of orange and blue bolts slashed overhead as Riverstone found himself in the middle of another crossfire. Somewhere farther off he heard more bodies drop. He breathed a short sigh of relief, thanking his benefactor for being such a good shot.

Riverstone took a mental inventory. Monday didn't have a gun. He was paralyzed just like he was. Harry was dead. Harlowe was back at the ship with Leucadia and Ian and that worthless Simon Bolt. The sound of his ally's weapon was quite different. Much more powerful, like his dad's Ruger .22 caliber blinker pistol compared to Harlowe's dad's .44 magnum Desert Eagle. The freaks fired orange bolts while the more potent shots were intense blue bolts of light.

"STAND DOWN!" a woman's voice shouted out.

Lu? What the . . . That means Harlowe can't be far away.

With all the strength he could muster, Riverstone managed to move his pinky toe. Hardly helpful. Another effort, however, turned him over. It wasn't much, but it was enough to allow him to see the Humvee clearly. A Dak near the hood of the car raised its weapon above its ugly head. It was only a ruse. The Dak flinched, but before the freak could pull the trigger, a sizzling blue bolt dropped the ugly goon where it stood.

That's a way, girlfriend . . .

A moment of tense silence followed before the sound of a rear-door gate opened on one of the Humvees. Just when he thought things were looking up, one of the Daks' beasts jumped out from the open tailgate. It was as mean and ugly as the others that had chased them back at the box canyon. It howled a terrible scream as its jaws snapped, displaying its lethal set of razored teeth and dripping hot, vile, dark drool. Riverstone squeezed his eyes shut, praying the nightmare would go away.

It didn't.

The giant Dakadude let out a low, sinister laugh before it spoke in its alien tongue. A Dak translation was unnecessary. The beast quickly zeroed in on Riverstone, lying helpless in the sand. Jolts of fear shot through his skull like sharp knives as he recalled what the other beasts' favorite human body part was. The beast charged, but the giant Dak snatched its collar in mid-flight and held it firm in its claws.

Riverstone forced himself to control his bowels while he listened to Leucadia answer the alien as though she understood the Dakadude fluently. "It matters little whether you can stop us here or not, Sar. The ship has been released. You are too late. We have the Gamadin technology and it is ours."

Riverstone couldn't see any change of expression on the alien's face. Such ugliness was void of emotion. But he did believe he saw a change in its stance, and Leucadia must have seen it too. "You piece of drak. Look at you, you worthless grogan pile of excrement," she continued.

That's it, Lu, don't sugarcoat it.

"You're scared. You think we are weak and unprepared, that you destroyed the Gamadin soldiers. They were only a small contingent of our Gamadin army, Sar. As sure as I stand here, we trained the thousands more that will destroy the Fhaal empire and its cowardly armada of worthless ships. You are waiting for your main force to add to your strength, otherwise you would have killed Millawanda by now. You didn't realize what you were up against until it was too late.

"You didn't anticipate such power, did you? You thought the tales of the ancients were exaggerated. Well, now you know, Sar. Yes, someone is late, and it is the Fhaal. The Gamadin *are* ready. Look at them. Your weapons only paralyzed them. They still glow with the power of the galactic core. Can you match this strength?"

The giant's eyes widened. "Ah, yes. I can see you have tried," Leucadia went on. "The bodies of your soldiers lie pathetically about, killed trying to slay the mighty Gamadin. So you know it is a force to be reckoned with. Now leave us, drak, or die here in disgrace . . . a failure to the Fhaal."

Before the Dak commander spoke again, three more black Humvees came out of the darkness and stopped a safe distance from the first one. Doors flew open, and out poured the giant's backups. Sar ordered them to surround the sand trap, cutting off any escape.

The commander's deep voice rumbled through the cold night air. Riverstone didn't have to be an interstellar linguist to figure out that the giant had called Leucadia's bluff, and now the ball was in her court.

"Like *drak* I'll drop my weapons," Leucadia shot back. "Your numbers mean nothing to Gamadin." Then something dropped from the sky and landed with a heavy thump on the top of Sar's Hummer. "One twitch, one wrong move, Sar, and I'll unleash my chinneroth on you."

Mowgi was in his most fully charged dragon mode yet. Riverstone didn't think he had ever seen the undog so torqued . . . and spread out. Mowgi's wings had expanded to over thirty feet from tip to tip. When he opened his mouth wide and screamed, Sar's beast cowered at the foot of the commander's black boot.

Sar grabbed the chain leash from his subordinate and released his pet, then kicked the beast toward the raging chinner. The reluctant beast charged Mowgi, but before it could pounce, its head was ripped clean from its neck by the chinner's powerful claw. Riverstone was aghast, watching the head bounce across the grass, coming to a rest against the commander's boot.

Sar kicked the twitching head away in disgust, and then all was silent again.

Out of nowhere, something grabbed Riverstone by his pants and began carrying him, together with Monday, away from the sand pit like he was a suitcase. He looked down and saw two round flat feet connected to spindly tube legs and figured the only thing that fit that description was a robob. Riverstone turned slightly and saw Monday's bewildered eyes wide open. Thankfully, Monday was still alive and in as much shock as Riverstone was at seeing himself being carried away by a stickman.

After a trek to the far side of the fairway, they came to the place where Leucadia had parked the rover. The robobs stretched Riverstone and Monday out in the back loading bed as though they were a couple of dead bodies. The China-hats were silent and proficient as they checked their patients and then picked up a crystalline blue ball, which they touched to each one's chest.

Riverstone still couldn't move, but the ball seemed to have relaxed him. Leucadia then came into view. She ordered Mowgi to keep an eye on Sar and then she looked at Riverstone. "Are you okay?" was all she asked.

Riverstone tried to speak but couldn't. All he could do was blink an affirmative.

"The robob has given you something to neutralize the paralytic affects of the Fhaal stun weapon. It will take a while, but you'll be alright in a few hours. The robobs will take you and Monday back to the ship. Tell Harlowe he must leave Earth immediately before the Fhaal strike force arrives."

Riverstone's eyes displayed his mental confusion, wondering why Leucadia couldn't tell Harlowe herself. She glanced down and saw his anxiety. "I must stay here and protect your escape. You must go now and be with Harlowe. That's where you belong, Matt. That's where you've always belonged."

His eyes grew wide in protest. She had to come along. They needed her.

"My place is here, where my parents left a vast empire. I know they were killed." She stopped a moment to gather herself. "Their work on Earth must continue. My place is here; your fate is with Harlowe and the stars, Matt."

She leaned her face closer to both Riverstone's and Monday's. "I must have you do one last thing. It will be difficult, but the fate of the planet depends on your success. Blink to show me you understand."

Reluctantly, both of them blinked.

"Good. You must tell Harlowe I was killed saving you and Monday. And you must be convincing. He can never know I'm still here on Earth."

Their eyes widened to show their protest, but Leucadia insisted. "You must tell Harlowe that you saw me die. Harlowe must believe I am dead or he will not take Millawanda safely away from Earth. You know him like a brother, Matt. He would search for me endlessly if he thought I was alive somewhere. You cannot allow this to happen. Millawanda must leave the planet or she will die. If she dies, Earth dies with her. Have I made myself understood?"

Monday blinked his acceptance. Riverstone could not bring himself to blink yes. She shook him again. "No, Matthew, please. Think of the billions you must save. Think of Lakewood or it truly will not be a home to return to. You saw what happened to my mother and father. Your parents will also die a horrible death and you could have prevented it."

His eyes welled up and it was difficult for Riverstone to see her through his tears. This time he blinked his cooperation.

Leucadia looked at them both one more time. "There is a small auto sequencer on the side of the center control room chair. You will easily recognize it. It is the only button just below the armrest. Press it once. It will guide the ship to a predetermined landing site my mother programmed into Millawanda's memory. That is where she planned to train her new Gamadin force."

Her tears fell on him as she gently kissed Riverstone on his head and then on the lips. "Good-bye, Matthew, and you, Monday Platter." She kissed him too. "The world's hopes go with you all." She nodded to the robob driver and called out as they left, "Tell Harlowe I love him. Tell him I will love him forever."

With every fiber in his body, Riverstone tried to sit up and object, but neither his mouth nor his body would cooperate. The robob driver put the pedal to the metal, and a second later they were racing flat out across the desert at three hundred miles an hour on their way back to the ship.

Chapter Fifty-Six

CYLINDERS

THE CALL FROM HQ alerted Sergeant Michael Defoe through his tiny ear com that a fast unidentified vehicle was headed his way. If the vehicle entered his section, his team was to use all means necessary to stop it from entering the ship's perimeter. Defoe rapped his tunic mike quietly two times. Message received.

He snapped the top grommet of his desert jacket to keep out the chill of a cold desert night as he prowled the desert landscape with his GIII Night Eagle optics. Hours before, his Delta Force company, Alpha-Bravo, had dug in around the southern quadrant of the ship. He saw only small mounds, prickly branches, and tufts of dry grass. He nodded with satisfaction. *Good to go.* His men were invisible to the untrained eye. They were scattered from as far out as fifty yards to within a few inches of the shimmering blue barrier. First light was still two hours away. They owned the night.

The best scenario was to do their job before the sun came up. "You heard it. Everyone on his toes. Radio check." An instant later, various clicks came over Defoe's headset. Brevity was their reply.

Alpha-Bravo, along with Baker, Charlie, and Delta companies, had been the first assault teams to reach the depression six hours earlier. They had choppered in from the four directions of the compass and put down a mile and a half from the alien target. They were to move silently into the saddle and secure their position near the saucer-shaped object, then await further orders. They located a prime observation point and monitored all movement related to the alien vessel. They were to use all diligence to capture any unauthorized personnel trying to enter or leave the depression. No exceptions. The use of deadly force was authorized only if they were fired upon or danger to their lives was imminent. They were to notify headquarters immediately if the disk made any unusual movements. And if there was a breach in the barrier, no one was to enter the saucer's perimeter without his Biosafety Level 4 protection suit.

Satisfied that his team was secure, Defoe returned to observing the ship and its perimeter for any changes, like he had repeated a hundred times during the night. Except for the rhythmic pulse of the ring of light around the edge of the vessel, there was no movement that he could detect anywhere. All was still.

Defoe switched to an alternate channel so he could remain up to speed on the incoming unidentifieds. "That's a confirm, Michaelson. You have an unidentified vehicle headed your way?" the voice said.

Corporal Billy Michaelson replied affirmatively.

"Well, why didn't you stop it?" the voice shouted in disbelief.

Corporal Michaelson said he and three others had tried. They gave chase in half-tracks and Humvees, but the unidentified was too fast over the desert terrain. "It didn't have wheels, Gunny! We couldn't keep up with it through Oberson's Wash. We even lost two vehicles."

"And it's coming this way?"

"Roger that. It's headed north for the saddle. It should be in Defoe's sights in a matter of seconds."

Defoe clicked back to his Alpha channel with a hard snap. He was going to smash some heads when they got back to HQ. *Of all the mindless retards,* he thought, unleashing his safety loop from his Beretta. *Michaelson had to be dozing off in his jeep for someone to get by the outer perimeter as easily as that. Did Alpha have to take care of everything?*

Defoe knew the terrain. He had studied the topos thoroughly. Oberson's Wash was three miles to the west. *Man, this wasn't Iraq. It was America's own backyard! You didn't mess up in your own backyard unless you were a retarded maggot like Michaelson.*

After switching off his light and folding his map back into his pocket, Defoe clicked on his mike. "Rascal, Faceman," he said in a low hushed voice, "front and center." Two clicks came back, indicating orders understood. A short moment later a bush moved. Defoe's men appeared: their helmets were covered with native brush and prickly thorns and their faces, like his, were painted with non-reflective camouflage grease.

Silently, the three stepped cautiously along the ridgeline. Faceman stopped suddenly in his tracks. He showed Defoe and Rascal the long cylinder he had spotted in the sand.

It wasn't one of theirs.

With his right hand, Defoe silently indicated for Faceman to flag it with a marker. If it was a booby trap, they would take care of it at first light. Faceman followed instructions, removing a wire flag from the side of his pack and placing it beside the cylinder. Before they had gone another ten feet, they discovered four more cylinders, just like the first, and marked them as well.

Faceman took point again. Stepping carefully as he surveyed the path ahead with his night optics, he pointed the muzzle of his HK over the field, silently indicating to the others that the cylinders seemed to be everywhere.

Defoe confirmed the observation at the same moment that something flew over the top of the ridge and into the saddle. "Sonava . . ." He didn't mean to break the silence, but what he saw wasn't in any reference books. Without taking his eyes off the wheel-less vehicle, Defoe barked at his men to hit the deck.

Defoe and his men readied their weapons. There was no time to hide as the vehicle came into range. They had only a split second to sight on the vehicle's driver. To their dismay, no human was at the controls. Both driver and passenger looked robotic. The only humans they saw were laid out flat in back of the vehicle.

The humans are being kidnapped for dissection!

"Now, men!" Defoe commanded.

Just after he issued his order to fire, Defoe glimpsed movement on the ground all around their position. The vehicle appeared to be slowing down, but it was still coming in at a good clip. Defoe took his eye away from his night vision optics. A dull, almost imperceptible blue glow flashed momentarily, and then it was gone. Immediately following that—or maybe at the same instant, he wasn't sure—he heard a sharp click from Faceman's direction. It wasn't the crack a dry twig makes when broken, or the banging of small rocks together. It was the click of metal upon metal. Then all was silent again.

Defoe wondered what was going on. Faceman and Rascal should have blasted the vehicle out of the sky by now, he thought. After several long seconds had passed, more than enough time for such action, Defoe shouted into his mike to open fire. He waved his hand, motioning his subordinates to strike, but no one fired a single round. *Why didn't they shoot?* He scanned the starlit desert with his optics. Faceman and Rascal were out cold, lying belly up in the dirt. *What happened to them?*

The vehicle kept coming down the ridge, unmolested.

It was up to him. Like wound-up springs, Defoe's legs were tense, pumped with adrenalin. He was going to nail the maggots if it was the last thing he did.

Then, the instant he was about to fire his HK at nearly point-blank range, a blue glow flashed behind him and jerked him backward as though he were a ball on a tether string. Then more blue light surrounded him and the world went blank.

The wheel-less vehicle continued on unimpeded, and it passed through the blue shimmering barrier like it wasn't even there.

* * *

In his report to HQ, Sergeant Defoe couldn't explain why no trace was found of the many gold-colored cylinders his team had flagged in the area that night.

Chapter Fifty-Seven

BAD NEWS

Harlowe and Ian bolted out the control room the moment they saw the ship's sensor screen display the rover coming over the top of the ridge. On a dead run, they headed for the ramp the instant they materialized on the lower-level pad. By the time they had exited the giant hatchway, the rover was already waiting for them at the bottom of the ramp.

"Why is a robob driving?" Ian asked as they bounded toward the car.

When they saw no movement from the two passengers and felt an eerie silence hanging like a shroud over the vehicle, they knew something was wrong. Suddenly their mirth at seeing their friends alive was replaced by a godawful dread as they cautiously approached the car.

Harlowe's stomach squeezed another notch tighter as he and Ian checked the bodies stretched out in the back.

Ian touched Monday first. "He's alive, Harlowe."

Harlowe didn't have to feel Riverstone's pulse. He was already groaning. "Is that you, Harlowe?"

"Yeah, pard. You okay?" Harlowe replied as he checked Riverstone superficially for injuries.

"No. I feel like throwing up," was Riverstone's straight answer. "Where's Lu?"

Harlowe lifted Riverstone to a sitting position. He was weak and struggling to stay awake. Both he and Monday looked like they had been through ten rounds with the Rock.

"Daks . . .," Riverstone muttered. "They found us, Harlowe."

Harlowe's face was a mixture of fear and relief at seeing his life-long friend alive. "Where's Lu, Matt?" he asked again. "She went after you. Where is she?"

Riverstone nodded as he pointed with his right thumb behind him. "Back there," he breathed. His head fell on his chest. But Harlowe couldn't let him pass out. Not yet. He needed to know what had happened to Leucadia.

He lifted Riverstone's chin, helping him stay awake as another robob popped out of nowhere and clickity-clacked over to Monday. The stickman scanned his body for injuries with a palm-sized crystalline ball, and then he shot him with a tube filled with blue fluid. The robob followed the same procedure with Riverstone. Almost immediately, he responded in a more coherent way. "Harry's dead, Harlowe. Mrs. M too," he said with a raspy throat.

"For sure? You saw them?"

Riverstone's eyes focused on Harlowe. "Yeah, I saw them, pard," he told him. His eyes started to tear up. "The Daks killed them. They hit us at Harry's," he added. "They skinned them alive, Harlowe. It was awful." He tried to steady his voice, but was too heartbroken at the loss of his dear friends. "We didn't have a chance, Harlowe. They found us with the com. They used our own technology against us. They will find us here too."

Harlowe held Riverstone by the shoulders as he drifted in and out. "Lu? Where is she, Matt?" He had to know.

Riverstone fought to stay awake. He took a deep breath, then went on. "Lu . . . didn't make it." Their eyes locked as the tears in Riverstone's eyes told the story. "The Daks had us. She came to help us escape. She died in my arms, Harlowe." He took in a long breath before adding, "The last thing she said was 'Tell Harlowe I will love him forever.'"

Riverstone stopped for a moment to gather himself. "Platter and I were coming back to the ship when the Daks found us again. It was the big ugly guy we saw in the canyon." Harlowe nodded, seeing the fear in Riverstone's eyes. He would never forget such evil. "He found us. He shot Monday and me. The Daks had us dead, too, until Lu showed up. She saved us from getting our brains blown away. I didn't understand what she said to him, Harlowe, but from the sound of it, she told the Dak off, big-time. Lu was something, Harlowe. You would have been so proud of her. The Daks were scared, brah. I mean *really* scared."

He swallowed, fighting to stay coherent before he went on. "She and ol' Mowgi didn't back down. Millawanda is what the freaks are after. They know she's the only power strong enough to stop them. With the ship destroyed, they are unstoppable."

Harlowe's heartbroken gaze drifted back toward the lights of Las Vegas.

"No, Harlowe," Riverstone warned. He could see the determination in his friend's face. "You can't go back. It's too late. She's gone. The ship is everything now. We have to leave Earth, Harlowe. That's what Lu said. You have to take Millawanda away from Earth. Her survival depends on it."

Riverstone reached out to Harlowe and looked him in the eye. "Listen, I'm going with you, pard. Somehow we have to pull it off. The Daks are out there. They want us to leave the ship unguarded so they can take Millie for themselves. They want this ship, and if they get it, there will be no Lakewood, no planet to come back to. I know that now. We must keep Mrs. M's promise. It's for Lu, too."

Several long moments went by before Harlowe finally spoke. "Alright." He nodded toward the heavens. "For Lu. For Harry. For Mrs. M. For our families. We'll do it to save our home from these toads!"

They embraced for a long tender moment before Harlowe gave the robobs the thumbs-up to raise the rover into the ship. Once inside the utility room, the robobs would transfer Riverstone and Monday to the nearest sickbay for further treatment.

Ian, who hadn't slept in two days, was showing signs of sleep deprivation. His eyes were red and swollen. "Go get some sleep, Wiz," Harlowe said.

"What about you?" Ian asked.

Harlowe told Ian he would be along shortly. He needed a moment alone. Ian dragged his body up the ramp without protest as Harlowe turned and walked out into the desert. With his mind in a fog of pain, he wandered aimlessly. Far above his head, the ship's massive hull looked over him, but he was too far away from the barrier to hear its quiet pulsing.

He looked out across the still darkness toward the glow of lights on the horizon, pleading for a way to go to her, to be with her one last time. His eyes filled with tears as the chill settled deep inside his bones. Suddenly, he wasn't cold anymore. He turned around. Someone felt near. A sweet scent replaced the sage of the desert. Then warm, caring arms encircled him. His shoulders slumped as he drank in her presence. She came around and he saw her, facing him. "Mrs. M . . .," he said. He stared at her bright green eyes in wonder, his mind confused as she led him to a nearby rock and they sat together. He never doubted that she was real.

Don't be sad, Harlowe.

"Lu . . . I need her."

You must go on without her. Your place is not here. She stared at the heavens. *It's out there now.*

Harlowe nodded as he wiped his tears with the back of his hand. His gaze took him back to the lights. A thousand more nights and a thousand more miles of a desert full of stars would not lessen the pain inside him.

They need you, Harlowe. You must survive, that is your destiny. You must save the Gamadin.

"But how?"

Another vision came to his side. It was Harry. He put a warm hand on his shoulder. *"It's up to you now, son. You must begin the resurrection."*

Harlowe closed his eyes, fighting back the dull aching pain he felt all over his body. When he opened them again, the visions were gone. He was alone again. A short distance away, Harry and Mrs. M were standing together arm and arm. Mrs. M's face was lit up as if a candle glowed in front of her face. *Good-bye, Harlowe,* she said to him.

"I won't let you down," Harlowe promised her one last time. "I'll save Millawanda and free Neeja for you."

Harry returned a confident wink and a pride-filled smile. *God-speed, son.*

Then, holding on to each other, they moved on across the desert and faded away.

Good-bye, Harry. Good-bye, Mrs. M., Harlowe thought as he watched them go. He cried a little along the way back to the ramp. His mind was made up. He didn't know what Gamadin meant, but somehow, somewhere, deep inside him he knew his destiny had been chosen for him and there was no going back.

Chapter Fifty-Eight

SITTING DUCKS

THE PINK TONES of first light were just coming over the distant mountains to the east when General Gunn, swagger stick in hand, hands on hips, looked down defiantly at the disk from his bunker high on the ridge. Standing with him were Captain Walker, Lieutenant Poole, and the contingent of four astrophysicists.

Like a chameleon, the alien vessel seemed to borrow color from the world surrounding it. In sharp contrast with the flying saucer's subtle tones, the desert-colored armored tanks and mechanized artillery batteries were dull yet menacing as they lay in quiet wait around the perimeter of the saddle, the alien target caught in each one's crosshairs.

Above, two Air Force Hueys cut across the general's line of sight. They were delivering more troops to positions along the ridge, while higher up, three squadrons of F-16 Falcons blazed white contrails across the cloudless sky as they circled in their constant holding patterns between twelve and fifteen thousand feet, ready in a moment to launch a rocket attack on the saucer when ordered.

All was quiet down in the saddle when General Gunn gave the command, "Let's get it over with, captain."

"Yes, sir."

Captain Walker signaled to another soldier in the bunker, who then radioed to another soldier down in the saddle. Seconds later, troops scrambled for safety all around the saddleback depression. When all were in their proper places, a whistle blew. A voice barked, "Fire!" and an armor-piercing uranium-tipped shell from an A1 Abrams tank shot toward the disk and exploded. At that range the explosive shell should have destroyed whatever it struck. But when the smoke cleared, the saucer was completely unharmed, its hull fully intact, its golden skin flawless. No explosive weapon, missile, or cutting device could penetrate its protective field. The general's numerous futile attempts to break through the barrier were symbolized by the worthless white-hot bits of shrapnel from the expended shell that lay smoldering in the sand around the perimeter of the ship.

A soldier dressed in desert fatigues came running up the hill, shouting the results that they all had heard a dozen times before this morning. "No effect, general. The shell didn't even leave a mark," he reported.

General Gunn summarily dismissed the results with a swift crack of his swagger stick against the sandbag edge of the bunker. He had tried everything from torches to lasers to plastique on the barrier. Given enough time he thought he could find a way, but time was running out. The alien ships were nearing the moon's orbital plane. There was no more time for failure; he didn't have that luxury. He needed results, not excuses, and if the young felons inside the disk wouldn't cooperate, he had no alternative but to destroy them and the ship.

Doctor Shaffer let out a heavy sigh of relief. He was vehemently opposed to any type of forceful action against the saucer. "No disrespect, sir, but I protest this action," Shaffer lashed out. The general turned around, taken aback by Shaffer's sudden outburst. "This is lunacy. This vessel has taken no hostile action toward us, and here we are trying to destroy it."

Gunn fought to keep his composure. "I've heard all the rhetoric before, doctor."

"We should try every available means to establish contact first, sir."

"We tried that last night, Doctor. You were there. Pylott will not lower the barrier," Gunn explained.

"But tank shells aren't exactly what I would call hello-how-are-you's, general."

"No choice," the general rebutted, "I understand your position. But you saw what happened back there," he continued, pointing his swagger stick eastward toward Utah. "If that thing starts to go ape, we're in a world of hurt."

Doctor McCarty stepped forward. "We know that, general, but you've got a lot of good men out there. We all know what it's capable of, right? So let's try again to reason with Pylott. You said yourself the boy seemed levelheaded. Maybe he needs more time to think his situation through. Once he understands that there is no way he can fly this ship, he'll see it our way, I'm sure. They should know the incoming alien forces are almost here, general. They could be as frightened of us as we are of them."

General Gunn didn't address the scientists' concerns right away. He continued to stare down at the alien craft as if trying to arrive at a decision through some spiritual means. "One hour," he said at last. "I'll give you that much time for your team to swap spit with Pylott, and then I have to do what I have to do, understand, gentlemen? One hour." The general's gaze never left the disk.

* * *

General Gunn, accompanied by Captain Walker and Lieutenant Poole, stepped firmly to the barrier wall. He wanted to see for himself the results of the most recent attempts to penetrate the force field.

The general rested his hands on his pearl-handled sidearm. "Alright, gentlemen," he snapped disgustedly. "Can't the world's mightiest military find a way into this spaceship! What do we have to do, nuke the salad plate?" he thundered, kicking up sand at the barrier. The gritty particles of dirt stopped instantly before the barrier and fell unceremoniously to the ground, where a foot-high heap of hot shrapnel rested against the barrier. It was a fitting reminder of his past failures.

"Doctor Zagorsky says nothing from Earth will harm it except, perhaps, something nuclear, sir," Lieutenant Poole added.

"That's nuts! He knows we can't do that. We've got two million civilians twenty miles down the fallout path from here."

"Yes, sir, he knows," the lieutenant replied, "but with the right precautions, he says a low-yield nuclear warhead is a viable option, sir."

From the ground, the barrier went up to a thin band of bright blue light that pulsed two hundred feet above their heads and circled the entire perimeter of the disk. A low, faint hum throbbed like a heart at rest as the barrier dimmed slightly and brightened. Zagorsky had explained that, according to his team's calculations, the light appeared to be the source of the barrier's power. If they could somehow disable the light, the barrier would dissolve.

"It may come to that, lieutenant. Contact the Pentagon for clearance," the general ordered. Then he asked, "How's Alpha-Bravo doing?" as he continued to probe the lighted barrier.

"Sergeant Defoe and his men are doing fine, sir," the captain replied. "They were flown to Nellis this morning and given complete physicals. All tests are negative, sir. The men were roughed up a little bit, but nothing was broken. They're eager to return to duty, sir."

General Gunn nodded with pride. "Good men. Make sure they get decent chow tonight."

"Yes, sir."

The general stepped back from the barrier and pondered. How does an alien man-of-war end up in the hands of young men? Maybe Pylott and his friends weren't the killers they were made out to be. Then again, the Harry's Casino connection could be wrong. There had to be some logical reason for it all, some common thread that would tie it all together. What made the saucer come here in the first place? More importantly, what did this have to do with the other alien ships en route to Earth?

He had to get control of the saucer. He had to make the Pylott kid understand before things got out of hand.

"General!" a voice called out.

Gunn turned and saw Doctor Shaffer with a pair of binoculars in his hand, standing at the edge of the barrier. "Someone's coming down the ramp, general. It looks like the Pylott kid again."

Gunn adjusted his Ray-Bans. "Well, let's hope the boy's come to his senses," the general muttered as he moved toward the ship.

Gunn waited with mixed emotions as Pylott strode up to the barrier and glanced skyward a moment, looking troubled, before turning back to the group. Gunn felt there was definitely a change in the young man's attitude. He seemed nervous, and Gunn thought he could play off that weakness.

Pylott studied their faces in silence until he came to Carole Rodale. "You know why we're here, don't you?" he asked.

General Gunn intervened before she could respond. "Forget the pleasantries, Pylott, we don't have a lot of time. Now turn off the barrier."

"Don't interrupt me, general." The young man's quick, plain-spoken response took the general by surprise. He had read him wrong. He was not emotionally distraught. His clear blue eyes held them all. "I came here to warn you. Earth is in danger. You must allow us to leave without interference."

"And if we don't?" the general asked.

"Look, general, I didn't come here to bargain. There's a group of Dak attack ships a short distance from Earth, and they're not coming to make nice. They want this ship, and if they don't get her, they'll try to destroy her and Earth along with her. I made a promise that I wouldn't let that happen. I'm goin' to keep it. So with or without your consent, this ship is taking off, and there is nothing you can do about it."

"I'm warning you," Gunn countered, "if you make one move to lift this salad plate off the ground, I'll turn it into subatomic dust."

"Please, general," Doctor Rodale pleaded, "this young man has obviously come here to help us. Let him."

Shaffer leaned forward to challenge the young man. "How can you be so certain those ships are hostile? Weren't you the ones who disfigured the desert? You could be the hostile ones, not them."

"No!" Rodale interceded on the boy's behalf. "They are not here to kill us. I know it. They're here to help."

"As I told the general last night, what happened in Utah was an accident," Pylott explained. "We had to break the ship out from the mesa to free her. We had no choice."

"What makes you think you can take on a squadron of alien attack ships, then?" General Gunn asked. "They'll make lizard waste out of you, son."

"That's a chance we have to take."

"How do we know you're telling the truth?" Shaffer interrupted, still convinced the aliens were harmless. "The incoming squadron has done nothing to indicate a hostile intent, whereas you have a laundry list of deaths surrounding your actions, son."

Pylott addressed Shaffer coldly. "I don't care what you believe." The scientists were taken aback by the kid's sudden force of will. "I know what I have to do. You can believe what you want."

"I believe you," Rodale interjected.

"Thanks, ma'am, but we're running out of time. I have to go. I came here to warn you. When this ship takes off, I'll have no control over what she might do to your men on the ground or the jets in the sky if they get too close to her. I would order your men away from the saddle, general," he said, making eye contact with Gunn, and Gunn alone.

"Take me with you, son," Gunn offered. "I can help. At least I can keep you from getting blown to pieces in the first ten seconds."

Suddenly the blue shimmer of the force field grew brighter.

"What's happening?" asked Shaffer.

"She senses danger," the young man replied. "It may already be too late. Daks are on the planet. Last night they killed Harry Mars, his wife, and his daughter—my girlfriend. My guess is that they will do what they can to try and stop us from leaving before their main battle group arrives."

Behind them, the landing pods of the saucer began to retract as Pylott glanced at Gunn. "General?"

"But this ship," Doctor Zagorsky protested, "how can you survive against them?"

Harlowe searched the sky anxiously. "Last time, general. Clear your people out of the area. I'm not asking."

Harlowe turned and began running toward the center ramp.

Rodale called after him, "Our prayers are with you, Harlowe Pylott!"

All three landing pods disappeared inside the hull, leaving no trace of their existence.

The young man glanced back, briefly. He felt the message from her heart and silently mouthed the words *Thank you* before he turned back toward the ship.

"I cannot allow you to lift off, Pylott!" Gunn shouted after him as he slammed his fist against the barrier. Harlowe kept running toward the stairway, unaffected by the threats.

A split second later a focused bolt of bright orange light shot down from the heavens and struck the southern outer section of the saddle. General Gunn watched helplessly as an entire brigade of military hardware and soldiers vaporized before his eyes.

"My men . . . my men . . .," he cried out, his face contorted in anguish.

Pylott stopped running, appearing momentarily at a loss as to what to do next.

Then a second and third bolt of intense heat blasted the eastern ridgeline, destroying artillery and tanks and more good men. One right, one left. The bolts were zeroing in on the saucer. Another bolt or two and the enemy would find his mark.

"My men!" the general kept shouting just before a burst of orange light touched the barrier. When the dust cleared, Gunn and everyone around him were spread out flat on the desert sand. No one was moving.

Chapter Fifty-Nine

PURSUIT

Dr. Ed McCarty looked into the vacant brown eyes of a young soldier. He was just a kid, he thought. With a bloody hand, the scientist wiped the dust from the soldier's pupils so his eyelids would close. The bunker had been completely razed. Everywhere was the stench of smoke and burning flesh. All McCarty could remember seeing was an orange flash, then nothing.

A moaning voice cried out. He wondered how many other voices would never cry out again.

Pushing the body of the dead soldier off his chest, McCarty thought of Tom Shaffer and the others down by the saucer's rim. They all had been talking to the young man on the other side of the barrier when the attack began. He prayed that his friends and colleagues had survived the blast.

McCarty rolled over and focused on what had once been part of the bunker wall. Two rows of torn-up sandbags a foot high were all that was left of the five-foot barrier. If he could hoist himself over the top, he figured he could see what had happened to the ship down in the saddle.

As to his own condition, McCarty was uncertain. He felt a deep gash across his forehead, but that didn't matter. He had to reach the wall before he thought about anything else.

He gritted his teeth and forced his mind to move his legs and arms. He kept clawing his way forward, over more broken bodies, knowing that time was against him. *Doctor Zagorsky? Tom? Where's*

Tom? What happened to Tom? They were down there by the ship. You said that. You're repeating yourself, McCarty. Keep your head on or you won't make it to the wall.

When McCarty got to the wall, he didn't think he had the strength to raise himself. Taking two deep breaths and thinking about his friends gave him the inner strength he needed. He grabbed hold, pulled himself up, and laid himself across the wall. He blinked the dirty irritants from his eyes and looked down below. The saucer was still there.

Just then an orange bolt rocketed down from the sky and exploded against the far outer rim of the saucer. The ground shook. He could feel the impact through the wall. The bolt detonated with such force that a tank two hundred feet away dug into the side of the ridge and melted to the ground with all inside. The disk heaved up slightly then fell back, appearing to absorb the energy, and balanced on its lighted stairway. Amazingly, the ship appeared to be undamaged, but how many such bolts could its barrier absorb?

Then, unbelievably, McCarty saw someone emerge from under the saucer's hull and run back toward the barrier. It was the Pylott boy. The kid hesitated briefly at the barrier, opening a small hole in the field to allow him to pass through. Pylott went straight for the bodies on the ground, checking them one by one. He turned up their faces and felt the side of their necks. Who were they? From this distance he couldn't identify anyone; they all looked the same—like lumps of dirt.

Why doesn't the boy get back behind the barrier? McCarty wondered, just as another bolt came from the sky, narrowly missing the ship. He looked up and saw the unimaginable. It was another alien ship. It was huge and drifting down. Its outer gun turrets fired volleys of hot bolts at the saucer. "Get back!" McCarty tried to scream, but his voice was powerless against the background of orange-colored death. "You can't save them. Save yourself. Save your ship, boy!"

From somewhere, McCarty didn't see where, two small mechanical robots—mere sticks on round flat feet, with circular glowing heads—sprinted through the hole in the barrier. Following Pylott's command, the robots picked up one of the bodies like it weighed nothing at all and carried it back through the barrier. Pylott was the last one through. He must have known the bolt was coming his way because he dove through the opening just as it struck. When the dust cleared enough for McCarty to see, Pylott, the body, and the robots had all disappeared.

Then the giant disk began to rise. When it was a few hundred feet off the ground, it turned 180 degrees on its axis and shot westward across the desert like a bullet. In a blink of an eye, the disk veered straight up at an unfathomable speed and raced into the heavens. The enemy alien ship, because of its mass, could not respond as quickly. It lagged a bit as it doggedly climbed after the saucer.

A squadron of F-16s tried to keep pace with the second vessel, but even those Mach-III aircraft, full afterburners blazing, could not keep up with the slower ship. Each F-16 was a Volkswagen chasing after a Formula 1 race car. A second squadron was in a better position to intercept the larger alien craft, but they were vaporized to ash when their drive pods cracked wide open in their hot pursuit of the saucer. A heartbeat later, both alien vessels had left Earth's atmosphere.

McCarty's eyes rolled back in his head and he dropped into the bunker among the dead soldiers.

Chapter Sixty

HIDDEN BUTTON

Searing projectiles of orange plasma continued to pound the sitting ship as Ian waited frantically for Harlowe to return to the bridge. He would not touch a single control before his friend was safely inside and the center ramp was secured.

Riverstone materialized off the pad at the same moment the ship shook violently from a direct hit. He fell to the floor and rolled over. "Daks?"

Ian climbed back into his seat. "They're attacking the ship."

Riverstone crawled to the center chair to lift himself up. "Where's Harlowe?"

"Outside."

"He's *what*?"

"Outside, warning the soldiers," Ian shouted back.

"What about Platter and the toad?"

Ian didn't know where Simon was. He had left the bridge some time ago. "If Platter's not with you, I don't know where he is."

Riverstone was worried. "Harlowe should be here." Anyone outside was toast.

"He was trying to warn the general," Ian said, righting his glasses back on his face. His eyes were racing over the many screens and readouts, most of which he still had no idea how to read. They were all Chinese.

"The general?"

"I can't explain. I'm trying to get Millie ready to lift off. Don't bother me now. Harlowe's trying to save the troops from getting slaughtered."

Riverstone stared out the massive windows. "It's a massacre out there. Why aren't we blowing up like the rest of those dudes?" It looked as though Harlowe was too late. Fire from the alien blasts had engulfed the saddle. The military all around the perimeter of the ship was on fire. Thousands were already dead. The troops didn't have a chance. The saddle was a killing field of humanity.

"The barrier is still protecting us."

"For how long?"

Ian didn't know. The ship shook again, sending the two of them crashing to the floor.

Riverstone helped Ian back to his chair. "We can't take many more of those. We have to lift off, Wiz. We're target practice sitting here."

"What, and leave Harlowe? Besides, if we do, you'll have to do it, Riverstone."

"Me? I can't a fly a kite. You know that."

"You're the only one who can." Ian pushed Riverstone toward the center chair. "Sit there and I'll tell you what to do."

Riverstone was scared stiff as he sat himself down in the center chair, regretting all those days he had ditched Farnducky's physics class. *Stay cool, toad!*

At first he didn't know where to rest his arms. There were too many activators, control levers, and lighted buttons. What if he touched something wrong? *You're sprouting wings, toad.*

Out of curiosity, he leaned over the right side of the chair, looking for the clear activator button Lu had told him about. *Cool, there it is.* He edged his hand down the side and was about to press it when Ian screamed at him, "Don't touch *anything*, suckwad!"

Riverstone jerked his hand away. "I'm not. Don't worry."

"You don't know what you're doing. You might hit the wrong button. Maybe we should wait for Harlowe after all. He has to be on his way."

"Maybe he got hit by the Daks," Riverstone said.

"No. I saw him on the overhead. He was dragging a body back from outside the barrier. I don't know who it was. The clothes were charred. It was a man, though; I'm sure of that. Harlowe got him back behind the barrier before the next blast hit. I saw that much. After the blast, the overhead blanked out. We're starting to lose instrumentation on the panel too."

"Why does it matter? You don't know what most of them do anyway," Riverstone pointed out.

"I can tell when we're going to hit a mountain. That helps."

"Okay. That helps. Does that button still have power?"

"Yeah, I think so. It's this one over here."

"Good. Mark it with a sticky note. We might need it soon."

"Okay. I think we're ready. You ready?"

"No, I'm not ready." Another blast rocked the ship. "Not without Harlowe. Think of something, Wiz!"

"Yeah, yeah, we can't leave him," Ian said before he bolted for the floor disk that would blink him down to the lower level.

"Wait! Where are you going, Wiz?" Riverstone said, trying to grab him.

"Chill out!"

"Chill out? The whole planet's going up in flames!"

"I'm blinking down. When Harlowe's in, I'll blink back up."

Riverstone thrust a pointed fist at the disk. "DO IT!"

* * *

Astonishingly, Ian was back in a matter of moments, leaping back to the center chair. "Harlowe was already coming up the ramp. The robobs had the body," he explained.

Riverstone sighed heavily. "Sweet, he can take over."

A horrific blast shook Millawanda like never before.

"We don't have time," Ian countered. "You're it, pard."

Riverstone stared out at the world on fire. "What do I do, Wiz?"

"Okay," Ian said, "when I say go, start sliding your finger along the first blue bar there on your left armrest."

"This one here, right?" As Ian concentrated on the console, Riverstone's finger slyly found Lu's button.

Ian nodded. "Now easy. Start at the bottom and slowly slide your finger forward. We should lift straight up." He nodded again. "Go ahead, do it now."

Ian looked outside to make sure the ship was moving.

"How am I doing?" Riverstone asked.

Ian was amazed. "Wow! You're doing great, pard. You're keeping her nice and steady. Harlowe was shaking all over the place the first time he tried it, and he practiced for hours before we blasted out of the mesa. I can't believe it. You're a natural, pard."

Riverstone's heart was thumping a million times a second as he leaned back in the chair, the sweat rolling down his face in rivers. He watched in awe as the ship rose out of the blazing fires that engulfed the saddle. Within seconds, the Millawanda was climbing out of the smoke and breaking past the sound barrier at incredible speed.

"Really nothing to it, Wiz. Just takes a little concentration is all."

"Who's flying the ship?" Harlowe's voice called out from behind them.

Ian and Riverstone turned and saw Harlowe stepping off the pad, his face full of unexpected surprise.

Ian pointed at Riverstone. "He is."

Harlowe came up behind the center chair. "You?"

Before Riverstone could defend himself, Ian came to his defense. "He's doing a good job, Harlowe. He could give you lessons. Look how steady he's keeping the helm. You were all over the place. He's doing it without any practice too."

Harlowe stood beside Ian's chair to view their progress. They were rising so rapidly that the bright blue sky had already turned black, and a zillion stars filled Millawanda's massive wraparound windows. Harlowe kept looking between the stars and the read-outs on the console, wondering how Riverstone really was guiding the ship like a seasoned veteran. "Something's whack." He wasn't buying it.

Riverstone tried to act innocent but the sweat from his face was too revealing. He couldn't get his mouth to work well enough to put up an adequate defense.

Harlowe ran his finger along the accelerator and steering bars and lighted knobs. Nothing happened. The ship remained constant and steadily increased its speed while maintaining a specified heading. The ship did not flip or wobble once. "What gives, toad?" Harlowe asked again.

Riverstone inhaled and spoke uneasily, like a kid caught with his hand in a cookie jar. "Well, before Lu . . . ah . . . well, you know, before she . . ."

"Go on. So tell us what you did."

Ian looked at Harlowe and said, "I think Riverstone's trying to say that Lu told him to do something before she . . ."

Riverstone quickly nodded. "Wiz is right." He leaned over the right side of the center chair and pointed at the auto button. "She told me to press this. She said her mom had pre-programmed it to take the ship and the crew to a place where they could train. She said it was all arranged to fly there on its own."

"Lu told you that, huh?" Harlowe asked.

"You think I could come up with a lie like that?" Riverstone replied.

Harlowe needed zero time to think that one over. "No. That's way beyond your simple brain," he agreed. "So where are we going, Captain Julian Starr?"

Riverstone moved out of the center chair into the one immediately to the right. "I have no idea. You can have the chair back, pard. That's as close to captain as I want to be."

Boooom!

Suddenly, a bright flash of intensity exploded across the bow, jolting the ship and everyone inside. Harlowe barely had time to grab on to the center chair before the next bolt struck the ship broadside.

Chapter Sixty-One

HUNTING DAKS

HOURS LATER, THE light of a billion stars reflected off Harlowe's face as he gazed outward through the massive forward windows. The ship's predetermined course had taken them . . . *Where?* He didn't know. They could be anywhere. Had the ship turned toward the outer planets? How far away was Earth? Were they far enough away to save it? Maybe. How would he know? At this point, however, none of that really mattered much. The promise he made to Mrs. M was at least partially complete. Millawanda had left Earth.

Harlowe lifted his mangled left hand that he had crushed against the console when a Dak ship finally caught up with them. A robob had encased his hand in a translucent flexible splint up to his forearm.

How long had they survived? A few hours? That's as far back as Harlowe could remember. He couldn't think straight, even if he concentrated. He examined his fingers through the membrane. The fingers had been straightened. Though he felt no pain when he moved them, they were as cumbersome as if he was wearing a ski mitten. He wiped a mixture of sweat and blood from his forehead with the arm of his torn blue uniform. He was careful not to accidentally touch his nose. It was broken, angling left, like his hand. A short while ago, a robob had injected him with more painkiller. He was feeling all right now, but he knew that was only temporary.

When he looked out the side observation window, Harlowe saw a tiny speck moving among the glittering dots. He took a deep breath and leaned back in his chair, resigned to the fact that maybe their luck had run out.

Forgetting the speck for the moment, his gaze turned to the control bridge. It was a depressing sight. A smoky haze of deterioration filled the room while the front control panel, where his nose had been implanted earlier, was burning and shorting out. Even the computer screen above him was fading in and out more often now.

He wondered how Ian and Riverstone were holding up. Ian was out cold on the floor behind his chair. He hadn't moved since two Dak cruisers hit them at the same time. His only pair of eyes were lying twisted and shattered all over the forward console, along with the blood where his face hit. Harlowe didn't know how he would replace his eyes. Optometrists were pretty scarce in deep space.

After that, Harlowe had had no choice but to divert the last of Millie's power to her protective shields. When he did, their seat restraints released, catching them by surprise and sending them slamming into things in the control room. Before the robobs could help Ian, they themselves collapsed on the floor next to him in a pile of mechanical tubes. It was like they had run out of gas. They didn't even have the energy to reduce themselves back to cylinders. Ian had to be hurting, Harlowe thought, not knowing, however, whether he was alive or dead.

Riverstone was somewhere in the ship. He said he was going to the utility room, why, Harlowe didn't know. That was Riverstone for you. He had gotten pretty banged up on the last go-round with the Dak attack ships. His right forearm was broken in two places. His right knee was shattered too. The robobs, who were on their last clickity-clack, didn't have the energy to perform their usual surgical miracles. But they did manage to get his knee functioning well enough that he could walk, albeit with a stiff limp.

Riverstone was irate. He was sick and tired of being shot at, he had said, and he had an idea of how to put an end to the BS.

Harlowe twisted around in his chair. Only a few tiny lights flickered on the back wall here and there. Their once beautiful ship was completely defenseless. They were flying on empty, he mused. Weapons were . . . Well, he didn't know how to use them. They had no maneuverability, either, because the course was still fixed. That hadn't deviated.

But as he sat there trying to think of what they could have done differently to change the outcome, Harlowe comforted himself with the thought that they had taken the battle away from Earth. That was the important thing. They had saved Earth. *Mission accomplished, Mrs. M.* That part anyway. And Lakewood was safe. He was proud of that.

For a short time in space he and Riverstone and Ian had held their own. He was proud of that too. After they led the Daks away from Earth, they should have been blown into subatomic particles by the time they passed the moon. But they hadn't.

How was that possible?

Out of the corner of his eye Harlowe saw another speck drift into position. The Daks were moving in for the kill, he told himself.

Fighting to stay conscious, Harlowe struggled out of his chair. He had to do something. He wasn't about to sit around and wait for the specks to finish them off. His fingers reached out for something, anything, to press or activate. More than likely, it would be the wrong thing, but even a wrong action was something.

Millawanda hesitated before she lurched forward. Harlowe felt her pain. Probably more than they knew, she was gutting it out like Baby would. *Yeah, she's just like Baby. She'll never let us down if she can help it.* The Daks would have to fill her with a million holes before she would quit. That's the only way they could kill her.

Harlowe fell backwards into his chair, too exhausted to stand for long. He squinted, searching the starscape for movement. "Where are you, toads?" he said, snarling at the screen. *What did Riverstone say Lu called them? Stupid draks! or some such thing.*

The Dak ship had been coming toward them a second before, making its final approach. Could it be above the window? Or maybe they were below the perimeter edge of the hull, out of sight. Harlowe wasn't sure.

He wiped more salty sweat from around his eyes. It was a continuous process to clear his vision as he stared intently out at a galaxy of tiny lights. The Dak specks were hidden among the stars. He kept waiting for something to move against the backdrop, but nothing did. The cosmos was still.

He turned the ship slowly around on its axis, hoping to see movement. That much he could do. As long as he didn't deviate from the prescribed course, he could spin the ship around like a top if he wanted to. Millie didn't care. She was keeping her heading at fifteen thousand miles per second, regardless. Talk about a hardheaded woman, he snickered. In Earth terms that was an unheard-of speed, but in the business of space warfare, it was a crawl. They might as well have been standing still. After one careful revolution, Harlowe raised his head to the overhead screen and begged in a strained, exhausted voice, "Find the Daks' ship, Millie."

In response, the screen went blank briefly. Harlowe heard some static, and finally an image of a long, slender cruiser came into view. Unlike the saucer, it was as clean and shiny as if it had just been through the Del Amo Car Wash off Bellflower. Harlowe grinned with satisfaction.

"Here they come," Harlowe said aloud to himself.

"Who's coming?" asked a familiar voice from behind him.

Harlowe rotated the broken center chair around toward the voice. Coming through the burning haze, Riverstone winced and hobbled along, using something long for a crutch. Wide golden bands supported his forearm and knee. *Robob patchwork at its finest,* Harlowe mused.

"Daks," Harlowe answered, nodding toward the windows.

Riverstone panned the room. "Look at this place. It's a mess! I leave for a couple of minutes, the place is in shambles. Why didn't you get a robob to clean it up? Do I have to do everything?" he mock-complained. He rested for a moment against the arm of the command chair next to Harlowe as he asked, "Weapons still down?"

"They were never up."

Harlowe wiped his eyes yet again. He couldn't see clearly enough as to what Riverstone had supporting his weight. He kept squinting, opening and closing his eyes in a poor imitation of Mr. Magoo. "What are you holding?" he asked.

"It's a rifle, dummy," Riverstone retorted. "Don't you recognize it?"

"You shoot that thing in here and we won't have to worry about the suckwads out there."

"You're so clueless sometimes, Pylott. You like to pretend you're a captain, but you're just a piece of Dak pet food."

"Insult me like that again, I'll break your other knee." He pointed at the rifle. "Listen, the last time we shot that thing, Monday rearranged the landscape."

Riverstone looked a little concerned. "Where is he, by the way?"

"Sick bay."

"And our movie star?"

"Looking for his shrink."

Riverstone shook his head, limping across the control room to stand at the forward windows.

Harlowe got out of his chair, creaking along only slightly better than Riverstone. "So, you got a plan?"

Riverstone held up the alien weapon. "Yeah, I'm going hunting for Dak."

"Dak, huh?"

"Yeah, interested?" He was too beat-up to add more.

Harlowe glanced though the window. The bright specks he had been searching for were moving against the background of stars. *There you are.* The Dak ships were lining up, making their approach. They seemed unstoppable.

Riverstone turned, standing at the doorway. "Well, are you going to help me, or are you just going to whine all day?"

Harlowe grudgingly moved toward the door where Riverstone was waiting.

"Think it will work?" Harlowe asked.

"Yeah, it will work," Riverstone grunted, trying to squeeze through the tight opening that led to the master cabin.

Harlowe grabbed an edge of the cabin door with his good hand and pulled. It was a struggle, but after a few four-letter grunts, he and Riverstone managed to slide it open enough to squeeze their way through.

They shuffled across the adjoining room together to another door along the outer bulkhead of the ship.

Riverstone pressed an activator on the left side of a small obser-vation window and waited. When the light at the side of the door turned blue, it meant that the force field had been activated and they could go out the door and into space. They had practiced simi-lar outings while Millawanda was still inside the cavern. Riverstone was about to step outside when Harlowe asked a simple question. "What if there's not enough juice?"

"Then we're screwed" was Riverstone's short answer. Throwing caution to the wind, he pressed the activator a second time. Like the door to the cabin, the outside door slid open only partially. There was only enough space to get a hand through. "We need to talk to maintenance about this," Riverstone joked. He grabbed the edge of the door and slid it open, wide enough for them to squeeze through.

To Harlowe's relief, Millie still had enough "juice" in her force field because they didn't get sucked out through the opening.

Riverstone slid through first, and Harlowe followed. Both their faces twisted with disgust as they looked out over the top of the ship and the damaged outer hull. The structural integrity appeared to depend on chewing gum and baling wire. Long black streaks crisscrossed the golden hull in many different directions. Sections of dura-metal were buckled near the upper control dome. Another few feet and the blast would have sliced through to the bridge.

In the distance, large electrical arcs were flashing close to the perimeter where the ship had suffered massive hits from the Dak plas-cannons. There was more. To their left were two black holes where the ship had taken direct hits. The damage seemed to be everywhere.

Careful not to step through an open breach, they dragged themselves along the hull. Their only protection was the tenuous force field.

Harlowe gazed up at the starry heavens and said, "Nice view."

Riverstone kept his eyes forward, looking for a spot to set up. They were so exhausted and wasted that every few steps they had to stop and catch their breath. Harlowe had to fall to one knee to catch his.

"You can't rest now, dummy," Riverstone said, helping him to stand.

"It's the altitude," Harlowe wheezed. He coughed and spit up a wad of blood.

Riverstone wiped Harlowe's mouth with his sleeve. "Just a little farther, pard."

They gritted their way for another hundred yards before Riverstone found his spot. "This is cool."

They looked like two tiny ants, alone on the massive bruised and lacerated hull.

A Dak cruiser now loomed bright and huge against the stellar heavens. Compared to Millawanda, it appeared to be a hundred times larger in every aspect, and infinitely more powerful.

"The Daks are sure taking their sweet time," Harlowe remarked.

"They just want to be sure," Riverstone added.

Together they watched the giant Dak ship coming closer. Riverstone pushed Harlowe around and told him to sit up straight, his legs outstretched before him. Harlowe followed instructions, too weary to resist.

Riverstone sat behind Harlowe, placed the barrel of the rifle on Harlowe's right shoulder, and took aim. The end of the barrel moved up and down as Riverstone tried to put a bead on the giant Dak ship moving in for the kill. A barn door would have been an easier target. The barrel fell off the side of Harlowe's shoulder twice before Harlowe had the idea to hold the barrel with his right hand.

"I can't see with your hand over the sight, toad," Riverstone said.

"Does it matter?"

"It matters if I'm hunting Daks. Move it."

After a long moment, Riverstone fired. The intense blue bolt streaked off in the right direction but missed by a planetary orbit.

"You need to do better," Harlowe said.

"My right eye's shut," Riverstone countered.

"Use your left one."

"That's my bad eye."

"It's your good one now."

Riverstone wiggled around, putting the butt of the rifle to his left shoulder as Harlowe grabbed the barrel with his bandaged hand and transferred it to his left side to accommodate Riverstone's new position. At that moment the giant Dak ship fired an orange bolt of intense energy. The ball of concentrated light came right at them and passed under the ship, missing them by a fraction.

"He's a better shot than you," Harlowe remarked. He noticed a small green light blinking on the side of the weapon's stock. "What's that light mean?" he asked.

Riverstone turned the rifle sideways and studied the blinking light. He shrugged. "I lost the instructions."

"Better make the next shot count, pard," Harlowe said, "in case you don't have many bullets left."

Riverstone nodded. It was a sound suggestion. As he turned the rifle upright again, Harlowe pressed a button on the side of the receiver, making a small scope deploy from the top.

"That helps," Riverstone said.

Weaving back and forth, Riverstone placed the illuminated crosshairs on the Dak ship that seemed to hang out in front of them like a giant silver whale, and fired.

Suddenly, the entire stellar night exploded into a ball of white light so strong that Riverstone and Harlowe had to cover their eyes from the flash. It was strange how the Dak ship went nuclear in the silent vacuum of space. It was like watching a *Star Wars* battle scene in a theater with no surround sound. After a long moment the white-hot pieces of debris came streaking by, some bouncing off Millawanda's damaged hull and flying away. The shield was still strong enough to protect them.

Riverstone stared at his weapon with awe. "Did I do that?" he wondered aloud.

Harlowe turned around, unimpressed. "Three to go, moron," he said unemotionally.

They had to hurry. Two giant cruisers were veering off, and a fourth Dak vessel was still a mere speck. It seemed to be holding back, waiting for the final results to come in.

"We surprised them. Quick, before they get out of range," Harlowe urged, steadying the Gamadin rifle back on his shoulder.

Riverstone squeezed off two more rounds, hitting the nearest cruiser broadside as it was making its turn. One shot tore a hole through the middle of the ship. Masses of fiery debris were exploding out the far side of its hull. The second round hit aft. The Gamadin bolts seemed to penetrate the defense shields like they were nonexistent. Huge vents of escaping gas were exiting out the blast holes.

"Keep shooting," Harlowe demanded.

"They might be crippled," Riverstone countered.

Harlowe didn't care. "Forget them. Think of Mrs. M, Harry, and Lu when you're pulling the trigger," he reminded him.

Riverstone clenched his teeth. More good advice. Three more rapid-fire rounds and the wounded Dak cruiser exploded like the first. Riverstone wasn't finished. The third Dak ship had already made its turn and was gathering speed in an effort to make its escape. All Riverstone could see was the tail end.

Harlowe said, "Shoot one up his bootie for Mowgi."

One round of intense blue light was all that was necessary as another ball of exploding light lit up the star-studded night.

They traded high fives.

"Dak soup," Riverstone said proudly. "Any more?"

"Yeah, there's one hovering over there to the right, far out of range. Let's send him a message."

"Aye, aye, captain."

Riverstone lifted the rifle back to Harlowe's shoulder and peered through the scope. "I can barely see it."

"Anywhere close, then. He'll get the point," Harlowe assured him.

Riverstone studied his rifle. The tiny green light was out. "I think we shot our wad, brah."

Harlowe waved his bum paw at the speck. "Try it anyway."

After checking the rifle thoroughly, Riverstone wet his lips and took careful aim. Harlowe felt a jolt push him forward and sideways. Riverstone lunged over the top of Harlowe, still holding the Gamadin weapon. Tumbling around on the ship's hull, they looked like a bad comedy act.

Harlowe was about to baptize Riverstone with a string of four-letter names when a sudden light lit up the cosmos, like a star gone nova. Shock and awe were painted over their faces. "Nice shot, pard!" Harlowe shouted, lying sideways, weak and out of breath.

Riverstone stared at his rifle, dumbfounded. "What's up with that?" The tiny green light was still out. He was as shocked as Harlowe, yet there was the last Dak ship looking like an exploding star.

As they both marveled at the final throes of the Dakadude ship expanding into a brilliant ball of celestial fire, Harlowe put a hand on Riverstone's shoulder and said with a warm but very relieved smile, "If you were a doe, I'd kiss you."

"If you were one, I'd let you."

They continued to lie on top of the hull a while longer, taking in the peace and beauty of the stars as they tried to gather enough strength to make it back to the control room.

"We should have died, you know," Riverstone said.

Harlowe didn't disagree. "A strange turn of events."

"Yeah, and they had weapons they knew how to use."

Harlowe laughed a little. "So do we." He twisted around and pulled a piece of blackened metal out from under his back. "They're really no different than the gangs."

"They're not cholos, Pylott."

Harlowe stared blankly at the stars. The dying sparks of the recent explosions were nearly a faded memory. "Someone will be asking what happened here. The Daks sent their best to destroy the Gamadin. What do you think is going through the head of that ugly toad-head commander about now?"

Riverstone didn't really care. He was fresh out of guesses.

Harlowe turned and looked Riverstone in the eye. "We just messed up their plans big-time, pard."

Riverstone grunted, then after a short struggle to catch his breath, he said, "They'll be back, you know. With an attitude." He left it unsaid that the Daks had messed up their plans a little too.

Harlowe forced a grin as he came to his knees and gave Riverstone a hand. They tried several times, but neither one could lift himself beyond a sitting position. Then, two robobs came out of nowhere to help them stand. The two humans, with their mechanical assistants, limped like old men back toward the open doorway.

"What now, captain?" Riverstone asked.

"We find a beach," Harlowe replied, gritting his teeth. "And catch some rays."

Riverstone liked the plan. "With warm, clear water."

"And surf," Harlowe added.

"Don't forget the babes, pard. Lots of hot babes . . ."

Harlowe nudged Riverstone in the side as they stepped through the doorway. "That's the plan then. We'll gather the boys and hit the sand."

But Riverstone could see in Harlowe's fixated eyes that the surf and babes were as far from his mind as they were from Lakewood. The rumble had only just begun . . .

THE END OF THE BEGINNING

Book II

GAMADIN™

Mons

Spring, 2010

BE SURE AND join Harlowe and the boys in Book II, *Gamadin: Mons*, coming in Spring of 2010. Millawanda has parked them on a planet with no life, no breathable atmosphere, and no In-and-Out burgers at the edge of the solar system's largest extinct volcano. They're broken, hungry, and lost, with no knowledge or skills as to operating the powerful ancient technology. Survival, then, becomes a minute-to-minute existence. If that were not enough, a military presence conscripts their souls, while back home, their families must contend with a hostile government that wants its property back!